THE DARKNET FILE

MAX TOMLINSON

THE DARKNET FILE

Third Edition, May 2019
©2017 Max Tomlinson

All rights reserved. This book may not be reproduced in any form, in whole or in part, by any means, electronic or mechanical, without written permission from the author, except by a reviewer who wishes to quote brief passages in connection with a review written for inclusion in a magazine, newspaper or broadcast.

SENDERO Press
San Francisco, California

Cover by Marianne Nowicki – Nowicki Productions

Visit the author's web site for updates:
http://maxtomlinson.wordpress.com/

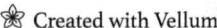 Created with Vellum

Treachery will come home to the traitor.
Romanian proverb

PROLOGUE

Northern Iraq, near the Syrian border

Besma heard gunfire off in the distance, popping on the warm night wind. She stopped for a moment on the dark road leading to her village, her arms aching from the bags full of onions and leeks she carried.

"Besma—what's that?" her brother Havi asked, standing next to her, staggering under the weight of a five-kilo bag of rice cradled in his small arms.

Cocking her head to a cobalt sky pierced with stars, she heard automatic rifle shots cracking louder, along with the roar of engines. Prickles of fear spread across her back. She imagined the jihadi fighters laughing as they waved their weapons from the back of their pickup trucks, their eyes wild from the pills they took.

"They're here, Havi," she whispered to the six-year-old, doing her best to control the trembling in her voice.

Jihad Nation.

The jihadis were coming. In their eyes, Besma and her people, Yazidis, weren't fit to live. They were non-Muslims. Infidels.

She drew a deep breath. "Run for the shop, Havi."

They picked up their feet, their flip-flops slapping, but were hampered by the weight of the food they'd been sent to fetch. Besma could run. She was fourteen, with limbs that grew longer every day, it seemed. But she kept a slower pace with Havi.

"Faster, Havi! It's not that far!"

"I can't!" Havi shouted, swerving off the dirt road as the bag of rice seemed to pull him off course.

Bursts of automatic gunfire grew louder, as did the whine of the trucks. And now she could hear them, screaming for holy jihad. *Death to the devil worshipers!*

"Give the sack to me," Besma gasped, stopping, hooking both of her plastic sacks onto her hands as she squatted and curled up her forearms, taking the precious bag of rice from her brother. "You run ahead. Warn the others."

Havi disappeared in front of her into the darkness, his short bare legs moving in a dusty blur. She wondered for one terrible moment if she would ever see him again.

She ran, too, laden down with the food. The plastic handles cut into her fingers like knives.

Even so, she began to pick up speed.

As she and Havi drew closer to the village, so did the jihadis, roaring with laughter, gunfire breaking the otherwise serene night. The single light over her father's shop appeared in the darkness. Then she saw her uncle, standing by the door with two men, rifles ready. All the other men were gone, off to the south, or in the refugee camps, trying to rescue the women and children the jihadis had taken. The men by the shop checked their weapons and talked in anxious torrents, then moved in haste, shepherding the women and children into her father's print shop. She saw Havi go in, but not before stopping to look her way.

Finally, she too reached the shop, where a boy about her age, with dark eyes and thick eyebrows, slung his rifle over his shoulder and helped her carry the food. "Get inside, Besma! You must calm the others."

"Yes, yes."

"Do you have your Koran?"

"Inside."

"Keep it with you."

It was rumored that if you could recite the Koran, they wouldn't behead you. She had been learning verses, and teaching them to Havi.

Soon they were locked inside the shop, huddled in the back, about fifteen of them, women, girls, and children. Besma's mother shot her a worried glance from under her black-and-white-checked scarf, blinking rapidly. She hugged Havi as she rocked back and forth, whispering prayers to Ezid—their God—to protect her son.

"Don't worry, Mother," Besma said. "The jihadis don't harm children."

Her mother frowned as she ratcheted up her prayers. It was clear she didn't believe her.

Outside, in the dirt square across the street from her father's shop, they heard trucks screeching to a halt amidst the chatter of weapons, the jihadis screaming that Allah would have his vengeance on the infidels.

"We must be strong and pray," Besma said as she gathered with the others, her heart a piston that felt as if it would break if it beat any harder. Crouching, she put her arms around her mother and another woman from the village, who was battling tears as she clung to her own daughter. Havi crouched in the middle of it all.

"Give me your cell phone," Besma said to her mother. With fumbling fingers, her mother produced a cracked phone from within her dark robe. It fell on the old tile floor and Besma scooped it back up, found the speed dial, and the number she needed. She pressed it with a shaking finger and held the phone to her ear.

Outside in the square the gun battle began, but with only a few of their men and so many jihadis, Besma feared it would be short.

The phone droned on. No answer. No rollover to voicemail. Her father was out of range. Last she heard, he was at a refugee camp in Raqqa, looking for women and children who had escaped the jihadis.

And then, as quickly as it began, the gun battle in the square was over. The jihadis shouted in victory.

It was all Besma and her people could do not to cry out in anguish. She wondered if the young man with the thick eyebrows, who had looked at her so kindly, was now dead.

The fighters searched the village, going from door to door while Besma and the others cowered in the back of the shop in silent fear.

It didn't take long for the shop doors to rattle violently.

"In here!" one man shouted. "I can smell them!"

Soon the jihadis smashed in the glass and metal door to her father's shop.

They stood there, more terrifying in real life, wild hair and long beards, all in black, holding their AK-47s, as they leered at the women, especially the younger ones. One man in a long afghan headdress bounded over, headed for her little brother.

"You!" he said. "Stand up like a man!" Havi trembled.

Besma reached for the man's arm. "Please," she said. "He's only a boy."

"Well, he's mine now," the man said to Besma in thick guttural Arabic. He licked his cracked lips and gave a wicked grin. "And look at *you*! Dark like an Arab. But with eyes as blue as the noon sky. A Yazidi princess. God is good to the victor."

"She is indeed a prize, Hassan al-Hassan!" another man said. The man in the headdress was clearly the leader.

The other men laughed as they picked out girls, fighting over them, some offering to pay for the privilege of taking them first. Several hovered around Besma, ogling her bare legs in her shorts. Unheard of for a Muslim woman. Besma fought the hammering in her chest, summoning up the courage her father said they must all have, even if it was buried so deep she might have to dig forever.

Havi eyed her, terrified, as he stood by Hassan al-Hassan.

She must do whatever it took to stay by his side. "Take me with you," she said. "I want to be with you."

"Of course you're mine," he laughed. "Until I'm done with you."

"Thank you," Besma said, bowing, putting her hands together in prayer. "Thank you." Then, "Take her, too," she said, her head still bowed, indicating her mother next to her. "She is the best cook you will ever have. She can make any dish you desire."

"That old hag?" Hassan al-Hassan laughed. Standing back, he raised his AK-47. As Besma's mother shrank, her arms over her head, pleading, he brought the butt of his rifle down on her, cracking her mother's skull. The women and children screamed and Besma battled waves of nausea as her mother fell to the floor, lifeless.

Havi yelped, as if he, too, had been struck, and could feel the blow.

She fought the gagging in her stomach, the roar of panic in her ears, the tears pulling at her eyes. She must stay strong for Havi; she would do him no good by collapsing like a panicked animal.

"Take them to the trucks," Hassan al-Hassan said to the jihadis. "Her," he said, pointing his rifle barrel at Besma. "She's mine."

Besma clutched her brother as the two of them were pulled away. Her body shook uncontrollably, but she struggled to calm herself, knowing she must dig deep for that courage, if they were to live.

1

Place de la Sorbonne, Paris

"Maybe the contact isn't coming," Maggie said to Dara, lowering her sunglasses to check her wristwatch. "Kafka should've been here ten minutes ago." She adjusted the black hijab over her head, for the anonymity that was in it.

Dara's light-blue eyes, contrasting her Middle Eastern features but characteristic of her people, blinked in concern as she drained her demitasse, then set the cup down with a nervous clink. She brushed back her reddish-brown hair and gathered the blue-and-white polka-dotted scarf back around her head. "He must be stuck in Paris's fabled rush-hour traffic." Dara picked up her cell phone, tapping it on the edge of the round wrought-iron table. "He's not answering his phone either."

The two women sat outside in one of the crowded outdoor cafés lining the Place de la Sorbonne, early evening, waiting for the man who had promised to provide Maggie the information necessary to infiltrate the Darknet payment system of one of the largest Jihad Nation cells known. A high-ranking defector indeed. The mid-September sun had just gone down and the streets and sidewalk were bustling with commuters. There was a chill in the air, brought on by the recent rain that left the asphalt glistening.

"Maybe," Maggie said, unconvinced. She pushed her sunglasses back up her nose. Without the shades and hijab, one would have seen deep-brown eyes, though set in a face that was more Quechua Indian than Latin American, with fine high cheekbones and skin the color of copper. She was lucky to have the face for two reasons. As a woman, she'd inherited her Indian mother's classic beauty, and as a field operative, she could pass for many races. That was proving to be a boon for Operation Abraqa. With the smart black-leather jacket she'd picked up at La Piscine, black yoga pants, and alligator loafers, she looked the part—an upscale young Arab woman hanging out in the City of Light.

"We're at the drop-dead time," Maggie said. "Better try and call Kafka again."

Dara took a deep breath, punching a single number on her speed dial, and slipped the phone under her hijab next to her ear.

"No answer," she said after a moment, jiggling her foot as she twisted in the chair, looking around at the street and other cafés either side. "He might be stuck on the Metro—out of cell-phone range."

"Agency protocol says bail," Maggie said with a sigh. "We'll have to reschedule."

Dara clicked off her phone, tossed it on the table with a bump. "All that work!"

A gray-haired waiter in a black vest and white apron appeared, metal tray tucked under his arm. *"Plus de cafés, mesdames?"*

"Non, merci." Maggie said. *"L'addition, s'il vous plaît."*

He gave Maggie a genial nod as he reached into the pocket of his apron, retrieved a bill holder, set it upright on the table in front of her. *"Merci beaucoup, mademoiselle."*

"Well, at least I'm still a *mademoiselle*," Maggie said, getting her cash out, removing the silver money clip, peeling off euros. "I thought I was on the wrong side of twenty-five for that."

The joke didn't fly with Dara, who grimaced and stared at nothing. For her part, half a year's work had been invested in luring Kafka away. His defection from Jihad Nation would strike a major blow for her people, the Yazidis of northern Iraq, who were being slaughtered and kidnapped en masse by the terrorists.

"Don't sweat it, Dara," Maggie said. "This kind of thing happens all the time." It didn't, but what was the point?

"If you say so."

Maggie understood Dara's frustration. The opportunity to break Abraqa—the Darknet payment system—wasn't something that came along every day. They might not get another shot. How many more people would die as a result? How many beheadings? How many women sold into sexual slavery?

It had felt so tantalizingly close.

"Tell you what," Maggie said. "We'll give it five more minutes. But no longer."

Dara exhaled and nodded. "Thank you."

"Just keep it between us." Maggie said. "I've violated protocol before." And paid the price. Was *still* paying the price. It was all she could do not to keep eyeing her watch. But she was keeping a silent count in her head.

One minute.

The people at the next table were having a heated discussion about the Syrian refugees.

"Ruining France!" one hefty woman said, slamming her cup down.

Two minutes.

Dara consulted her phone again, looked up with a frown. "Still nothing from Kafka."

Three minutes. "We're out of here in two minutes if Kafka doesn't show," Maggie said to Dara.

Just then, a car came roaring up in front of the restaurant, skidding to a stop at an angle on the wet tarmac by their table. A rattling blue Citroën, with one white fender and a series of dents.

"That's him. It has to be," Dara said brightly, turning in her chair toward the street.

But Maggie wasn't so sure. Already she was resting her hand under the hem of her silk T-shirt, ready to draw her pistol if need be.

The car doors flew open simultaneously and two people leapt out, from the driver's side a man with a weather-beaten face, unshaved, wearing a black watch cap and a beat-up leather jacket, a drugged look in his sunken eyes.

From the passenger side a woman emerged, dressed entirely in black—jilbāb robe, gloves, and a full niqab over her head, covering everything but her eyes, which stared out in a daze. She wore a white headband with Arabic writing across the front. Strapped on a black sash around her middle were half a dozen black canisters, fused together with white electrical wire.

"Everybody down!" Maggie yelled in French as she

sprang up from her chair and reached under her T-shirt, pulling the subcompact Sig Sauer P238 from her holster bra—a procedure that took one point six seconds at the firing range.

"*Allahu Akbar!*" the woman in black shouted, staggering to the curb. *God is the Greatest!*

Her companion came around the front of the car, raising an AK-47.

Maggie brought the Sig up fast in both hands as she crouched down behind the table, flipping the safety off with her thumb.

The bar patrons shrieked. Some dove for the sidewalk; others started running.

The AK opened up, spraying the crowd indiscriminately. People screamed and fell as the street echoed with gunfire.

Maggie focused on the suicide bomber, keeping her arms straight, lining up the sight at the end of the short pistol on the woman's chest, while the man's machine gun filled the air with a *chock-chock-chock*, rattling in Maggie's ears as she squinted in concentration.

She fired five of the six rounds, holding one back despite the urge to empty the magazine, pulling the trigger gently for each shot the way she did every Thursday at the range.

The woman's niqab puffed out on one side as blood erupted from the eye slit, soaking the head covering before she threw her hands up in a twist and sank back to the ground, as if deflated.

The man with the machine gun stood spread-legged on the street, firing into the crowd hiding under the tables while he shouted euphoric chants in Arabic.

Kneeling, Maggie held her breath and fired the last shot at him.

He bolted sideways, hit in the shoulder.

But he wasn't down.

He kept firing, up in the air, screaming for holy jihad.

Maggie shoved the hot gun in her pocket and racked her brains for her next move. Then, more automatic gunfire boomed to her right. She turned to see two policemen in blue military fatigues sprinting toward them, one firing a submachine pistol at waist level. The other man's side cap flew off as he stopped, readying his weapon.

The man with the AK-47 collapsed in a hail of bullets. His head hit the street at the same time his machine gun did.

And then it was over, just the shots reverberating, subsiding, taken over by the cries of the terrified patrons and wounded victims.

"Everybody get out of here!" Maggie yelled, jumping up. There was no telling if the woman bomber was due to explode or whether Maggie had cut her mission short.

People fled in all directions.

"Come on, Dara!" Maggie shouted.

Then, on the sidewalk by the table, Maggie noticed Dara curled up and motionless.

"Dara!" she gasped, falling to her knees, pulling her friend up. Dara groaned in response, blood trickling out of the corner of her mouth. She was alive! Maggie hauled her to her feet, but it would be a colossal task getting Dara out of here.

A big man with a blond crew cut came bounding over, peeling off his windbreaker. He wore a tight blue T-shirt and had the physique of a body builder. "I'll help!"

"I've got her!" Maggie shouted back. She scanned the pile of blood-soaked bodies and saw the waiter rolling in agony under an old woman in a blue coat and high heels, clearly dead. "Help him!" she yelled, pointing.

The man pulled the waiter from under the dead woman, carried him off.

"Come on, Dara." Dara was in a state of open-mouthed shock, her face streaked with blood, but she could move, albeit unsteadily and with assistance.

"Arm around me," Maggie said, leading her out into the street. The two policemen were now on handheld radios, calling for ambulances and a bomb squad.

In the distance the whoop of sirens resounded off the stately apartment buildings, but it was Dara's desperate gasping that filled Maggie's ears. She was close to death. Warm blood soaked through the hip of Maggie's pants as she clutched her friend and guided her out of bomb danger. Dara stumbled alongside in a haze, sucking in labored breaths that didn't seem to come fast enough.

2

"Hang on, Dara," Maggie whispered in her friend's ear as she gripped her hand, hunched forward in the ambulance winding in and out of traffic down rue de Four. With her other hand, Maggie pressed down on a thick blood-soaked bandage on Dara's chest. The wailing of the siren filled the traffic-jammed street with an electronic whoop that reverberated inside the vehicle.

Dara moaned, a sound barely audible over the siren and the oxygen mask hissing on her face. Her eyes opened for a moment, blue and glazed, giving Maggie a fearful stare, hinting that she understood death was a possibility.

"We'll be there soon," Maggie said, squeezing Dara's clammy fingers.

A *paramédique* in green scrubs and neon-red sneakers sat perched on the bench seat doubling as a second bed alongside Dara's gurney, administering QuikClot and bandages to another shooting victim. The middle-aged man helped him by gripping the bandage in place on his neck with an unusual calmness. His large belly jiggled in a once-white shirt mostly red now as the ambulance careened around a bus.

"How soon?" Dara wheezed through her mask.

Soon was a fluid term. Hospital Necker, the nearest emergency facility, was a five-minute drive from Café de la Nouvelle in the middle of the night at high speed with no obstacles. But Paris's rush-hour traffic tripled that time, according to the ambulance driver. He was skillful and fearless, using the oncoming lane to corkscrew in and out when he could.

Dara's head bobbed to the side as she lapsed into unconsciousness. She'd been shot at least twice, but the chest wound had received the *paramédique's* primary attention. He'd filled the gaping lesion with QuikClot powder and not spared the bandages. But a sucking chest wound was still that—not a strong indication of survival.

Maggie gulped back her anxiety as she pressed down on the bandage. Dara awoke, moaned through her mask. Her head jerked and she twisted against the restraints.

"Don't you have anything to kill the pain?" Maggie shouted in French to the paramedic. "Any ready-to-use morphine shots?"

"I've got my hands a bit full at the moment," he snapped, taping the bandage on the portly man's neck.

Dara cried and shook.

"I can take care of it!" Maggie shouted. "Where are they?"

Without looking at Maggie, he said: "You sure you know what you're doing?"

"I've got an EMT certification," she lied. "Back in the US."

He nodded at a yellow soft pack about the length of a shoebox and half as tall on the shelf above the gurney.

Maggie hopped up, grabbed an overhead bar to steady herself as the ambulance lurched out into an oncoming lane amidst a blare of horns. She nabbed the yellow pack and sat back down, unzipping it in a hurry, rifling through the contents until she found several ready-to-administer morphine-sulfate injection units in a side pouch. She extracted one, pulled the plastic cap off with her teeth as she lifted Dara's soggy abaya cloak to expose her thigh, midriff, and bloody underwear.

"Let me see that!" the tech shouted at Maggie, his shaved head turned her way, his hands still on his patient's neck.

She held up the disposable one-shot syringe. He squinted to read the label.

"That's good," he said, turning his attention back to the big man.

"Can you lift your butt, girlfriend?" Maggie said to Dara.

Dara grunted, then did her best to arch her back, to no avail. Maggie jabbed the side of Dara's buttock through her blood-smeared panties, pushing the plunger in slowly, grabbing the overhead bar again with her free hand as the vehicle rocked. Dara exhaled a blast of air, as if a mountain of suffering had been lifted, and her body slumped back down onto the gurney. Maggie pulled the needle out gently, recapped it, tossed the unit into the trash bin on the wall, then resumed her position at the head of the gurney in the jump seat, holding Dara's now-limp hand.

"*Shukran*," Dara puffed through her oxygen mask, thanking her. She had relapsed into Arabic.

"You're welcome," Maggie replied in Arabic, patting her hand. Watching fretfully as the tension eased out of Dara's face, she bent her head down and pulled off Dara's head scarf, speaking directly into her ear. "Feel any better?" She caressed Dara's head, stroking her matted, damp hair.

Dara raised her hand to her mask, pulling it half off. "Better enough to know that I'm not going to make it."

"Don't even think that," Maggie said. "We'll be there any minute." But even as she said it, she knew what the reality most likely was.

"No, we won't. It's my time. I can feel it."

Dara's voice contained such a note of finality that Maggie didn't doubt her. She pulled the oxygen mask back over Dara's face and chewed her lip as she ran through options. Then she bent back down. "Don't pull your mask off again. Just nod *yes* or *no* in answer to my questions. The phone Kafka gave you, the one you two use to communicate with, is it in your pocket?"

Dara nodded, tried to reach it.

"No," Maggie said. "I'll get it."

When she retrieved the phone, she said, "Is there a password? Security gesture?"

Dara gulped as she made a sign in the air with a shaky hand, an upside down L. Maggie executed it on the phone and it unlocked the screen.

"Do you know if Kafka's tracking you?" Maggie slipped Dara's phone into her jacket pocket.

Dara shrugged. She wasn't technical.

"Do you think Kafka set up the suicide-bomber attack?"

Dara shook her head no.

"So someone in his Jihad Nation cell found out about him? That he was planning to defect?"

Yes.

"Any idea who?"

Another shrug.

"Do you think you can still trust Kafka?"

Dara gritted her teeth while the ambulance cut a sharp corner before she shrugged again.

"*Maybe* you can still trust him?" Maggie asked.

Yes.

"Have you ever met him in person?"

No.

"Videoconference?"

She held up one shaking finger.

Dara tried to pull the mask off her mouth. Maggie intercepted. "No! Keep breathing. How many live phone calls have you had with Kafka?"

She seemed to think about that.

"Less than five?" Maggie said.

Yes.

"Does he have a picture of you?"

Nodded *yes.*

"And you've got one of him, I know. I've seen it."

Another nod.

"What makes you think you can trust him?"

Again Dara motioned to move the mask. Maggie pulled it to one side, put her ear close to Dara's mouth.

"I just . . . know," she said in a tortured voice.

Maggie replaced the oxygen mask firmly over Dara's mouth. "Are you positive Kafka has access to those Darknet folders?"

A weak smile appeared. *Yes.*

"Do you think I can pass as you, Dara? Physically? Long enough to meet Kafka?"

Dara nodded. Then she coughed. Blood splattered the inside of her oxygen mask. The sound of gurgling followed.

"I'm going to need your laptop," Maggie said. "Waleed has to let me have it."

Dara spluttered and the inside of her mask became a percolator of blood. She tried to raise her hand to her neck. She wouldn't last much longer. Maggie put her hand over

Dara's and squeezed, then realized Dara was indicating a gold pendant hanging around her neck. "The pendant?"

Dara had slumped to the side and her hand fell on her chest, motionless.

"Oh my God," Maggie said, pulling back the mask, trying to wipe the blood from Dara's mouth, blood that wouldn't stop bubbling up from her chest. "Can't you help her?" she said to the attendant. "*Please?*"

He turned around quickly, swiped Maggie's arm out of the way to get a look at Dara, then hopped up and powered on the defibrillator mounted to the wall behind the driver. "Clear her chest!" he shouted.

Maggie opened Dara's abaya and pulled the soggy bandages out of the way as the paramedic pressed the two black pads to her chest. An electric snap made her torso bounce, but it was dead muscle memory.

Repeated attempts did nothing.

The only sound coming from Dara was the whisper of the oxygen mask on the side of her bloody face.

"She's dead," he said, "I'm sorry." Tossing the paddles aside, he returned to the other patient.

This was no time to stand on decorum. Maggie brushed Dara's hand away, yanked the chain and pendant off in one swift movement, and quickly slipped them into her pocket where Dara's phone was. She felt through Dara's robe until she located her wallet. She took that as well. For the time being, no one would know who Dara was. Her only contacts in Paris were the Incognito group she worked for and the aunt she lived with. Nothing on her body would identify her.

Maggie pulled the abaya cloak back over Dara's body and buttoned it before removing the oxygen mask. She cleaned Dara's face with an antiseptic wipe. Then she turned off the oxygen, the relative silence enveloping her with a sense of defeat and despair.

She slumped back in the jump seat, stroking Dara's hair. Hung her head. Tears welled up, even though she was trained for this eventuality, had been party to failed operations before. The death of a colleague was no stranger. It came with the territory. But this was different. Dara had taken such a risk for her people, slaughtered and raped by the jihadists. Drawing Kafka out, getting him to commit to a defection that would cripple Jihad Nation financially. Her companions, the volunteers of Incognito, the notorious international network of activists and hacktivists, took risks, too, but it was Dara who put her life on the line. Literally.

They'd gotten so close. Kafka—whoever he was—was a strong candidate for defection. In the time she'd known Dara, Maggie had learned to trust her instincts, and Dara knew Kafka better than anyone. If she believed Kafka was still ripe, then Maggie believed that too. If she'd learned anything in this business, it was to trust her instincts. Truth was a fickle beast. You had to trust your gut.

The ambulance swerved into the vehicle dock at Hospital Necker with a screech of tires, jerking to a halt.

The paramedic flung open the back door of the ambulance and the driver leapt out to assist him.

Dara's phone vibrated in Maggie's pocket.

Maggie pulled the phone and swiped the upside down L security gesture with her finger.

Incoming call from Kafka—the no-show defector who had somehow caused this huge tragedy.

Her heart thumped wildly.

She couldn't talk to him, not if she was going to continue the operation posing as Dara, leveraging everything Dara had given her. There was no way Maggie could mimic Dara's voice, accent, her command of Arabic. She let the call roll over to voicemail, then immediately retrieved it, pressing the phone close to her ear. A youngish man with a cultured Baghdad accent left a beseeching message in a dialect Maggie could just follow.

"Did you get away safe, *habiti*? God, I pray that you did. I'm so terrified that you didn't. I had no idea they were going to do that. How could I know? Madmen! You know I would never allow that, my dear *habiti*. Please, *please* call me as soon as you get this. I *must* speak to you before I go mad." Then one last sentence before he clicked off: "*La astatee'a an a'aeesh bedonak.*" *I can't live without you.*

Kafka's use of the word *habiti*—an Arabic term of endearment—gave Maggie pause, as did the last sentence. She scrolled back through previous texts to get a feel for the language Dara and Kafka used.

Many of the interactions contained romantic terms. A revelation. Dara had always been vague on her communications with Kafka, merely saying she was grooming him after he'd shown interest in her when she'd reached out to him at Incognito. But in addition to his desire to get his parents safely out of Iraq, there was enough side conversation about his wish to meet Dara to make Maggie wonder.

She switched the phone keyboard to Arabic and struggled to pick out a message. Arabic was much more difficult to write than speak, and it was challenging enough to speak. Slowly, she typed: "Dearest *habibi,* I was wounded, but God willing I am alive ... but they are watching me and I cannot call ... too dangerous ... you do understand? ... text only ... please be safe and wait for me to call."

Then she typed one final phrase, one she had seen Dara use over and over in her texts to Kafka: *"Enta kol shay'a."* *You are my all.*

She closed her text messenger and went through Dara's recent call list until she found the number of her contact at Incognito. She pressed the speed dial and Waleed answered on the first ring.

She pictured the young muscular Arab with his wild hair and passionate, intense eyes.

"Are you all right?" he said breathlessly in Arab dialect. "We're watching the news now. I can't believe it! Thank God you called, Dara. We were so worried..."

"Waleed," Maggie said, drawing in air, not wanting to deliver the wretched news. "It's Maggie."

After a pause, Waleed said, "Oh." Then, "No. But no!"

"I don't know what to say. Except that I'm so sorry."

There was a gap while the paramedic and driver got the big man on a stretcher and lugged him away.

"Those bastards!" Waleed hissed into her ear. "Those murdering bastards."

"I need to ask you a huge favor."

"What?" Waleed's voice sounded distant.

"If anyone asks, Dara is in intensive care. She's alive, fighting for her life, but can't accept visitors. Is that very clear?"

She could almost see Waleed nodding in agreement. "Dara's not dead. Yes, I see what you're doing. Yes. Got it."

"It's very important that you don't tell anyone the truth. I debated whether to tell you. But I decided you needed to know."

A distant siren whined.

"You have my word."

"I'll tell Dara's aunt next. I'm going to call her now. I'll swing by later when I get the chance. I need to pick up some of Dara's things."

"Yes," he said in a hollow tone. "It's best that *you* tell Aunt Amina."

Maggie dialed Aunt Amina, taking another deep breath, preparing herself for more emotional carnage.

No answer. A sick kind of relief fell over Maggie, knowing she'd only have to call Amina later.

A squeal of tires and the flash of blue lights alerted her to a police car pulling up behind the ambulance. A compact Renault, headlights blinding. Turning to one side, Maggie pulled the Sig Sauer from her jacket pocket, shoved it into the trash bin full of medical waste on the wall of the ambulance. While she was at it, she pulled her own phone, removed the battery, dumped both items in the trash as well. She didn't need two phones on her. That might look suspicious if she were searched. She still had Dara's phone, the one that counted.

The doors to the police car opened and two blue-clad National Police officers emerged.

Maggie waited for the policemen, wondering what feelings Dara had truly harbored for her mysterious would-be defector.

3

"Get off the motorway," the man called Kafka said in halting French to the taxi driver. "Then let me out."

"Here?" the *chauffeur de taxi* said, squinting in the rearview mirror. The tall Arab man with fine features was wearing sunglasses, even though it was early evening. The man's face was taut, although he did a good job of concealing his nervousness.

"Yes," Kafka said. The truth was, he'd changed his mind —about running. His masters would find him eventually. His life would be worth nothing. Less than nothing considering what they'd do to him before they ended it. His parents too. But now, it was the worst of all worlds: He was blown.

"I see," the cabbie said, a smirk now on his unshaven face as he took the off-ramp in northern Paris. He had been eyeing the Arab with suspicion ever since he picked him up outside the Denfer-Rochereau metro, where multiple police vans had been parked as they searched trains after the shooting at the café in the *place de la*

Sorbonne. "It's still thirty euros," he reminded his passenger. "You agreed."

"Yes, yes," Kafka said. Blatant thievery. But it was the least of his worries.

The cabbie pulled over on the edge of La Courneuve, where the middle-class suburb gave way to vacant lots and forgotten buildings. The runway lights and tower of Le Bourget Airport loomed in the distance.

Kafka handed the cabbie two twenty-euro notes, told him to keep the change. A ludicrous tip but he didn't need an irate taxi driver calling the police about some Arab with a daypack getting out in the middle of nowhere so soon after the shooting. The cabbie drove off without thanking him, a whine of gears as he fled the poor neighborhood tucked away in the shadows of the wealthy city.

Kafka stood in a shantytown that kept rematerializing even though the authorities cleared it out every few years. The Roma who occupied the slum were too tough, too mean, to take their efforts with anything less than amused disdain and increased vigor.

Kafka could blend in here. He couldn't go to the safe house. His masters had sent suicide bombers to the rendezvous. He'd make his own way. Hide for a day. Let the dust settle.

He pulled the knit watch cap down over his ears, hiding more of his classic features. He was a pale-skinned Arab, in his thirties, trim, tall, and his striking good looks drew too much attention for his own good. He wasn't being bigheaded; he just needed to be incognito. What a choice of word: Incognito—the very place Dara had worked.

He thanked Allah that she was still alive, albeit in serious condition.

Madmen! *His* madmen.

Jihad Nation. How had they found out? That he was going to run? Either someone betrayed him or they always suspected him. He was never truly one of them. How could he be? He wasn't insane. He couldn't go back to Iraq without knowing exactly what lay in store. He'd make contact in a day or two. Play stupid. Play along.

But if he didn't return home, his parents, living in Mosul, a city ruled by Jihad Nation now, would pay the price. His defection would have carried his mother and father to safety, but now it was up in the air, at best. At worst, cut off. Over.

Dara. Thank God she was still alive. Although they'd never met in person, he'd become attached. He thought of her soothing voice, calm and reassuring, speaking his language well, and her dark features and long hair, accentuated by piercing blue eyes. He'd spent too much time looking at the photographs she'd sent him.

He heard sirens in the distance as he walked down a dirt road. It was starting to rain again as night took hold. Winter was coming early this year.

Kafka—a name so ingrained he thought of it when he thought of himself now. He no longer recognized who he used to be. That didn't matter. He didn't want to be who he used to be. He needed to become someone new again. If he wanted to survive. If he wanted his parents to survive.

He'd do what he always did, whatever it took. It had always been that way. And it was that way now.

He headed into the slum. It would be his home tonight.

4

"What did you do with the gun?" Captain Bellard asked Maggie in French, for the second time. "The one you shot the suicide bomber with?"

"I tossed it," she said, also for the second time.

The two of them were sitting in the captain's glass-walled office in *Sous-Direction Anti-Terroriste* headquarters on rue de Villiers in Levallois-Perret. SDAT was the elite counter-terrorist task force of the French National Police and their building was a sleek, modern structure, more reminiscent of a four-star hotel than some grimy police station where interviews were conducted in dirty rooms with questionable stains on the walls. It was late and the rest of the floor sat in empty dark silence.

She'd been there for several hours, with no end in sight.

"You tossed it," Captain Bellard repeated. He was a smallish man in his early forties with sleepless brown eyes that drilled through you. His short dark hair was thatched and said he didn't think much of haircuts. His pale skin took a back seat to the five-o'clock shadow that enhanced his angular features. Bellard wore an off-the-rack light blue suit. Despite his size he was muscular and reasonably good-looking, depending on your mood. But Maggie wasn't in the mood. Kafka might be about to take off for Iraq any minute, and she needed to intercept him. Meanwhile, she and Bellard kept going round and round on the same questions.

"What kind of gun did you use?" Bellard asked.

"Sig Sauer—P238. I'm pretty sure I already said that."

"Where did you get it?"

"On the street," Maggie said. "In a bar. Rue d'Aboukir. As I said, it's not that hard. Not as hard as you think. But we've been through this. We really need to get moving before Kafka runs. And the sooner you get hold of my handler, the sooner we can do that."

Bellard gave an impatient stare. "What was the name of the bar?"

One more time. The age old police technique of asking you the same questions over and over, hoping to trip you in a lie. Maggie had already explained how, as a Forensic Accounting Agent, the op was to provide analysis on Abraqa, a Darknet network used by Jihad Nation to move huge sums of money to fund terrorist activities. Dara had catfished Kafka at Incognito, and passed the info on to one of Maggie's French contacts in the hopes of finding someone to fund and help drive the operation. Maggie had invested the last two weeks working with Dara, lining up Agency resources to hopefully crack Abraqa.

And now, she and Bellard, back at the gun question. She hoped she hadn't made a mistake in asking for him when the police questioned her. She brushed her hair back in exasperation. "I don't remember the name of the bar—and it's not important."

"Oh, I see—it's not important. Why, thank you."

"Look," she said. "I came to you, told you a lot more than I was authorized to."

"More than you were *authorized to*? Your agency ran a covert operation—in Paris—without our consent, and you tell me what's *important*? What you're *authorized* to say?"

Maggie put her hands up in a gesture of appeasement. "Bad choice of words. I'm tired and my French is a little rusty. I understand your frustration."

"*You understand my frustration?*" Bellard nabbed a blue-and-white pack of Gauloise cigarettes and tapped out a smoke with a snap of the wrist, stuck the cigarette between his thin lips. "You're not in California now." He picked up a gold cigarette lighter, flicked it, bent down over a tapered flame, sat back up, blowing smoke which she wanted to fan away but didn't. Bellard tapped ash into a ceramic ashtray. "Let me ask what your people would do in my position. If I were running a clandestine op in *your* country."

She gave him a wry squint. "You're saying it doesn't happen?"

"Ah," he said, pointing the cigarette at her. "But you were caught."

Maggie wanted to say that it was not her idea to exclude SDAT from Operation Abraqa, that she *had* recommended they participate, but that the Agency did things its own way, which generally meant keeping everyone in the dark, especially competing intelligence agencies.

"I obviously did not expect a shooting situation," she said. "I told you, this was meant to be a first interview with a potential terrorist who might want to defect. I was to evaluate what he knew and report back. That was it. I have no other people here. I need your help—and you need mine—if we want to catch this Kafka. Someone found out about his meeting with Dara and sent suicide bombers instead. Now, will you please call my boss, Ed Linden?"

Bellard shook his head, clearly annoyed. "Who the hell do you think you are?" He smashed out the cigarette, left it broken and smoking in the ashtray, then picked up the phone, punched a single digit and said, "I have a person helping me with my enquiries. She will be staying with us overnight. Request a female officer to conduct a thorough search before we process her. Fine. Thank you."

Maggie's nerves shot into overdrive. She stood up. "Are you *serious*? You're holding me? After I came to you?"

"I need time to gather information. We'll continue in the morning. Have you eaten?"

"What were you thinking of—some microwaveable treat in my cell? Will I get a plastic knife or will it be taken away? Go to hell."

Bellard gave a smirk. "I understand your frustration."

Maggie sat back down, vibrating with anger. She was exhausted. She caught her breath. Bellard was only trying to do his job, one he'd been blind-sided at. "Look, I wanted SDAT brought into the Abraqa op. I was told it was too early. That we were still at the fact-finding stage. You know how it is—everyone is so secretive. Why, you'd think we were secret agents or something." She smiled.

"Per French law, we can hold you for up to five days." Bellard consulted his wristwatch. "We'll continue in the morning."

Five days. Maggie could do the time standing on her head but Operation Abraqa couldn't. They needed to nab Kafka, cut off Jihad Nation's funding.

And Dara's death couldn't be concealed for that long.

"Captain," she said. "I have a favor to ask."

Bellard gave a bemused smile. "Only an American would ask such a thing at this very moment."

"I know. But will you please agree *not* to divulge that Dara is dead? And communicate that bit of misinformation to Hospital Necker so they keep it under wraps? If Kafka hangs around in Paris, we can use Dara as bait . . . we don't want all of her work to go down the toilet."

Bellard nodded as he seemed to give that some thought. "Yes," he said. "That's wise—not to disclose that Dara is dead. Yes." He wrote something down on his pad of paper.

"Thank you." It wasn't much but it was all she was going to get for now.

She heard the elevator ding out in the hallway and guards chatting. They arrived at the door of Bellard's office. Dressed in blue with SDAT patches on their shoulders—white panther heads on black, bearing fangs—one guard was a pretty young woman with blonde hair up in a swirl and twinkling blue eyes. She had a wicked-looking collapsible metal baton hanging on her web belt. She gave Maggie a friendly smile, then turned to Bellard.

"Is this our prisoner, *Capitaine*?"

THE PRETTY BLONDE guard took her belongings, catalogued them, handed Maggie a receipt. Maggie tried to hang onto Dara's phone, saying she needed it to call her husband, that her little boy back home was sick with the flu, but her request, of course, was denied. She powered the phone down, handed it over. But she would need that phone back, if she were ever to get hold of Kafka.

She knew she would not sleep, even though she was physically shattered. She kicked off her shoes and climbed under the single blanket in the stark windowless cell. She had a straight-line view of the stainless steel toilet with no seat. A hint of urine hung in the air. The overhead light blazed down. Ambience.

What did she know? That Dara had fostered some sort of romantic connection with Kafka. She and Dara had not spoken about that part of the relationship. It was an eye-opener. From Maggie's text with him in the ambulance earlier, posing as Dara, she believed it was genuine. Dara had said she never met Kafka in person. That meant the relationship was probably along the lines of infatuation on Kafka's part, an online romance. Arab men who grew up in repressive cultures were susceptible to that sort of thing. Maggie could leverage that.

Then she wondered, once again, who had sent the suicide bombers?

Someone at Incognito? They were anarchists. Couldn't be ruled out. But it wasn't their style. Their MO was to screw up someone's banking profile, leak their financial data. And Dara was very careful about what information was disseminated, even careful with what she let Maggie know.

Someone on Maggie's side of the fence? Unlikely. Everyone at the Agency was thoroughly vetted and every op had hurdles of security clearances. And who knew about Abraqa? Not many.

There had been one hint of a mole—or maybe just an information slip-up—on her last op. Someone had betrayed Maggie's position when she was on the run in Ecuador. Unfortunately, the man who could answer that question was now dead.

It was more likely someone with Jihad Nation had found out about Kafka and Dara. But who?

Maggie shut her eyes and saw blurred lines, then the

gunfight playing on her eyelids, while the distant clatter of automatic rifle fire reverberated in her ears. Café patrons fell screaming, the suicide bomber's haunted eyes staring out of the slit of her naqib as she staggered for the café. Maggie's Sig Sauer popping in her hands, each shot measured. Dara was on the ground, curled up, then gasping in the ambulance. Until she stopped.

Dara's death was still fresh, but not yet real, even though Maggie's shirt and tights were stiff with her friend's dried blood.

What was real was the fact that Maggie had violated protocol, exceeded the drop-dead time for the meeting. What would have happened had she and Dara left the café on time? Dara would still be alive. Maggie soaked up guilt like a dry sponge absorbed water. Tears pulled at her eyes.

Stop. What good would that do?

Then she heard footsteps, coming down the hallway outside her cell. Light enough not to be a man's. They stopped outside her cell. Followed by the electric whir of the door lock.

Here it comes, Maggie thought, another time-honored police trick—let you fall asleep, then wake you up, question you when you're bleary, off your guard.

Throwing off her blanket, Maggie sat up, slipped her shoes back on.

The electronic door slid open. The blonde guard stood there with Maggie's belongings in a blue plastic basket.

"What's going on?" Maggie said in French, rubbing her eyes.

"You're leaving us," she said.

"Leaving you how?" Maggie said. "Am I first in line for the guillotine tomorrow morning?"

The girl laughed as she set Maggie's box of things on the bunk. "Not this time. Someone arranged for your release."

Well, Maggie thought, every dog has its day. And she could be a bitch. She probably owed her boss Ed about ten dinners. And how the man could put the food away.

Going through the box, the first thing she checked was Dara's phone, which she slipped into the pocket of her leather jacket. She hadn't even taken the thing off; it was still sticky on one side with Dara's blood. That made her shudder. She'd like to get hold of Dara's laptop too. That was probably at Dara's aunt's house. Or Incognito.

"The captain wants a word with you before you leave," the guard said.

It was almost two AM.

∽

"I'll have someone drive you to your hotel," Captain Bellard said, sitting at his desk, hands folded behind his head, not making eye contact. His unshaven face was slightly pink. Embarrassed.

Ed, her boss, had managed to get hold of Bellard's superior and short-circuit Maggie's stint in a cell.

"Thanks for not hitting me with a phone book, at least," she said with a smile.

Bellard grinned.

"Seriously," she said. "No hard feelings, hey?"

"We'll resume our interview at ten o'clock tomorrow morning."

Maggie's spirits dropped. It seemed Ed's efforts had only gone so far. She was still on the hook with Bellard.

"Very well," she said. But she would be on the phone to

Ed as soon as she got out of here. As soon as she got another phone. She wouldn't use Dara's. It might be bugged.

Bellard pressed an intercom button on his desk phone. "I need a vehicle escort." He returned his attention to Maggie and drummed on his desk, one beat for each hand. Maggie didn't mind another ride in a police car at this time of night.

"You did well out there today," Bellard said. "You shoot as well as you speak French. Where did you learn French anyway?"

Now he wanted to be friends. Well, she thought, you catch more flies with honey than vinegar. "Here and there. I grew up speaking Spanish so I had an advantage."

He sat back in his chair, tapping the arms, looking at her. "You're Spanish?"

"Born in Ecuador. But I'm a US citizen. My father's a Yankee."

He scrutinized Maggie's face, with its high cheekbones, deep-set brown eyes. Dark skin, long black hair. "Ah, you're part Indian."

"My mother was Quechua." Quechua Indians, descended from the Incas, were indigenous to many Andean countries.

"Do you think this Kafka set you and Dara up?"

"I don't think so," she said. "Dara spent a lot of time vetting him."

"And where is Dara's phone?" Bellard said.

"On the café table last I saw," Maggie lied. "With Dara dying in front of me, I didn't think to take it." She gave a theatrical sigh.

Bellard pursed his lips and nodded, wrote that down on his pad of perfectly aligned notes.

Maggie cleared her throat. "May I ask where we stand on Hospital Necker giving out details on Dara's death?"

"They won't release any info."

"Thank you," she said with a weary smile. "If we work together, we can salvage this op."

Bellard returned the smile as his eyes briefly scoured her upright figure in her black tights, T-shirt, and leather jacket. The drying blood probably wouldn't bother a man who had undoubtedly seen much worse.

"Ten AM tomorrow," he said.

"I'm looking forward to it."

He gave a wry smile. "Of course you are."

∾

It wasn't until two-thirty AM that Maggie finally got back to the Shangri La hotel on rue Philibert Lucot in the 13th Arrondissement. She had to ring the bell to wake up the night desk clerk, a young woman with a pixie haircut slumped over a text book. Maggie's head was splitting. In her room on the third floor, with its wild apricot and blue paisley wallpaper that hurt the eye, Maggie pulled Dara's phone from her sticky leather jacket, peeled off the jacket, dumped it on the bathroom floor, along with her blood-stained tights and T-shirt, destined for the trash.

The day came back at her in jarring flashes.

She raided the minibar in her room, spending a small fortune to fill a tumbler. She sat on the bed in her underwear, gulped an inch of Johnnie Walker. She needed a shower but had a few things to do first.

If Kafka was worth his salt, he'd be tracking the phone he'd given to Dara. Maggie powered up Dara's phone, saw no new messages, downloaded MockLoc, an app that mimicked GPS locations. She looked up Hospital Necker, plugged the location coordinates for it into MockLoc, in case Kafka *was* monitoring Dara. If he was he'd see her at the hospital.

She powered down Dara's phone for the time being.

Using her room phone she made a call to Hospital Necker. No information on the shooting victim she'd arrived with. Good. Dara's death was still under wraps.

She called Ed, her supervisor, on his personal phone back in San Francisco from the phone in her room.

"Hey, Maggie," he said, sounding a little surprised she wasn't calling on his work phone. He was no doubt dealing with the many fires that had been created by the shooting.

"Did you order a pizza?" she said. *Safe to talk?*

"No. You?"

"No."

"You at your hotel?"

"I am. I even have a toilet with a seat now. Thanks."

"Cool," Ed said, and she could hear him sucking on a cigarette long distance. She could picture him, looking like an unmade bed, hair smashed, untrimmed beard, glasses askew on his chubby face. "See you tomorrow."

"But I have an appointment tomorrow," she said, meaning Bellard at ten AM.

"No you don't." Ed hung up.

What did Ed mean by that?

Before her next call, she gulped another half inch of Scotch and took a deep breath.

Aunt Amina answered, groggy. Maggie braced herself.

"Oh, hello, Maggie!" Dara's aunt said with forced cheerfulness that only made Maggie feel more miserable. "With the news, I was worried. I can't seem to get hold of Dara. Are you two out somewhere?"

There was a long silence. In the street outside her hotel room a couple of stories below, Maggie heard excited young voices chatting away in Vietnamese, heels clicking on down the street.

Had she followed protocol, would Dara still be alive? She downed another inch of whiskey.

"I'm afraid . . . I have some very bad news," Maggie said.

There was a long stillness.

"Oh," was all Amina said.

It was one of the hardest phone calls Maggie ever had to make. But she secured Amina's promise to not discuss Dara's death. Maggie could only imagine how hard it would be, keeping that grief to oneself. Amina didn't cry. Her people, the Yazidis, had seen so much, they were hardened to death. Dara's passing was just another example of how brutal life was.

"And now I have a huge favor to ask, Amina . . ."

Amina said, quietly: "Of course."

"Is Dara's laptop in your apartment?"

"Let me check." She put the phone down. A minute later she picked it up again.

"In her room."

That was what Maggie wanted to hear. "I'll pick it up first thing in the morning."

There was another pause. "So you can continue where you and Dara left off." Amina exhaled. "Yes, that *is* what my niece would have wished. To keep fighting for our people."

Maggie said goodbye, hung up and guzzled more whiskey before stepping into a long hot shower that had no regard for the planet's dwindling water supplies. She stood under the jets, letting hot needles of water drill into her face until it was numb, and the vision of bodies tumbling at the café and Dara's sickening demise blurred.

When she emerged from the shower, she found the red light blinking on the phone by her bed. Wrapping her wet hair and a towel and gathering her robe around her, Maggie called reception.

"There's a man waiting for you in the lobby, mademoiselle," the girl at the front desk said.

All Maggie wanted to do was finish off the lesser liquors in the minibar and crawl between the sheets for a few hours, pretend that today never happened.

"Is he a *flic*?"

"No, he's not a policeman. He's an American. He's actually quite entertaining."

"Does he sound like a cowboy?"

"Oh, yes. He certainly does."

John Rae had the ability to charm most women. Even Maggie from time to time. But she wasn't going to ask him up with her in a bathrobe, not at almost four in the morning.

"I'll be right down."

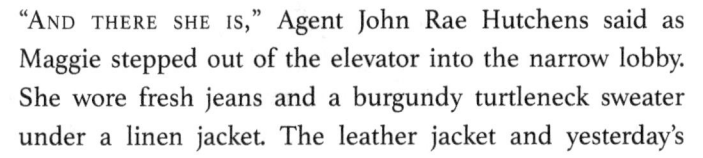

~

"And there she is," Agent John Rae Hutchens said as Maggie stepped out of the elevator into the narrow lobby. She wore fresh jeans and a burgundy turtleneck sweater under a linen jacket. The leather jacket and yesterday's outfit had been relegated to the trash.

John Rae wore a slim-fitting dark blue suit over a black silk T-shirt and tasseled loafers. His longish sandy colored hair was combed back behind his ears and the designer stubble he'd sported last week had morphed into a neatly trimmed goatee. Doing his best young Brad Pitt impression.

Always easy to look at. He stood up as she went to greet him. "Remind me not to challenge you to a duel."

"Too soon," Maggie said, giving him a platonic peck on the cheek, intending to keep it that way, although it was sometimes tempting to let things slide. "Way too soon."

"The sooner the better." He squeezed her shoulder, dropped his voice. "How you holding up?"

She stood back. "If I had my way, I'd be in bed by now." She gave a tired smile. "*Alone.* So I hope this is important."

"Important enough the powers that be scheduled a private flight for me from Berlin."

"Berlin?"

"The Class Four thing I'm on?" John was one of the Agency's top operatives. Class Four was so hush-hush even JR probably didn't know what it was about yet. "We're still ramping up. So I have spare cycles. Which means they sent me to pick you up. Take you home."

"Take me home?" she said.

"Your home away from home. Langley."

A post mortem of the shooting with Agency brass. Oh joy.

"When?"

"We get on a C-130 leaving Le Bourget eight-oh-five AM tomorrow. We'll be keeping a bunch of army regulars coming back from Kandahar company."

"I'm supposed to meet Captain Bellard at ten AM for ongoing questioning."

"Not anymore," he said.

So *that's* what Ed meant when he said he'd see Maggie tomorrow. "If I blow Bellard off, JR, it won't do our rapport any good."

John Rae grinned at Maggie's use of his nickname. "I hear you but you are talking about *The* Captain Bellard—a complete *however-you-say-it* in French. Walder figures Bellard's going to hang us out to dry over the unauthorized op by making an example of you." Walder was Director of Field Operations, John Rae's boss, Ed's boss too. "Walder doesn't want that."

That could doom any chance of Abraqa continuing. "There's a little hole-in-the wall Vietnamese place down the street," she said. "Open all night. I haven't had anything to eat since lunch yesterday."

∽

A NEW SONG had just started and two young Vietnamese women, one in a black leather miniskirt, the other in a clingy beige knit minidress, hopped up from their crowded Formica table and danced in front of the fish tank in the corner. Their friends clapped along to the beat and shouted encouragement.

John Rae watched, obviously savoring the moment, before he turned back to Maggie. "Paris is pretty cool."

"What we need to do," Maggie said as she munched a hot onion pancake that was well worth the calories, "is to 'transfer' Dara to the American Hospital of Paris—a *keep-alive*." A keep-alive fabricated a scenario in which a dead person appeared to still be alive. "We get Bellard to play along, then we can lure Kafka. If he's still here, that is . . ."

Maggie caught the disheartening frown on John Rae's face.

"Maggie," he said, swigging Tiger beer, "you need to see the cold gray light of dawn."

She picked up her glass of Chablis, took a swallow. On top of the minibar binge, her head was buzzing, which at least meant her headache had been pushed into the background, along with the images of the shooting. "Has Abraqa been cancelled yet?"

"It's only a formality."

She set her glass down. "What have you heard?"

"Nothing. I just know how it works. The fact that you saved about one hundred lives is going to be a dim memory once the French start sending nastygrams to Washington. Since SDAT weren't informed about the operation, they're going to be out for blood." John Rae drank some more beer. "Yours, in this case. Abraqa was never high-priority. You were the only agent on it, because you pushed. Well, good for you. But it's over. Now the Agency's going to run for cover."

She straightened her napkin. "I'm not prepared to throw in the towel yet. Any way we can take a later flight? I think we can sway Bellard."

John Rae shook his head. "I'm escorting you to Le Bourget first thing. Orders."

"And you always follow those, right?" She drank wine, gave a wink.

"When your ass is in a sling, I do." He set his bottle down.

The tinny pop song came to an end and the girls sat down amidst rounds of applause.

Maggie let out a hard sigh. "If we can break Abraqa, we stop close to a billion dollars of Jihad Nation money being funneled through the Darknet."

"Ours is not the reason why," John Rae said.

"Dara gave her life for this. Her people are being raped and beheaded, nine-year-old girls sold into sexual slavery by Jihad Nation. But all the Agency is focused on is damage control."

John Rae turned his bottle on the table. "You're top

notch, Maggie, but you need to let go when something flames out on you. Like it just did. I'm on your side but you need to see that. When we get back home we can see if anyone will listen to you—but don't get your hopes up. You're getting on that plane with me. In about four hours."

Maggie saw it was futile to argue at this time.

"I need to swing by Dara's aunt's place first thing, though," she said. "On the way to the airport. Amina's the only family Dara has–*had*–outside of Iraq. She also has Dara's laptop. There's a ton of data on that."

John Rae frowned as he peeled the label of his bottle. "If we can fit it in before we head to Le Bourget, fine. But it means an early start. We're getting on that eight-oh-five flight."

She drained her wine. She'd gotten that much out of John Rae. He was a good guy. If they didn't work so closely together, it would be a different story between the two of them. She wondered if he'd break rules for her then.

A new song had started and the two Vietnamese women were back up, dancing, pulling their friends out of their chairs. Everyone was laughing. For some Paris was a different city right now.

∽

Across town, Kafka rolled over on the rough wooden floor of an abandoned house. The snoring of a vagrant in another room was not keeping him awake. He had not been sleeping. Not only was it too cold, without a blanket or mattress, but he would not let himself become a victim of whoever might wander in. So he'd wait until morning, the stench of urine and human waste permeating his thoughts.

He'd have to contact his masters at some point. Even

though he felt like disappearing. But his mother. His father. Jihad Nation had them in their clutches any time they wanted them.

They had him where they wanted him.

And then there was Dara. Was she in intensive care? Was she...

He'd find out more tomorrow, when the day began.

He adjusted his shoulder bag under his head, a hard pillow to be sure, and listened to the rush of the motorway in the distance, while the man in the other room snored.

5

Dara's aunt Amina lived in a small one-bedroom walk-up off the Boulevard Barbès. Compared to what she had left behind in northern Iraq, however, where her people were being decimated by Jihad Nation, it was heaven. No rolling blackouts. No food shortages (unless you factored in shortages of cash). No crazed jihadis at the door.

Around the corner the street market was already setting up for the day underneath the elevated Metro line when Maggie and John Rae pulled up in a cab.

"Wait here," Maggie instructed the driver in French, then switched to English and told John Rae the same. John Rae tapped his wristwatch as she jumped out, dashed across the street, dodging an irate bicyclist who shook his fist at her.

Upstairs, on the fourth floor, the door to Amina's apartment opened as soon as Maggie reached the landing. Aunt Amina peered out, her big hair hennaed and sprayed, the scent drifting out into the hallway. She was completely made up, including dark red lipstick. She wore a blue pant suit that hugged her full figure and a thick gold chain over her ample bosom.

Amina was not the shy and retiring type. But one look at her face close up revealed that her mascara had run and been reapplied.

"Amina," Maggie said, giving her a deep hug, "I don't know what to say."

Amina showed Maggie into the tiny apartment where a large fabric wall hanging and a healthy spider plant in a green ceramic pot on the polished hardwood floor fought off the gloom. She had already set up a small shrine with Dara's photograph and a flickering candle in the corner of the room.

"Sit down, Maggie," Amina said in a husky voice. "Have some tea."

Maggie felt like a rat for having to grab Dara's laptop and run.

"I can't, Amina. I'm flying back home in an hour. When I return I'll spend more time. I want you to know that the company I work for will pay for Dara's funeral services." Maggie hoped so, anyway. She retrieved a white envelope from the breast pocket of her jacket, which contained several hundred euros she'd withdrawn from her account at the ATM on the way here. She handed it over. "In the meantime, this will hopefully cover immediate living expenses." Amina owned a small tea room where Yazidi people met but it was more of a calling than a source of income. Without Dara's outside earnings as an IT consultant she would soon be in dire straits, living in Paris.

Amina took the envelope. "Thank you."

But despite the customary grieving, something seemed wrong. Maggie held Amina at arm's length and scrutinized her desolate face.

"Amina—is something else the matter?"

Amina looked down at her gleaming black flats. "I think I did something very stupid, Maggie."

~

"What do you mean she gave the laptop away?" John Rae said as Maggie climbed back into the cab. More vendors were arriving and setting up market stalls in the street. The cab driver was watching a video on a tablet fixed to the dash and didn't seem to mind as long as the meter was running.

"Waleed stopped by her place earlier and picked it up," Maggie said. "Amina told him she'd already agreed to give it to me but he insisted it was Incognito's property—which it is. He got difficult—something he's good at—threatening to sue her and saying he'd have her deported." Maggie shook her head. "As if he would. But she fell for it. In the end, Amina handed it over."

"Well, it was a noble effort, Maggie." John Rae leaned forward to the driver and said, "Airport. Le Bourget," splitting each syllable into a separate word, making him sound a little like Herman Munster.

The driver nodded, started the engine.

"Wait a minute, JR," Maggie said. "Going back without that laptop is calling it quits. There's info on it that'll keep Operation Abraqa going."

"That's how we roll at the agency, Maggie."

"Well, it can roll without me." She instructed the driver in French to hold off. He obliged, sat back, turned off the engine, watched the Simpsons in French with half an eye.

"No, no, no, no," John Rae said. "It's not a damn suggestion. It's an order. From on high. You're coming back with me." He raised his eyebrows. "Copy that?"

The cab driver's eyes darted back and forth between the two of them in the rearview mirror, as he obviously wondered how to proceed.

"I'm serious, Maggie. If we aren't on that C-130 and talking to the brass first thing tomorrow, you can kiss any chance at all of getting Abraqa resurrected."

Punt.

"Whatever," Maggie said. "Let's just go, then."

"Thanks for seeing it my way." He leaned forward and said to the driver: "Air. Port. Now."

The cab started up again, spun around and headed down Boulevard Barbès, stopping at the light to turn right.

"Since when does the cabbie stop at a red light in this city?" John Rae said. "Maggie, please tell this guy we need to get there today."

Maggie leaned forward and spoke calmly in French: "This jerk is threatening me. Please pull over at the Metro station so I can jump out of the car. Then I want you to take off. Take him to Le Bourget. Don't let him argue. Pretend you don't understand what he's saying."

The cab driver blinked into the rearview as he absorbed that. "Will he be all right?"

"Oh, yes. He won't hurt you. He's just being a complete asshole with me right now. Well, he is American." She laughed.

The driver laughed too.

John Rae laughed as well. "I'm just glad we're all friends again."

They set off. And stopped in front of the Barbès—Rochechouart Metro station.

Maggie flung open the door, hopped out, slammed the door. "See you at the airport, JR." She sprang into a run in her jeans and sneakers, heading for the Metro entrance already thick with morning commuters.

"You're starting to piss me off!" John Rae shouted out the cab window as the vehicle swerved off into traffic.

She pushed through the crowd, down into the subway.

6

Incognito's Paris office was near the Bastille, several flights up a narrow seventeenth century building full of Internet startups, entrepreneurs and assorted hand-to-mouth enterprises. Few were open as Maggie climbed the stairs but Incognito was, thanks to the dedication of its volunteer "hacktivists" who made it their mission to antagonize the establishment as well as select enemies. Maggie knew they would not be deterred by the demise of one of their key members. In fact, quite the opposite.

She stood in the open doorway, metal music grating from a PC at the far end of the room overlooking a narrow alley. At a pair of desks against a wall underneath the poster of a smiley face with a wry smirk and sunglasses—Incognito's logo—two of the people Maggie knew well enough to say hello to were busy clacking away on keyboards.

Standing behind the two was the man she needed to see.

Waleed, a well-built Arab man in his thirties, with a week's worth of brown beard and a knit cap, pointed at one of the screens. Ever since the November 2015 Paris attacks, Incognito had been focused on the deactivation of Twitter accounts used by Jihad Nation. Two days ago they had reached 100,000, a number proudly scrawled across a white marker board with several exclamation marks after it.

Operation Abraqa, the effort to cripple Jihad Nation's Darknet Bitcoin payment system, was originally Dara's brainchild. Maggie had learned of the endeavor and pushed the Agency to assist and fund it, in return for Jihad Nation's Darknet information.

When she knocked on the open door frame, Waleed turned, saw her. He wore a faded Rolling Stones T-shirt, the lapping tongue a hint of what it once was, and his brown eyes were intense, as always. Around his neck hung the silver Iman Ali Islamic sword on a thin chain she had never seen him without.

Waleed gave Maggie a stare that wasn't particularly friendly. The two hackers stopped their work momentarily to look up at her as well; they eyed each other questioningly.

"What are you doing here?" Waleed said to Maggie in rough French. He was fluent enough but cared little for the pronunciation.

"I need Dara's laptop. But you already know that. Dara's aunt told you as much this morning—when you stopped by. But you took it anyway. After you threatened her with deportation."

Waleed placed his hands on his hips. "It's not your operation to worry about anymore."

"I put many, many hours into it. Saw it got the funding it needed. It wouldn't have gotten off the ground without me."

"Things have changed since Dara died. That laptop is the property of Incognito."

"With a good deal of software on it provided by my people. I promise I will take excellent care of the machine and have it returned by private courier in a matter of days—as soon as I harvest key files off of it. I won't delete a thing. And I will provide you any analysis I come up with, and keep you in the loop."

"Keep me in the loop?" Waleed laughed. "Do you really expect me to believe that?"

"Things actually go better for me when someone else gets the credit."

"Do you know what kind of reputation your agency enjoys?" He held up a thumb and forefinger, forming a zero. "I didn't want you part of this in the first place. It was Dara. Well, whatever agreement she made with you died with her."

"I went out on a limb to get Abraqa noticed, Waleed. It won't be easy getting my people to move forward now, after the shooting. I'm going to need all the help I can get. That laptop is key."

"I'll let you know." Waleed returned his focus to the screens the two hackers were working on. He pointed at one, said to one of the workers: "Hold off on deleting that one for now. We'll monitor who follows him."

"I have to get on a flight in less than an hour, Waleed," Maggie said.

He gave a casual shrug, not looking at her. "When you take risks, you have to be prepared to suffer the consequences."

"How far do you think you and your friends are going to get without our help?"

"We get as far as we get. It has always been that way."

"You don't have access to satellites, software—I'm going to have to deactivate what's on Dara's laptop, you know . . ." She crossed her arms again, sitting back on the desk. "And I'm going to push ahead, with or without you. I'm going to nail those guys, trash their payment system that's funneling a billion dollars to murderers while you sit here, deleting Twitter accounts. And in that time how many innocent people will die? How many more slaughtered? How many girls raped? Taken as child brides?"

"You need to leave. Before I throw you out."

"How far do you think *you'll* get?" Maggie reached into her jacket pocket, came out with Dara's cell phone, held it suspended between thumb and forefinger. "Without this?"

Waleed's mouth fell open for a moment.

"That's right," Maggie said. "Security gesture, password, text history. I've already texted Kafka once. That's why we need to work together."

"That phone is the property of Incognito."

Maggie slipped the phone back in her pocket. "Kafka gave it to Dara. And she gave it to me. On her deathbed."

Waleed narrowed his eyes. "You think I couldn't take that thing away from you?"

"It's debatable," she said. Daily runs, trips to the gym, Special Agent training said as much.

Waleed took a step toward Maggie. She reached into her pocket and quickly pulled her house keys, working the tip of one between her index and middle finger. Raising a reinforced fist, she showed him an inch and a half of impromptu stiletto.

Waleed froze.

She lowered her hand. The two volunteers had stopped typing again and were watching, one of them open-mouthed.

"This makes no sense," Maggie said. "We're on the same side." She needed to get to the airport. "OK, I tried. Thanks for nothing. But all you've done is slow me down. I do need to ask a favor, though."

"A favor?" He shook his head.

"I need to remind you and the others here not to discuss Dara's death. Not with friends or family, even amongst yourselves. For now, Dara is still in the ICU, but stable. You can't say which hospital yet, but you spoke with her family and she is looking forward to returning to work at Incognito as soon as possible. Can you update your web page with that info today?"

Walled gave a shrug. "Fine."

"My sympathies for Dara. I'll be back for her funeral. I'll keep you posted." Maggie turned, strode through the doorway.

She heard Waleed's determined footsteps thumping through the door behind her.

"Maggie."

She stopped on the landing.

He leaned over the rail. "You promise to send Dara's laptop back once you get what you need?"

She gave a sigh of relief.

Dara's laptop was a beat-up MacBook with a bumper sticker across the lid that read *Wage Beauty*. When Maggie slipped the computer into the cushioned laptop compartment of Dara's SwissGear backpack, she found a granola bar with a yellow post-it stuck to it with a note from Aunt Amina, telling Dara to stay strong "for our people." She took a deep breath when she saw that.

"Don't lose this," Waleed said, holding up a one-inch long digital key fob on a chain so Maggie could log onto the Incognito network.

Maggie took the fob, added it to her key ring, careful not to break a thumbnail.

"She was my responsibility too." Waleed placed the

power cord into one of the pockets of the backpack, zipped it up, handed to Maggie. "You are Dara now."

Maggie borrowed Waleed's phone and let John Rae know she was en route.

Taking off in 15, John Rae texted back. *With or without you.*

Still pissed. Well, she'd earned that.

On her way to the airport, Maggie switched on Dara's phone in the back of the cab, checked the voicemail. Nothing. Good. Kafka was honoring her no-call rule. But there was a text from him:

I pray you are safe. please let me know you are well.

She texted back, struggling with the Arabic: *alive, thank God, but still very weak.*

To her surprise Kafka texted her back immediately: *I must see you. Where are you? Hospital Necker?*

Damn. *Was* he tracking her? It was a good thing she had set up MockLoc.

She replied, *still in ICU. should not even be on phone. they'll take it away if they find it. not allowed visitors, only aunt. wait for me to contact you. don't know when. but promise I will.*

I want to see you, he wrote.

She replied: *I want that too. but be patient. please.*

As you wish. Thank God you are all right.

must go, she replied. *enta kol shay'a.* You are my all—the phrase Dara used when signing off to Kafka.

Hopefully that would hold him for a while. But how long could Dara "stay" in the ICU?

As the cab approached Le Bourget, she saw the huge camouflage tail of a C-130 US military transport appear above the buildings. Still here. A flush of encouragement offset the weariness of very little sleep. Leaping from the boxy Renault after tossing the driver several bills, she flung

Dara's backpack over her shoulder and once again leveraged her running skills to get her through the airport.

She found John Rae waiting for her, with his carry-on, plus the one she'd left in the cab.

"Don't you ever pull a stunt like that on me again, little sister," he said, his eyes darkening.

"I think you'll find it was worth it, JR. And I did make the flight."

He picked up his carry-on, left hers sitting on its rollers. "Hurry the hell up." He turned, headed off.

7

Northern Iraq, on the outskirts of Mosul

The pickup trucks juddered to a halt inside the walls of the compound just before dawn. Dust wafted up from the tires, coating the occupants huddled together in the backs of the vehicles with a fine layer of sand. In the desert night the air had grown cold, so cold Besma and her brother Havi were shivering, not just from the fear of death.

They lay in the bed of one truck with eight other girls and children, and a lanky jihadi guard with one empty eye socket whose lips quivered hungrily whenever he looked at Besma. Besma clasped her arms tight around her little brother. She lifted her head cautiously and when the guard looked away, peered out over the side of the truck. One boy had had his skull cracked for such an offense and moaned listlessly by the tailgate, his head in a pool of sticky blood that attracted flies now the truck had come to a stop. Her heart thumped, out of control—for him and the rest of them.

From what little she could see, three or four low buildings formed the compound, an old school by the looks of it, with the red, white and black Iraqi flag still painted over the door. Bombed at one time, the main structure had been rebuilt with crooked cinderblock and had a lopsided roof. All the windows were boarded up.

"Where are we, Besma?" her six-year-old brother whispered. He trembled in her arms.

"I think we are near Mosul," she said softly, so as not to be heard by One-eye. She stroked her brother's soft hair. She had glimpsed a road sign during one of her braver moments when she had risked lifting her head, while bouncing along the potholed highway. They'd left her village several hours ago, heading west, so that put them close to Mosul as well. Mosul was now one of the Jihad Nation strongholds.

The doors to the cab of their truck squealed open and men leapt out.

"Everybody out!" screamed One-eye, slamming down the tailgate. He wore a long Afghan style turban and had a scraggly dust-caked beard. He brandished a Kalashnikov, pointing it at one girl. She was about thirteen, almost Besma's age. She flinched and quickly got out of the truck, a stream of urine running down her leg.

"Out, you Yazidi dogs!"

In the truck bed, up against the back of the cab, Besma and Havi crouched, waiting their turn.

"I'm scared," Havi murmured into her chest.

What was there to say? "I know you are, Havi," she said, squeezing him close. They clambered to the rear of the truck. "We all are. But remember what *Dadi* told us. We must be brave."

"They killed mother, didn't they, Besma?"

She didn't answer. She wasn't ready to face it herself.

"I said 'everybody out'!" One-eye shouted again, lurching around the side of the truck. His one good eye met up with Besma's fearful stare. "That means you too, Sabia!"

The name alone made her shudder; *sabia* was a slave captured during war. The underlying connotation: a sex slave. She stuffed her fear down deep inside and climbed out with Havi.

She gave her little brother one final embrace before helping him down to the ground. "We will probably be separated, Havi. Remember what I told you."

"Surah Al-Maun," he said, naming a verse of the Koran, his small body shaking in his shorts and thin T-shirt. He had lost a flip-flop.

"Good boy," she said, slipping off her flip-flops and kicking them over to him. "Recite it perfectly. No fear in your voice now." Knowing the Koran could mean the difference between life and death. Besma had sung the verse Al-Maun along with Havi several times on the trip, locking it into his memory.

"Get moving, already!" One-eye shouted at Besma. "When you're my wife, you'll listen. There will be no doubt of that."

"Get in a line!" another jihadi shouted, brandishing his AK-47. "Girls here!" He pointed his gun to one side of him. "Boys there!"

The rest of the jihadis were climbing out of the back of the truck they had been riding in.

"I love you, Havi," Besma said, pushing him away, knowing no mercy would be shown for any infraction.

As they were split into two groups, more fighters emerged from the main building, a sandstone-colored affair. They were primarily jihadis, many in full Afghan-style costumes, as well as a few ominous looking individuals dressed in black fatigues with black knit caps. One was light-skinned, obviously Caucasian, a foreign fighter. He had a red beard. But there were two women as well, dressed head to toe in black, including niqabs which covered everything but their eyes, visible only through veiled slits, making the women look eerily sinister. They wielded short Kalashnikov automatic rifles. Besma had heard stories of the Al-Khansa female police, brutal in their enforcement of the standards of strict Sharia law for women. They walked quietly while the men swaggered, laughed and smoked, some chatting on cell phones. A chill crawled up Besma's spine as one woman eyed her shorts, revealing her bare legs and feet.

But it was one lone woman who truly took Besma by surprise, in camouflage fatigues and a short black hijab over her head, with a black headband and white Arabic writing across the front. A black scarf with similar writing covered her mouth and nose but much more of her face was visible than the two Al-Khansa women. She was a Caucasian as well, with pale skin and green eyes, a teenager as evidenced by the blotches of acne on her forehead. She was also a good twenty kilos overweight. She wore expensive-looking Columbia hiking boots. Besma suspected she was one of the Terror Brides she'd heard about, radicalized over the Internet and brought in to marry Jihad Nation fighters.

She lumbered up to the line of girls and stood there with her hands on her substantial hips and scrutinized them, one by one, smirking with her eyes as she went from one fearful girl to another. She had a cold petulant stare.

It stopped on Besma.

"Name," she demanded in clumsy Arabic. She was an Ameriki.

"Besma," Besma whispered.

"No!" The girl lunged forward, striking Besma across the face with the heel of her hand. It packed a solid blow and knocked her to the ground. "*Sharmoota!* Your name is *Sharmoota!*"

Whore.

Besma sat up on the hard dirt, rubbing her cheek.

"Up!" the American girl shouted. "Up, *Sharmoota!*"

Besma climbed to her feet, her head ringing. She shook it off and stood up straight. The Terror Bride stood with her hands on her hips again, a self-satisfied grin showing through her scarf. She turned her head this way and that for signs of approval from the others. None came.

Just then Hassan al-Hassan came striding over, dressed in black, except for dirty white sneakers adorning his feet and a khaki ammunition belt over his robe. Besma immediately recognized him by his arrogant strut as the man who killed her mother with the butt of his rifle. He had removed his black headdress and his hair hung long and unkempt. His beard was thick, like a beehive. She knew she would hate him more than any other man, and for the rest of her life, however long that might be.

"What is happening here, Abeer?" he said to the American girl. He spoke slowly, Besma assumed, so that the girl could follow.

"*Sharmoota*," she said, pointing at Besma's bare legs.

The man nodded as he studied Besma's legs, his eyes moving up her body, taking her in. He had thick lips. He reached for her face, holding her chin in his fingers.

"You again," he said with an appreciative nod.

Besma trembled, fighting to keep from shaking. *Be brave*, her father had said.

"How old are you?" he said.

"Fourteen."

"Look down when I talk to you."

Besma did.

"Do you know who I am?"

"You're Hassan al-Hassan," she said quietly. "The leader."

He seemed to be studying her.

"Strike her!" Abeer said. "Strike the *sharmoota*."

"It seems you already did that," he said.

"Sell her! Sell her in the slave market."

"Do *not* tell me what to do, woman," Hassan said to Abeer. "Go inside now."

"But..."

He jerked his head to one side, glaring at her over his shoulder. "Don't make me say it again."

The girl named Abeer lowered her head, waddled back to the main building. The other men and the two Al-Khansa women seemed pleased with that outcome. Abeer was not popular.

"Take this one over there," Hassan said to the Al-Khansa women, letting go of Besma roughly.

A flood of panic welled in Besma's chest as the two women each grabbed one of her arms and frog-marched her over to the group of girls and boys destined to be sold as sex slaves or, at best, ransomed back to their families. Tears sprang up and she struggled to keep them in. It wouldn't help Havi to see her weeping.

The men were already gathered around, saying they would take this or that girl for wives if the girls were lucky. Others would be bounty, sold or traded. Several men gawked at Besma. One wanted to know if she was a virgin. Meanwhile the Al-Khansa women inspected the line of boys, of which there were five. Two boys were taller than the others, close to puberty. The boy with the fractured skull had been left motionless in the bed of the truck.

A weak sun started to glow above the jagged stone wall in the east.

"Remove your shirts!" One woman waved her AK at the two tall boys.

They eyed each other nervously.

"Do it now!" the woman screamed.

The boys did as they were told, hunching forward, shirtless.

"Hands above your head!" the other female officer instructed them.

The boys obeyed. The slightly taller boy's skinny arms shook as he raised them above his head.

"Aha!" the first woman shouted, turning to alert the men. "Come! Come!"

Three men came sauntering over. One was the Caucasian man with the red beard.

"See!" the woman shouted. "He has hair!"

The taller boy had faint wisps of underarm hair. Too old for conversion to Islam.

The two boys were told to lower their arms while the men broke out cigarettes. At first the boy was merely bewildered, looking back and forth at the men, as if they might be discussing who would take him under their wing.

"You take him," Hassan al-Hassan said to the Caucasian fighter. "You need the experience."

"*Allāhu Akbar*," the man said. Then he said to the boy, "Let's go for a walk." He unsnapped the holster on his hip.

The boy's face froze. He broke out in tears.

"Don't be a coward," the man said. He drew his pistol and pointed toward the gate of the compound. The boy stepped forward reluctantly, slumped over, head down.

Besma's insides churned. She couldn't pull her eyes away from her brother at the end of the line, where one of the men was now questioning him. She strained her ears to listen but couldn't make out what he was saying over the pre-morning wind blowing in from across the desert. She prayed silently to the Peacock Angel of their faith that Havi would answer their questions well, that they would let him live.

From behind the wall, they heard a single shot, and the foreign jihadi who had led the boy away, yelling: "God is great!"

A pale orange sun edged higher, throwing slanted shadows across the compound.

8

The military flight to Washington started off with two dozen Army regulars more than ready to celebrate after their deployment to Kunar province. Two of the soldiers were women, their faces tanned, youthful, but matured with having witnessed what their sisters back home could only imagine. Someone broke out a guitar and sang "La Bamba" to the roaring of the engines as the plane reached altitude. Others joined in. Somehow a bottle of Jack Daniels appeared, floating up and down the lines of jump seats either side of the skeleton fuselage. The bottle was drained in minutes. Then one of the girls, a California blonde with a toothpaste ad smile, produced a fifth of Wild Turkey from her duffel bag.

"Who's your buddy?" she yelled.

The music and laughter only got louder. The bottle came John Rae's way. He took a healthy swig, passed the bottle to Maggie, not looking at her. Still pissed off.

She took the bottle, handed it on to the next man.

"Maybe you could cut me a little slack, JR," she said to

the back of John Rae's head. "Dara gave her life for this op. I needed that laptop. And I still made the damn flight."

John Rae turned to look at her. "Abraqa's dead. Stop dreaming."

Not one word about what she went through, or the death of her friend. She thought she and JR went a little deeper than that.

She extracted her own laptop from her carry-on and staggered up to the front of the plane, rolling with turbulence, where she showed one of the two blue-suited Air Force attendants her agency ID and requested secure satellite access. The woman had Maggie power up her machine, logged her in. The military transport had full MILSATCOM. Maggie locked herself in a toilet, put the seat lid down, sat on it, opened the laptop on her thighs. Plugging in her headphones, she fired up the Agency's secure chat client and dialed Ed Linden.

A still photo of her boss appeared while she waited for a connection, showing him to be a heavyset but intelligent-looking man in his forties with dark hair combed to one side, dark-framed glasses and a trim beard. In the photo he wore a white shirt and a blue tie and had the confident look of a rested professional.

Ed answered, presenting the calamity of a man she was much more familiar with.

He was obviously sitting in some hotel room, hair disheveled, glasses askew on his round face. His beard was bordering on mountain man. He wore a white undershirt. Smoke curled up in front of the screen from an unseen cigarette. He blinked to focus.

"Did you order a pizza?" he said. *Safe to talk?*

"Bacon with extra bacon. Where the heck is it?"

"I ate it," Ed said, smoking.

"I have no doubt."

"We can't all be beautiful, twenty-seven-year-old Ecuadorian models."

"Half Ecuadorian," she said. "And I never modeled. But you got the rest of it right."

He tapped his cigarette somewhere off camera. Then he squinted. "Are you calling from the John in the plane?"

"Call it *ambience.*"

"About as much as the Holiday Inn, Langley, I bet. We're waiting for you to show up so you can amuse us with your latest escapade."

"Will Walder be there?"

"Of course."

A full grilling. Ugh. "Anyone else?"

"I'm hoping for a special guest to drop by. I'm planning a little informal get-together beforehand in the hopes that the top brass won't be too critical. That we can save what's left of Abraqa."

"And how is that looking?"

Ed took a puff. "You want an honest answer?"

"Ed—we need to do a *keep-alive*. On Dara."

He tapped the hidden cigarette again. "Let's talk about that when we see how your post mortem goes."

"Don't go limp on me, Ed. If Dara's death gets out, Abraqa's blown."

Ed frowned, smoked. "Best bring me up to speed."

She did.

"So you snagged Dara's phone," he said. "*And* spoke to Kafka."

"Texted him but, yeah—got Dara's laptop, too."

"Nice." Ed raised his eyebrows in appreciation. "Is Kafka tracking the phone?"

"He gave it to Dara so I'm assuming so. I'll verify when I get a moment. But I've got that covered."

"OK," Ed said. "I'll do forty-eight hours on the keep-alive. That should go in under the radar. It'll bridge us until we get the official word, see if we're going to continue."

Dealing with bureaucrats could be trickier than suicide bombers. Politics. "I'm only going to bug you again to extend it."

"Walder's got Forensic Accounting under the microscope, Maggs. It's all I can do to keep next year's budget from getting axed." The cigarette bounced in Ed's mouth as he made entries on his keyboard. "How do you spell Dara's last name again?"

"N-e-z-a-n," Maggie said. "Dara Nezan."

"She'll be in a private room at the American Hospital of Paris later today. No visitors. There'll be a guard on the door."

"Make sure that guard isn't some Marine who looks and sounds like the All-American boy."

"You think I was born yesterday?"

"I think you're the only guy in the Agency who knows what he's doing. Everyone else is focused on damage control."

"Just don't go taking that $200,000 job at that Internet startup on me."

She had gotten very close to quitting after the Quito op, but then relented. "They wouldn't give me my own parking spot near the front of the building, Ed. Can you believe it?"

"Bastards." Ed shook his head. "See you in the afternoon. Ciao."

Ed hung up.

Abraqa was still limping along. She had Ed's limited support.

9

Mosul, Iraq

The university was closed again. Akram Tijani studied the empty campus through the morning haze from the balcony of his apartment building. He wondered if he would ever teach again.

His eyes were drawn to the line of pickup trucks and armored vehicles crawling along University Highway below, all flying the black flags of Jihad Nation.

Jihad Nation had come to liberate. To bring order.

What a hideous joke.

"I'm just going out for a moment, Akram."

Akram, turning from the balcony railing, saw his wife of many years wearing her burqa. It still took him by surprise. She hadn't worn the thing for decades, favoring her simple light housedresses and scarves for public. But of course she wouldn't be safe on the streets in that kind of garb anymore. Not with the jihadis in charge.

"No," he said. "You're not going anywhere, *habiti*."

"We need bread."

"I'll go."

He could see her shoulders slump inside the restrictive garment. "I need to get out of this apartment for a few minutes."

"Perhaps later," he said. "If we see people go out walking. After dinner."

"You always say that. It doesn't happen."

"Sit out on the veranda here. That's almost like going out."

"No, it's not. You know it isn't. And even so I still have to wear this, in case anyone sees me."

He sighed in agreement. "I don't know what to say. But it's too dangerous for you to go out."

"Any word from our son?"

"Not today."

"I'm worried about him over there, in Paris. That shooting. On the news. Do you think . . . ?"

"No," he said abruptly. He was worried too. More than worried. His son, working for the jihadis. Insanity. It was like riding a tiger—one could never dismount. But Kafka promised them he would get them to a better life. Out of Iraq. To the west. "Take that silly thing off." Akram headed to the hall closet. "I'll go fetch bread. Maybe they'll have some ice cream."

His wife removed the hood at the same time he pulled his light white windbreaker from the closet, slipped it on over his Izod shirt. "Where are my glasses?"

Her soft features, plump but still attractive, were marred by lines of sleeplessness and worry. "They're on your head, you silly man." She actually divulged a smile, one of the few he'd seen since the jihadis came. He returned it, glad for the small respite.

"I'll be back soon," he said, giving her a peck on the cheek. "Don't let anyone in."

"I know, I know."

He turned to the door of their apartment, just as he heard noises out in the hallway. Any sound these days was cause for alarm.

"Akram," she said. "What's that?"

"Just the boy delivering water." They hadn't had water from the taps for days. Even so Akram's insides churned with anxiety.

"Do be careful."

Akram opened the front door and jumped to see two men, heads and faces covered in full scarves, carrying AK-47s.

Jihadis.

He went for the money in his pocket, the smaller bundle he carried for bribes.

"Collecting taxes?" he said. "I am happy to pay."

"Akram Tijani?" one man said. "Father of Kafka Tijani?"

"Yes," he said, the rapid beating of his heart making his arm shake as he held the door partially closed.

"Come with us," the man barked. "You and your wife."

"My wife is not here," he lied, praying that she had overheard the situation and secreted herself somewhere. Her weak heart would not handle what these men might have in store.

"You let your wife out alone?" the taller of the two men said. "That is a violation of Sharia Law."

"She went out with her brother," he said.

"Akram," his wife said, coming out into the hallway

behind him now, wearing just a floral housedress and sandals. Her hair had been brushed. "Who is it . . . "

And then she saw them. Her face dropped. "No!"

Akram turned back to see the tall man's eyes blazing through the slits in his scarf.

"You lied to me," the man hissed.

"It was a mistake."

"Allah will not call you to account for thoughtlessness in your oaths, but for the intention in your hearts."

"I said it was a mistake."

"You're coming with us. Both of you." He jerked his head at Akram's wife. "Put on a burqa, woman."

Akram cleared his throat, shaking visibly. "My son reports to the deputy emir. He is Kafka Tijani, as you have duly noted yourselves. He has quite an important position."

"And that is exactly why you two are coming with us," the taller man said. "To make sure your son realizes where his allegiances lie, eh?"

"No!" Behind him, Akram heard his wife gasp then spin on her heels, clacking away across the tiles. Where did she think she was going to run to?

"Get back here, woman!" one jihadi shouted, knocking the door wide open with a crash against the wall, marching angrily into the apartment. He strode across the tile floor, his rifle slung over his shoulder, into the bedroom where Akram's wife had fled. Akram beseeched his wife to calm down, knowing resistance was the worst course of action with these people. One lived at their mercy.

Soon, amidst cries and whimpers, the jihadi brought his wife back out, gripping her soft, fleshy arm in his dirty fingers. Her face streamed with tears as he pushed her roughly, telling her to stop her noise or feel the back of his hand. Akram was powerless to stop him.

10

"For she's a jolly good fellow—which nobody can deny!"

The casual reception was held in one of the Agency's more private conference rooms, with selected staff, primarily those who would be attending the Abraqa post mortem later that afternoon. The blinds were drawn. Ed had a cake wheeled in and made one of his better off-the-cuff speeches, extolling Maggie's virtues as a field op. When he was good, he was good.

Maggie, blushing from the attention and two days of sleep deprivation, gave a shy smile as she read the message on top of the cake out to the throng. *Maggie: 1- Jihad Nation: 0.*

Rounds of applause.

The irony of the dedication didn't escape her. At last count, four were dead—five if you counted Dara, whose demise would be secret for another forty-odd hours. The body count rose to seven if you included the two jihadists, as yet unidentified.

"I don't know what to say," she said, looking around the

gray room at the twenty or so beaming faces. She was determined to play along. Ed had staged this celebration not only to congratulate her, but to hopefully build support before the top brass could put Operation Abraqa on the back burner. "Except 'thank you'. As you know, nobody here works alone—although it sure feels that way sometimes." Laughter bounced around the room. "The contact I worked with comes from a part of northern Iraq where over twenty-five hundred women, some as young as nine, have been sold as sex slaves. An equal number of men have been shot or beheaded." The room chilled into silence. "That's only the tip of the iceberg. Jihad Nation are doing the same all over the Middle East. If we can break their covert payment system, we'll put a serious dent in the genocide, if not cripple Jihad Nation for a good long time. And you all play a part." Maggie gazed around the conference room, engaging as many eyes as possible. "I look forward to completing the operation and know the Agency will give it the priority it deserves." She held up a spatula. "Now, the important part—who wants cake?"

"Better give the first piece to your boss," someone said.

Ed grinned, rubbing his belly good-naturedly for the crowd before he pulled one of the bottles of champagne out of the waste paper basket doubling as an ice bucket, sitting on the conference table.

"I'll drink to that," he said as he popped the dripping bottle and began to fill plastic flutes.

John Rae entered the room in his well-fitting blue suit, fresh white shirt and skinny tie. Maggie breathed a sigh of relief. After their falling-out, she worried he might not show. She didn't need—or want—to lose her key supporter. *And* friend. She winked at him, received a taut smile in return, along with a lazy wave—very cool, but friendly enough. He looked good, hair swept back with a hint of gel, fit and trim. He didn't look like he'd been up half the night drinking with Army regulars. He strode over to the corner of the room where his boss was standing. Meanwhile Ed handed out glasses of champagne and greeted Agency desk jockeys by first name. People lined up for cake and champagne and Maggie was thoroughly over congratulated. But if someone called her 'killer' one more time, she thought she might scream. She kept a smile plastered on her face and returned every insincere wish with genuine thanks. If it kept Abraqa and Forensic Accounting going, so be it.

She found she kept looking John Rae's way, hoping they'd get a chance to chat. He was in an intense discussion with Eric Walder, director of the clandestine Field Operations. With his slender build, frizzy hair and ordinary gray suit, Walder looked like a bookkeeper at a tire emporium. He was anything but. You didn't run an intelligence empire by being politically inept and not making exactly the right move at exactly the right time, every time, whether it benefitted the American people or not. Walder was Ed's boss, too, and had his department in the cross hairs. Maggie had had a run-in with Walder and it was John Rae who smoothed things over. John Rae had gone to bat for her more than once. A lot of men at the Agency hit on her. Not John Rae, even though they kidded around. In a different setting who knew where the two of them might be. There had been plenty of electricity. But now, damage had been done. She'd taken off after Dara's laptop in Paris, made him look like a fool. If Abraqa were to continue, she'd need his help.

Just then a tall woman in a conservative blue pant suit entered the room, filling the doorway. She was accompanied by a short man with a comb-over carrying an attaché case. A hush fell over the conversations. Maggie did a double take.

The woman was statuesque, with sharp, elegant features framed by perfectly coiffed white-gray helmet hair. Maggie had never met her in person but half the country saw her regularly on CNN and read about her in the Washington Post.

Ed sauntered over, refilling Maggie's glass. "Looks like the guest of honor has arrived. I was getting worried she wouldn't show."

"Senator Brahms," Maggie said, sipping champagne. She nodded at the woman, now chatting with Walder while John Rae checked his watch. "What is she doing here? Besides freeloading cake and champagne?"

"She was on site to see Walder so I invited her. Five bucks says she wants to congratulate you, *Killer*."

"US Senate Select Committee on Intelligence," Maggie said. "She's major league. Maybe Abraqa has some support after all."

"Not to mention Forensic Accounting." Ed showed Maggie crossed fingers and grinned.

Maggie's eyes connected with Senator Brahms. The senator raised her glass and smiled firmly from across the room. "Well, it was nice knowing you and the other little people," Maggie said to Ed. "What was your name again?"

"Typical. Ditched now that you've got a big time political buddy."

"I think your little dog and pony show might have paid off, Ed. I better go suck up to Senator Brahms."

"Knock 'em dead, Maggs."

But before Maggie could take a step, she saw Senator Brahms marching her way. The mountain was coming to Mohammed.

Senator Brahms was a good three inches taller than Maggie, not to mention four decades older and remarkably well-preserved. The steely smile and firm handshake only added to her intimidating presence. People around her and Maggie automatically gave them a circle of room.

"Agent de la Cruz," Senator Brahms said. "I am *delighted* Ed Linden invited me to your little shindig. I know these things are usually kept discreet but it *is* a privilege to meet a real live hero." She held Maggie's hand the entire time she spoke.

"I'm the one who's honored, Senator," Maggie said, finally getting her hand back. "I've supported you ever since I could vote. You were instrumental in getting Abraqa funded as well."

"Call me Joyce," she said, clicking plastic flutes with Maggie. "And thanks for the vote. I'm certainly going to need your support in the upcoming election. It's turning into a barroom brawl and I've got some fierce opposition. You make sure to let me know if I can ever return the favor." She was already eyeing the time on the wall clock. Across the room Maggie saw the comb-over man, standing next to Director Walder, trying to catch Senator Brahms's eye. Her assistant, no doubt.

"Since you mention it, Senator, Operation Abraqa can use your help to continue to completion. The situation of Yazidi women and girls being sold into slavery by Jihad Nation is dire. And I know how you feel about women's rights around the world. That's why you've always had my vote."

Senator Brahms's smile flattened. "As a matter of fact, that's something I actually wanted to talk to you about—woman to woman."

"O-kay," Maggie said slowly. She stood cross-legged, took a slow drink of champagne, trying to get a read on Brahms. This wasn't feeling like the boost Ed expected.

"As you know, women's rights are first and foremost on my agenda. Always have been. But the situation that occurred in Paris is highly sensitive, bearing in mind the aftermath of last year's shootings. And now Belgium!" She shook her head. "The amount of flak we're taking with our Muslim allies is simply unbelievable. So rest assured Abraqa is going to get my attention *after* the election. But for now, I need you to be patient."

The old saw about not offending Muslims. "Patient," Maggie repeated. "*How* patient?"

Senator Brahms tilted her head down and stared directly into Maggie's eyes. "It's only a matter of time before the press finds out who you are. In this morning's White House press briefing, a reporter asked if anyone knows anything about the mysterious female who pulled out a gun and shot a suicide bomber five times. There's not a TV show, magazine or publisher that isn't going to want to talk to you. But the timing couldn't be worse. We *must* avoid any publicity. Since I championed Abraqa on the Senate Committee, it's about to come back to bite me. I wanted to tell you in person, because I respect all you've done."

No, Maggie thought, you wanted to do your best to shut me up. "I think you might be over-reacting, Senator. I wore a hijab and sunglasses during the—ah—operation. I spoke French, posed as an Arab."

Senator Brahms gave an irritated frown. "Well, it's still not a risk we want to take."

We. "Senator, Abraqa has a shot for a real breakthrough —but only if we act quickly . . ."

Brahms cut her off. "I need your support here and now, Maggie—it's okay to call you Maggie?—and I hope I can count on it." She gave Maggie another piercing stare. "Rest assured I'm going to circle back. But this is a much bigger issue than it appears."

Maggie's indignation began to rise. "What could be more important than nine-year-old girls being sold as sex slaves by a terrorist organization?"

"Believe me, Maggie, there *are* bigger things." She shot Maggie a hot look that told her she had had enough of the conversation. The senator turned, nodded at her assistant. He strode over and joined the two of them with an obsequious smile, clasping his briefcase in front of him. Senator Brahms handed her nearly full glass of champagne to him before shaking Maggie's hand again. "Keep up the good work, Maggie. I'll be looking forward to hearing about your *next* operation."

It was clear the next operation would not be Abraqa.

And as soon as she had appeared, Senator Brahms was gone, escorted out of the conference room. Half the room seemed to follow.

Then Maggie saw that John Rae was gone too. She let out a hard sigh, drained her glass.

Sidelined.

Not even.

Dead in the water.

Then she saw Director Walder strolling across the room, a smirk plastered on his face.

"I want to offer my personal congratulations, Agent de la Cruz," he said, hands in his pockets, no attempt to shake Maggie's hand. His tone was anything but congratulatory and the cool look in his eyes confirmed it.

Maggie didn't reply at first, wanting to stay calm, something Ed had told her to strive for in situations where she seemed to do just the opposite. She reached over to the conference table, yanked a nearly empty bottle of champagne from of the watery wastepaper basket and refilled her glass, setting the empty bottle on the table with a *thunk*. "I guess I'd like to hear it from you, Director," she said. "What *is* the status of Operation Abraqa?"

Director Walder rattled change in his pocket. "That wasn't made clear?"

"I didn't realize Senator Brahms ran the Agency."

Walder frowned as he scratched the top of his head before putting his hand back in his pocket. "Don't be so naïve. Senator Brahms runs the committee that butters our bread. We've had enough bad press in the last year to last us a lifetime. We don't need to climb into bed with Incognito and the likes of Edward Snowden right before an important election."

"Everyone knew Incognito was part of this op."

"That was before seven people were shot and killed. One of them by a Forensic Accounting agent not authorized to carry a weapon."

"Good thing I had that weapon. Might've been a whole lot more casualties, otherwise."

"Do you have any idea how unhappy the French are with Washington? SDAT are livid we ran Abraqa right under their nose. It was supposed to be information gathering only—not the Shootout at the OK Corral."

"Exactly why I suggested we bring SDAT in from day one." But Maggie knew how it worked—competing agencies never shared juicy intel. "With their help, the situation in Paris might even have been prevented."

Walder's eyes slitted. "You're paid to do a technical job. Not make policy decisions."

"So now we back down, right when Abraqa has a chance at success? Because we don't want to risk Brahms being asked a question she can't answer on Meet the Press? When is the Agency going to be committed to the things it says it's committed to? Not politicians who can't wait to go out and make ten times as much as lobbyists when they're done not doing the jobs they were elected to do?"

Walder rubbed his face, lowered his tone. "Your shooting saved lives. You did a hell of a job and I'm glad we have agents like you. So I'm going to disregard your comments."

Ed came lumbering over, obviously sensing trouble.

"What's going on, guys?" he said, barging into the conversation.

Walder glowered at Maggie but spoke to Ed. "You might want to teach your people the meaning of the word 'teamwork', Ed." He turned abruptly and left, his suit jacket swinging, and strode out of the room.

Ed glared at Maggie with narrowed eyes. "What the hell, Maggs?"

11

"Want to tell me what that was all about, Maggie?" Ed said, hands on his hips. His stomach hung over his belt in a bulge of blue Oxford shirt.

The last attendee had filed out of the conference room. What little was left of Maggie's cake sat dejected on the cart, all the edge and corner pieces gone. The conference table was littered with half-empty champagne flutes.

"Director Walder basically parroted what Senator Brahms told me, to—ah—'be patient' on Operation Abraqa."

"Crap." Ed rubbed his hand through his unruly hair. "And here I thought Brahms was going to ask you for a photo op."

"Not today. Nice try on the cake and speech, Ed, and inviting Brahms, but she used it as an opportunity to shut us down."

"It must be the Incognito connection," Ed said.

"Brahms knew about that when we requested funding."

"That was before you turned into six-gun Maggie. The plan was always to have Abraqa be low-key. That's why Incognito was tolerated. Once bullets flew, Brahms and her lily-livered companions do what they do best—scatter like chickens."

"I think it's more than that, Ed."

Ed found a half-empty bottle of champagne on the conference table, refilled his flute, held out the bottle for Maggie. She shook her head no. She needed her wits about her.

"Don't go paranoid on me, Maggs." Ed drained his glass, went over to the cart where he cut himself a doorstop of cake and proceeded to attack it, standing over the cart.

"So now what?" she said.

Ed spoke with his mouth full. "You're back on the Acorn probe."

"Oh, come on," Maggie said. "Acorn is nothing but a keep-busy project. A yoyo."

"Well, based on the way you sweet-talked my boss, you're lucky to have that. It's going to take some serious finessing to get Walder to ever listen to one of our proposals again."

"So what does that mean for Dara's keep-alive in the American Hospital of Paris?"

"It runs out. In about forty hours."

"Ed, once Dara's death is official, our advantage over Kafka dies with her. I can still string him along for the time being. It's too good to waste." She wasn't giving up. She had to ping Kafka soon.

"Walder needs to cool off. Thanks for pissing him off, by the way."

"Can't you push for another forty-eight hours, just as

protocol for winding down Abraqa? To safeguard Dara's family?"

Ed shook his head. "Not with Brahms calling the shots."

"Maybe you could talk to Houseman?" Houseman was Deputy Director of Field Ops.

Ed frowned. "Tell you what *might* work, Maggs..."

"I'm all ears."

He drew a breath. "Your father..."

She heard the brakes screech inside her head. "No," she said. "And *hell*, no."

"Hear me out, Maggs. Your old man is with the State Department, right? And everyone knows he's worked *pretty closely* with Brahms." Ed gave a sly smile.

Maggie started. The way in which Ed said *pretty closely* made her realize just how far her father's womanizing had progressed over the years. Wasn't it enough that he'd knocked up Maggie's mother, a poor Indian woman he met while stationed in Quito? Left her and *Mami* standing barefoot when he took off back to the US?

"Now he's sleeping with elder stateswomen senators," Maggie said, taking an angry swig. "I'm just so proud of him."

"Sorry, Maggs," Ed whispered. "I thought you knew."

"What a piece of work," she said through her teeth, trying to stifle her humiliation. "How long did *that* go on for?"

"They worked together on the Lebanon desk, Maggie. Years ago."

Maggie hadn't spoken to her father in years. He hadn't even made her graduation from Stanford when she received her MBA in finance and computer science. He sent sporadic checks when she was a girl and brought Maggie to the US when her mother died back in the nineties, when Maggie was seven. But that was his guilt at work. He was a *Poncho*, a white Latino who went native when he was abroad and his hormones were raging but came scurrying back home to his Wonder Bread wife, who produced a white-skinned son he lavished goodies on while he distanced himself from his half-Indian daughter. If Maggie had detested the man before she even knew about Senator Brahms, she certainly had no plans to ever talk to the son of a bitch again now. Except on his deathbed where she could tell him exactly what she really thought about him. How he broke her *mami's* heart.

Hers too.

"I think I'd rather ask Jack the Ripper for a back rub, Ed."

Ed raised his eyebrows. "What if Jack could save Abraqa?"

Maggie let air flutter out between her lips. Calm down. "I guess the *pendejo* does owe me."

"Bingo."

"But to tell you the truth, Ed, I'm not sure my old man will cave. I haven't exactly been very gracious to him over the years."

"Dinner at Moshi's when we get back to SF says he will. So suck it up and play the *nice* card. You call him and I'll see Dara's keep-alive gets approved for another forty-eight hours. That gives us almost four days. How's that?"

"What the hell." She remembered the day she found her mother dead in their hut up in the Andes.

"It's a 'what the hell' kind of operation, Maggie."

"I guess it always was."

"Those are the best kind," Ed said, picking up a plastic knife, sizing up another wedge of cake.

"No wonder you can't snag a dinner date," Maggie said.

"If I'm calling my old man, you're calling it quits on the death cake for a while."

"Deal." Ed set the knife down on the frosting-smeared cardboard platter. He picked up a napkin from a stack and wiped his hands. "Let me know what your old man says."

12

Paris, near Gare du Nord train station

Kafka passed El Mushir market for the third time that morning, peering inside. He stopped, pretending to browse the eggplants on the rack between the sidewalk and the open front of the shop. His nerves were brittle—an understatement. Through the ramshackle shop, beyond the cluttered shelves of spices and imported goods, plastic boots hanging from the ceiling, even the stuffed head of a white Oryx for sale, he saw the man he had been looking for, stooped over, stocking a shelf with tins. The old shopkeeper was finally on his own, no one else in the store.

Kafka had observed the shop all morning. He knew his masters. They watched those who were doing their bidding.

But he was relatively sure he was not being followed now.

He picked up an eggplant, craning his neck to catch the old man's eye.

As if sensing his look, the old man stopped his stacking, turned his head to look directly into Kafka's eyes from down the aisle. His light-skinned face was wrinkled and stubbled with gray. A beige knit prayer-style cap sat on his head.

Kafka did not even know his name, nor did he want to.

The old man raised himself from his crouch, one hand supporting a weary back. He did not seem much taller for standing up. A long green apron reached past his knees.

Kafka gave him a questioning look.

The old shopkeeper shuffled to the front of the shop, a limp in his walk, went behind the counter. Kafka stayed out front on the sidewalk. If he had to run, this was the place to be.

The man gestured for Kafka to come inside.

Kafka shook his head.

The shopkeeper shrugged, bent down behind the counter, and Kafka put one hand inside his coat to grasp the polymer handle of the compact Caracal 9 mm jammed down the front of his waistband. He didn't bother with the safety mechanism because it was off. These Caracals had been recalled due to faulty safeties that often let the gun fire regardless. But the pistol was the only weapon Kafka could lay his hands on at short notice.

The old man stood up, a crumpled paper bag in his hand. He held it up for Kafka to see.

Again, Kafka shook his head.

The shopkeeper shuffled to the front of the shop, stood across from him at the rack of vegetables.

"All is well?" Kafka asked in Arabic.

"*Alhamdulillah.*" Praise be to God.

Kafka repeated the phrase, right hand still on the handle

of his gun inside his coat, and reached over and took the paper bag with his left. He didn't have to open it to know what was inside.

He put the bag with the phone in his pocket, grabbed an apple, turned, and quickly left. He looked over his shoulder, to make sure he wasn't being followed. He no longer trusted anyone.

∾

THE PASSWORD for the old school Nokia cell phone was written on the back of the bag in blue ballpoint pen:

٣٤١٢

1-2-3-4.

Kafka dialed and listened to the single voicemail while he ate his apple outside Gare du Nord. He kept his back to a wall, eyes to the street.

"Call this number," was all that the voicemail said. Kafka called.

"It's about time, Kafka," Hassan al-Hassan said in guttural Arabic. No doubt from that god-forsaken camp outside of Mosul. That hellhole Kafka had been to, to videotape executions that he had to put up on social media for Jihad Nation. The bite of apple in Kafka's mouth remained unchewed for a moment. He forced it down, as if it were stone.

"It's good to hear your voice again, Sayidi," he said, using the formal method of addressing a superior.

"Of course it is," Hassan al-Hassan said, the sarcasm thick, even as it travelled the miles. "Did you try to betray us, *friend*?"

With a flash of terror Kafka realized, perhaps he too was supposed to have been killed in the café blast that never happened. He tossed the apple, steadied himself against the wall while his heart pounded.

"But no, Hassan al-Hassan!" he said. "I would never..."

"Good. I have someone here who wants to say hello."

What was he talking about?

A well-known voice came over the phone. A woman.

"Hello, *habibi*," his mother said in a quaking voice. "Your father and I are well. Please don't worry..."

Kafka's heart sank. They had taken his parents hostage. To ensure his cooperation.

Hassan al-Hassan spoke again. "Do we understand each other clearly, Kafka?"

"Please don't harm them. My mother has a weak heart."

"No one is going to harm anyone," Hassan al-Hassan said. "As long as you do exactly as I say."

"You have my word, Hassan al-Hassan."

"Good," Hassan al-Hassan said. "Have you contacted Dara?"

13

Standing by the window of her hotel room next to Dulles International, Maggie stared at the cell phone in her hand. The hum of a plane taking off throbbed through double panes and she looked up for a moment, witnessing its heavy ascent into a morning sky dull with haze.

She had jumped through a leaded glass window in Quito to evade a firefight, sprayed a suicide bomber with bullets from a Sig Sauer, done any number of things necessary to get the job done.

What was so damn hard about one phone call?

When was she going to forgive Robert de la Cruz for abandoning her and her mother, leaving them to fend for themselves in the slums of Otavalo? For letting *Mami* die alone?

Enough. She called the cell phone number she had for him. And got a piercing *subscriber no longer available* message.

She called her father's house in Alexandria, Virginia. A woman answered, not Elise, the iron maiden her father was manacled to, who gave no quarter when Maggie was brought to the US as a girl after *Mami* died. Who promptly shipped Maggie off to boarding school at the first opportunity. This woman had a husky Eastern European accent and was young. She must be the new maid. Dad did like them exotic.

Maggie asked for Mr. de la Cruz.

"Robert just left. Who is this?"

Robert. So the hired help now called her father by first name. Maybe that was the new protocol for maids who threw in the odd blowjob in the laundry room.

"Maggie. His daughter."

"Maggie?" It was as if Maggie had said she was Typhoid Mary. "I've heard about you."

"Look," Maggie said. "I don't have my father's new cell phone number."

"He doesn't like to give that number out."

Maggie sucked in an exasperated breath. "I know I haven't spoken to my father in a while but I really need to now." The term *father* still sounded odd, coming out of her mouth.

"*Quite* a while."

"And who are *you*?" Maggie said.

"Stefania. Your father and I were married two months ago."

Another plane groaned into the sky. Maggie might as well have been slapped across the face. "Ah . . . congratulations. I hate to ask but . . ."

"Elise died earlier this year. Lymphoma."

"God. I am sorry."

"I wonder. But at least you're up to speed now. Perhaps you should call home once in a while."

"How can I get hold of my father?" Then she remembered to add, "Please?"

"He's meeting clients for dinner," Stefania said. "What exactly do you want?"

Clients? Her father was with the State Department. "It's important. I'm only in town for the day. I fly back to San Francisco in the morning."

"Give me your number and I'll have him call you."

Witch with a capital B. She gave Stefania her number. "I do appreciate it."

"Of course you do," Stefania said, hanging up.

Maggie wondered if her father was being taken for a ride. And then she wondered if that made her protective. Then she figured the old goat could fend for himself.

While she waited for her father to call, Maggie plugged in Dara's laptop to recharge and made coffee in the coffee maker by the sink, where she washed her face with warm water, rinsing with cold. Maybe she could just keep going without sleep altogether.

After two plastic cups of watery, but desperately needed coffee she checked her watch. Maybe dear old Dad was stuck in traffic. Maybe he was busy.

Maybe he didn't want to talk to her.

She stripped down to comfort level and climbed into bed with Dara's laptop, hooking up Dara's phone with a mini USB cable. She dug through the phone's OS, scanning the active apps. She stopped at one, unsigned, meaning it wasn't from the online store. That gave her pause.

The app name was *nbd*. With a little investigation she saw it was pinging the SIM card every thirty minutes. Spyware 101. She bet it would report back if anyone tried to remove the SIM card. It was also probably logging GPS location. It was a good thing she had set MockLoc to fake out the GPS coordinates before she left France.

She realized that *nbd* was an abbreviation of the Arabic word 'noobed'. The word for *pulse*.

Kafka had given Dara the phone. She suspected he would monitor it.

She looked up the American Hospital of Paris, changed the GPS coordinates on MockLoc accordingly. Dara's new home. Then she powered the phone down. Dara was in critical care and would not be able to get to her phone. Maggie could get away with that for a while.

It was midnight in Paris so she wasn't going to ping Kafka just now. She set an alarm for five AM to do that.

On Dara's laptop she found a hidden master folder—Abraqa. One document was labeled Darknet. Maggie clicked on it. Password protected. Maggie tried a password or two she suspected Dara might use. No luck. She plugged her IKON network card into Dara's laptop and logged onto GITHUB, spent longer than she cared for locating a suitable copy of WordCracker that wasn't infected with a Trojan virus. She downloaded it, went to work opening the Darknet file.

Once inside, she found a document named Kafka. That kind of find always elicited a thrill. Another document was named Mosul—a city in Iraq, currently under Jihad Nation control. There were more documents, too.

A treasure trove of information. She'd have to digest it quickly.

She fired up a Tor browser for the privacy that was in it and headed over to Al-Media, a news gathering organization heavily maligned in the US but the first with Middle Eastern news.

It took a moment to mentally translate from Modern Standard Arabic into English.

She clicked *Breaking News*.

Paris Blast Kills 6.

There was a picture of Maggie helping Dara into an ambulance, Maggie's head covered in her black hijab and her eyes masked by sunglasses.

No one had taken responsibility for the attack yet. Odd.

Regarding Maggie:

Who is this woman? Her shooting most likely saved countless lives by foiling a bomb blast. The waiter at the cafe said she spoke French and appeared to be Middle Eastern, as was her companion, who is thought to be a member of Incognito, the hacker organization currently running a campaign against Jihad Nation. Incognito declined to state the woman's name out of respect for her safety but say she is recuperating from multiple gunshot wounds. An unconfirmed report maintains that the woman is in critical condition at the American Hospital of Paris but expected to make a full recovery.

The world did not know of Dara's demise yet. The keep-alive was doing its job. Al-Media already knew about Dara moving to the American Hospital of Paris, though. Good disinformation traveled fast.

All good, Maggie thought.

Another sidebar read: *Was mystery shooter with French Intelligence?*

SDAT wouldn't mind taking credit for thwarting a terrorist attack for now. And that would only take the focus off Maggie. And maybe open a door for a coalition with Bellard.

A grainy photo of the man who had been driving the suicide vehicle appeared under the snap of Maggie and Dara, a mug shot provided by Turkish authorities who had kicked him out of the country last year, deported back home to Saudi Arabia.

The woman, the man's wife, was Saudi as well. There was another photo of the very same man and a woman, who, from her shape and size and intense stare, was the one Maggie had gunned down. They were coming through Charles de Gaulle airport three days earlier from Riyadh, dressed in western clothes, except the woman wore a hijab. They had used fake Turkish passports and were on student visas.

Saudi Arabia, Maggie thought. She was not that surprised. America's supposed ally was, after all, the leading exporter of terrorists.

Maggie pulled up a search window and entered three words: Senator Joyce Brahms.

14

An hour and a half later Maggie checked her cell phone to make sure it wasn't on vibrate. It wasn't. Her father hadn't called.

His new wife Stefania said he was meeting clients for dinner. On the rare occasions Maggie had gone to dinner with her father in Washington, it always at the Golden Eagle Steakhouse, the city's premier watering hole for politicos and lobbyists and her father's favorite restaurant to boot. As a girl, fresh from her mountain village outside Quito, she recalled sitting in a plush leather booth in the Golden Eagle, trying to eat a T-bone that would have fed a family back home.

She telephoned the restaurant and said she was Robert de la Cruz's secretary and that one of his clients was running late and would they possibly be able to move his reservation. They said that unfortunately they would be unable to move Mr. de la Cruz's eight o'clock reservation at such late notice. Should they cancel? She said no, promised to be there on time, thanked them, and hung up.

So her father had an eight o'clock reservation at the

Golden Eagle. That gave her two hours. She took a twenty-minute nap, followed by a long hot shower. She pressed her gray pinstripe skirt suit and a white cotton blouse, donned them with black heels. After that she went down to the lobby, had a real cup of coffee that picked her right up, before time to grab a cab to the Golden Eagle.

She found a stool at the bar with a good vantage point, where she ordered a glass of Malbec from the 1,200-bottle wine selection.

At 7:50 a man came in she had not seen in years. Tall, still slender and fit-looking, he wore a dark gray suit, light gray shirt and dark blue tie, all of which complemented distinguished salt-and-pepper hair that had receded since the last time she saw him. Chiseled folds around his mouth added self-assurance. He did a double-take when he saw her sitting at the bar.

"Maggie?"

From the tone of his voice it was obvious he had received no message from his lovely wife. Maggie's appearance was a complete surprise.

"Hi, Dad!" She added a magnificent smile.

He broke into a grin. "Are you here to see *me*?"

She sipped from her glass of wine. "I know you have an appointment and I'm sorry to interrupt."

"Not at all." He came forward, gave her a peck on the cheek. He stood back to appreciate her. "You're more beautiful every time I see you. Which isn't nearly enough."

"You're holding up pretty well yourself, old man."

He dropped his voice. "You must be in town for an Agency meeting?"

"I was. Thought I'd check in."

He furrowed his brow. "I heard some news about you and Paris? Is it true?"

"You always did have your ear close to the ground."

"It's the only way to stay alive in this town. And, whatever you may think, you're still my daughter. I must say, I am proud of my girl. And relieved you're safe."

She blushed. "I hope it's being kept discreet."

He made a zipper over his mouth. "How did you find out where I was?"

"I called your house. I don't have your new cell."

"You spoke to Stefania?" He stammered, looked down at his gleaming Oxford shoes. "She didn't call."

Because she's a bitch and a half, Maggie thought. "Congratulations are in order, I gather."

He looked up, obviously sheepish over his new bride.

"Sorry to hear about Elise," she said.

"I debated whether to tell you, Maggie. But, quite honestly, the two of you were never the best of friends. And I've heard so little from you over the years, I didn't want to contact you over bad news."

"I understand."

"I'm just so pleased to see you. What else can you tell me?"

"Well, that op is kind of what I wanted to talk to you about," she said quietly, setting her long-stemmed glass on the bar. "I have a favor to ask."

His smile faded. He looked at his watch. "I'm due to meet clients in a few minutes..."

"I'll make it quick. The operation is getting the ax. There's a ticking clock. I was hoping you could call Senator Brahms. She's driving it from the funding committee and needs a little push. I know you used to work closely with her." She stared straight into her father's eyes and gave him a knowing look. Screw it. He owed her.

Her father winced before he covered it up with a weak

smile. "Probably shouldn't tell me much more, Maggie. I don't have Agency security clearance. It's really not something I can do anyhow."

"Maybe we can have a drink after your dinner tonight? I'm just staying at the Airport Hilton."

Now he frowned. "It promises to be a late night, sweetie."

She was getting the brush-off.

Hardball.

"Oh well, I should have known I need three months' lead time." She hopped down from the stool, straightened her skirt. "You don't want to be late for your eight o'clock reservation."

He squinted at her. "You knew I had an eight o'clock dinner?"

"You think I can't find things out? Like about you and Senator Brahms?"

He flinched again.

Maggie said, "Stefania let slip that you were going to dinner with clients. I figured out the rest."

"You were always smarter than the law allows."

She squeezed his hand. "I'm headed back to SF tomorrow. Give me a call if you can think of a way to change Brahms's mind."

He looked at her in a way that conveyed he was reading her disappointment. Perfect. "One moment, Maggie." He went over to the maître d' and had a quiet word with him, then returned while the man scurried off to a back room at the side of the main dining room.

"I'm now tied up in traffic," he said to Maggie. "You've got five minutes."

"Where are your clients?" she said. "I thought they'd be hovering around the bar about now."

"VIP room," he said. "Private entrance so they aren't seen coming and going."

"These aren't your normal State Department types then?"

"I quit the State Department."

That was news. "I hadn't heard."

"I thought you kept track of such things," he said drily. "I'm working for BlackWeb."

She reared back in surprise. "I thought you hated lobbyists. And everything they stood for."

"We all conform in the end."

"You didn't just conform. You got on your knees. *Defense* lobbyists?"

"It was right after Elise passed. She had political aspirations for me and I did my best to honor them. But she's gone. My time is running out. I need to take care of myself."

He always did. Maggie wondered if Stefania had steered him toward the big money of Washington lobbies.

"Life is just full of surprises," she said. "Okay, here's my elevator pitch."

In less than two minutes Maggie was able to bring her father up to speed.

He waved for the barman, pointing at Maggie's glass. She shook her head no. Her father ordered a double Black Label, neat, for himself. The drink came quickly and he drank off a third. "So you want me to contact Senator Brahms and ask her to reconsider her stance on Operation Abraqa. When her reelection is on shaky ground." Her father twisted his glass on the bar.

"Brahms will survive. The Yazidi won't."

Her father lifted his glass, drank off another third. "What I have to say is going to be heartily denied if it ever reaches the light of day. *Claro?*" Her father spoke perfect

Spanish, although he ran like a deer from his Hispanic heritage.

"*Claro,*" she said.

"Senator Brahms's election coffers would be empty if it weren't for the Worthington Group."

"The Worthington Group. Aren't they lobbyists for the Saudis?"

"See?" he said, taking another sip. "My girl is no dummy."

It clicked into place. "And the Saudis don't want to promote anybody who's going to come down hard on Islamic terrorism. Because the Saudis fund Jihad Nation. While they sell us oil."

Her father tapped his temple. "Your mother's beauty and my brains. What a combo."

She shook her head. "But how can you accept that?"

"Accept what? That you're beautiful and brilliant? I'm your father. I paid for your college. Undergrad *and* grad school. Even though you never bothered to thank me. Even though you won't talk to me. Unless you want something—like you do right now."

"I know, I know. You could have bought a fifty-foot Sea-Ray for what Stanford and Berkeley cost," she said. "You told me—more than once. But how the hell can you accept the fact that the Saudis get away with funding terrorism and US politicians?"

"Ever since 9/11, this gar-*bage* has been going on." He consulted his watch. "I really have to go now, Maggie."

"So you're not going to talk to Brahms?"

"How can I? I have no real sway. Not over something like this."

Maggie shrugged. "I guess I could call her and tell her no one wants *The New York Times* to hear about her connections to Saudi lobbyists at election time. Worthington Group, right?"

Her father shook his head. "That would affect you very badly in the long run. People like Brahms wield incredible power and could destroy you. Don't."

"Then I'll opt for Plan B."

"Plan B?"

"Going back to Paris," Maggie said. "Even if I have to run Abraqa on my own."

Her father's eyes widened. "Don't be crazy, Maggie. You'll get yourself killed. Those people are insane."

"I'm going to nail those bastards—pardon my French. Unlike you, I'm still at a point where I don't mind sticking my neck out."

Robert de la Cruz took another hit of scotch. "You'll need an army."

"I've made a few friends along the way, too, you know." Maggie swirled her glass of wine.

He took a deep breath and dropped his voice. "Please don't, Maggie."

"What's the alternative? Walk away? Like you did with *Mami* and me all those years ago? Left us in a one-room hut waiting for you to come back, while you skedaddled back to Elise? And your political career that never happened?"

The maître d' approached her father and excused himself. "I'm so sorry, Mister de la Cruz . . . should we begin serving the appetizer?"

"I'll be there in a moment, Charles, thank you." The maître d' floated away.

Her father downed the last of his whiskey. "This is going to cost me, Maggie," he said, snapping the glass on the bar. "But maybe now you'll finally realize how much I've been trying to make things up to you."

A jolt of relief made her sit up straight. "You're going to call Brahms?"

"Not promising anything but I'll do what I can."

Maggie climbed out of the chair, went over, gave her father a kiss on the cheek.

"*You're a prince*," she said in Spanish. "*Gracias.*"

"*De nada, Magdalena.*" He smiled. "But I know what I am. Now, I've got to run before I lose *my* job."

15

At 4:45 AM, after the first real night's sleep since the Paris café attack, the hotel wake-up call pulled Maggie out of a near coma. It took her a moment to recall where she was—the Airport Hilton by Dulles International. She fumbled for the telephone by the bedside, answered it, thanked the automated service before she realized it was automated. Climbing out of bed she stumbled over to the bathroom where she made coffee. She needed to ping Kafka to keep the Dara ruse going, in the hopes that Abraqa was going to continue.

Maggie had prepared the skeletons of some basic texts the night before in a word file. Even though she'd been learning Arabic for over a year, working with a different alphabet, and writing from right to left didn't come naturally. And the more she played Dara, the more she risked being caught out.

She powered up Dara's phone and connected.

There was a text waiting:

KAFKA: *are you there? I pray that you are recovering*

She typed a response: *critical care. so many drugs. but better, yes - slowly*

Kafka answered almost immediately, giving her a jolt of both encouragement and apprehension.

KAFKA: *alhamdulillah! Where are you?*

Per the tracker app Kafka had buried on Dara's phone, he should have been able to tell where she was, more or less. She had fudged the GPS coordinates to show she was at the American Hospital of Paris. Maybe he was testing her.

DARA: *American Hospital*

KAFKA: *safe to call?*

DARA: *guard on door. nurses, doctors in and out. risky just to text. if i stop texting at any time you will know someone has come in.*

KAFKA: *must speak to you soon*

That's what she was afraid of. She'd have to put him off.

DARA: *too soon. too risky. not well, plz be patient, habibi*

KAFKA: *can't stay in paris much longer. have to get back*

Her blood pressure ramped up. That very thought had been plaguing her.

DARA: *but what about us?*

KAFKA: *when can we talk? so much to say*

DARA: *will try but not now - they have IV in me, not easy to move*

KAFKA: *must see you*

DARA: *you must promise not to come here. promise me that, habibi*

There was a lengthy pause.

KAFKA: *I promise. I will wait to hear your voice. The memory of it lingers.*

And that was the problem. How to recreate Dara's voice and continue this charade?

KAFKA: *I want to finally see you in person. I think about*

that time on skype.

The Skype call wasn't in Dara's notes. But on her deathbed she said she had done one videoconference with Kafka.

DARA: *I'll try to call tomorrow. don't leave. enta kol shay'a.* You are my all.

Signing off, she powered down the phone.

How long could she string Kafka along? She had to keep him in Paris—until the op was formally reapproved. Until a plan had been put in place. Until she could return.

She hung up, took a shower, letting the hot jets push the shooting one more day into the past. Letting Dara's dying face fade one more day back into her memory. Even so, she could hear the shots, see the bodies falling. How long would it take? Weeks? Months? She forced herself to focus on the task at hand—how to have a live conversation with Kafka and sound like Dara.

While she was getting dressed an idea came to her.

She pulled her laptop over onto the bed and did a Google search for the name: Elizabeth Stotz.

There she was on LinkedIn. Elizabeth Stotz was still at the DLI: Defense Language Institute in Monterey, where Maggie had taken Arabic.

She called Ed. He was staying in the same hotel. He answered the phone on the third ring, his voice thick with sleep.

"Please tell me this isn't an emergency, Maggs."

"Isn't everything?"

"You talk to your old man?"

"He's good with talking to Senator Brahms. I think we can extend Dara's keep-alive at the American Hospital of Paris."

"Slow down. Is Brahms a done deal?"

"It's going to happen, Ed." She hoped so, anyway. "In the meantime, I got Kafka breathing down my neck for a live phone call. Simple texts aren't cutting it anymore."

"Maggie, we need to get Abraqa officially reauthorized before we interact with a hot person."

"We don't have that luxury, Ed. Kafka's going to skedaddle if I don't whisper sweet nothings into his ear real time soon."

She heard Ed light a cigarette, breathe in poison. Exhale. "Can *you* pull it off, Maggs?"

"I wish."

"You were at DLI learning Arabic for *how* long? I should know. I had it approved. Unless you were off at the beach the whole time."

"I don't sound anything like Dara," she said.

"You're the techie. Use voice conversion."

"It takes forever to reconstruct speech digitally with voice modulation and it's not flexible enough. We need to be able to speak to him on the fly."

"A man in the throes of desire is going to hear what he wants to hear, Maggs."

True enough. Ed had spent the better part of two years being toyed with by an Irish girl who dumped him once he got her a US work permit using Agency contacts. The result was Ed smoking two packs a day and gaining thirty pounds.

"Here's another wrinkle, Ed. My Arabic isn't bad but it's MSA—Modern Standard Arabic. Spoken Arabic is a whole different animal. Think BBC English versus Alabama good-old-boys. Kafka speaks Baghdadi—one of the four major dialects. I can fake the written, using Dara's old texts as guides—but Kafka'll spot me before I finish a sentence if I open my mouth."

"Then we need to punt, Maggs," Ed said. "Push back best

you can. Make the bastard wait."

"Kafka needs convincing now—before he runs. We need a stand-in who sounds like Dara on the phone—with me feeding her the lines."

"Can you use Aunt Amina? She knows—knew—Dara."

"Not a bad idea but Amina sounds nothing like Dara." Maggie continued. "We need someone who sounds like Dara and speaks fluent Baghdadi Arabic. *And* has Agency clearance."

Ed took a drag on his cigarette. "Does she have to do card tricks, too? Ride a unicycle?"

"When I took Arabic at DLI, we went out drinking with the instructors. One of them did impressions—Katherine Hepburn, Meryl Streep, Rosie Perez—you name it, she nailed her. Had us in stitches. Her name is Elizabeth Stotz. She could do Dara in a heartbeat."

"Stotz?" She heard Ed fumbling for a pen.

"I can't very well call her two AM her time," Maggie said. "But if you expedite it first thing in the morning, get the authorizations and clearances, I can get down to Monterey and hopefully see her tomorrow."

"*Tomorrow?*"

"I'm going to head out now and catch the first flight back to SF."

She could almost hear what Ed was about to say: Here she was, going ahead without proper authorization. "I know what you're thinking, Ed," she said. "This isn't the way we're supposed to do it."

"Walder is going to remind me of that when I meet him tomorrow before I head back myself." She heard Ed suck on his cigarette. "Is this stunt going to work, Maggs?"

"It has before. And like you said yourself, Ed—desire is the hook. Kafka wants to believe."

16

"Ready?" Maggie asked, holding up Dara's cell phone.

The three of them—Maggie, Ed and Elizabeth Stotz—stood in a dimly-lit stairwell on the fifth floor in the Agency's San Francisco office on Golden Gate Avenue. Ed was the lookout.

"Ready as I'll ever be," Elizabeth said. She was a tall woman just under thirty, with straight blonde hair and bright blue eyes that danced when she spoke. One of the Arabic instructors at the Defense Language Institute in Monterey, she had been picked up and driven to the City while Ed's plane was in the air. She wore gray Levis, tan suede boots and a loose sea green cable knit sweater.

Maggie had run Elizabeth through Dara's voicemails and Elizabeth had come up with a very acceptable imitation of Dara's sensuous voice. Human memory was imperfect. Kafka had spoken to Dara infrequently and the passage of time, the stress of his situation, combined with the noise of a cell phone call, all made the hoax more credible.

Maggie plugged ear buds into the phone, popping one

into her right ear while Elizabeth did the same with her left. They stood next to each other in the stairwell.

"Ready, set . . ." Maggie said, about to press the Call Recorder button on the phone's setting screen. Still in her gray skirt suit she was feeling the wear and tear from a day's worth of cross-country travel and the prep for making voice contact with Kafka.

"Whoa," Ed said, holding up a big paw. His yellow tie, the one he wore far too often, was askew on his blue Oxford shirt. "Run me through this little stunt one more time first."

"We call Kafka, and Liz here, posing as Dara, uses the basic script we've written as a guide." Elizabeth held up the yellow-lined pad with half a dozen sentences and phrases Maggie and Elizabeth had translated to Arabic. "After a short phone call, enough to hopefully satisfy Kafka, 'Dara' pretends to be interrupted by a nurse or doctor or some other hospital employee entering the stairwell in the American Hospital of Paris. The echo in here should be enough to represent that. Then 'Dara' begs off the call. You—Ed—make sure we don't have any interruptions, which we shouldn't, this time of day. I put a sign on the door leading to the stairwell. If anyone surprises us, it'll be from another floor and we'll have time to react. Is Mobile Ops tracking Kafka's number?"

"They better be," Ed said, standing by the stairwell door. "You have your GPS mocker set?"

"MockLoc is still set for the coordinates of the American Hospital of Paris," Maggie said. "If Kafka, or anyone else, is monitoring Dara's phone, that's the location they'll see."

"Let me hear Elizabeth do Dara one more time," Ed said.

Elizabeth rounded her mouth into an oval shape, blinked as she concentrated, spoke a throaty phrase in Arabic, sounding to Maggie, eerily close to Dara.

"Unbelievable," Maggie said. A chill slipped down her back as the simulated voice of her dead friend reverberated through her. "You're in the wrong line of work, Liz."

"It's not work if you're having . . . *fun*," Elizabeth said in a breathy voice, sounding like Marilyn Monroe now.

Ed gave a thumbs-up. "Let's do it, ladies."

Maggie selected Kafka's number from the speed dial, hit it, holding the phone up in the palm of her hand. The call dialed and rang in the earphones with a foreign *beep-beep* tone.

Two rings.

Three.

Elizabeth eyed Maggie, raising her eyebrows.

After all this work, Maggie prayed Kafka was available.

There was a click.

"Dara?" a cultured voice said in Arabic. "Is that you? Is that really you?"

Heart pumping, Maggie nodded for Elizabeth to go ahead.

"It's me, *habibi*," she whispered, so close to Dara's musical lilt that Maggie found herself studying Elizabeth's lips as she spoke. "It's so good to hear your voice again!"

"And you. God be praised. How are you feeling?"

"The doctors are concerned about some inflammation around one wound but I am recovering." Maggie wanted to plant the seed of a possible infection to support any future delays she might have to incur.

"Where are you?"

"Didn't I tell you? The American Hospital of Paris."

"It's echoing."

"I'm in a stairwell. They posted a plainclothes policeman on the door to my room, for my protection, and he stepped away for a moment."

"What room are you in?"

Elizabeth eyed Maggie and Maggie displayed three consecutive fingerings.

"Room 213," Elizabeth said. "But I'm not allowed visitors. And I mustn't stay on the phone long."

"When will they be releasing you?"

Once again Elizabeth questioned Maggie with her eyes, pressing the earbud to her ear. Maggie made a gesture, showing three, then all five fingers.

"Three days at best, I am told," Elizabeth said. "But it might not be until the end of the week."

Another pause, much too long for Maggie's liking. She pointed at a sentence on the notepad, motioned for Elizabeth to recite it.

"Where are *you*, *habibi*?" Elizabeth said.

"I can't say."

Shit, Maggie thought.

"When will I see you?" Elizabeth asked.

"My masters are growing suspicious. They have told me to head back home. I don't have long. A couple of days at most."

"Back to Mosul?" It had been in Dara's notes.

"Yes," he said. "I can't stay in Paris much longer."

Maggie didn't like the sound of that. She pressed the phone's mute button, said to Elizabeth, "Tell him you're going to try to get out early, that you'll fake your recovery if you have to. We can always stall him later." She unmuted the phone and gestured for Elizabeth to continue.

Elizabeth said, "I'll tell the doctors I'm feeling better, *habibi*. I'll try to get out in a couple of days. With all that's been happening, I need the strength of seeing you again. Please wait for me."

There was a pause. "I have something to tell you," Kafka said, sounding final.

Maggie didn't like the sound of that.

"What is it?" Elizabeth gasped.

Kafka took a deep breath. "I can't go through with it."

Maggie felt an alarm sound, deep inside. She mouthed the words Elizabeth was to say.

"About coming over to us?" Elizabeth said.

There was a pause. "Yes."

"But *why*?"

"My parents," Kafka said in a defeated voice. "Jihad Nation are holding them. Until I return."

Maggie whispered to Elizabeth what she was to say.

"You think your masters might harm them?" Elizabeth said.

"I have no doubt . . . if I don't return to Mosul soon. It's standard procedure. They can't afford me slipping away with all that I know. My mother has a heart condition. Just being held is a risk for her."

Damn, Maggie thought. She muted the phone in her palm. "He's ready to bolt. Tell him you have to see him, if only for a little while, before he goes back to Iraq. Lay it on thick."

Elizabeth nodded and Maggie unmuted the phone again.

"I understand, my dearest," Elizabeth said. "But couldn't we at least meet briefly? Before you go? All this time and . . ." She feigned a sniffle.

"I want that, too," Kafka said. "But I don't see how . . ."

Maggie held up the locket that dangled around her neck for Elizabeth to see, the one she had taken off Dara's body.

"I'm holding your locket, *habibi*," Elizabeth said tearfully. "Near my heart."

A knot of emotion caught Kafka's voice. "I wish it could be..."

Maggie made a cranking motion with her free hand. *Turn it up!*

Elizabeth gave a nod of acknowledgement before she burst into Academy-worthy tears. "Oh, *habibi*, after all this—we are not going to meet? Oh, I am not strong enough for this news! I was kept alive for a purpose. Surely not this! Please don't forsake me..." More convincing tears, ones that had Ed shaking his head. "Oh, I don't want to live!" Elizabeth sobbed, as if uncontrollably.

"Hush, hush," Kafka said. "It pains me to hear you weep. If you can get out of there tomorrow, I'll wait."

Maggie mouthed what Elizabeth was to say next. Elizabeth confirmed with a nod.

"I can't possibly get out of hospital tomorrow," she said. "I'm so weak. And the doctors would never agree to it. Perhaps the day after."

After a long pause, Kafka spoke. "Very well."

"Do you promise, *habibi*?" Elizabeth cried. "Do you mean it?"

"But I must return home after that. I simply must."

Maggie checked her wristwatch. The call had gone on far too long. She motioned for Ed to open and shut the stairwell door, part of the deception. Ed pulled the door open, stomped several times in place on the metal stairwell, let the door slam shut.

Elizabeth followed Ed's cue. "Oh my God, *habibi*, someone's coming! I'll text when I can."

"Tell me what you always tell me," Kafka said in a quavering voice.

Elizabeth turned to Maggie, her face a mask of sudden panic.

Maggie muted the phone, whispered it to her, unmuted the phone.

"*You are my all*," Elizabeth said.

Maggie hung up.

All three of them let out a respective breath.

"That seemed to fly," Ed said. "I couldn't understand a single word Liz was saying but she almost had *me* in tears."

"I think he bought it," Maggie said. "Thanks to Liz. But he's scared to death for his parents. And for good reason. We've got to grab him before he runs." Truth was, she couldn't help but feel for Kafka's plight. His parents—prisoners of Jihad Nation. And here he was, a pawn in a shell game.

Ed frowned. "We *still* don't have authorization." He pulled a cell phone from his pocket, dialed a number. "Were you are able to get a trace on that call?" he asked someone, then swore mightily and hung up. "Kafka's location services were turned off!" Ed jammed the phone back in his pocket. "We don't know where he was calling from. We better hope he's not playing *us*."

Maggie looked at her watch. Six PM. "Let's go get a drink," she said. "Figure this thing out."

17

"Who do we have on duty outside of Dara's hospital room for the keep-alive?" Maggie asked Ed, drinking a Coca-Cola of all things. She was probably the first person to order a nonalcoholic drink in the One-Two Club since 1971 but she needed to keep a clear head. The rest of the bar's clientele were more than making up for her, however, focused on serious discount drinking in one of the last of the Tenderloin's hardcore alky hangouts. Layers of dust on untouched bottles of top-shelf liquor attested to the ambience. Dean Martin crooned on the jukebox. The One-Two was Ed's preferred haunt to discuss business; no other agency types around, and no one else was paying attention.

Elizabeth was being driven back to Monterey in the back of a black SUV with tinted windows.

"A French contractor," Ed said, scooping up peanuts from a bowl on the bar. "I specifically requested it."

"Can we grab Kafka if he tries to pay a visit?" Maggie asked.

"Not after your shootout at Café de la Nouvelle," Ed said,

chewing, excavating more nuts. "SDAT would have to buy off, and make any arrest. I've been trying to sweet talk Bellard back into the op but, frankly, it's going to require more lubricant.'"

"Surely the progress we just made will help change Bellard's mind. He's going to get a terrorist handed over to him without lifting a finger."

"There's still Senator Brahms to consider. She has yet to give Walder the official go-ahead. So we have to hold our proverbial horses." He tipped more nuts into his mouth.

"Ed, if Kafka runs, we can kiss Abraqa goodbye. And maybe Forensic Accounting as well."

"I'm hip." Ed wiped his hands on a bar napkin, drank some beer.

"We only need a skeleton team. Once you get Bellard on board, John Rae and myself will cover our end. He can push Walder too."

Ed squinted at her. "You sure John Rae's good with this?"

Truth was, she wasn't. Things were still cool between them. She hadn't spoken to John Rae since the flight back, before her so-called celebration in Langley. After she'd left him in a Paris cab.

"John Rae won't want to be left out of an op like this," she said.

"He just flew back to Berlin."

He did? That knocked her off kilter. "That's right. He was there on some Class Four when he was tasked to come and —uh—escort me back home."

"Reporting directly to Walder on something hush-hush."

She hoped that didn't mean JR would be tied up when she needed him.

"Well," she said, "he's only a hop, skip and jump away from Paris then, isn't he?"

Ed slurped his beer, removed his glasses, rubbed his face with a fresh napkin, put his glasses back on. "If Abraqa is resurrected, Maggie, SDAT will lead it. A peace offering. It'll also be easier to get it approved if we aren't on the hook."

Maggie hated to give up control but the operation needed to get going any way possible. Otherwise they would lose Kafka and the Yazidi people would suffer. "All I ask is that we get first crack at interviewing Kafka. Once I know how Abraqa's Darknet works, then SDAT can have him." Poor Kafka. She didn't want to throw him to the wolves. But Dara and her people came first. Kafka was a big boy. He had walked into this world with his eyes open. He would have to deal with the consequences.

"Roger that."

Maggie sipped her Coke, realizing how much she didn't care for the sickly sweet taste and non-alcoholic aspect. "I need to get back over to Paris ... get this op set up."

"Walder will nail my testicles to the floor if I approve anything smelling remotely of Abraqa without his OK. And I can't ask until Brahms calls him. I just got back from DC a few hours ago and Walder's little tantrum this morning is still ringing in my ears."

Maggie gave a deep sigh. "Jesus H. Christ," she said, pushing her Coke to one side.

Ed flagged down the barman. "But, Maggs, you do have a lot of comp time coming. If you were to, say, take a few days off to go to Paris to see your friend's auntie, well, I've got nothing pressing for you right now." He raised his eyebrows at Maggie. "Do I?"

Maggie narrowed her eyes at Ed. "You willing to take that risk, Bud?"

"Looks like I'm going to be on the phone all night kissing Bellard's ass—but I've got nothing better to do. And Forensic Accounting does need the win."

Maggie smiled.

The barman appeared, an old geezer with the face of a bloodhound.

"Give me a shot of something that burns," Ed said.

"Something that burns," the barman said, looking below the counter, clanking bottles.

Maggie said, "Oh, by the way, Ed, I was thinking of taking some comp time, starting tomorrow. I wanted to visit my friend's aunt. She . . ."

"Send me an email, Maggs," Ed interrupted. He dropped his voice. "I can't reimburse you for any expenses, not yet anyway. You'll have to put any impromptu trip on your own credit card."

Maggie grabbed Ed's face, kissed him on the lips. "Now was that so damn hard?"

The barman set a shot glass down on the bar, filled it to the brim from a bottle of Fighting Cock bourbon. Maggie grabbed the shot glass before Ed could, downed it. The lingering after-burn reminded her of moped fuel.

"Good Lord, Ed. What're you trying to do? Go blind?"

18

Pulling her carry-on behind her, Maggie hopped BART and took the subway back to 16th and Mission where she walked the block up to her Edwardian apartment building on Valencia, savoring San Francisco on an Indian Summer night, that rare time when the City was warm and balmy. The old Hispanic neighborhood was fast becoming gentrified. Working in Paris meant she hadn't been home in a while to her third-floor flat that rent control kept within her budget.

She collected an armload of mail and headed upstairs, where she let herself in, flicking on lights, and was just about to set her mail down on the mahogany side table when she noticed a cut vase containing a mixed bouquet that cost a hundred bucks if it cost a dime, sitting on the black tile countertop to the kitchenette. Roses and carnations and lilies, in purple, pink and lavender. There was even a hint of blue. Her heart beat a little faster, and that annoyed her as much as it pleased her. She and Sebi were history. But who else could have sent them? Only the guy who knew her favorite flowers and made a point to remember. Damn him anyway.

She set her mail down, went over to the counter, picked up the card attached. There was a yellow post-it stuck on top, from Helena, her cleaning lady, who explained that they had arrived when she was freshening up the flat yesterday, prior to Maggie's return.

The flowers *were* from Sebi, of course.

Welcome home. Just thinking of you. Right. Was Sebi just thinking of her when he entertained some groupie in Maggie's apartment when Maggie was in Quito a couple of months ago? The one who left hot pink lipstick on one of Maggie's wineglasses she found in her dishwasher? It hadn't been the first time, either. Maggie had given Sebi his marching orders after that, making herself a new rule—no more musicians.

She went through her mail, trying not to think about Sebi and the way he would strut out on stage with his Elvis curl and his guitar slung low, ready to rock the house. She had almost gotten him out of her mind when she saw a letter addressed to her from the very same. There was no getting away from Sebi today. She tore it open, angry at herself for wanting to see what was inside.

A cashier's check.

Five thousand dollars. And a note.

Long past due!

S.

P.S. In lieu of interest, I propose buying you a cup of coffee at Higher Grounds. I won't even open my mouth. I'll just sit there and smile pleasantly while you drink it.

Maggie had lent Sebi the money to buy a Les Paul Goldtop over two years ago. She had never thought she would ever see the money again, Sebi being Sebi. But he was making good. Well, well.

Still, she had a new rule. No more musicians.

She pulled open the old sash windows. The sheer curtains billowed, letting the cooling night air disperse the stuffiness of the locked-up apartment. She straightened the Diego Rivera look-alike that a no-name artist in Buenos Aires had sold her, went into her bedroom, stripped off her business attire, slid into her black Lycra running shorts, pink tank top, and stepped into her duct-taped ASICS sockless. She grabbed her phone and earbuds to catch up on her voicemail on her personal phone—the one she left behind—then locked up the apartment, and fifteen minutes later was sprinting through Golden Gate Park, heading to Ocean Beach, her shoes kicking the fog crawling around her ankles.

One of her voicemails was from Sebi. When it rained, it poured. Secretly she was thrilled, although she would never admit it to anyone.

Sebi sounded good. Not drunk. Or coked up. He sounded like the old Sebi, and she bet he looked good too, because he always did, even when he was a mess, but especially when he wasn't. Like when she first saw him swaggering out on stage with his band, *Los Perros de Caza,* and she thought, yep, that one's got it, and then he tore into a Spanish version of Rattlesnake Shake, which he played like a demon, flirting with her the whole time he ripped out a solo. And it was shameless.

He had some big news. He would love to meet her—for coffee. *Just coffee.*

She thought about all the times she'd come home from assignments and she'd meet Sebi, at El Rio or some other dive in the Mission with his rock 'n' roll friends, and the two of them would have too much to drink, too fast, knowing what was going to happen as soon as they got back to her place, on the floor on the way to the bedroom more often than not, tearing each other's clothes off, consuming each other with wet mouths and hot hands. And every knot in her body would pop at his guitar player's touch. Now she was going home to an empty apartment. But that's the way things had to be. She didn't return Sebi's call.

The run helped clear her head. Even as she still felt the five shots spitting out of her pistol, and could still see the black-robed woman tumbling dead, and it still jarred her senses. Kafka was the man in her life now. She'd be Dara until she saw this through.

~

AFTER A LONG HOT shower Maggie slipped on her kimono. She grabbed a cold Corona and punched in the numbers to the keypad on her reinforced office door, which whirred open and let her into her cyber sanctuary, a seven by nine room facing the light well, buzzing and flashing with machines. She dimmed the lights, dialed in KRZZ and listened to Alex Cuba sing as he played his six-string. It made her think of Sebi. She kicked her bare heels up on the desk, beside her 24-inch monitors, and pulled a keyboard onto her lap. She fired up the Agency's secure client. Pinged JRAE83. It rang and rang. She needed JR's help in Paris.

Come on, JR. Don't let me down.

Finally John Rae answered, sitting down at a table in a corporate hotel in a pair of shorts and a sweaty tank top. He must have just worked out. She'd never really seen him that way before. He was trim, nicely muscled. Brushing his long hair back behind his ear. Thinking about Sebi had put her in a mood.

"Hey, Maggs."

"Do I know that hotel?" she said.

"All Hiltons look the same."

He was back in Berlin, last she heard. "I'm betting it's about seven AM in Berlin."

"It's meant to be a classified op."

"I don't know much more beyond that," she said. "If it makes you feel any better."

"You're back in SF. I know that kimono, too. I saw you in it when that guitar-player accused me of hitting on you and wanted to punch me through the wall. Fun times."

"Sebi's history."

"Sure he is."

"I'm looking for a helping hand in Paris."

JR frowned. "Don't start packing yet, Boo Boo."

"Why? What have you heard?" John Rae was a font of intel.

He shook his head. "I'm not falling for some half-dressed woman trying to pump me for information."

"Interesting choice of words."

"Bottom line: You're not going until the word is official. And it's not."

Maggie let out a sigh and re-crossed her ankles. "Brahms is going to approve Abraqa. SDAT is going to get control, removing our level of commitment. It's all falling into place, JR."

"The question is, will it?"

She looked at him sideways. "Why wouldn't it?"

He picked up a glass of orange juice and drank, his Adam's apple bouncing. He set the glass back down. "No talking out of class, homie."

There was a time, not too long ago, when he might have told her what he knew.

Maggie related the events of the last twelve hours to him—connecting with Kafka, Elizabeth filling in for Dara on the phone call, Ed working on bringing Bellard and SDAT in.

"It's not too late to get in on the action," she said. "You're a few hours from Paris. This'll be quick. I meet up with Kafka, and you and Bellard's Neanderthals grab him. Done."

John Rae shook his head.

Maggie suppressed a sigh. "You could easily talk Walder into it," she said. "With Bellard taking the heat. This is a major score. All ready to go."

"Not quite. This one's got hair on it."

"Come on, JR."

"There'll be other ops."

A wave of disappointment washed over her. Her voice cracked. "I don't care about the others yet, JR. But I really care about this one."

"You're pushing too hard. You need to learn how to finesse things."

"Like you did the Quito op? Played me for a damn fool? All I did was leave you in a fucking taxi cab."

"That's not what this is about," John Rae said.

"So you say. But you still owe me one, Bud."

"And I'm good for it. Just not this time."

She let out a heavy sigh. "OK, guess I'll call you when I get to Paris."

"Don't go."

"You don't get to tell me what to do unless you join the op, JR."

Now it was John Rae's turn to sigh. "Watch out for Bellard."

"How about you tell me *why*?"

"How about I *can't*? I shouldn't have even told you that."

"OK," she said, more than disappointed. "I'll let you go. Thanks for the head's up."

"Anytime."

"Right."

"Don't go away sore."

"Just go away?" She grinned. "Never mind. I'll get over it."

Maggie hung up, the image of John Rae fading as her frustration level rose. But her feelings weren't important. She'd focus on what she *could* do. And she could do plenty. She just wasn't exactly sure what. Not yet.

She'd get dressed soon, pack, get ready to head back to Paris on the early flight. In the meantime, she transferred a selfie from Dara's phone to her laptop. Dara was sitting in a restaurant, smiling. Maggie opened it up in her photo editor, turned up the music, and went to work on the image.

She could do plenty.

∽

JUST BEFORE SUNRISE, her carry-on freshly packed, Maggie let herself quietly out onto Valencia Street where the Yellow cab was puffing exhaust, waiting to take her to SFO. She stepped down to the sidewalk, keeping an eye out for any homeless types who sometimes slept in the lee of the stairs and tended to scare the holy bejesus out of her.

And sure enough, Maggie startled when across the street a figure appeared, emerging from the doorway to Starlite Bakery. They opened early. The smell of fresh baked bread wafted across.

Then she relaxed. Somewhat.

It was Sebi, his telltale taut stance, one hand jammed into the pocket of his ripped-beyond-belief leather jacket, the other holding a bag of what had to be pastries. He knew she salivated over Starlite scones. His hair gleamed for a moment in the streetlight. He was growing it out, combing it back, Rockabilly style, ducktail and all. Her heart pulsated when she saw his eyes crinkle.

He crossed the street in a brisk walk.

"Hey, Sebi," she said, her voice just a little shaky. "What's the haps?"

"Hey, *chica*." He gave his customary smirk of a smile. "I'm not really a stalker. I just wanted to catch you before you went to work. I didn't want to bug you so early. Thought I'd wait until you left." He held up the bag and raised his eyebrows. "Blueberry scones?"

"I have to catch a flight," she said. He looked good—eyes clear, cheeks lean and shaven, not sunken, the first sign that he was partying too hard. He had just the right amount of muscle on his slender frame. His shoulders were set; he'd been working out. He had a relaxed, confident air.

"Oh," he said, looking at her carry-on, assuming a frown. "Taking off again."

"I guess you wanted to talk," she said.

"Since you didn't answer my phone call. Or my note."

She took a breath. "Thanks for the flowers. *And* the check."

"You were due."

The cab window whirred down and a grizzled old geezer leaned out, his unshaven face turned. "You wanted to go to the airport, right?" he said to Maggie.

"I do," she said. "In just a minute." She turned back to Sebi.

"Where did you get five K?" she asked. "Rob a bank?"

He laughed, showing white even teeth. "We got signed," he said. "999 Records."

"Get away!" Sebi's band had been hunting a record deal for years. "But that's great, Seb. When?"

"Last week." He grinned. "We're already in the studio. Finished laying down the demos yesterday."

She felt a pang. "And you didn't tell me?"

"Didn't want to brag. And I kind of wanted to tell you in person. Besides," he said, "you aren't exactly talking to me much, these days—not that I blame you. Well, not too much."

"I've been tied up with work."

"You just better come to the record release party," he said. "Even if you don't talk to me. You did pay for half my gear."

She laughed. "Are you sure you want to use your advance to pay me back right now? I could always wait until your album hits number one."

"Cash the check now," he said, smiling. "Get it while it's there."

Their eyes met.

"Anytime you're ready," the cabbie said, arm hanging out over the door of the cab.

"You could always put my bag in the trunk," Maggie said to him. "While I say goodbye to my friend here."

The cabbie gave a theatrical sigh, ignored her.

"You look good," she said to Sebi. And he did.

"You too—but that's a given."

She wasn't going to respond to that.

"You're not sleeping," she said. Sebi didn't, in general, when he was either under some kind of chemical assistance or was wrapped up in a music project. This looked like the latter. It was good to see.

"Been on a creative jag," he said. "Alexis wants ten new songs."

Alexis. Alexis was a tall redhead who got what she wanted. She was a rep with 999 Records and Sebi had been trying to get her attention for years. Maggie found herself just a little bit jealous. When Sebi got a woman's attention, it was generally for one reason.

But that wasn't her concern anymore. Right?

"I won't ask where you're going," Sebi said. He knew the rules about what she could and could not talk about. "I just hope it's mundane."

"It is," she lied. "Business meeting."

"Are you sure you need a cab?" the cabbie said to Maggie.

"Turn the damn meter on," she said. "And while you're at it, close the window. Next time, I use Uber."

The cabbie swore, turned on the meter as the window hummed back up.

Sebi grinned. "Get rid of that clown. I can take you to the airport. We can talk on the way. You can eat your scone." He raised his eyebrows again. "*Blueberry* . . ."

She actually thought about it. How she wanted to spend just a few minutes with the new, improved Sebastian. But she didn't want any more pink lipstick on her stemware.

"Is that really such a good idea, Sebi?" she heard herself say.

"I think it's one of my better ones."

She shook her head. "I guess I need to think about it."

She saw his shoulders slump. "Come on, Maggs. Give me a freakin' break here. I haven't touched a line for months. *Los Perros* are killing it in the studio. I've finally caught a wave. But it's not that much fun on my own. I want to share it with you."

If only he'd said something like that before.

Her voice cracked. "I need some time, Sebi." But the finality of her tone gave her away, she feared.

Sebi's chest fell. "OK," he said. "OK. Got it. Call me when you get back?"

"Sure," she said, without enough conviction to generate a smile out of him. He was getting let down, gently, in his eyes. He leaned forward, squeezed her shoulder with his strong guitar player's hand. Then he handed her the pastry bag. "Take care of yourself out there."

19

Northern Iraq, near Mosul: Hassan al-Hassan's Jihad Nation encampment

"Do you know your verses, boy?" the gangly jihadist with one eye yelled. "Do you know the Koran?"

The small boy in the crewcut trembled before him, standing in line with two others, including Besma's brother, Havi.

Although it was late morning, a hard grayness obscured the mottled sky. The wind blew sharp, swirls of dirt dancing across the camp.

"No, sir," the boy muttered, one bare foot crossed over the other as he looked down at the ground.

"What good is he?" One-eye shouted. He turned to the group of jihadists, most of them mulling around the girls not yet selected, of which Besma was one: "Another godless Yazidi!"

One of the two Al-Khansa women came marching over,

her automatic rifle slung over her shoulder, and led the little boy away, taking him to the girls that seemed destined for the sex slave market. Some men were flirting with them, on their cell phones, laying claims, making deals.

Two boys left. All stood to attention, trembling. Poor Havi. Besma could see him trying to stay brave, his eyes shut, his lips moving silently. *Dadi* said he was a man, but that was to flatter him, make him strong. And with his curly black hair, long eyelashes and blue eyes, he looked so vulnerable. Just six years old. A baby! Besma hoped he was reciting the verses to himself that they had learned together.

She'd heard stories of the other Yazidi girls, some not even ten years old, being raped by a dozen men before they were sold or ransomed back to their fathers.

She prayed silently to Melek Taus, the Peacock Angel, and begged for a quick death if that was to be her fate, and to save her little brother. If Havi had to become a Muslim, she asked that he would become a good man, not a killer. But she knew what Jihad Nation did with converts. Once they were brainwashed, they became suicide bombers.

One-eye approached the next boy, a lad with a big nose and crooked stare.

"Abbas!" one jihadi shouted at One-eye. "He looks just like you! Have you been dipping your wick in a Yazidi honeypot?"

Laughter all around. One-eye grimaced at first, then broke into a grin. "I will be soon enough!"

More laughter.

"Enough of that kind of talk!"

Everybody turned.

Hassan al-Hassan had emerged from the building, and stood, legs apart, hands on his hips. He wore his black outfit and dirty white sneakers, his uncombed hair and thick beard fluttering in the breeze.

It was difficult to tell what the two Al-Khansa women thought but their stoic lack of movement implied that they agreed with him.

One-eye returned to the boy. "Do you know your verses?" he yelled. "Do you know the Koran?"

The boy stood to attention, arms straight by his side. Then he spoke in an awkward stammer:

"And who ... thinks ... of what has been told ..."

His face erupted with tears.

"Disgraceful!" One-eye struck the boy with his fist, driving him to the ground. "You insult the noble Koran with your clumsy attempt!" The other woman in black was waiting. She led the boy to the group of unwanted.

"We'll have to dig a bigger grave!" One-eye said, moving over to Havi. Besma's eyes fluttered with fear. She felt as if she might faint. She fought it, for Havi's sake.

"Do you know your verses, boy?" One-eye bellowed at Havi.

Quaking, eyes clamped shut, arms strapped to his side with fright, Havi lifted up his shaking head, then announced in a clear voice, "In The Name of Allah, The Beneficent, The Merciful:"

He tilted his head back and sang:

"Seest thou one who denies the Judgment?
Then such is the man who repulses the orphan,
And encourages not the feeding of the indigent.
So woe to the worshippers
Who are neglectful of their prayers ..."

Besma found herself silently whispering the words along with her brother, relief flowing like water as he executed the verse flawlessly. When Havi was done, silence loomed around the courtyard for a moment, punctuated by the morning wind blowing up clouds of dust. The jihadists had all stopped to watch and listen.

"Good job," One-eye said to Havi. "Well recited."

Hassan al-Hassan strode over to the line of boys. One-eye scurried out of his way.

"Excellent!" Hassan said to Havi. "*The small kindnesses* —a perfect surah for a young man. Reminding us that it is not enough just to be a good Muslim, but that we must take heed of those less fortunate than ourselves. Beautifully recited. By a heathen no less. God is great!"

Small fists clenched by his side, Havi stared down at the ground. He still wore the big flip-flops that Besma had given him.

"God is great, sir," he said quietly.

Hassan squatted down in front of Havi. "Look at me, boy."

Besma watched her little brother lift his head and open his eyes, blinking rapidly.

"Don't be afraid, boy. What is your name?"

"Havi, sir."

"Who taught you that surah, boy? The one you sang so well?"

"My sister, sir." Havi pointed at Besma, standing with those destined for slavery or ransom.

Hassan stood up, turned, looked at Besma. "Did she now? And what is your sister's name?"

"Besma, sir. She taught me other verses as well. Would you like to hear them?"

"Later, perhaps." Hassan spoke to one of the women in black. "Clean these two up." He indicated Havi and Besma. "Put her in something that covers her shamefulness." Besma still wore her shorts. "This boy will be perfect for training. Bring them both to my quarters."

Besma's young body shook as it released a torrent of tension. The women in black gathered her and Havi together and led them away.

They were taken to an open garage on the other side of the compound where a cement sink occupied the far corner. The two of them disrobed and washed in water from buckets. They were given used clothes to wear, a small robe and sandals for Havi and a dirty burqa for herself that smelled of livestock. The sound of a car engine grinding caught Besma's guarded attention. She peered over to the camp entrance as she pulled the garment over her head. A sedan was bouncing into camp, its chassis squealing, causing a fair amount of commotion. The taller of the two Al-Kahnsa women, who had big feet, stepped out beyond the roof of the parking structure to watch.

As Besma bathed her little brother, she craned her neck to see. An old Mercedes with dented fenders pulled up in front of the main building in a spin of dust. A jihadi with an AK-47 climbed out of the front, opened the rear door and motioned for the occupants to get out.

There were two middle-aged Arabs, a man and a woman. He was portly, clean shaven, wearing gold framed glasses which glinted in the sun, his short sleeve shirt tucked into gray slacks. The woman wore a fine light burqa, made of silk judging by the way it hung on her. The man steadied the woman, who was clearly petrified. He himself was shaking.

Hassan al-Hassan went over to them, speaking to the couple in what appeared to be firm tones. Besma could not hear what they were saying but they were clearly being admonished. The woman appeared to faint; the man caught her. They were taken around the back of the main building by the man with the Kalashnikov, the husband holding his wife's trembling arm.

The tall woman in black returned to the sinks.

"Who is that?" the other woman, who had been watching Besma and Havi, said.

"Kafka's parents," the taller woman whispered. "Hassan al-Hassan must have seized them. To ensure his return."

Both women shook their heads ominously, the hoods of their burqas moving to and fro.

"Are they to live?" the shorter woman said.

The tall woman shrugged. "Who knows?"

"Is Kafka still on the run?" the shorter woman said.

"Still hiding in Paris, I gather."

The short woman lowered her voice to a whisper. "They say he fell for a Yazidi woman there who tried to lure him away."

"No!"

The shorter woman shook her head and clucked. Then she noticed Besma listening.

"You there! Stop dawdling! Hurry up."

Besma resumed rubbing Havi's hair dry with a towel. For the moment, the two of them were still alive. That seemed to be the best one could hope for in this life.

20

When Maggie checked into the Hotel Shangri-La on rue Philibert Lucot, she plugged in her laptop and hung her clothes up in the free-standing pressboard closet, admiring the new lavender patterned wallpaper and puffy white vinyl headboard replete with chrome studs. The cottage cheese ceiling glitter added a certain something as well; she just wasn't quite sure what. She shook her head and smiled. It was mid-morning.

She felt rested, having popped for a business class seat from SFO to De Gaulle and sleeping most of the flight. Maybe she would be reimbursed. If not, she considered it almost a freebie, thanks to Sebi's unexpected loan repayment.

She powered up Dara's phone, checked for messages. One pending from Kafka. Her pulse quickened. He was still communicating. That was good.

KAFKA: *how are you today?*
DARA: *had a difficult night, habibi*
KAFKA: *why?*
DARA: *temperature - an infection? one wound is weeping.*

She'd keep laying the groundwork for a potential delay in leaving the hospital. Hopefully, not scare him off.

KAFKA: *sorry to hear that*

DARA: *waiting to see doctor. they don't make the rounds until late morning. I just need some rest ... will chat later*

She signed off, powered down.

With any luck, the longer Kafka waited, the longer he'd keep waiting, like a gambler trying to win his money back. But for Kafka, it wasn't money he was losing but precious time.

She checked her work phone.

A note from Ed. Bellard was receptive to leading the op. But there were conditions. He was still waiting to hear back from Walder. The world could come to an end while someone waited for authorization. Maggie hoped Senator Brahms was going to come through. Ed wanted to know if Maggie had contacted John Rae.

Not a word from John Rae, though. Not that she really expected anything after last night's downbeat phone call in SF. She'd have to work on that.

Maggie called Captain Bellard, SDAT. He answered on the second ring.

"You're *here*?" he said. "In Paris?"

"I am," she said. "I take it you've spoken to Ed?"

"Café Lepic," Bellard said. He gave her the location. "One hour." He rang off. A man of few words.

She left her private phone on the nightstand to recharge, pocketed her work phone, slipped Dara's phone into a side pocket in the SwissGear backpack containing Dara's laptop. She threw that over her shoulder and took it down to the front desk.

At reception Madame Nguyen bore an air of rosewater. It complemented the blue frock with the white lace trim at the neck and her soft blue cardigan with the Kleenex stuffed in the sleeve. She and her husband had run this little hotel for decades. Maggie had always had her unspoken trust.

"I need somewhere safe for this, madame."

Madame Nguyen peered at the pack through cat-eye spectacles. "Too big for the safe. I'll have Vinh take care of it. Set it there, please."

Maggie set the bag by the desk. "I also don't want anyone to know about this—except for you and your husband, of course."

Madame Nguyen understood that Maggie's work was confidential. "Of course."

"Oh, and this is for you." Maggie slipped her a folded one hundred Euro note. "In case I forget before I leave. I'm always in such a rush, it seems." One always tipped the concierge, especially if one appreciated the service.

Maggie hailed a cab and headed over to Café Lepic, slugging along the Périph, the ring round the city. They passed the Bois de Boulogne and she savored a brief glimpse of restful green. Gray clouds hung in the sky. The cab took her near SDAT Headquarters, north of the central city, outside of the arrondissments and Paris's administrative limits. Bellard had picked a meeting spot convenient for him. She got out half a block from the café, following a basic rule—never pull up at an assigned address. They didn't call it the Kill Zone for nothing. She didn't see any suspicious people lurking as she walked up the busy sidewalk to the café. Despite traffic, she was only five minutes late.

Lepic was a workingman's café bar, with its long narrow counter, old black-and-white tile floor, fluorescent lights, dairy cases of drinks and sandwiches, and a few stools, all taken. Most patrons stood as they drank their mid-morning coffee, one elderly gent in an overcoat appending his with a small snifter of Pernod.

Bellard was leaning at a small counter in the back, next to a flight of stairs. He wore a dark blue suit today, jacket buttoned, white short-collared shirt, no tie. He maintained that compact but formidable look Maggie had first noticed about him. Already a shadow of beard darkened his pale face. He consulted his watch as Maggie approached.

"You're late," he said in French.

"I don't know if anyone has ever brought this to your attention but Paris has a complicated relationship with its traffic. I haven't even changed from the flight." She wore the jeans, Cuban heel boots, red turtleneck and leather jacket she had worn on the plane. Bellard was trying to act tough, establish dominance. Put her in her place. So much for being welcomed with open arms.

She ordered a *noisette*–an espresso with a dash of milk. "I take it Ed brought you up to speed on Abraqa?"

"Not really much in the way of speed on your end, is there?" Bellard drank from a tall glass of Americano. "Not with your director of Operations dragging his feet."

"We're still waiting on official approval." Maggie took a sip of her *noisette*. "But we're moving ahead all the same—unofficially. And we've made real progress."

"You Americans." Bellard gave a smirk. "*We've made real progress! We get the job done!*"

Maggie did her best to ignore the slight. "I'm ready to get started anytime you are."

"You're not planning on skipping town this time?"

She was wondering if that would come up. "You did put me in a cell." She gave a sly smile as she drank her coffee. "Besides, I had no choice. I was escorted back to Washington. Orders."

"I'm not going to be the brunt of your agency's politics. Who knows when Walder's fabulous approval will come through? Will it be delivered on a silver platter? Will it take weeks? Or will it never happen at all?"

Bellard did have a point. "I don't see a problem. But we should get started. We don't have a lot of time..."

"Oh, you don't see a problem? That's good. Because it's *my* operation. Is that understood?"

Maggie picked up her coffee and took a breath while her irritation settled. "I'm more than happy to work with you."

"You're happy to work with me?" Bellard set his glass down with a loud *clink* that caused one of the other café-goers to stop mid-conversation and look their way. "You need to be happy to work *for* me. Do exactly as I say. Or get on the next flight out of France."

Maggie counted to three. "Fine." She dropped her voice. "But Kafka is not your garden variety terrorist. He has the key to turn off Jihad Nation's money spigot. We have to play our cards right."

"Let me tell you how it works. SDAT will apprehend Kafka, and he will stay *here*." Bellard pressed his finger on the countertop for emphasis. "You assist. But he's mine."

"Ed did stipulate we get to interview Kafka first, correct? Long enough to get information on Abraqa's Darknet? Passwords, server locations, file structure, processes? Your people are welcome to sit in. After that he's all yours."

"*D'accord*," Bellard grunted, checking his watch. "I have to get back for a meeting. Do you have Dara's phone?"

She blinked in surprise. "Why?"

Bellard put his hand out.

She assumed a deadpan face, then feigned disbelief. "Oh, you want me to *give* you Dara's phone." In the back of her mind, Maggie had anticipated something like this. That's why the phone was with Madame Nguyen.

"Phone," Bellard said through his teeth.

"We've already made voice contact. Kafka isn't stupid. We've got to handle the communication with kid gloves. I'll take care of that part. You take care of the rest."

"Phone."

"Blow it and he'll run. He's on the verge of running now."

Hand still up, Bellard said: "I hope I haven't made a mistake with you."

"I'm not giving you Dara's phone, *ami*. I don't even have it on me."

Bellard dropped his hand, glared at her. "Where is it?"

Maggie continued: "Dara did the initial legwork on this op, grooming Kafka, with *my* assistance. I've been in contact with him since her death. *I've* maintained the relationship. Built it up. How are you going to mimic Dara's voice? We've taken care of that. Communication doesn't get any more sensitive."

His angular face reddened. "I want that phone."

"Dara's phone and I don't separate."

"Do I have to put you on the next flight back to Washington?"

She wasn't going to get anywhere with Bellard right now. She drained her coffee, which now tasted bitter. She jammed her hands in the pockets of her jacket. "Let's take a break. I'll sync up with Ed, get back to you this afternoon. We'll work this out."

She left Bellard glowering, went out into the hubbub of lunchtime traffic, both motor and pedestrian. She'd collect her thoughts before calling Ed. She headed toward the center of the city.

A small white Peugeot pulled up, squealing to a stop in the middle of the street. Doors opened and two people got out. A woman and a man.

"Good afternoon," the woman said to Maggie in a harsh Northern French accent as she strode toward her. She was tall, lanky, in her forties, with a short fluffy brown retro haircut, and was wearing black stovepipe jeans, a black T-shirt, and a baggy denim jacket faded to a pale blue that no doubt concealed a weapon. She wasn't pretty but she was attractive in that way French women were when they didn't work at it too much. The man who followed her was a skinny kid with acne, wearing a tight black ball cap, who looked like he might have gotten out of the police academy that morning. He wore a voluminous dark blue windbreaker that billowed, showing a glimpse of pistol hanging under his armpit. He was smoking what remained of a cigarette, staring at Maggie through wraparound sunglasses.

Maggie stopped.

"If you two are meant to be undercover," she said in French. "It's not working."

The woman returned a flat non-smile and nodded at the wall behind Maggie. "We need to search you."

"And I need to see a badge."

The woman flashed her SDAT ID for a nanosecond, put it away. "Up against the wall. Or we can go down to the station. It's up to you."

Maggie assumed the position, legs apart, hands against a wall bumpy with hardened untrimmed mortar oozing out between the bricks. The woman patted her down efficiently.

"Did Bellard have you two waiting the whole time?" Maggie said, head turned halfway. The kid glowered at her, holding the butt of his smoke with his thumb and forefinger.

"No questions," the woman said, pulling Maggie's work phone from her jacket pocket. "You can turn back around now."

Maggie did. "That's not the phone you're after."

The woman pocketed Maggie's phone. "You can go."

"That phone is for work. I'm going to need it."

"You can file a report to have it returned."

"If you try to access it without the correct code," Maggie said, "it'll deactivate."

"I'll make a note." She gave a cold smile, turned and headed back out to the car, its doors still open, engine running, a bored-looking man at the wheel. The young cop took one final drag on his cigarette before he flicked the butt at Maggie's feet where it spit embers.

The two got into the car which took off with a screech of tires.

～

Kafka showed his forged French National Identity card to the hospital receptionist. He wore a dark brown suit, white shirt and tie, his dark hair plastered down close to his head. Tinted black-framed glasses completed the disguise. He carried a bunch of white lilies.

"Katy Charron, please," he said in his best French, a bit of a struggle.

"And you are Madame Charron's husband, monsieur?"

"Brother."

"I see." The stout woman in the white lab coat sitting behind the counter picked her glasses up from the chain around her neck and slid them on her face as she consulted the computer screen. "Yes, five-twenty-one. The elevator is over there."

"*Merci*." He gave a slight bow and proceeded to the security guard, who verified his ID, then instructed Kafka to put everything on the conveyer belt, just like at the airport, even the flowers. Kafka gathered his belongings on the other side of the machine and entered the elevator where the guard selected the fifth floor.

On the fifth floor Kafka disembarked, walked purposefully past a doctor holding a clipboard, then found the stairwell, where he took the stairs down to the second floor.

The inner stairwell door was unlocked. He'd had his doubts but, so far so good. He opened it, peered out, saw no one coming either way, and emerged, holding his bouquet. Room 213 was on the west side of the floor. He headed that way, adopting a suitably confused expression, a man looking for a hospital room.

He saw the man seated outside Room 213 before the man saw him. Young, early twenties, short dark back-and-sides haircut, muscular build. Levis and a roomy green gabardine car coat, roomy enough to conceal a weapon. The right age to be a junior policeman standing guard. He was chewing gum and checking his cell phone.

Kafka walked down the hall toward him, checking room numbers.

He got to 213. The door was shut.

The man stood up, put his phone in his pocket.

"Can I help you?" the cop said in French.

"I wanted to visit my coworker," Kafka said, indicating the door to 213. "Dara Nezan."

The young man's eyes narrowed. Khafa spotted the bulge of a pistol under his arm. "Who told you she was here, monsieur?"

"A work acquaintance—at Incognito—where we both work."

"May I see some ID?" the young man said.

Kafka had another fake French National ID ready. He presented it.

The young man looked at it, then at him.

"No visitors," he said, handing back the ID.

"But I've taken off work!"

"Sorry. No visitors."

"Can I drop off my flowers, at least?"

The cop softened his tone. "The nurses don't like flowers or plants in the room. The air, you see. Possibility of infection. She's had a rough time of it." He shrugged. "Sorry, sir."

Typical western police, Kafka thought. *Soft. Weak.*

"I'm sorry to have disturbed you," he said.

"Good day, sir."

Kafka left, headed down the hallway, ducking back into the stairwell and hurtling down the stairs for the first floor exit. He knew he might set off an alarm when he exited but he could pass that off as general visitor stupidity if anyone stopped him. But they wouldn't. He'd be long gone.

His curiosity was satisfied. The police put a guard on Dara, as she had said, and that made complete sense, considering the shootings.

Dara was in that room. Waiting for him. Tomorrow, hopefully, she'd be discharged.

He tossed the flowers into a trash bin on a lamppost.

He'd stay in Paris a while longer. He must see her. But he must be careful. He mustn't let his emotions take control.

∽

Back at the Shangri La, Maggie called Ed via the Agency's VOIP client, sitting on her bed against the white vinyl headboard, the MacBook open on her lap.

"So Ballard decided to play hardball," Ed said angrily, coughing through a cloud of smoke on the webcam. First cigarette of the day. It was early morning his time and Maggie'd woken him. Under different circumstances his striped pajamas might have elicited a comment out of her. "I did my best," Ed continued, hacking. "But France's foreign minister filed a formal complaint with the White House over the café attack. Said we caused an international incident. The National Security Advisor called Walder personally and chewed him out."

"So Bellard is feeling his oats," Maggie said. "Thinks he can do what he wants."

"That seems to be the case."

"The problem is that Bellard thinks he can pull it off on his own. But he can't. If we switch contacts now, he'll scare Kafka off."

"Let me make some calls, Maggs. Sit tight."

One step forward, one step back. "I'll be waiting on your call," she said.

Maggie did a hundred sit-ups. She drank a cup of instant coffee.

Ed skyped her on her laptop. There was a pause while he came into focus, smoke billowing on the other side of the webcam.

"You're not gonna like this, Maggs."

Maggie had not been expecting great news. And here it was. "Ed," she said. "I am *not* giving Dara's phone to Bellard."

"Bellard's still going to need you," Ed said. "He's just throwing his weight around. Well, you did ditch his interview last time."

"Because you had John Rae pick me up!"

"Thank Walder for that."

"Ed, Bellard won't realize what he's doing until it's too late."

"It's not like we really have a choice, Maggs. The op *was* conducted on French soil. The phone is technically their evidence. You're working under NOC—no official cover. So this is the way Walder wants to play it. Let SDAT take Abraqa."

"You spoke to Walder?"

"Yes."

The shoe dropped. "Walder wants to stand back and watch SDAT hose it up. Let Abraqa go down in flames. Leave them with the charred remains. The French sent a nastygram to the White House so he's going to teach them a lesson. Only they don't know it yet." Maggie shook her head. Office politics on steroids.

Ed took a drag on his cigarette. "Welcome to the wonderful world of intelligence, Maggie."

SDAT didn't care about the Yazidi genocide. They weren't up to speed on the Darknet angle. All they wanted to do was grab Kafka, throw him in jail. If they managed to catch him.

She didn't bother to say she'd wanted SDAT involved in the first place again. But she'd like to have known who sent those suicide bombers. In the middle of all this bureaucratic bullshit, that little detail kept getting ignored.

Going off half-cocked wasn't going to help Dara's people. Maggie needed to stay cool, even though she was being gutted.

"So Maggie," Ed said, smoking. "You've got Dara's phone?"

"I thought you had it."

"No games, Maggie. I'll do my best to salvage what we

can. Try and get you a spot on Bellard's team. Wait for his call. Then give him the goddamn phone."

"How the hell is he going to call me? His flatfoots took my work phone."

Ed sighed. "He'll have to call you at your hotel."

What could she do? "You call the shots, Ed."

"That's the ticket, Maggs. If we're going to get anything at all, we are going to have to bend over on this one."

They signed off.

A slew of choice words shot through Maggie's head while she regretted not taking that sweet job at Delta Financial again. She let the anger pass, powered up Dara's phone. Nothing from Kafka. Good enough. Everything was on hold for the moment anyway. She set Dara's phone in airplane mode and, with Dara's laptop in its backpack over one shoulder, her own work laptop folded under her arm, went downstairs to the front desk.

"Would you mind putting these somewhere safe, madame?" Maggie asked, handing Madame Nguyen Dara's phone and her work laptop. Madame Nguyen slipped the phone into the pocket of her cardigan and carefully took Maggie's laptop.

Maggie took the Metro over to the Bastille, quicker than a taxi with Paris traffic.

Incognito's door was shut. And locked. Good. They were learning.

She knocked. Waleed answered the door, a cell phone in one hand as he shouted at someone in rough French. "We're paying for four hundred gigabits per second—and getting half that!" Today he wore his faded Metallica T-shirt. And the ever-present Iman sword on a chain. He looked at Maggie in surprise.

Maggie held up the backpack with Dara's laptop. Waleed was pleased.

They spent some time syncing up while volunteer hacktivists worked the computers.

There had been several inquiries about Dara at Incognito, which were responded to with the same stock answer: Dara was recovering and expected to be back at work next week.

"Do you know if Kafka was one of those callers?" Maggie asked.

"Not sure," Waleed said. "Only Dara knew Kafka's voice." And Maggie.

"Do you have recordings of those calls?" she asked.

"When you are taken to court as often as we are, your lawyers insist you record every single telephone call," Waleed said. "We use Skype."

Sitting down at the desk under the poster of the smiley face with its smirk and sunglasses, Waleed logged into a server and pulled up folders of archived calls, organized by date and subject. Under a folder labeled Dara, he selected several recent MP3 files.

The first was a genuine call from a reporter at *Le Figaro*. A woman. The second was a crazy person saying Dara was being punished by God and would die for it. The last was from a flower delivery service, two days ago. The soft educated tenor of the man's voice gave Maggie the chills. He spoke French but with a Middle Eastern accent.

"That's Kafka," she said.

Waleed rewound the call. A young woman with Incognito had replied to Kafka, saying, "Dara is recovering. She is expected to return next week."

"Do you know what hospital she's in, please?"

"I can't give any information out, monsieur."

"Do you have her home address?"

"We do not give that information out, monsieur. May I take a message?"

The caller hung up.

Kafka was doing his due diligence. Smart. But perhaps he didn't trust Dara one hundred per cent.

"Why are you listening to that call?" a twenty-something female at a nearby desk said, startling Maggie. She had purple braids and a nose ring. Her voice was the same one they had just listened to on the recorded phone call with Kafka.

"Trying to track down who made that call requesting Dara's hospital information, Dani," Waleed said. "Do you know anything else about it?"

"Only that he called again about two hours ago. I was the only one here. You guys went out for coffee. You forgot my latte, remember?" She grimaced.

Right after Maggie spoke to Kafka. She looked at Dani. "But that call wasn't logged."

"We don't always have time to archive them until end of day," Waleed said. He pulled the keyboard onto his lap, dug into the file structure, retrieved a time-stamped folder of today's calls. "Here we go—eleven-oh-three this morning."

He played the call back.

"This is Maison Hermès chocolatiers. We have a delivery for Dara Nezan and need to confirm an address."

Kafka again.

Dani replied that Dara was recovering well and expected to return to work next week.

"Is she still at the American Hospital?"

"I can't give out any information, monsieur."

Kafka hung up.

Checking up on Dara again—on Maggie as Dara—verifying her story. The last text exchange between them was before that call. Getting suspicious?

"Thanks," Maggie said to Waleed, standing up. "I'll let you know about Dara's funeral."

∽

"ANY MESSAGES FOR ME, MADAME?" Maggie stood in the narrow lobby of the Shangri-La, noting the new poster of an elephant and tiger walking past a fantasy depiction of a mystical temple in a cheap gold frame.

"No, but the police were here, mademoiselle," a flustered Madame Nguyen said. "They said you had something of theirs. They searched your room. I protested, but, they had a warrant..."

Maggie caught her breath. "A tall woman and a young man?"

Madame Nguyen nodded sheepishly.

"Did they take anything?"

"The cell phone on your nightstand," Madame Nguyen said. "I'm so sorry. Vinh and I watched them the whole time." She held up a piece of pink paper. "They left a receipt."

Maggie took the receipt, read it. *Sous-Direction Anti-Terroriste.* SDAT. Now they had two of her phones. But not Dara's.

"Did they take anything else, madame?"

"They asked if I had anything of yours in storage. But, of course, I had nothing, did I?" She gave a knowing smile.

Dara's phone was still safe, as was Maggie's laptop. "I'm very sorry for the intrusion, madame. Do I need to find a new hotel?"

Madame Nguyen squinted through her cat's-eye glasses

and dropped her voice. "Does this have anything to do with that shooting? At Place de la Sorbonne? A few days ago?"

"Can I trust you to keep what I say between you and me, madame?"

Madame Nguyen gave a taut smile. "I always respect my clients' privacy."

Maggie told her what she had to, which was a fair amount of fiction and just enough fact to hold it together.

"I see," Madame Nguyen said. "Do you think the police will be back, mademoiselle?"

"Not if I can help it. If so, I'll move to another hotel. But I do like it here."

Madame Nguyen seemed to mull that over. "Do you need your phone and laptop now? That you left for safe-keeping?"

"Just the phone, please." Madame Nguyen went off, downstairs to the basement where Vinh was banging away with a hammer. She returned, handed her Dara's phone.

"If you need to leave it again," she said, "you can give it to either me or Vinh."

"Thank you so much, madame."

Madame Nguyen straightened her cardigan and smiled. "I do hope you like the upgrades, mademoiselle. Vinh has been working very hard on redecorating the rooms, you know."

"And he's done a wonderful job," Maggie said.

21

When Au Bon Pho, the hole-in-the-wall eatery down the street from the Shangri-La, ran out of the Malbec, Maggie thought of switching to white wine. It would be easier on her head come the morning.

Maybe a nice Chablis.

Enough, she told herself. And enough of the boisterous diners who kept arriving and didn't seem to have a care in the world while Vietnamese pop music blasted from plastic loudspeakers.

Bellard was to have Dara's phone. But once he did, that would be the end of Abraqa.

But there were always options, she told herself.

In the meantime she needed to get hold of Aunt Amina, see about making funeral arrangements for Dara. She couldn't call her from inside this boom box. Maggie popped the last bite of a spring roll into her mouth, tossed euros on the plastic bill tray and left.

Outside, she glanced around. She'd let her guard down this afternoon. A growing throng of twentysomethings were hovering outside the restaurant, chatting, laughing, snapping photos of each other on their smartphones. Maggie turned the collar of her leather jacket up against the chilling night air, headed down rue Philibert Lucot.

She got her throwaway phone out and punched in Aunt Amina's number from memory. But, just as she was about to dial, that prickly feeling crawled up the back of her neck.

She put the phone away, turned around. Slowly.

And saw a compact man, wearing a dark windbreaker, hands in pockets, shoulders hunched forward as he marched behind her. The glow of a cigarette in his mouth. His working-class swagger and silhouetted ball cap took her back to Café Lepic this afternoon. He must have been waiting in a doorway or hidden amongst the others outside the restaurant.

That sobered her right up.

At the corner she turned right, broke into an easy jog in her sneaks. But losing Bellard's people would only be temporary. They knew where she was staying.

She'd have to switch hotels. Damn.

She ducked into an alley, pulling her house keys. If people ever wondered why she carried her keys on her person when she traveled, there was a reason. She worked the Yale key between her index and middle finger, made a fist and stood sideways, left shoulder facing the street, left fist up to parry. Legs apart, right fist back, ready to strike.

She heard him coming, footfalls soft and quick. Catching up.

Then his footsteps slowed. Not as dumb as he looked. He'd seen the entrance to the alley, had a good idea where'd she'd gone.

She waited, her right arm vibrating.

There was a second or two of tense anticipation. Down the street, a high-pitched horn honked.

He came lurking around the corner. The French SDAT punk, his windbreaker now open, his left hand inside, ready to pull a weapon. Still had his silly wraparound shades on.

"I can hit you before you pull that gun," she said.

He stared at her.

"When someone tries to pull a gun on you at short range, you have a twenty-one foot advantage if you rush him," she said. "That's about seven meters."

He stood there, hand in his coat, waiting.

"Why are you following me?" she said.

"Phone," he said.

"Tell Bellard there are ways to get it besides having some punk try to pull a damn gun on me. Tell Bellard if he wants the phone, he has to work with *me*. Now, do you have all that or do I need to write it down?"

"Got it," he said between clenched teeth.

"The gun goes on the ground," she said. "Slowly." Her hand was in the air, key out, ready to strike. "Anything funny, I let you have it."

He stared at her through the wraparounds. Finally his hand came out of his coat, the gun loose and down.

"On the ground," she said again.

He squatted, set the pistol on the sidewalk.

"Now stand back," Maggie said.

He did.

She picked up the gun, ejected the clip, tossed it, just as a car screeched around the corner up the street off rue Philibert Lucot. Maggie stopped where she was, listened to an engine whine up to the alley. The small white Peugeot she'd seen that afternoon appeared, two people inside. The passenger door flew open and the tall woman got out, the one who had taken Maggie's work phone earlier that day. She wore a car coat and a scowl. She came marching over, looking at the kid curiously, then at the gun in Maggie's hand.

"I already gave your pal here a message for Bellard," Maggie said. "And if I see either one of you outside my hotel, or following me, he'll never see that phone. Ever."

She handed the empty gun back by the barrel.

∽

BACK IN HER ROOM, Maggie threw her belongings into her bag, no folding or planning, and headed downstairs. She told Madame Nguyen she'd be moving on. Maggie wasn't going to risk SDAT making another appearance.

"I'm not worried about a refund," she said. "Consider it a small apology for all the harassment."

"I'm very sorry to hear it, mademoiselle." Maggie heard the relief in her voice, though.

"I'll be back some other time, madame. When I'm not so popular." She got out her phone, pulled up a browser, typed in *booking.com*. Now for a real challenge—find a hotel in Paris at eleven o'clock at night.

"Going somewhere, darlin'?"

Maggie turned.

John Rae Hutchens. Wearing his tan pigskin jacket, snug blue jeans, cowboy boots and a smirk. He had his sandy hair pulled back in a short tail. His goatee was neatly trimmed.

"JR—what the hell?"

"Looks like I almost missed you."

"Well, if you think you're escorting me back to the US of A again, you've got another thing coming. This trip was paid for by me, myself and I. I'm calling it a vacation, for lack of a better word. Which means the only one who tells me when to leave is me, myself or I."

"Same here," John Rae said, jamming his hands in his jacket pockets. "Thought I'd take a little break too. Nothing going on in Berlin right now. Figured you could show me around Paris." He grinned.

She squinted at him. "You're not here to take me back?"

"Not in the slightest."

"Then clue me in, if it's not too much trouble."

"Is that restaurant still open down the street? I just got off the plane and I'm famished. "

Maggie looked down at her carry-on on wheels.

"Vinh can put that in the basement, mademoiselle," Madame Nguyen said. "You won't find another hotel at this time of night anyway. Not one you'd want to close your eyes in."

22

Once they got a table, Maggie started in on the Chablis while John Rae demolished an order of Bo Nuong Ha, marinated beef grilled on skewers, which was as close to Bar-B-Q as he was going to get in a Vietnamese restaurant. While he ate Maggie brought him up to speed on Bellard.

"How do you say someone is a complete and utter asswipe in French?" he asked, taking a slug of Saigon Special beer.

"Did Ed call you?"

"He did. I knew you weren't going to get much cooperation. I tried to warn you. When you called me from SF."

"You did, but I'm curious: how did you know?"

"That's for me to know and you to ponder."

He wasn't going to tell. "So why the change of heart, JR?" She sipped wine while the pop music played and clubbers took a break to refuel. A noisy table of eight had just left so the restaurant was lively but not insane. "I thought you were a no-go on Abraqa."

"I guess I really don't want to see you back in a cell, even if you did leave me in a cab. And Bellard is on the verge of doing just that if his punks are harassing you on the street multiple times per day."

"But isn't Walder going to be upset?"

"Walder trusts me to run with certain things. Truth is, if I can help you pull off a quick win with Abraqa, let's just say he's not going to turn his nose up at free intel and brownie points. And Walder, for all his faults, does not like his people pushed around. Even you. And, besides, Senator Brahms finally came through."

Relief. She made a mental note to kiss her father next time she saw him, for pushing Brahms. "So that must have helped sway Walder's mind."

"That's why I'm here." John Rae raised his beer. "Maybe we get some juicy intel. Maybe you break Abraqa Darknet. And . . ." He drank. ". . . maybe you keep your butt out of a French jail. I hear they have Turkish toilets. Is that true?"

"Just stainless steel," she said. "But no seats. Helps build quads."

"Barbaric."

"I figure we've got a couple of days to nab Kafka."

"If it hasn't happened by then, he'll be gone and you'll be going home."

She was feeling giddy. Not just because of the wine, but because it looked like a visible course of action again. And, well, John Rae.

"There's still Bellard to deal with," she said.

"Right. But, unlike you, I have a rapport with him."

"Even though you speak French like Popeye the Sailor?"

John Rae took another drink of beer. "Bellard and I worked together in Marseille two years ago. At the time it was Hamas. Now Hamas seem like sweet little granny ladies, compared to Jihad Nation."

"Explain how Bellard is going to change his tune on letting me handle the communication on Abraqa," she said.

"Bellard's going to realize he can't land Kafka on his own. I'm going to convince him. Ultimately, Bellard is a cop. That's what SDAT are. Police. Busting heads is how they roll. Especially when jihadists are trying to blow up their city. If I were French—God forbid—I'd be pretty freakin' annoyed right now too. He knows I get that. He'll listen to me."

"What it comes down to," she said, "is that Bellard will listen to *you*. Another guy."

"Bellard is sexist."

"I forgot how progressive you are."

John Rae smiled. "Maybe because it won't be just *you*." John Rae pointed the tip of his beer bottle at Maggie. "It'll be you *and* me. And a couple of friends, if I need them."

"Some of your off-the-books friends?" John Rae had a shadowy network of people he could call in. They worked for cash and they shunned paperwork. "Well," she said, "all I can say is 'thanks'."

He took a drink of beer. "Maybe I just don't like standing by while some girl gets all the glory."

"You're supposed to say 'woman' now, JR."

"You are that."

Their eyes met for a moment.

"I'm going to hit the little boys' room," John Rae said. "Then I'm going to call Bellard, leave him a voicemail, speaking slowly, so he can understand. Tell him I can deliver Kafka, but it comes with conditions. Number one is you handle bringing Kafka in."

"What hotel are you staying at?"

John Rae gave a sheepish smile. "Do you think Madame Nguyen has an extra room?"

"So that's what this is really all about. If all you wanted was to get into my pants, you could have just said so."

"I thought the pants thing was a given."

"The answer's still 'no'."

John Rae sat back, drained his beer. "Story of my life."

Truth was, they both knew it was better this way.

"I guess you're sleeping on my floor then," she said. "I'll see if Madame Nguyen has an electric cattle prod I can borrow."

But John Rae was an honorable guy in that department. It was a relief to have him on this op. He downplayed it all of course. That was just his way.

John Rae sat up, waived the empty beer bottle at the waiter for a fresh one.

"In that case," Maggie said. "I think I'm going to have another glass of this kinky-poo Chablis."

∽

It was late when the two of them half-stumbled into Maggie's room, where Maggie searched for the switch to the puffy pink bedside lamp. She found it and the room was bathed in soft light. She set Dara's phone down on the nightstand.

John Rae, swaying an inch or two, eyed the white vinyl headboard with the chrome studs while Maggie stood back up. She was wavering a little too.

"Headboard reminds me of the Camaro I bought when I was sixteen," John Rae said. "Drove it down to Tijuana and got it upholstered just like that."

"Classy." She kicked off her sneaks and twiddled her blue-nailed toes. That caught his eye.

Maggie winked, kneeled down in front of the minibar,

clanking through bottles, having a little trouble reading the labels as the letters were moving around on her. "Would monsieur care for a nightcap?"

"Fuckin' *oui*. Bourbon."

She clanked. "Ixnay on the ourbonbay."

"Otch-scay?"

She found a mini bottle of Johnnie Walker, stood up, catching her balance, twisted off the tiny cap, handed him the bottle. She uncapped a small Gordon's gin for herself.

"To Abraqa," John Rae said, holding up his little bottle.

His blue eyes met her brown ones. *Current.*

She raised her own bottle. They clinked, downed the contents. Maggie gave a small gasp at the shot.

She took his empty and set it on the dresser along with hers. Then she was back down on her hands and knees, searching through the fridge.

It was all John Rae could do not to eye her fine derriere in her well-fitting black yoga pants. He shook off the thought that came to him often enough. Mental cold shower.

She rose back up with another whiskey for him and a vodka for herself this time. "Hold these." She turned, stumbled half a step, found the radio on the dresser, dialed in some smooth jazz, set the volume low. She came swerving back. Close. He could smell her. Some people smelled fantastic, even if they'd almost been jumped, been running around Paris all day and night. She was one of them. There was exactly one woman like her on the planet.

They touched bottles gently. Drank. Their eyes locked.

She gave a little breath again, an appreciative frown. "I think I like the vodka over the gin."

"Hairdresser's drinks."

"Because you're so macho."

"Damn straight."

"Were you staring at my butt?" Maggie asked, smiling with her eyes practically shut, head tilted back now.

"When?" he said in a stiff voice.

She gave a smirk. "Don't pretend you don't know when. Just now."

"No," he said, his pulse rate escalating.

"Yeah, you were."

"Not at all."

"Never?" She came up close, looking directly into his eyes. "You've *never* checked out my butt?"

He cleared his throat. "Only for professional reasons. I was covering. In case you fell over. You've been drinking. You were in a precarious position. I was worried about your safety."

She set her bottle down on the dresser, put her hands on her hips. Her breasts jutted out. *Good Lord.* She wiggled her toes. "And what were you going to do if I came into harm's way?"

He cleared his throat. "I was going to come to your assistance."

She moved in closer, brushing against him, woozy, eyes closed. "I'm glad you were watching me, if only for my own safety."

He could feel the heat coming off of her. Smell her sweet natural woman's perfume.

So close to heaven.

"This would be your cue, JR," she said.

"I'm probably an idiot for asking this, but, what about the guitar player?"

She gave him a sly squint. "Check out the shred of decency on JR. You think Sebi would do the same for you?"

"No," John Rae said. "I couldn't care less about him. I

was just thinking about you. If he's what you want, that's none of my business."

JR was old school.

"Sebi's history," she said. Her eyes got shiny.

She didn't have to ask twice. His arms went around her, soft but firm, as if he'd done it a hundred times.

"In that case..." John Rae said.

They swayed, listening to Miles Davis.

She unbuttoned two buttons of his shirt, nuzzled his firm chest with her soft lips. She undid another button and put her warm, soft cheek on his bare chest. His heart was thumping away.

To Maggie, he glowed. He gave off a raw scent that went straight to her groin, filling it with blood and something else. He was still wearing his jacket. His heart was pounding right next to her face, strong and sure. She always knew he would be like this. She just never thought either one of them would find out.

They moved together to the music.

"Thanks," she said, slurring the word.

"For what?" He nuzzled the top of her head, kissed her sweetly on her forehead. "Dancing like a white guy?"

"You know," she whispered, her head on his chest, reaching down his shirt, unbuttoning the last button. He had a six-pack and a fine layer of hair that led down to his waistband. She unbuckled the belt, heard him gulp, his face in her hair, kissing the top of her ear, setting it on fire.

She got his zipper down. She reached for him.

"Wow," she said, head on his chest.

"I have wanted you since the moment I first saw you," he said in a husky voice.

"Shut up." But she was getting wet.

He didn't speak. He didn't want to say another word, mess up the moment.

They danced while she fondled him.

"This is a one-time thing," she said. "You know that, right, JR?" She honestly didn't know what she wanted, just that, at this point, she'd keep things simple.

His head nodded on top of hers and he kissed her ear again, then her neck. His fingers were through her hair, brushing it back off her forehead.

They looked at each other in the dim pink light before a primal hunger pulled them back together like kissing magnet dolls. He pulled away, took her chin in his hand, smiled, parted her lips with his thumb, ever so slightly. And then his mouth was on hers again and he tasted good, and hot, like she knew he would, like food, like beer, but mostly like him. She found his tongue and he wasn't clumsy, not at all. She responded, probing his mouth with her own tongue, realized how long it had been. He lifted her up with ease and she wrapped her legs around his waist. Warm spasms shot down the small of her back in anticipation—through her bottom, straight to her toes as her feet curled around his back, locking over his firm ass. He leaned back, just touching the wall, holding her upright, resting her groin on his. She rubbed herself against him while he stood there, legs apart. Holding onto his shoulder with one hand, she reached down underneath her butt with the other. He was hard, as hard could be, his underwear taut over his crotch. Her hand slipped underneath the elastic waistband and circled around him, stroking him slowly.

He was breathing heavily.

"All these clothes," she said. She leaned back, legs holding onto him like a vice.

"What do you recommend?"

"Take them off?"

"That would work—wouldn't it?"

"You first," she whispered. "I get to watch."

"Yes, ma'am," he murmured.

"When I said this was a one-time thing, JR, I meant it's once, fast and furious, then once again, slow and delicious. That's what I meant."

"Let me write that down."

"It's OK. I'll remind you."

She held onto his neck while his hands grabbed the firm curves of her thighs, found their way up her midriff, burrowing under her sweater. He cupped her breasts, outside her bra, massaging her through the lace, his thumbs circling her nipples expertly. She was generating steam heat. She unhooked one arm and, pulling her sweater up, exposed her breasts still encased in bra. She hugged his face into her cleavage.

Reaching behind her back, she unhooked her bra, let her breasts jiggle free, relishing the way they fell into his warm hands. Then his hot tongue was all over them.

On the nightstand, Dara's phone vibrated.

No, she thought. *No!*

John Rae stopped doing what he was doing, looked up into her eyes.

"It's him," she said.

"Kafka," John Rae said. "I thought you were calling him tomorrow."

"Me too."

The phone buzzed again while they watched each other, the moment slipping away.

"I have to get that," she said, brushing her tousled hair out of her face, pulling her sweater back down over her swelling breasts.

"You better get that," he agreed, letting her down. He exhaled deeply.

KAFKA: *must talk to you*

Maggie had to think fast. Her head was swimming with the drinks and muggy thoughts of what had been about to happen.

DARA: *can't, still in hospital. was asleep*

KAFKA: *are you getting out tomorrow?*

DARA: *not now. one wound puffy. docs want to watch it*

There was a pause. Maggie heard John Rae zipping up his trousers. The party was over.

KAFKA: *I have to leave tomorrow*

No! Maggie thought.

DARA: *iraq?*

KAFKA: *Yes.*

No way. Not Now.

DARA: *your parents worry you*

KAFKA: *Yes.*

DARA: *one more day, habibi. just one more day. please!*

KAFKA: *but how?*

DARA: *you simply stay. that's how. you don't leave me*

KAFKA: *but ...*

DARA: *don't you want me? like I want you?*

Pause.

KAFKA: *yes, but ...*

DARA: *then you must wait*

John Rae came over, peered over Maggie's shoulder. The conversation was in Arabic script, so completely unintelligible to him.

"What's the deal?" he whispered, as if Kafka might be able to hear the two of them talking.

"He's going to bolt," Maggie said, sucking in air. "Tomorrow."

"We need more time. Another day."

"I know."

"Promise him anything."

"I think I just did."

KAFKA: *I cannot. I am so sorry. I must leave tomorrow.*

"It's time for the *pièce de résistance*," Maggie said. She retrieved the JPEG image file she'd photoshopped for this very situation. Created from a selfie she'd found on Dara's phone and transferred back. The original was taken at a restaurant but that context she'd removed. Now Dara was set against a hospital bed, which had taken a while to find. Shy smile, hair slightly messed. A little bare neck and the hint of one shoulder. Blouse touched up blue-green with a higher collar to resemble a hospital gown. Dara had been pretty, to be sure. Maggie had shaded underneath Dara's eyes to simulate weariness. As a final touch, she had roughened the photo appearance using her photo editor, making it grainy and just a little harder to discern. A comely Dara, happy and hopeful, recovering, with a hint of intimacy to get Kafka's blood flowing. Nothing overt. Her hope was that Kafka wouldn't see anything too forward. He was, after all, a Muslim, and if his radicalization was anything to go by, most likely straight-laced. According to Dara, they had only ever traded formal photos on two occasions.

But men were still men.

"Nice work," John Rae whispered over Maggie's shoulder.

"Think he'll buy it?"

"Only if he has a pulse."

"OK, then," Maggie said. "Dara—do your thing."

DARA: *i'm sure i will be discharged day after tomorrow. just look at me!*

Maggie attached the photo to her next text message, and

hit *send*. Seconds crawled while the image transmitted and she imagined Kafka studying the picture. "Come on, Kafka," she whispered, her heart rate belying her still pose, sitting on the bed. "Take the bait."

Finally, a single word came back.

KAFKA: *Jamillah!*

Beautiful.

Maggie sat back, sighing with relief.

DARA: *why, thank you!* :)

"Things seem to be getting pretty out of hand," John Rae joked.

"Now you know what Muslim sexting is, JR. Let's see if we can get him to send one back. Get him to buy into the fantasy." Get a fresh look at their problem child while they were at it.

DARA: *and may i have one of you? it's been so long*

No response. Had she overplayed her hand?

KAFKA: *1 sec*

She brushed her hair back while a photo downloaded. A coarse selfie of Kafka appeared. In a dark room with a mottled, stained wall behind him, wallpaper peeling off in strips. Lit only by a camera flash. Was he in a slum of some sort? An abandoned house?

"Cool digs," John Rae said.

But there was Kafka, in need of a shave, his chiseled face made even more gaunt by lines of stress and apprehension. Forcing a smile.

DARA: *very handsome!*

KAFKA: *Now I know you are lying. I'm too worried for my parents*

DARA: *where are you?*

KAFKA: *paris*

She wanted to know exactly where but didn't want to push too hard.

KAFKA: *do you mean it? About getting out?*

DARA: *i will get out day after tomorrow. even if i have to walk out*

KAFKA: *Promise?*

DARA: *promise!*

Finally, the response came.

KAFKA: *then I shall wait . . .*

"Woo-hoo!"

"Keep your voice down, Maggs. It's three in the morning."

KAFKA: *shall I meet you?*

The hospital was out. Kafka had already been there, according to John Rae. In disguise. He'd tested the keep-alive.

"He wants to meet me," she said. "We need somewhere where he'll trust me unconditionally."

"How about Aunt Amina's?"

"I don't want to get her involved."

"You won't have to. Bellard can set up a flytrap." A flytrap was a house or apartment set up to resemble a person's living quarters.

"That works," Maggie said.

DARA: *do you know where my auntie lives, habibi?*

Maggie waited. Somewhere upstairs, a toilet flushed. Someone stomping around, woken up.

KAFKA: *montmarte, correct?*

DARA: *yes, i'll let you know when i'm home*

She waited. And waited.

KAFKA: *will I talk to you tomorrow?*

He was back under her control now. But she needed to make sure he didn't have a change of heart.

DARA: *yes*

KAFKA: *until then*

She let out a breath she wasn't aware she'd been holding so long.

DARA: *enta kol shay'a*

She signed off, set Dara's phone down. She stood up, turned around. "The fish is on the line."

"We need to get hold of Bellard," John Rae said, pulling his cell phone from his jacket pocket. "Get this puppy rolling." He hit dial, put the phone to his ear.

"We need to get Elizabeth on site, too. We'll need her telephony magic."

"We can fly her in. We have until the day after tomorrow —thanks to you."

"Thank Dara."

Maggie took a good look at John Rae tucking his shirt in with one hand. Now she knew what was underneath. Only a few minutes earlier the two them had been headed down a very different path. That course had been changed. It felt as if someone had opened the window, pulled back the curtains, let a blast of cold air into the room.

Probably for the best.

But what a sweet start before the brakes were applied.

23

"And there he goes," Maggie said. "Leaving the hospital."

Maggie, John Rae and Bellard were huddled around Maggie's laptop on the round table in the corner of Bellard's office at SDAT headquarters. It was early the next morning, the floor near empty and unlit, as they watched rough black-and-white closed-circuit TV footage of a man exiting the American Hospital of Paris the day before. The man in the video was tall, slim, wearing a dark suit, dark hair combed down. He carried a bunch of lilies. He turned abruptly where the path from the hospital stairwell exit met the sidewalk, revealing his profile for a moment. Prominent nose, thick-framed glasses. He marched briskly out of camera view.

"That's Kafka," Maggie said, pausing the video Field Ops had given her access to. "Although he's done a good job of looking like someone else. Fake glasses, change of hairstyle."

"So you know what this Kafka looks like?" Bellard asked Maggie, sitting forward now, next to her. His attitude had changed dramatically since consulting with John Rae and realizing how tantalizing close the Agency had gotten to Kafka.

"We traded photos only a few hours ago," Maggie said. "I sent one of Dara I'd altered to look like she was in the hospital."

"I see." Bellard took a sip of coffee from a plastic vending machine cup.

"The flowers were found half a block down Victor Hugo in the trash," John Rae said. "Kafka was posing as the brother of another patient. Showed a false National ID at the desk. Took the elevator up to the fifth floor, walked down to the second, where Dara's room is. He was stopped by one of our contractors. Kafka asked for Dara, said he was a work acquaintance at Incognito. He presented another fake ID. He left when challenged."

Maggie leaned over the desk, brushing her hair back, verifying the timestamp. She was back to her prosperous young Arab look, with black leggings, long gray cashmere sweater working as a dress, her black crocodile Gucci loafers. Her hijab was in a shoulder bag hanging over the chair.

"So Kafka bought it," Bellard said in accented English, leaning back, looking at Maggie. "He fell for your *keep-alive*. And your text chats."

"It seems that way." Maggie smiled.

"Quick thinking on Maggie's part," John Rae said. "Getting Ed to set up the keep-alive in the first place." He'd been promoting Maggie's efforts since they had sat down with Bellard that morning. Bellard, contentious at first, was now being receptive, thanks to John Rae's persistence. "Maggie's been staying in constant contact with Kafka since the shooting, keeping him on the hook—keeping him here in

Paris." John Rae was chewing gum, leaning back in his chair—casual, wearing sneakers, 501's and a black long-sleeve T-shirt. Maggie thought of him briefly with fewer clothes, scant hours ago, in a physical clinch she still savored. She banished the memory. "Maggie's also brought in a language resource who can stand in as Dara on phone calls with Kafka. We're flying her in from California as we speak. You can't afford *not* to have Maggie on this effort, Bellard."

Bellard folded his hands over his stomach. He said to John Rae, "And you can guarantee your support as well?"

"That's why I'm here," John Rae said.

"Walder has approved this?"

John Rae gave a sheepish grin. "Define 'approved'."

"In writing."

John Rae made a *comme ci, comme ça* motion with his hand. "Let's just say I have a lot of leeway although my name —and especially Walder's—will be nowhere on this op in any official capacity. Walder wants Kafka caught but he wants it off the Agency books. Politics. So Abraqa is officially your baby."

Bellard pursed his lips. "And Maggie here? What does she get? The first interview with Kafka? That's it?"

Maggie and Bellard exchanged knowing glances. She hoped she could trust Bellard to deliver on his promise.

Maggie said: "Forensic Accounting gets the first interview with Kafka. And others, as necessary, until I understand how to gain access to Abraqa Darknet. The process overview, logins, passwords, IP addresses. That can be done here in this facility, with you or your people sitting in. He's all yours after that."

Did she feel good throwing Kafka under the bus? He had been lured into this situation for his parents' sake and he cared for Dara. But he had served Jihad Nation, helped them further the Yazidi genocide. Ending that took priority.

Bellard sat back, eyes half-lidded. "SDAT makes the arrest. We hold him—here. To clarify, Kafka is ours, not yours. No question. After your interviews, you are gone, poof!" He made a little motion with his hand.

"That suits us," Maggie said.

"I want it in writing."

"This is way below the radar, Bellard," Maggie said. "No paper trail."

"I want an email at least." Bellard pressed an imaginary button on his desk. "From Walder."

"I told you," John Rae said. "Walder's not going to put his name anywhere near this. Not after getting his ass chewed out by the National Security Advisor. But you have our word."

"I need *something*," Bellard said. "There's been too much —ah—volatility in the way our departments work together. My boss has a lot of egg on his face."

"How about an email—from Ed?" Maggie had already cleared it with him prior to meeting with Bellard this morning. Good old Ed was prepared to stick his neck out. One more time.

Bellard stared at a poster of a white sandy beach on the wall for a moment.

"*D'accord*," he said, raising his eyebrows, looking at Maggie, then John Rae, then back at Maggie. "You get Abraqa Darknet. I get Kafka. The operation is mine. My instructions will be followed to the letter."

Maggie took a quiet breath. Dara had died giving birth to Abraqa. Maggie had been both midwife and wet nurse. And Bellard was going to be the proud poppa, handing out the cigars.

But, if it was the only way Abraqa was to survive, and Dara's mission be fulfilled, so be it.

"Deal," she said. She stood up, put her hand out across the desk.

Bellard sat there for a moment before he gave up a begrudged smile and finally sat forward, reaching out, taking her hand.

24

SDAT Computer Lab: two days later, early morning

"THE FLYTRAP IS READY," Bellard said, standing at the door to the SDAT *Salle Informatique* on the second floor. He had just entered the lab.

"You've inspected it?" Maggie asked. She wore her young prosperous Arab look again—alligator loafers, black leggings, newer patent leather jacket. In her bag she had a pair of Nike sneakers. She and Elizabeth Stotz, flown in the previous day from California to stand in for Dara on phone calls to Kafka, sat side-by-side at workstations. Assisting them was an SDAT tech, a big man in a crewcut and a snug uniform who was nosily working a keyboard, surrounded by stacks of electronic equipment. The room was rushing with air conditioners doing battle against spinning hard drives and numerous electronic heat sources. Flashing lights added to the mayhem.

Equipe Abraqa—Team Abraqa—led by Bellard, had spent the previous day setting up the sting, preparing officers, lining up resources, going over procedures. Maggie had Dara's phone on the work surface, hooked up to computers, along with a set of headphones around her neck, a pair of earbuds and adapter. The tech had pulled up a Kurdish soap opera on YouTube on one of his machines. The video was paused, ready to simulate Aunt Amina's apartment.

Elizabeth sat at her own laptop, her long legs wrapped in paisley toreador pants. A yellow notepad full of Arabic scribbles lay in front of her. John Rae leaned against a worksurface, arms crossed in his pigskin jacket.

"Of course I checked out the flytrap," Bellard said. They were speaking English so everyone could participate. Bellard buttoned up his suit jacket against the manmade chill. "There's plenty of litter." *Litter* was staged personal effects to make a location seem genuine—photographs, belongings. "Everything is in order. Have no fear."

"Where exactly is this flytrap?" Maggie asked.

"Montmartre."

"Yes, but *where*?"

"Rue des Martyrs," Bellard said. "Near La Cigalle. Not too far from *le Musée de l'érotisme*." He grinned, hands in the pockets of his light blue slacks.

A small jolt of alarm caught Maggie. She typed the street name into a browser and pulled up Google maps.

"Dara's aunt lives off Boulevard Barbès," she said.

"Not bad at such short notice, eh?" Bellard was obviously pleased with himself.

Maggie eyed the map. "It's half a kilometer away. Too far." Not the way they would have done it.

Bellard rattled change in his pocket. "Did you not say

that Kafka doesn't know the exact location of Aunt Amina's apartment?"

"He's implied that. And I've been through Dara's texts and saw no record of her telling him. But Kafka is tracking Dara, so he might have gotten a pretty good idea where Aunt Amina lives. He's checked out Dara's hospital room, called Incognito, so he's no dummy. He could be testing us. I don't want him smelling a rat."

Bellard seemed to think that over, then pulled his cell phone, dialed a number. He instructed someone in French that they needed a new flytrap set up, ASAP, on Boulevard Barbès. That someone ranted on the other end for a good twenty seconds before Bellard hung up, his face turning red.

"I don't speak French but that sure sounded like a big fat 'no' on any new flytrap," John Rae said.

Bellard grimaced. "They can have it ready by tomorrow." He focused on Maggie: "But Dara is due out of the hospital today."

"Correct."

"If Kafka calls, can we stall him? Tell him it's taking time to be discharged? Drag it out another day?"

"We've already pushed Kafka as far as we can," Maggie said. "Any further delay might well scare him right off."

"*D'accord*," Bellard said. "Get hold of Dara's aunt. We'll just have to use her apartment for Kafka's capture."

Ninety-seven percent of her said Kafka was a genuine defector. But who were those suicide bombers who attacked the café? The fact that Kafka hadn't run said he probably didn't know either. If he was in on the potential bombing, he'd be gone. But she didn't know anything for sure. "I don't want Aunt Amina in harm's way."

John Rae agreed. Elizabeth worked on her notes, staying out of the discussion.

Bellard made a stone face. "I have a duty to capture Kafka."

"You have a duty to protect citizens, too," Maggie said.

"Do not tell me what my duty as a Frenchman is," he said, narrowing his eyes. "And this Amina is just another illegal immigrant anyway."

Maggie's ire rose. "And that makes it all right to put her in danger?" She was getting edgy. There had been too many interruptions and change of plans.

John Rae jumped in. "This is how I see it, guys, Maggie calls Amina, gives her the heads-up so that if Kafka makes contact today, we'll plan to grab him *out front* of Aunt Amina's. If there's a delay we use the new flytrap tomorrow."

"We also have to account for the fact that Kafka picks a different location," Maggie said. "He might not want to meet at her apartment. I wouldn't. I'd want to meet somewhere else. In public."

"I thought you and Kafka have built a level of trust," Bellard said to Maggie.

"Yes. But we still have to be prepared for multiple scenarios." It was basic procedure. But she didn't say so.

"Where is Kafka?" Bellard asked.

Maggie shrugged. It was making her nervous that she hadn't heard from him yet.

"I suggest we call."

"No," Maggie said. "Kafka calls *us*."

Bellard's eyes hardened.

John Rae saw the interaction, said to Bellard: "If Kafka thinks *he's* calling the shots, he's more likely to buy into the sting."

"Very well." Bellard put his hands in his pockets. "But it means drawing up a new arrest plan."

They spent the next hour in front of a dry erase board.

Amina would be moved out of her apartment. Officers would be posted inside, as well as outside, to wait for Kafka. Bellard made phone calls, putting the resources into play.

Maggie, John Rae and Bellard would monitor the capture from a van. If Maggie had to meet Kafka in person, she could do that, staying in touch via Rino phone and a wireless throat mic. Elizabeth would join them in the van.

It was coming together.

"All we need now," Maggie said, "is for our guest of honor to call."

Bellard checked his watch, rubbed his hands together.

"Anybody got a deck of cards?" John Rae asked.

Hours later, the lab was littered with half-filled plastic coffee cups, paper towels, and half-eaten vending machine sandwiches. No one was hungry. John Rae was telling Elizabeth a joke about a penguin.

It was 2:44 PM when Dara's phone blipped with an incoming text.

Everybody froze.

25

"This is it," Maggie said, sitting up, reading the text on Dara's phone.

KAFKA: *are you there?*

Yes, she typed, using the Arabic script keyboard. *Finally out of the hospital! At my aunt's.*

KAFKA: *Safe to talk?*

Maggie eyed the computer tech, who was watching her intently, poised over his keyboard.

DARA: *Yes.* Maggie nodded at Elizabeth, who was donning her headphones.

KAFKA: *I will call you*

"Get ready," Maggie said, signaling the others. She pointed at the lab tech who clicked Play on the YouTube video fed into the audio mix, filling the background of her headphones with a Turkish soap opera. A mother and daughter were having a heart-to-heart talk in Arabic while syrupy strings played tear-jerking music.

Dara's cell phone vipped on the table, and Maggie pulled her chair up next to Elizabeth's. Elizabeth got into position, adjusting her headphones and throat mic. John

Rae moved closer. Bellard rebuttoned his jacket for the umpteenth time.

The tech raised a finger, hit Record on one of his computers.

Maggie answered the call, giving Elizabeth the go-ahead.

"*Alsalamu 'alakum!*" Elizabeth said in a breathless, excited rendition of Dara's voice that still astounded Maggie for its accuracy. The tech adjusted a digital dial on his application, adding a level of static, muddying up the call quality just enough.

"God be praised," Kafka said. "You sound well!"

"It's so good to hear your voice."

"Are you at your auntie's?"

"I arrived not long ago."

"In Montmartre?"

"Yes." Maggie made eye contact with Bellard and John Rae. She had set MockLoc on Dara's phone to the GPS coordinates of Aunt Amina's apartment.

"What are you doing?" Kafka asked.

"Oh, just having tea." Elizabeth drank nosily from a cup for effect. "Watching television."

"What are you watching?"

Elizabeth looked over at Maggie. Why was Kafka being so inquisitive? Doing his due diligence?

"Some silly soap opera," Elizabeth said in Dara's voice.

"Do you really watch such things?" There was a tone of admonition.

"My auntie likes them."

"Is she there?" Kafka asked. "Your auntie?"

Elizabeth and Maggie's eyes connected again and Maggie nodded *yes*, then motioned for Elizabeth to go ahead. "Yes, *habibi*. She's in the kitchen."

"I would like to say hello, if I may. I've never had the pleasure."

Elizabeth gave Maggie an *oh, shit!* look.

Maggie pointed to herself. Elizabeth nodded. Maggie caught the tech's eye, gave him a signal to mic her in. He adjusted another dial.

"Let me just go fetch her," Elizabeth said. She stood up, placed her hand partially over her throat microphone, and shouted in Kurmanji: "Amina! Kafka wants to say 'hello'."

Maggie put on a deep voice while the tech toyed with a setting, adding a touch of echo, and said, "Coming!" before stepping deliberately over to the table so that her footsteps might register.

"Is that Auntie Amina?" Kafka said in a sweet voice.

"*As-salam alaykom*," Maggie said in basic Arabic, channeling her best fifty-year-old Yazidi woman.

"*Wa 'alaykum salaam ya Amina*," Kafka replied. "I've heard so much about you."

Maggie didn't know whether that was even true. Perhaps Kafka was testing her. She forced a laugh. "Arabic is not my mother tongue. I only speak a little classical. Unlike Dara, who speaks Baghdadi with ease."

"Say something in Kurmanji, Auntie Amina," Kafka said.

Testing her, to be sure.

"*Xwa-legell*, Kafka," Maggie said. Thank God Dara had taught her a phrase or two.

"I have no idea what you just said but it sounds wonderful."

Maggie switched back to Arabic, not feeling too bad about nailing Kafka now. He was going to get what he deserved. "I'm preparing a special meal—Adana kebab. I hope we see you today."

"That sounds wonderful, too."

"Let me give you back to Dara."

Maggie nodded at Elizabeth, who tightened the headset over her ears. Maggie sat back down.

"Well," Elizabeth said in Dara's voice, laughing like a schoolgirl. "When *will* we see you? How soon?"

"I can be there in an hour."

Elizabeth eyed Maggie. Maggie translated for Bellard and John Rae. Bellard jacked his thumb down, then showed six fingers. He needed time to get everyone in place.

"Auntie has just started to prepare the meal, *habibi*. She will be mortified if it's not ready when you arrive. And I need a nap. I am so tired after getting out of the hospital. Best make it later. Six o'clock?"

"Six o'clock it is."

"I can't wait."

"And I."

Maggie grabbed a pencil and circled a particular note on Elizabeth's notepad.

"Oh," Elizabeth said, reading. "You'll need directions, won't you?"

"You're on Boulevard Barbès, correct?"

"Just off of it. Rue Bevric. Down the street from the Metro." Elizabeth consulted the yellow pad, read off an address. "*Ma ʿ al-salāmah.*"

Maggie hung up the phone.

Elizabeth jumped up from her seat, gave her and the tech a high five while John Rae and Bellard hooted with glee.

Maggie's enthusiasm, however, was more tempered. Kafka was acting more suspicious than she'd expected and that worried her.

∼

Kafka hung up his phone, looked around at the crumbling walls of the abandoned house he was staying in, sleeping on a sheet of cardboard with a throwaway blanket. The mold had given him a headache. The rats scurrying back and forth all night made it impossible to sleep. His arms were covered with spider bites.

He would meet Dara in a few hours. His mind was set.

He pulled on the blond wig, combed the shiny hair into place with his fingers. Pulled a white ball cap on over the wig, with its red, white and blue French Le Coq rooster gripping a soccer ball in its talons. Dress like a patriot to blend in.

Then he checked his Caracal 9C, slipped the pistol carefully into his waistband. The faulty safety switch remained a concern. He slid a spare fifteen-round magazine in his jacket pocket.

He stood up straight, arms by his side, and closed his eyes. He attempted to calm himself.

When he first 'met' Dara, killing her had been the last thing on his mind.

He had entertained the thought they might be sweethearts. Indeed, she had fostered that notion. He had allowed himself to become infatuated. Dara was beautiful, intelligent, spoke Arabic, and had worked tirelessly to get him to come over. She had sensed he wasn't a true jihadist.

If there ever was a tragedy on this earth, having to ending Dara's life was it.

But now he had no choice. Hassan al-Hassan held his parents hostage.

If they were to live, he must atone for his transgression, execute Dara, send proof. A photo.

What if Hassan al-Hassan killed his parents anyway?

After Kafka killed the woman he once thought so much of? What a mess. What a damn mess.

He slipped on his sunglasses.

Too late for regrets. He had made his decision.

It was time.

26

After slapping hands all around the computer room, the Abraqa team reconvened to Bellard's office, where Bellard got on the office phone, his tone turning serious.

"Bring the van to the side entrance. Tell the support team already in position to be on the lookout for the person in the photo that was distributed. But be aware, he may be in disguise." Bellard hung up the phone, looked at John Rae and Elizabeth, then Maggie.

"How about the two officers slotted for Aunt Amina's apartment?" she asked.

"They're in position. Aunt Amina has left. She's at her tea shop, out of the way. But we're going to grab Kafka before he gets inside the building anyway."

"I know." Maggie got out her work phone, which Bellard's people had finally returned to her, and called Aunt Amina, to check in on her.

"Operation Abraqa is live," Bellard said, standing up, rubbing his hands.

27

They were ready.

But Kafka was almost half an hour late.

No one was saying it, but everyone was thinking it: What if he didn't show?

The windowless van, bearing a faded red cow painted on the side over the name of a fictitious Paris butcher's shop, was parked down Boulevard Barbès. From the back seat Maggie could just see the corner of the side street Aunt Amina lived on, a length of four-story buildings constructed during the late nineteenth century when Napoleon renovated the city. An eclectic mix of modern shop fronts at street level contrasted with the stately architecture.

As evening approached, the open-air market along the elevated Metro line on Barbès—Rochechouart had reached full swing, despite the cool weather and sharp wind. The odd spot of rain landed here and there. Clouds churned low in the sky. Even so, Parisians were out, strolling from stall to stall, sampling delicacies, listening to lively Middle Eastern music piped through outdoor speakers. The atmosphere was distinctly south of the Mediterranean, with tantalizing smells to match.

Five others occupied the van along with Maggie, making the air inside close and well-breathed. Behind the wheel sat a driver in a dark blue windbreaker, working a toothpick. Next to him, in the passenger seat, Bellard consulted a Garmin Rino two-way radio, scrolling through its tiny screen. The high end device featured GPS, electronic compass, camera and had a range of two miles, supported by dual antennae.

Next to Maggie sat Elizabeth, wearing a wireless headset, her ever-present yellow pad full of notes on her lap. In the back bench seat behind Maggie sat John Rae, along with an SDAT tech who worked a small array of digital equipment mounted to a metal frame.

"Hurry up and wait," she heard John Rae say, as if sensing her concern.

Maggie turned around to give John Rae a smile. With the pigskin jacket he seemed to wear in every part of the globe he was assigned to, John Rae sported a blue beret. Along with the goatee, it helped tone down his Anglo features. His young Brad Pitt hairstyle was tucked back behind his ears. Maggie kept finding herself taking a moment whenever she looked at him now, reminiscing about their aborted encounter. But work was work, and coworkers were just that. John Rae returned her smile, despite the fact that Bellard had relegated him to an "advisory role", meaning he would not participate in Kafka's capture.

Maggie was ready to meet Kafka, if it came to that, in a smart new abaya pulled over her black leggings and a white, loose-fitting T-shirt, finished off with black Nike women's 5.0 running sneakers, each shoe weighing in at a few ounces.

She had changed out of her chic loafers in case things came down to a chase. On her head she wore a black leopard print hijab, which would set the department back one hundred and twenty-five euros if she could get it approved, along with a sheer black face veil that she had unfastened. Under the hijab she wore wireless earbuds and a wireless throat mic, which would allow her to talk on Dara's cell phone as well as with the rest of the team hands free.

Dara's phone rested on her knee, awaiting Kafka's call.

Two agents were posted near the Metro stop behind them, watching out. The tall female cop who had searched Maggie was stationed in Amina's apartment on the third floor, along with another agent, in the event that Kafka made it that far. The kid who had almost pulled the gun on Maggie stood across the street from the side street to Dara's apartment building, in a blue hoodie and sunglasses, sipping a soft drink from a paper cup. Maggie and he had acknowledged each other at the beginning of the op today. Maggie had put her hand out and said, '*sans rancune*'. No hard feelings. The young man, whose name was Remi, had taken her hand, given it a single wooden shake as he looked away. Good enough, Maggie thought. He was OK—just green. She could see him through the windshield, craning his neck, scanning the street.

On the Rino Bellard had issued her, she enlarged the grainy photo of Kafka, sent to "Dara" when she was allegedly in the hospital. Thirties, olive skin, half-lidded hazel colored eyes with prominent lashes, accentuating a long face with elegant features. The rest of Bellard's team had a copy of the photo on their phones as well. One problem was that Kafka looked like many other Parisians around the street market at the moment.

"Kafka's over half an hour late," Bellard finally said,

breaking the silence. "We should call."

"A few more minutes," Maggie said.

"A few more minutes." Bellard tapped his radio.

"Hang in there, darlin'," she heard John Rae say behind her.

"I told you not to call me that unless we're in bed together and . . ." Maggie caught herself. She'd have to find another joke. That one cut too close for comfort now.

John Rae said: "I guess it's a woman's prerogative to change her mind."

"I'm impressed, JR. You know a word like prerogative *and* can use it in a sentence."

"I don't have a clue what it means. I just know it impresses the ladies."

Elizabeth turned to grin at John Rae. "Who are you calling a lady, buddy?"

"Everyone's a comedian." Maggie checked the time again on her phone. Thirty-five minutes late. Kafka had been dying to meet Dara. He'd be early, if anything.

The radio in Bellard's hand crackled. Everyone jumped. Bellard punched a button and spoke speakerphone style. "*Allez-y, mon petit,*" he said. *Mon petit* was the team's nickname for Remi, the junior agent in the blue hoodie posted across from Aunt Amina's.

"*Un van de DHL vient de s'arrêter à l'extérieur du bâtiment,*" Remi said.

Maggie translated for JR. A DHL van had just pulled up outside Amina's apartment building.

"Some guy in a DHL uniform is getting out," Remi said. "Carrying a couple of packages."

"Stand by, everyone," Bellard said into his Rino.

"Dude just went into the building with the packages."

Maggie leaned across the front seat, spoke into the phone, which was now in conference mode. "You get a good look at him, Remi?"

"Tall. Yellow uniform, cap, glasses."

Maggie translated for John Rae. "Could be our Kafka. In disguise."

Several tense minutes went by during which Bellard issued commands, primarily to the two agents stationed inside Amina's apartment. Then, Remi spoke again.

The DHL man had exited the apartment building, without packages.

"Well, that was kind of exciting," John Rae said, sitting back.

A tense breath escaped Maggie's lips.

"Time to contact Kafka," Bellard said.

"Yes," Maggie said. "I'll text him."

DARA: *are you running late, habibi?*

No response.

Two minutes later, she tried again.

DARA: *just wondering where you are—give me a call when you think you'll arrive—so looking forward to it!*

She sat back.

"Shit," she said out loud.

∼

KAFKA HAD SEEN the young punk in the blue hood loitering across the street from Rue Bevric when he checked the neighborhood out before his visit. Perhaps nothing, but he wasn't taking chances. Kafka circled the street market twice. Now, half an hour later, the kid was still there, drinking the same drink. Maybe he was waiting for someone. But it didn't look quite right.

Kafka's first instinct had been to flee. Then he thought of his parents, specifically his mother, at the hands of Hassan al-Hassan. Their deaths would be brutal.

He had waited this long. His masters didn't care if he died killing Dara, but he did. So he headed briskly down Boulevard de la Chapelle, the wide thoroughfare flanking the elevated Metro, to the next Metro stop, La Chapelle. About half a kilometer from Aunt Amina's, near the Gare du Nord. There was a small park on this side of the street, on the corner, across from the entrance to the Metro. It was surrounded with black decorative wrought iron fencing, dotted with trees, and populated with rough-looking people milling about. The area under the elevated Metro across the street was teeming with Syrian refugees sleeping out underneath. A place to run to, if need be. Kafka checked that he had a spare Metro ticket for quick entry. He did.

He found a spot next to a green circular Morris column next to the park, affording a good view and providing cover.

The phone in his pocket buzzed.

He retrieved it.

DARA: *are you running late, habibi?*

She was getting anxious. Good. He'd wait. He said a silent prayer for his mother.

Then, another text.

Dara: *just wondering where you are—give me a call when you think you'll arrive—so looking forward to it!*

Yes, he had feelings for her but weren't they just some imagined thing? What was she? An illusion he had created. Out of loneliness. If she had to die, she had to die. All illusions die.

His parents came first. His mother.

It was time.
He dialed Dara.

~

MAGGIE JOLTED upright in the van when the phone call came in.

Thank God. She thought he had slipped away.

"It's him," she said, sucking in a breath. "It's Kafka."

28

"Ready?" Maggie asked Elizabeth, sitting next to her in the bench seat in the back of the van. Elizabeth acknowledged with a quick nod. Maggie hit *answer call* on Dara's phone, which was resting on her knee.

"Alo, habibi," Elizabeth said, head tilted back, speaking into her headset. Her eyes closed, she held her mouth just so, rendering an excellent match for Dara's voice. "I was getting worried you weren't coming."

"I was delayed," Kafka said. "Then I got off at the wrong stop!" He laughed. "I swear I will never understand the Metro. I think I was just nervous—finally meeting you."

"I know what you mean," Elizabeth said in dialect. Maggie was able to follow the conversation easily enough. Speaking Baghdadi was another matter.

"When will we see you?" Elizabeth asked.

They could hear street noise in the background through their earphones, the sound of traffic. Kafka was outdoors.

"I think it might be better for the two of us to meet first,"

Kafka said. "Without your auntie. We can go to your auntie's for dinner afterwards."

That got Maggie's attention. She and Elizabeth traded glances. Then Maggie acknowledged Bellard, turned around in the passenger seat, arm on the seat back, clearly anxious for an update. She pressed *mute* on the phone.

"He's changed his mind about coming straight over," Maggie said. "He wants to meet Dara separately now."

Bellard swore in French.

"Tell him you're not feeling well, Liz," Maggie said. "You did just get out of the hospital." She unmuted the phone.

Elizabeth conveyed the message.

"Of course," Kafka said. "I understand."

"So?" Elizabeth said "You're coming over?"

There was another pause while a car honked. "I'll let you rest," Kafka said. Maggie's nerves tingled.

"Wait," Elizabeth said, sitting upright. "You're not coming over now?"

"After all we've been through," Kafka said, "It's important for us to talk. Just the two of us."

"But we've been waiting!"

"And I have been patient and waited for you. But there are a few things we must discuss."

"Aunt Amina is making Adana kebab—just for you. It's ready."

"Please extend my apologies. I'm sure it will be delicious in an hour if she puts it in the oven."

Maggie hit mute on the phone. "Tell him you can send Amina out for a while," she told Elizabeth. "You two can talk privately at the apartment."

Maggie unmuted the phone. Elizabeth relayed the message.

"I don't want to inconvenience your auntie," Kafka said.

"It's not a problem, *habibi*."

"It's not right. She's your aunt. She deserves respect. It's her home."

"But she needs some groceries anyway, *habibi*. She forgot the Urfa pepper. Can you believe that? We're so excited about your visit."

"She's your aunt!" he said in a stiff tone. "*You* can pick up the groceries." Then his voice softened. "There's a little café here near the park. We could have a coffee together. Wouldn't that be nice?"

Damn! Maggie hit mute again.

She translated for Bellard. "He wants to meet at a café. He's pretty firm. We can grab him there. I sense he's going to cancel otherwise. We can't afford to let him slip away."

"*Merde.*" Bellard rubbed his chin. "Where does he want to meet exactly?"

Maggie unmuted the phone again.

Elizabeth caught the cue. "Where are you, *habibi*?"

"I can meet you at Place de la Chapelle," Kafka said. "Across from the Metro station. It's not far from your auntie's. Less than half a kilometer away."

"Of course, I know it," Elizabeth said. "Give me twenty minutes. I'm moving a bit slow. I'm leaving now."

"Excellent! I'll be waiting near the Café Avril. It's next to the park. See you there." He hung up.

Maggie explained the rest of the phone call in English to everyone.

Behind her, John Rae said, "I don't like it much, Maggs."

"Neither do I, JR. But it could be legit."

"*Could* being the operative word," John Rae said.

She felt the same way. But Kafka was so close. "We were worried about Kafka entering Aunt Amina's apartment building—and the possible collateral damage. Now we can meet him out in public. This might work out better."

"Maybe," John Rae said. "But maybe Kafka spotted us and is playing us."

"That crossed my mind, too," Maggie said. "But I'm not about to lose this shot." She looked at Bellard. "I'll meet Kafka. But not with the whole team there. Like John Rae says, he might suspect something."

Bellard rubbed his eyes. "Two people." He picked up his Rino. "I'll put them in place. Place de la Chapelle. Café Avril."

"Not yet," Maggie said, putting her hand on Bellard's arm to stop him. "Kafka might indeed have spotted us. If so, he might be watching the café. I'll go first. Two guys follow me. We'll be in Rino contact. I'll give three taps when it's time to move in."

Bellard thought that over. "Very well."

Maggie took a breath. "And I want one of the two to be John Rae," she said.

Bellard flinched. "Absolutely not. John Rae is an advisor. He doesn't carry a weapon."

"John Rae and I have worked together before in tight situations and I just feel better with him behind me."

Bellard shook his head *no*.

Maggie switched to English, so that Bellard might save face.

"John Rae is coming."

"No," Bellard said. "No, he is not."

"Then it's no go." She held Dara's phone out to Bellard. "The op is all yours, after all. Just the way you wanted it."

Bellard looked at the phone in her hand, then back up at her with his mouth open. "You're not serious."

"I've been flexible, Bellard. More than. But we're walking

a tightrope. I want John Rae with me. And that's all there is to it."

Bellard grimaced, then finally turned to the driver. "I need your pistol."

Maggie felt John Rae's hand squeeze her shoulder. "I think you're my new best friend, Maggs," he whispered.

"You mean I wasn't before?" she said.

29

Maggie pulled her filigree face veil up over her mouth and nose, fastened it to her hijab. Just her eyes and eyebrows showed. A good likeness for Dara.

"Stay close but stay back," she said. "I don't want to scare Kafka off."

"Don't worry, Maggs," John Rae said, taking the driver's SP 2022 automatic, checking it for a full clip. "If you don't see us, don't sweat it. We'll be nearby. Place de la Chapelle."

"I know you will," she said. John Rae was planning to follow her from a distance, on the other side of the street. Remi had been dispatched on an alternate route.

Bellard was turned around in his seat, alert and ready: "We will be ready to move in, Maggie. Keep us updated as you go."

"You don't have to worry about that," she said, her heart beating firmly.

John Rae rose from his seat, came around, crouched by the sliding door. "Just remember, Maggie—a few hours from now, you'll be grilling Kafka." He raised his fist.

They bumped. Bellard raised his fist too in an uncharacteristic display of solidarity.

"*Merci, Capitaine,*" Maggie said, touching his fist with hers. "Once I confirm it's Kafka, I'll tap the Rino's call button three times." She stuffed her Rino in one pocket, Dara's phone in the other. Then she picked up a sack of groceries, a prop they had ready in the event she had to meet Kafka. It also contained a minuscule tracking device in the bottom, the size of a pencil dot.

John Rae heaved back the side door amidst a whoosh of traffic. "It's a milk run, Maggie."

"Seems I've heard that one before." She stepped out of the van into the busy street with her sack.

"*Pousse-toi!*" a voice yelled, right in front of her. *Out of the way!*

Maggie slammed herself back against the van, clutching her groceries. A youth on a skateboard rocketed around her on the sidewalk, rattling her nerves but good.

Calm down, she told herself. *Milk run.*

"Stay cool, Maggie," John Rae said behind her. She heard the van door slam shut. The sidewalk was dotted with splotches of rain. A stray spot hit her exposed face.

She took a breath of cold air. She was finally going to meet Kafka.

30

By the time Maggie reached the small park across from La Chapelle Metro station, sporadic drops of rain flew at a slant. Her muscles were warm, loosened up from the brisk walk. Trains clattered along tracks from the Gare du Nord station nearby.

The park was occupied by more than a few people, many of them appearing to loiter. She scanned the crowd from across the street, looking for anyone who might resemble Kafka, saw no one right off. A city of homeless were camped out under the elevated metro tracks across from the park, adjacent to where she stood. Refugees from Syria, arriving *en masse*, with nowhere to go. The sidewalks were busy with after-work foot traffic.

The last daylight had faded behind billowing clouds. Weak ambient light seeped from shops around the park. Headlights stood out. She squeezed the Garmin's call button in her pocket, the sack of groceries in her other hand.

"I'm here," she whispered. "No sign of our boy yet." Her throat mic was doing the work of transmitting.

"Right behind you," John Rae whispered. "Across the street. I see the Chapelle Metro stop."

She waited a moment. "Remi?"

"Not far from Café Avril," he said in French. "By a florist's."

Remi had gotten there quickly. The benefits of youth. But it made her nervous. She knew he was impulsive and he was green. He'd be eager to prove himself.

"Don't get too close yet, Remi," she said in French. "We don't want to spook him. Remember, I'll tap the call button three times once I've confirmed it's Kafka."

She scanned the people milling about across the street, one drinking from a paper bag.

A solo figure appeared from behind the round Morris column. A tall slender man. He was wearing a white ball cap, sunglasses and appeared to have blond hair. It gave her a start. But it made sense Kafka would wear a disguise.

He hadn't mentioned it during their phone call, however. She'd approach cautiously.

"I think I see him," she whispered in both French and English. She gave a brief description and location. It was slow-going, having to work in two languages.

"Maybe back off, Maggie," John Rae said. "This is starting to feel funky."

"Not on your life," she said. "We're so close."

"I'm almost there," John Rae said.

"*T'es là*, Remi?" she said.

"*Oui*," Remi said. "*Je le vois.*"

Remi saw him, too. "Heading across the street now," she whispered. "Remember, three taps when I'm sure." Again, she had to say it in English and French.

"Ten-four," John Rae said.

"I think it's him," Remi said in French.

"I know, Remi," she replied. "But wait for confirmation."

∼

Kafka stepped out from behind the Morris column. He squinted across Rue Marx Dormoy.

There. A woman in an abaya and hijab. Dara's height and build. Wearing a light veil. Carrying a bag of groceries. She was craning her neck, looking his way.

Dara.

His heart began to thump, annoying him for betraying his emotions. He had dreamed of this moment so many times, never planning it to be one where he would be taking her life.

Too late for second thoughts.

He saw her eyes lock onto his from across the street, do a slight double take. She didn't recognize him at first, in his wig and ball cap. But she was looking directly at him now.

Kafka drew a measured breath. His Caracal was nestled in his waistband, just inside his coat, within easy reach. His cell phone was in his left coat pocket. The camera was active. He'd let her cross the street, come to him. Shoot her. Get a photo of her dead. With all the people milling around, he'd be able to get across the street to the Metro after that, into the throng, lose himself. Then away.

She was heading to the corner of the street.

∼

Maggie approached the corner, waited for the green light, her heart racing. She started across the street holding her bag of groceries. She wished she had a gun. But Bellard had been emphatic. After the café shooting, any gunplay would be handled solely by his agents. Her nerves grew taut.

She finished crossing the street, turned across the front of the park.

The man was still by the Morris column, partially obscured by the black wrought iron fence surrounding the park.

She got within ten feet.

She slipped one hand in the pocket of her abaya, on her Rino, ready.

"Dara?" the man said.

"Kafka?"

A tentative smile crossed his face. "It's really you?"

He smiled. Then he reached inside his coat with one hand.

Going for a weapon!

"Gun!" she whispered to alert the team as she hurled the sack of groceries at him. "*Pistolet!*" The sack hit him full on, taking him more by surprise than anything else. He recoiled, banging up against the green advertising column. Groceries landed on the sidewalk as Maggie rushed him. She saw the hint of a small black automatic pistol appear in his hand from under his coat.

"*Je l'ai!*" She was well inside the range he needed to pull a gun and fire. "I got him!" She charged in, elbows up, fists ready.

"*Arrêtés!*" Remi yelled over her shoulder. Where the heck had *he* come from?

"Stay back, Remi! I got this!"

Remi pulled her roughly out of the way, bringing his gun out.

But Kafka was quicker and jammed his gun into Remi's gut.

"*Fais attention!*" Maggie shouted. Kafka's pistol went off, sounding like a firecracker, muffled by Remi's stomach. Remi flinched, his eyes squeezing shut, his gun bouncing from his shaking fingers, landing on the sidewalk with a *clunk*.

People in and around the park shouted and turned.

"Man down!" Maggie shouted. "Remi's shot! Call an ambulance."

"Got it!" Bellard replied. She could hear the van's engine whining over the radio.

Two more sloppy shots made Maggie duck as Kafka ran in the direction of the train station. Someone else screamed. Remi was rolling on the ground, grabbing his gut, gnashing his teeth.

"Kafka's heading north," Maggie said into the throat mic as she bent down on one knee to attend to Remi. "Gare du Nord is my bet."

"On my way," John Rae said.

"We're on our way, too!" Bellard announced. She could hear the van's engine rushing.

Kafka would have to wait. Damn it. Maggie focused on Remi. She took his hand. It was clammy.

"Hang in there, *mon petit*. Help is on the way."

"Go get him!" he said through gritted teeth. "Don't let Kafka get away."

"I'm not leaving you here alone," she said, feeling his skittish pulse. So close! They had been so close. If only Remi hadn't intervened.

People started to approach but hovered, giving her and Remi a wide circle of room.

John Rae came pounding up, gun out. "Which way?"

"You wait here with Remi," she said, grabbing Remi's

pistol from the sidewalk. She jumped up, spun on the heels of her sneakers, about to head toward Gare du Nord.

"I saw the man who shot your friend turn around across the street and head that way!" an older Middle Eastern man wearing a kufi cap said in Arabic. He obviously thought Maggie was Arabic, too, due to her dress. He pointed at the Metro station across the street.

"You saw him?" Maggie asked. Kafka must have doubled back to throw them off. Sly.

"I saw him toss his hat and a wig. He has dark hair. That way." He pointed toward La Chapelle Metro station.

"*Shukran*," she said, thanking him. Maggie turned, headed for the Metro.

"Be careful, Maggie!" John Rae yelled, crouched down by Remi.

31

Horns blared as Maggie dodged cars, crossing the hectic thoroughfare to the Metro station. Fat drops of rain were falling steadily out of a dark sky.

The area underneath the elevated station was a mass of cardboard and discarded mattresses. Dozens of homeless were now on their feet, moving about in agitation.

Maggie tore her veil and hijab off as she approached, gun in hand.

"Police!" she shouted. "Looking for a tall, slender man. Carrying a pistol possibly. Wearing a dark car coat. Dark hair. Arab."

"That way," an old woman said, pointing up the stairway to the elevated station entrance.

Overhead, Maggie heard a train screech onto the outbound platform.

"Did he go through the turnstiles?" she asked.

"He did!"

Christ. Maggie flew up the stairs, spoke to the station

agent, a sour-looking man with short gray hair and a sleepy stare, who let her through.

She arrived in time to see the train screeching off.

No one around. Kafka must have gotten on that train.

This couldn't be happening.

Back down to the station agent. "How far is the next station?" She pointed in the direction of the outbound train.

"Less than half a kilometer. Stalingrad."

"You need to stop that train. A man who boarded is a known terrorist."

"I'll need proper authorization." He gave a squint. "Badge?"

She had no badge on her. "No ID. I'm working with SDAT—anti-terrorist police."

He shook his head. "You're not French. That train is full of commuters. I need authorization."

She was wasting time. Maggie pivoted on her heels, thundered down the stairs as she engaged the team on her Rino while she undid her abaya with one hand. "Bellard," she said into her throat mic. "Kafka's on the train headed to Stalingrad station. Do whatever you can to stop that train."

"Will do," Bellard said. "We're headed there now. But traffic is a mess."

"Stalingrad," she said again. "On my way."

On a good day she could clock a quarter-mile in less than a minute and a half. Seventy-three seconds to be exact. She stepped out of her abaya and took off, dodging through the mattresses and cardboard and people, pumping her fists, the Sig Sauer in one. An earbud fell out.

Halfway to Stalingrad she crossed over the train tracks leading to Gare du Nord, underneath the elevated road she was on. She split a pair of strolling lovers apart.

"*Ah, la vache!*" the man shouted after her. Then he saw the gun in her hand.

Maggie shot up Boulevard de la Chapelle, stretching out her limbs, picking up speed, even with the wet sidewalk. Back home in San Francisco, it was five miles a day, rain or shine. This wasn't shine. She planted her feet firmly as she ran.

"Some good news," Bellard said, his voice coming in through one ear. "They stopped the train at Stalingrad."

"Good work," she gasped, the elevated Metro station ahead of her. She was moving fast.

"But some of the passengers were able to disembark before they could close the doors."

That wasn't good.

"Got it," she said.

She raced across the street, horn blasting as a car swerved around her on wet asphalt.

And then she was under Stalingrad station.

If La Chapelle was a homeless encampment, Stalingrad was a city. The number of migrants and refugees milling about required elbows and shouts for her to get through to the stairs up to the platform. Her blood was pumping between her ears.

She reached the top of the stairs, across from the turnstiles, and saw the man she most wanted to see just exiting a turnstile.

Kafka. More than a little surprised to see her. He wasn't carrying his gun but the moment he saw Maggie, he reached inside his coat.

She was less than a dozen feet away. He wouldn't be able to draw in time. He knew it too. She had the gun in her hand.

"Stop right there!"

But she wasn't about to shoot him and lose that precious information hidden in his brain.

He turned back around, attempted to push his way through the turnstile. A piercing alarm sounded as tall Plexiglas doors blocked his path.

Maggie closed the distance, slamming into Kafka, shoving him hard against the Plexiglas doors. He twisted around, teeth bared, and managed to smack her in the face with a fist.

It smarted. She dropped the gun. Head ringing, she grabbed his coat collar with both hands. Dara's death erupted inside her, a wellspring of fury rising like a geyser. She hauled him out and hurled him back into the turnstile doors with a crash. He grunted as she burrowed in, kicking and punching. She kneed him in the groin. Then she pulled a breathless Kafka back out, using centrifugal force to fling him back onto the elevated platform. He tumbled, landing on his hands and knees with a shout of pain.

A gun went off, barking like a metal beast, reverberating through the station, taking them both by surprise.

"Stop!" John Rae yelled in English, storming up the stairs, gun aimed at Kafka.

On his knees, Kafka pulled his own pistol, began to raise it.

John Rae walked up calmly, his face glistening. His beret was gone. His Sig Sauer was pointed directly at Kafka's chest.

Kafka seemed unsure of what to do, his pistol halfway up.

"Go ahead," John Rae said through his teeth. "Point that fucking thing at me. I'd love to shoot you right about now."

Kafka's face became a tortuous mask of indecision

before he finally nodded in defeat, put both hands up, the gun hooked on one thumb, in surrender.

Bellard and another SDAT agent came pounding up the stairs, running over to make the arrest.

Maggie moved in, took Kafka's gun.

"That's the smartest thing you've done all day," John Rae said to Kafka.

Kafka got to his feet, one knee of his slacks torn.

"Keep your hands up!" Bellard shouted, he and his man coming in with pistols aimed. Commuters spread around the far edges of the station as announcements reverberated.

Kafka complied, his shaking hands going into the air above his head.

His mouth fell open. He had gotten his first good look at Maggie.

"Where's Dara?" he said in Arabic, eyes wide in surprise.

"Dead," Maggie panted. "Dara's dead."

32

"We'll conduct this interview in English," Maggie said.

"Because you can't speak Arabic well enough?" Kafka replied, his voice spiked with contempt.

The two of them were in one of the sterile green interrogation rooms in the basement of SDAT headquarters, a windowless box bearing a hint of disinfectant. Kafka sat upright in a straight-back chair, his hands bound together in one long chain looped through an arm of the chair, loose but restrictive. His ankles were chained through the bottom rung. Maggie sat at a Formica table, across from him. Bellard and John Rae were monitoring the session from Bellard's office on the third floor, via a camera mounted in the ceiling in the corner of the room.

The temperature was 14°C. Even though Maggie wore her jacket, she was cold. Kafka wore just his shirt and trousers, torn at the knee, spotted with blood. She could tell he wasn't warm at all.

All part of the breaking-down process.

Kafka stared at the wall past her ear, stiff with rage, at

having been tricked into thinking Maggie was Dara. Maggie understood. She'd spent time in a similar place, after she realized Kafka had been intent on killing her—Dara.

"I speak Modern Standard Arabic well enough to conduct this interview," she said. "But our viewers don't speak *any* Arabic." She nodded at the camera. "And, truth be told, your French is a little wanting, friend." She smiled.

He looked away.

Maggie said: "But we need to move quickly. You and I don't have a lot of time before you're all theirs." Meaning SDAT. She raised her eyebrows.

Kafka continued to stare straight ahead but his mouth slackened.

"Oh, yeah," Maggie said. "You shot a cop. He's still alive, but what do you think that's going to mean?"

No answer.

"You're going to spend the rest of your life in a French prison," she said. "But if you work with me, I can still get your parents out of Mosul."

He looked at her for a moment.

"That's why you tried to kill Dara, isn't it?" Maggie said. "Because Jihad Nation are holding your parents?" He'd implied they were in danger in his texts. "They told you to kill Dara, clean up the mess you made when you tried to defect, didn't they?"

He gave a weak frown, the first sign she'd broken his shell.

"Do you know who I am?" she asked.

"I know you're a fake."

"Because I assumed your lover's identity?"

"She wasn't my *lover*," he said.

"No," Maggie said. "But you were hoping."

"To talk about Dara in such a manner shows utter disrespect for her memory."

"Even though you tried to kill her." Maggie shook her head. "Dara's the real reason you came to Paris. Oh, sure, you wanted a better life for your parents but let's not kid ourselves. What you wanted most of all was . . . Well, in honor of Dara's memory, what word *would* you like to use?"

"I have nothing to say."

"Let's talk about me again," Maggie said. "Do you have *any* idea who I am?"

"Some lackey on loan to French intelligence?"

"That's actually pretty close. I was working with Dara at Incognito. After she cat-fished you."

Kafka squinted at Maggie, incensed again.

"That's right," Maggie said. "She played *you*."

He looked away.

Maggie said, "What Dara really wanted was to strike a blow, cut off Abraqa, so that her people, the Yazidi, might escape Jihad Nation's genocide. And that's what I want. That's why Dara and I were working together, before she died in the café attack. When you didn't show up."

She could tell he wanted to know more.

Always leave them wanting more.

"So," she said. "I've got a little time with you before SDAT sends me on my way. If you and I move quickly, nail down Abraqa, we can get your parents out of Iraq. And my people can do their best to make sure you get as lenient a sentence as possible. They have some influence."

Kafka was looking at her again, obviously trying to get a read. Could he trust her?

"I know a little about your family," she said. "Your father is a university lecturer in Mosul. *Was.* Not working now, thanks to Jihad Nation shutting down the university, but still

. . ." She caught his look of upheaval. "They're not in Mosul anymore?" She eyed him sideways. "Did Jihadi Nation arrest them? They did, didn't they?"

He gave a deep sigh, hung his head. "Yes," he whispered.

She had managed to get him to show some raw feelings.

"I can't imagine what that must be like," she said softly. "Only that it must be hell. Pure hell."

She let that sink in.

"My people can get your parents out. Why make them pay for your mistake?"

He looked up at her. His eyes were glistening. Again she saw his anguish.

"You hungry?" she said. "There's a decent little café down the street. Middle Eastern. We could order takeout. Well, we'd have to." She smiled. "It's not like you're not going anywhere, are you?"

He gave a smirk. "What were you thinking? Adana kebabs? Is your auntie going to cook them?"

"You've still got a sense of humor."

He frowned.

"Want some coffee?" she asked. "I could use some. It's freezing in here."

No response.

Maggie continued: "While we are sitting here in this room, kept abnormally chill to keep you uncomfortable, think about this—it's really going to behoove you to be my friend."

"*Friend?*"

"Yes. Even though you shot an SDAT officer. A popular one, as it turns out. Even though you potentially organized the café bombing."

"I had nothing to do with that."

"I know that," she said. "And you know that." She

nodded at the camera in the ceiling. "But you're a perfect fit for it, my friend."

"Stop calling me your *friend*."

"I agree it's a stretch right now. But you are in some deep yogurt, and you need someone on your side. For your parents' well-being, if nothing else."

He raised his hands to the point where the chain through the arm in the chair became taut, demonstrating his lack of movement. "What kind of friend does *this*?"

"You tried to shoot me. What kind of friend does *that*?"

"Then I guess we're not friends, after all."

Maggie stood up, pushing her chair back, which squeaked on the floor. She zipped up her jacket, crossed her arms over her chest, walked a couple paces, then back.

"You're not a true jihadi. You're too smart, for one thing."

He looked up at Maggie. "Can you really get my parents out?"

A surge of victory flowed through her. She was breaking through.

"For a price," she said. "Access to those Darknet folders that contain the Bitcoin transactions that Jihad Nation uses to fund their efforts. And full knowledge of how the process works. I know Jihad Nation hired you because you had the technical savvy to set it up. But you need to make a decision to work with me—and work fast. As I've said, I only have so much time before I'm out of here."

He pressed his lips as he scanned her face. "How do I know this isn't all some sort of trick?"

"Dara," she said. "Our proxy. She's the only reason I'm trusting you. So you need to trust me just as much as you did her. Until you tried to kill her."

"My parents are being held in a camp manned by jihadi

fighters. A jail, essentially. What kind of guarantee can you give me that you can actually get them out?"

"Where? Mosul?"

"About twenty kilometers outside."

Another revelation. Things were going well. "We've got helicopters that cost the taxpayers forty million dollars apiece, loaded up with gadgets that would make your head spin. Heat cameras that can spot footprints half an hour after they've been made. A team of Navy Seals or Army Rangers, in one of those forty million dollar choppers, can be in and out in half an hour with your mother and father. On the way to Turkey. Then Europe. Or the US. Or wherever you prefer—within reason, of course." She uncrossed her arms, went over to the table, put both hands on it, leaned down, looked him in the eyes.

"*Hopefully* they make it out," he said. "Iraq is littered with military equipment that failed in its mission."

"We're talking the same people who killed Osama Bin Laden," she said, raising her eyebrows. "Compared to that, this op is child's play."

She watched Kafka take a deep breath, uncertainty flickering across his face.

"What's the alternative?" Maggie said. "Leave your parents at the mercy of Jihad Nation? *That* outcome is definitely guaranteed. We're not only the best hope you have—we're the *only* hope you have."

Finally Kafka nodded, seemingly in agreement. He held his hands up. "Can you take these off, then? Since you trust me so much?" He smiled, shook one ankle, rattling the chains.

Negotiations. "Let me see what I can do," she said. "Want some coffee now?"

He seemed to think about that. "Tea."

"Something to eat?"

He hesitated before he spoke. "Is it halal?"

"Absolutely. All kosher. I'll pick it up myself, from the little café I told you about." She patted the edge of the table.

"Thank you," he mumbled, looking at the floor.

She smiled. "Good. This is going to work out. I'll be back."

Kafka nodded once, and stared straight ahead. But his eyes had a softness to them that hadn't been there when they'd started.

~

"You're getting nowhere," Bellard said.

"Now just a minute," Maggie said, standing in Bellard's office, with its glass walls supposedly implying that all SDAT did was transparent. "I just made some pretty good headway. In only a few minutes. This is only the first interview."

Bellard was leaning back in his desk chair, hands clasped tightly behind his head, dark patches of perspiration in each armpit of his blue shirt. John Rae was slumped in a guest chair, his long legs stretched out, ending in his favorite pair of cowboy boots, mahogany brown with tooled leather and brass tips. Maggie could tell he wasn't enjoying his role as advisor. But that was the op.

"He's toying with you," Bellard said to Maggie.

"He told us where they're holding his parents. He's beginning to confide in me."

Bellard sat up, folded his hands over his desk. "He was supposed to be a friendly agent to begin with. A walk-in."

Maggie nodded. "The only person he thought he could trust is dead. And he was duped into meeting us."

"He shot one of my agents!"

"He shot at me, too, Bellard. He was ready to shoot John Rae."

"Neither of you are in the hospital at the moment, getting a 9mm bullet pulled from your intestines."

"I told Remi *three times* to hold off," Maggie said.

Bellard's nostrils flared.

"With all due respect," John Rae interrupted quietly, "I think Maggie's got a valid point. Kafka *is* talking to her. And, from where I sit, he wants to work with us. And we really should have anticipated more resistance in the first place." It was diplomatic of John Rae to use the word *we* since it was Bellard who put the plan together and his team had been undermanned. Not to mention that Remi rushed in to grab Kafka, despite Maggie's many warnings to wait.

"Well, you've had your interview," Bellard said to Maggie. "He's mine now."

"Wait a goddamn second," Maggie said. "I got ten minutes."

"You were lucky to get that."

"I handed Kafka to you, Bellard, all wrapped up in a red ribbon. I get him until I crack Abraqa. Then he's yours. That was the deal."

"That was before he shot one of my men."

"No," she said, shaking her head. "No."

Bellard looked at his watch.

"You want a pissing contest?" Maggie said. "You'll get one. Don't cross me on this."

Bellard took a deep breath through his nose, looked at her with a flat-lined mouth. "You'll get another chance—when I'm through."

"Look," Maggie said. "Just give me a little more time with

him now. Get some tea and food into him, soften him up a bit more. That'll benefit you, too."

They all seemed to be looking at the computer screen on Bellard's desk, the CC camera showing a sullen Kafka sitting in his chair.

"You can have him in the morning," she said. "Then I'll take him back. Good cop, bad cop."

"What's it going to hurt, Bellard?" John Rae said. He looked at his watch. "You and me can go out and grab a beer."

Bellard eyed John Rae as if he had asked him to shoot heroin. "We're on duty."

"Glass of wine, then," John Rae said. "Wine's not considered drinking in France, is it?"

Bellard shook his head and actually cracked a smile. John Rae had a way of getting people to like him.

"I could use a bite to eat, too," John Rae said. "Something that doesn't come out of a vending machine. I'm buying."

Standing up, Bellard grabbed his jacket from the back of his chair and slipped it on. "*D'accord.* I need to make a phone call first."

Thank you, John Rae, Maggie thought, giving him a wink. She grabbed her temporary ID, went out to order the food. She could have called it in but she needed the walk to clear her head. And she needed time for Kafka to ponder her offer. It was all part of the process.

THE CELL DOOR OPENED.

Kafka looked up from his chair, where he was still restrained. And saw four French police officers standing in the hall, three men and one woman, wearing blue fatigues. All had their faces covered. One tall man wore a ski mask, one short man a blue handkerchief tied around his mouth and nose, one older, heavy-set man some silly plastic mask with vertical red, white and blue stripes—the tricolor, something someone might wear to a party. The woman had blonde hair showing, with a red and white Paris St. Germain soccer scarf wrapped around her head like an Arab naqib, showing only her blue eyes.

All four guards stared at Kafka.

They wore plastic gloves. The man with the tricolor plastic mask had a dark blanket folded under one arm. The woman had a roll of masking tape in her hand.

Kafka's heart began to thud, more powerfully than his terrified body needed to survive. He was overcome by fear, immediately feeling weak and sickly.

The tall man in the balaclava entered the room first, staying close to the wall, then nodding at the woman who followed him in the same manner, out of range of the ceiling camera pointed at Kafka. Both guards stopped directly underneath the black camera.

The woman tore off a three-inch section of tape. The tall man squatted, wrapped his arms around her legs, lifted her up with a grunt. She placed the section of tape over the camera lens. Then she disconnected the black wire from the back of the camera.

Kafka tried to stand up. The chair scraped the linoleum floor, but his hands and ankles were held back by the chains.

He knew what was coming.

The tall man let the woman down, said to the other two guards, "*D'accord.*"

The two guards entered the room. One man placed a

radio on the floor, turned it on. A commercial for automobile insurance came on.

"Something else, I think," the woman said brightly. "A little party music for our friend, yes?"

They all laughed.

Kafka did not speak good French but his fearful intuition made up for any lack of understanding.

The short man squatted, turned the dial until he found a dance station, playing *Numa Numa*, of all things—a bouncy Eastern European song full of high, operatic voices at first, settling in on a grinding dance groove.

"That's it!" the young woman shouted, breaking into a playful dance, her arms and legs pumping as she twirled, her baton on her web belt swinging. It was as if she were out at a club. She was a good dancer. The little man who had set the radio down jumped in and started dancing with her, not well at all and laughing about it. The third man laughed and joined in too, crossing his arms and doing a jaunty Cossack dance, which caused much merriment as his tricolor mask tilted to and fro. The tall man joined in, getting the hang of it, and the dancers formed a circle.

The tall man broke away, came over, shoved the Formica table out of the way with an angry screech.

He stood directly in front of Kafka.

Chestnut eyes underneath thick brown eyebrows glared through the eyeholes of his ski mask.

This drove Kafka back down in his chair with fear, his breath coming and going in desperate gasps as blood pumped wildly in his head, out of control.

"Look up at me, you filthy Arab."

Fighting every natural instinct in his body, Kafka looked up. His head shook uncontrollably on his neck.

The tall man's fists clenched by his side.

"Did you enjoy shooting a policeman, you filthy fucking Arab? A *French*man?"

The three dancers broke their circle and began to wend their way over, still dancing. The two men had drawn their batons, the older man making figure eights in the air with his as he approached. The girl pulled more tape from the roll, giving Kafka a wicked look, smiling with her pretty blue eyes.

∼

It was 11:00 by the time Maggie got back to SDAT headquarters with the food. The mouthwatering scents emanating from the Styrofoam containers in the plastic bag she carried had her stomach growling as she rode down in the elevator with the tall slender officer with the chestnut eyes. She was feeling good about the progress she had made. It would take some finessing to work with Kafka, but she knew they could hammer out a deal.

"Oh, but that does smell delicious," the tall guard said in French as the elevator doors opened in the basement. His heavy eyebrows contrasted his otherwise delicate features. "Buzkashi's, am I right? On the corner?"

"Yes," she said. "It's a good thing they stay open late."

He put his hand out to hold the elevator door for Maggie. "*Après vous, mademoiselle.*"

"*Merci.*"

He accompanied her to the interrogation room where they were holding Kafka. He punched a code into the access pad to the right of the door.

"Do you need to inspect the prisoner's food?" Maggie asked holding up the plastic bag. "And I don't mean eat it." She smiled.

He smiled back. "No, I think we can trust you. Although I wouldn't mind."

She laughed. She couldn't get over how lax they were. None of this would've passed back home. But then again, sending a junior agent out in the line of fire wouldn't have been on the agenda either.

"You need to stand guard while we eat?"

"Only if you wish, mademoiselle. But I think it's fine." He spoke in that flirtatious manner common to Frenchmen, never missing the opportunity to be playful. American men could learn a thing or two.

"*Merci encore*," she said.

He stood back, held open the door.

"*Bon appétit*," the guard said as he shut the door.

Maggie's heart jumped.

Kafka lay on his side, still fettered to the chair, a gray blanket covering his head and torso.

A smear of blood on the floor told the rest of the story.

Under the blanket Kafka panted, his breath coming and going in little gurgles.

33

"Of course I had no idea such a thing would happen!" Bellard said.

Maggie wondered. She stood in front of Bellard's desk, her arms tightly crossed.

"They almost killed him," she said. "If he hadn't chewed through the masking tape sealing his mouth, he would've suffocated." Kafka's nostrils had become plugged with blood during the beating. "Let's hope he doesn't suffer from some kind of cerebral contusion and die." She shook her head, vibrating with anger.

"Medical personnel are evaluating him now," Bellard said.

Selfishly she thought, even if Kafka didn't die, he could suffer the equivalent of a stroke and be useless to her.

All that work.

"You can see what I see," Bellard said defensively, moving the computer mouse and backing up the recorded video on his computer to the point where the camera had blacked out. The time in question was less than ten minutes after Maggie had left to pick up food, which now sat untouched in a plastic bag on the corner of Bellard's desk. "Look," he said. "Nothing."

John Rae stood behind Maggie, arms crossed as well, stroking his goatee. It was past two AM. Everyone was tired and exasperated.

"Stay cool, Maggs," he whispered.

She took a deep breath. Bellard's tone did seem to imply he had not been aware of the beating until she had discovered it.

"Go back earlier," Maggie said. "Before the video blacks out."

"One more time," Bellard said with unmasked irritation. He backed up to Kafka sitting up, chained to his chair, head back, eyes closed. Grabbing a rest. The sound of the interrogation room door opening made him open his eyes. Eyes that soon rounded in shock.

What followed was the sound of soft footsteps entering the room. Multiple footsteps. Then, in close proximity to the camera, a muffled noise, followed by the blurry tip of a small thumb in a plastic glove partially blocking the lens.

The screen went black. Then the sound of a mechanical screw turning, or something similar. Someone detaching the video cable. Silence. That was the way Maggie had found the camera when she entered the cell—the lens taped over, the camera disconnected.

"I hope you're calling whatever passes for SDAT's internal affairs and beginning your investigation," Maggie said.

Bellard turned in his chair, sat back, eyes narrowing.

"There will be a full investigation," he said. "When I say."

"And no one's allowed to leave the building until that is done, right?"

He put his hands back behind his head. "Do *not* tell me how to do my job."

"Under-planning an operation handed to you on a platter. Assigning some pimply-faced kid to handle a crucial arrest. And now—*this*. Do you have any idea how much work went into this op? Dara lost her life."

Bellard's eyes turned to slits. "I suppose I'd have to go to Guantánamo Bay to learn how to do things properly."

"I had Kafka talking," Maggie said. "Good luck getting anything out of him now."

Bellard gave a nasty staccato laugh as he sat up in his chair. "Do you really think batting you're eyelashes at some terrorist who would behead his own mother for not following Sharia law is going to make him bend to your will? You American women don't have a problem with low self-esteem, do you?"

Maggie shook her head. "You can bet someone on my side of the fence is going to be giving you a call," she said. "You guys think you're hot shit, filing complaints against *us*? Well, you ain't seen nothing, *ami*."

"Maggs," John Rae whispered. "*Cool it*."

Bellard shot up out of his chair with such force that it rolled back, smacking the credenza. "Get out of my office!"

"Hey, guys," John Rae said calmly, stepping forward. "Let's just take it down a notch, huh?"

"Shut up!" Bellard said to John Rae as he picked up a phone and punched buttons. Someone answered. "*Capitaine* Bellard here," he said, switching to French. "I need officers. Be prepared for resistance." He slammed the phone down, turned to Maggie and John Rae, hands on his hips. One shirttail was halfway out.

"Seriously?" Maggie said. "Are your guards going to beat us senseless, too?"

"Enjoy your flight back to the US," Bellard said, sitting back down with a thump.

"We might have lost a little ground," John Rae said. "But it's not a showstopper. Tempers run high when an officer gets hit. I get that. But let's not lose sight of the original plan."

Bellard nodded as he pulled a pack of cigarettes from his shirt pocket, shook one out, put it in his mouth. "I'll crack Kafka," he said, pulling his lighter from his pocket, flicking it, lighting up his cigarette. He got it going, slipped the lighter back in his pocket. He took a deep drag, pulled the cigarette from his mouth, exhaled. Smoke billowed across the room. "I'll crack Abraqa. I don't need either one of you."

"Now that makes about as much sense as tits on a bull," John Rae said.

"What the hell does that mean?" Bellard sucked on his cigarette. "What damn language are you speaking?"

"Maggie's put a lot of legwork into this. There's no way you can replicate what she's done, the intel she got from Dara. You'll be starting from scratch."

"I'm tired of talking to both of you," Bellard said, taking a calmer puff on his cigarette.

They heard the elevator bell ding in the hallway. Excited voices. Footsteps came bounding down the hall.

Two men and one woman in blue appeared at Bellard's office door. All had their hands on the batons in their belts.

"Look," Maggie said in English, so that Bellard wouldn't lose face in front of the guards. "You may not think so, but you're going to need the Agency's help." She raised her eyebrows. "I'm sorry if I lost my temper."

Bellard smoked. "*D'accord*," he said to the guards in French. "Escort these two to the airport. If they give you any problem—*any* problem whatsoever—place them under arrest." He turned to Maggie and John Rae, switching back to English. "And you two better be on the next military flight out of France." He tapped his cigarette into an ashtray.

The guards came into the room and it suddenly became very crowded.

"Americans," Bellard said, sitting back in his chair.

∼

"WELL, THAT WENT WELL," Maggie said as she and John Rae were unceremoniously dumped off in front of the Shangri La hotel on rue Philibert Lucot. The blue and white French National police van roared off on a street devoid of traffic, glistening with recent rain. It was just after three in the morning.

John Rae jammed his hands in the pockets of his pigskin jacket. "At least you got us a reprieve."

A hasty phone call to her boss had resulted in Ed calling Bellard and negotiating the two of them being allowed to stay the night and gather their belongings. The next military flight wasn't until after eight AM anyway. In the meantime Ed was going to try for an extension. Bellard wouldn't want Washington to create a stink over Kafka's beating so Ed had some leverage.

They walked across the street to her hotel.

Once inside the small dark lobby, John Rae said to the night clerk: "My bag is in storage. Do you have a room for me?"

"So sorry, *monsieur*," the young woman said, hunched over her textbook. "All full."

Maggie sighed.

"Come on up," she said to John Rae.

John Rae gave her a look.

"You're sleeping on the floor," she said, punching the button for the tiny elevator. "I smell like a horse anyway, trying to break my quarter mile to Stalingrad Metro. I'm not fit to sleep with the homeless refugees."

"Sure you are," John Rae said.

Maggie shook her head. They got into the lift. "Once Bellard cools down," she said. "He'll realize he can't pull it off without us." But she didn't know. Bellard didn't really care about Abraqa. All he wanted was Kafka. And he had him.

34

Northern Iraq, outside Mosul—the Jihad Nation encampment

"Don't you dare move, *sharmoota*," Abeer said as she scrolled on her smart phone, sitting on the sofa, her dirty feet up on the brass tea table. "On your knees. No sitting back. Or you'll get the stick."

Abeer's gnarled walking stick leaned against the tattered arm of the sofa.

Up on her knees, Besma shook with exhaustion. How much longer before Hassan returned? How ironic to think she actually wanted him here. But Abeer was a meeker creature when he was around and her bullying would be curtailed. Hassan was interrogating the parents of the runaway man they spoke of, the one hiding in Paris. *Kafka*, Besma had heard him called.

She sat silently, on her knees, arms by her side, in the scratchy black robe that the women in black had given her, that smelled of other women. On the floor of Hassan al-

Hassan's private quarters, as she'd been ordered by Abeer. Her knees ached. Her back hurt.

The room was crowded with furniture, a bed with a cracked mirror over it, two ripped sofas, a big flat-screen television teetering on top of a bookcase. A giant teddy bear, of all things, staring down from another.

She would pray. Silently. It was all she had left. And for that, she needed the sun. And even though Hassan al-Hassan's room was shut off from light, the window boarded up with plywood, the sun was up there. Even though the air conditioner chugged away, the generator running during the day, she knew the relentless midday sun blistered down on everything in equal measure.

Besma had never felt the need to pray so strongly before.

Pray for Havi, at the madrassa, the school the jihadists had set up on the far side of the camp. Besma had gotten a glimpse when she went to the outside toilet, escorted by Hassan's private guard, thankful not to use the indoor one that stunk, with no wind to ventilate it. Men with wild hair and beards were showing boys—*little boys*—how to behead a prisoner with a toy sword, demonstrating on one of the men. Everybody laughing.

She shut her eyes now. The daily prayer of the Yazidi must not be performed in the presence of outsiders, and always in the direction of the sun. She would have to make allowances. Abeer sat nearby. The sun was hidden.

On her knees she cast her eyes up, facing the noon sun beyond the roof. A black Jihad Nation flag with white Arabic writing was pinned to the ceiling, draping in places like the inside of a Bedouin tent. She closed her eyes, directing her thoughts beyond that flag, to the sun.

Yazidis were descended from Adam. God created the

world and entrusted it to the seven angels. The most divine of them was the Peacock Angel, Melek Taus.

The Peacock Angel was beautiful and strong, with brilliant blue feathers sweeping back from his aristocratic forehead and a face of the noblest, purest features.

The jihadis called him Satan and said the Yazidis were devil worshippers. That was why her people must convert to Islam or die.

Convert or die.

She prayed silently for her *dayik*, her mother, for her poor dead soul, split into two when her life was snuffed out by Hassan's rifle butt. The loss of her mother was so great she had not fully grasped it yet. But one thing she knew was that she hated Hassan al-Hassan almost as much as she feared him.

Then she prayed for her *bawi*, her father, wherever he might be. The last she had heard he was off to Raqqa province, to pay ransom for girls and women taken hostage. Once he learned what had happened to mother, he would grieve. But when he found Besma and Havi were taken, he would go mad with worry. She prayed his grief would be bearable, that he would keep a clear head, and find them.

But most of all she prayed for Havi, to keep him from becoming one of *them*. A jihadi. To keep him from being one of their suicide bombers.

She did what she could to push her fear aside, the fear of what could happen to her at the hands of men who took young girls, did what they wanted with them, laughed while they did it, then passed them around before selling them like animals.

She'd met those who'd been raped and beaten. Some descended into a pit of despair, but others, the brave ones, lived with it, somehow, returned home, to care for their families. She prayed she would be strong like them, not let what might happen destroy her. Otherwise the jihadis would win.

She folded her hands discreetly and prayed, while Abeer texted on her cell phone. Besma intended to repeat her simple requests twenty-one times. Twenty-one was a sacred number.

Suddenly, the clattering of Abeer's smartphone on the brass table shook her out of her secret worship.

"I'm going to the toilet," Abeer announced, climbing out of the overstuffed sofa with an effort, overweight, looking foolish in her camouflage. Without her naqib she was not pretty, just young, a few years older than Besma, with mousy hair cut in a greasy bob, accentuating her nose, turned-up like a pig. Acne mottled her plump face. But she was an American, so still a prize.

"If you even move," Abeer hissed at Besma, picking up the knotted walking stick, brandishing it, "you'll get a beating, *whore*."

"I won't move," Besma said.

"No, you won't." Abeer jabbed Besma in the ribs with the end of the stick, almost knocking her over. Besma recovered.

Abeer, Hassan al-Hassan's terror bride, squeezed past the sofa too close to the bookcase with the big dusty TV on top, left the room, passing Hassan's guard in an afghan turban with an AK-47 who was manning the door. He squinted at Besma before the door was shut. The key turned in the lock.

Besma fell back on her heels. A precious minute or two on her own.

She stood up, her feet buzzing, and leaned back, hands on her hips, cracking out her back. Shaking the numbness and ache out of her limbs.

Relief!

She heard a blip. From the brass tea table.

Abeer's phone. Flashing. Someone sending her a text.

If Besma could use that phone, she could call her father. It had been done before. When security grew lax, someone managed to get hold of a phone and call for help. Then the people back home would arrange a ransom, buy the women and children back. Or they would know where their loved ones were, send help.

Besma eyed the phone on the low table, her chest grinding. She took a step closer, turned the phone to face her, and the blackened screen opened up. No security gesture required. Yes.

She picked up the phone, an ear cocked to the door. A text window flashed.

MOM: *Traci—are you OK? Are you there, hon?*

Besma could read a little English.

It was from Abeer's parents. In the United States.

MOM: *Please call—or answer—just to say that you're OK, Traci—please?*

Besma heard footsteps pounding down the hall. Her heart leapt. She turned the phone back the way it had been on the table, found the button on the side and, with trembling fingers, blacked the screen out.

Besma resumed her kneeling position on the floor by the corner of the bed.

The door unlocked. Abeer came in, eating an apple, the stick in the other hand. She glared at Besma. Hassan's guard, standing behind Abeer, looked at her suspiciously as well.

"What were you doing, whore?" Abeer held the stick lazily as she ate the apple.

"Nothing," Besma said in a whisper.

Abeer slammed the door, bit off a large piece of apple, a piece of pulp falling onto the floor.

"You moved," she said, chewing.

"No," Besma said.

"You're a liar."

Besma said nothing, heart pounding.

"Did you hear me?"

"Yes," Besma said.

"What are you?"

"I don't know," Besma said.

"A liar. You're a liar."

Besma kept silent, her heart racing.

"What are you?" Abeer said.

"A liar," Besma whispered, watching the stick twitch in Abeer's hand.

"Don't look at me, liar."

Shuddering, Besma fixed her gaze onto a palm tree on the threadbare Persian rug.

Abeer strode over, squeezing past the sofa and bookcase, crunching the apple. Her stick banged the edge of the brass table as she walked by.

Abeer's dirty feet came into view. Besma heard her bite the apple.

"Liar."

Besma didn't know what to do. Stay silent? Pulse skittering, she decided to do that.

"Whore."

Besma gulped.

"Did you hear me?"

"Yes."

"Say it."

"I'm a liar."

"And?"

"A whore."

"Together."

"I'm a liar and a whore."

"Yes. Yes, you are."

Abeer tossed the apple core in front of Besma.

It lay there.

"Are you hungry?"

"No," Besma said, although she was starving. But she didn't want to eat the apple core.

"You're lying again."

"No," Besma said. "I'm too frightened to be hungry." Almost true.

"Eat it," Abeer said. "Eat the apple core."

Besma gulped. "Please don't," she said.

The next thing Besma heard was the stick whooshing through the air before it connected with her ribs in a crack of bone. It hurt. Oh, God, it hurt.

Besma toppled over to one side, clutching her rib, biting her lip, trying not to cry like a baby. She prayed something wasn't broken.

"On your hands and knees, you liar. You whore."

Besma struggled back up onto her hands and knees.

"That's it. Like a dog. You're my dog."

Besma drew in a shallow breath because every single one she took made her side scream.

"Well—what are you waiting for?" Abeer said.

Besma drew another thin breath, contemplated the apple core.

"And while you're eating your lunch," Abeer said in her bastardized American Arabic, "Think of one thing: when Hassan al-Hassan returns and flirts with you, you will shun him. And when he takes you, and does what he wants, you will not give him any pleasure beyond what he takes for himself. If you do anything—anything to give him pleasure, I will know, and I will see you and your little brother dead. Got that?"

"Yes," Besma murmured.

"Louder."

"*Yes*."

"Good. Now eat my garbage."

Besma stared down at the apple core, the teeth marks on it already turning brown. Her stomach retched.

"Eat it, whore."

There were far worse things. Besma closed her eyes, opened her mouth, and bent her head down to the floor.

Then she heard voices outside the door. Hassan al-Hassan talking to his guard. A swell of relief overcame her.

"Get up!" Abeer hissed, clambering back up onto the sofa. "Move!"

Besma decided to stay right where she was, on her hands and knees in front of the apple core. Let Abeer pay.

The door opened. Hassan's heavy breathing filled her ears.

"What is going on here?"

"Nothing," Abeer said in a high voice.

"Don't tell me *nothing*, woman. I can see it's something. Tell me what's going on or feel the back of my hand. Why is she kneeling like that?"

"We were just playing a game."

"A *game*?" He slammed the door.

Hassan came up to Besma, took her chin roughly in his hand. His black fatigues were dusty and he smelled. "What kind of game is this?" He spotted the apple core on the floor and grimaced. "Did you do this?"

Besma shook her head *no*.

Hassan let go of her, turned slowly. "You'll do well not to play any more games, woman," he said to Abeer.

Abeer stared at her bare feet. "Yes, husband."

"Come here!" Hassan said to Besma.

She did so, standing, savoring the movement in her limbs if nothing else.

"Closer."

She obeyed.

He leaned over, his nose inches from her neck.

"Her robe stinks," he said to Abeer.

"She's Yazidi." Abeer laughed.

"What are you laughing at?" Hassan shouted, storming over to Abeer. She cowered, clutching her phone. "Put that thing down when I speak to you! Always playing with it like some toy! I forbid you to use it anymore!" He struck her, knocking the phone from her hand, sending it flying across the room, landing near Besma's feet. "You *stupid* Ameriki! I'll knock some sense into you."

Hassan proceeded to beat Abeer as she burrowed down into the sofa, holding her with one hand while he slapped her with the other repeatedly, generating cries and shrieks.

"Take your punishment, woman!"

As little as Besma cared for Abeer, she could not watch. And she prayed that Hassan would not unleash such anger upon her, or Havi. But the real reason she could not watch was because she was placing her bare foot on top of Abeer's smartphone and sliding it underneath the bed, as far as she could manage without having to stoop. A box of DVDs poked out from under the bedspread. With a shock she saw the cover of one video, a garish photograph of a naked white woman doing unspeakable things with two men, also naked. Could such an abomination truly exist? She shifted the box under the bed with her foot, pushing the phone back behind it. She hoped the battery would last long enough for her to make use of it.

She turned back around and stood to attention as the beating drew to a close.

"Sit up, woman!" Hassan al-Hassan shouted.

Abeer sat up, blood dripping from one corner of her mouth, her face streaked with tears.

"Let that be a lesson to you," Hassan said.

"Yes, husband," Abeer cried, wiping her face with her sleeve.

"Go get Besma a clean robe. Something decent. Not that filthy rag."

~

"ARE YOU ALL RIGHT?" Besma said to Abeer as Abeer wiped tears from her face.

They were standing in the hall down from Hassan al-Hassan's room. The air was hot and close.

"That was nothing," Abeer said. "Wait until it's you turn."

"I need the toilet," Besma said. It had been many hours. "Please."

Abeer gave a deep sigh, but led Besma toward the indoor bathroom that the women used. They stopped at a door where another guard, Mustafa, a short dark-skinned man with a big belly and a gray thatch of beard, stood outside, an automatic rifle slung over his shoulder. A smirk appeared when he saw Abeer's bloody lip. No one liked her.

There was no sound coming from the bathroom. No water splashing. They had to carry water inside. All the pipes had been stolen and sold for scrap, long before Jihad Nation took this facility.

Abeer tried the door handle. Locked.

"Who's in there?" she said to the guard.

He shrugged. "One of the new ones."

"How long has she been in there?"

"A while."

"I asked you *how long*?"

"I don't time them."

Abeer banged on the door. "Open up in there. You've been long enough."

There was no response.

"Open up in there!"

No response.

Abeer stood back, glowered at Mustafa. "Open this door."

He scowled, a woman giving him orders.

"Do you want me to go get Hassan al-Hassan?" Abeer said.

"No," Mustafa said. Now it was his turn to bang on the door and shout. Still no answer.

"She's going to get a beating for this," he said, standing back, kicking the door with a stocky leg

The lock ripped loose, the door flew open, hitting the wall.

Besma gasped when she saw Shayma, a girl she knew from her village, a year or two younger than her, in shorts and T-shirt like Besma had worn, sprawled on the floor of the bathroom. Shayma lay motionless, curled around a shining pool of blood. Her right wrist had been butchered open. A piece of broken blood-smeared mirror lay by her hand. Her head was twisted up to one side and her blue eyes were open, as was her mouth. She appeared to be staring at the ceiling. In the direction of the sun. She must have prayed before she took her own life.

Besma reeled back in shock.

"Oh my God!" Abeer said in English. Her hands flew to her mouth.

"She's gone and killed herself," Mustafa hissed. "I knew we should never have had a lock on that door." He turned to Besma as he unslung his rifle. "You can carry her out to the pit. Go get the wheelbarrow."

~

THE TWO AL-KHANSA women followed Besma back from the huge open grave, outside the walls of the compound, chiding her, telling her that her people were filth to kill themselves in such a way. Besma thought she might be sick again as she pushed the empty wheelbarrow, the blood in the tray attracting flies as she bounced it across the hard dirt. Her hands were sticky with the girl's blood, having had to load Shayma and ferry her out to the pit. It was almost more than she could bear. She recalled the vision of her people lining the mass grave in the midday sun, some old, some children, and so, so many. It was heart-rending when she accidentally tipped the barrow into the pit along with the flopping body and had to climb down at gunpoint, retrieve the wheelbarrow, standing on the stinking corpses of her people to hoist it back up. She looked away to avoid seeing the faces of anyone she might know. Her stomach wrenched when she saw a familiar bracelet on a withered wrist. Only the constant reminder that Havi needed her gave her the strength to complete the gruesome task. One of the Al-Khansa women joked about needing a bigger grave. Besma was exhausted and shook with fear as she climbed out of the pit.

How could human beings—women, no less—behave in

such a manner? Maybe they weren't human. Besma had to clean the bathroom floor with dirty towels, her gut a churning maelstrom.

Afterwards, she took a sponge bath with a rag and a scrap of soap that had hair on it, standing over the dead girl's bucket of filmy water. There was no usable sink. It lay in the corner, broken off the wall because the men had stood in it to wash their feet before prayers. Abeer and one of the Al-Khansa women watched Besma bathe with guarded eye. They remarked about her young body and her dainty breasts as she washed herself down.

"She'll fetch over a thousand," Abeer said.

"When the men are done with her," the woman in black said, laughing.

Besma was given a clean robe to wear and, as she combed her wet hair back, she took strength from the fact that she had hidden Abeer's cell phone under Hassan's bed. She would hopefully use it, even as she feared what Hassan would do to her when he had her alone.

Abeer led her back to Hassan al-Hassan's quarters and was surprised and relieved to see Havi sitting on the floor with Hassan al-Hassan, watching a video on his phone. Hassan grinned. Havi paid close attention to him but Besma saw that he was nervous, playing the student. He gave her a quick glance. He was coping. His youth was an advantage. She just hoped he wasn't becoming one of them.

"Pay attention now, Havi," Hassan said, and Havi craned his neck to look at the phone in Hassan's hand. The sounds of gunfire and men screaming popped from the tiny speaker.

Abeer and Besma sat on the floor and Besma realized what her little brother must be watching. It filled her with disbelief, numbing her emotionally and physically.

"We sent the infidels to their appointed fates, Havi," Hassan said. "Allah's justice was swift."

"Yes, Hassan al-Hassan."

"And *that* is holy jihad, Havi," Hassan said, tapping the phone, slipping it into the pocket of his black shirt.

Besma could only imagine what horrors they had been viewing.

"Are you hungry, Havi?" Hassan said, patting him on the back. "Are you hungry after your morning of instruction?"

"Yes," Havi said quietly.

"Yes, of course you are. You've worked hard. You will make a fine warrior." He clapped his hands to get Abeer's attention. "Bring us our meal." He clapped again. "Quick now."

"Yes, husband," Abeer said, standing up, eyes to the floor. She left the room.

"May I speak with my sister, Hassan al-Hassan?" Havi said.

"What a polite boy!" Hassan said, looking at Besma for the first time since her return, nodding with approval at her clean robe, scrubbed face, and freshly washed hair. "Yes, you may speak to your sister—your sister who taught you the noble verses."

Havi bowed and eyed Besma across the room. "Are you well, sister?"

"Allah be praised, yes, Havi. Am I to assume you have been learning your lessons well?"

"I hope so, Allah be praised."

She traded glances with her brother. Was he succumbing? She prayed not.

"I'm so very pleased for you," she said. "God is great."

Hassan al-Hassan beamed at Besma. "Do you know the Koran well, woman?"

"Not as well as I should, Hassan al-Hassan. But I try. When I can. I learn in order to teach Havi."

"Do you know the Al-Fatihah?"

Besma racked her brains. "*In the name of Allah, the Entirely Merciful, the Especially Merciful,*" she replied.

"Excellent." Hassan sat back, leaning against the bed. "Recite more. While we wait for our meal."

Thank God she knew more.

Thankfully, after a while the door opened, the guard outside holding it while Abeer came in with a brass tray of steaming plates.

"Your meal, husband." She set the tray down on the small stand in front of Hassan.

There was a platter of roasted goat meat in sauce, a dish of rice, bread, a pot of tea, two glasses. The aroma of the cooked meat set Besma's stomach growling, even though she had witnessed horrific sights not long before. She hadn't eaten properly since they were taken from their village. But she also understood that she might not be invited. The women frequently dined separately.

"You may leave now," Hassan said to Abeer, tearing off a piece of flat bread, dipping it in thick brown sauce, shoveling it into his mouth and chewing with his mouth open.

"May I not dine with you, husband?" Abeer said in a tight voice.

"Not now. And you need to dine less, woman." Hassan scooped meat up with a curl of bread, shoved it in his mouth. "You've gotten fat. Look at Besma here. Nice and slim she is."

"Yes, husband." Abeer cast an irritated glance at Besma before she left the room.

"Go on, Havi," Hassan said. "Eat!"

Havi dove in, using just his right hand, as was tradition,

for the left hand was unclean. Despite that, he ate quickly, faster than he could swallow, his cheeks bulging.

Besma sat, her stomach rumbling while man and boy devoured most of the meal, and slurped tea. Havi came up for air, looking at his sister with a sheepish frown. Then he said, "Hassan al-Hassan, might my sister join us?"

"Yes, yes," Hassan said, scooping up the last of the meat with a piece of bread. There was one piece of pita bread left.

Besma got up, approached, sat on her knees by the round brass tray. The bowl of sauce was almost gone.

"May I?" she said.

Hassan waved at her impatiently while he gulped tea.

She took the last piece of pita bread. Scooping up the remaining sauce, she ate the bread slowly, chewing each bite many times. Her empty stomach clamped onto the balls of food, almost hurting with relief.

But it was sustenance. And Havi had eaten his fill, and for that she was thankful.

After the midday meal, Havi was sent back to the madrassa, where he was to learn how to fire guns. Besma could not comprehend how a child could do such a thing. She had fired her father's pistol, an old forty-five automatic, and his rifle many times. She had gone hunting with him and quite enjoyed it. But she had been older than Havi was now.

But Havi was safe for the moment.

Besma sat alone in the room with Hassan al-Hassan.

Hassan al-Hassan's eyes fell upon her. He leaned back against a cushion.

Her pulse quickened.

"You are a very pretty girl," he said, his eyes half-lidded. "Do you know that?"

She swallowed hard. "Thank you, Hassan al-Hassan."

He stretched out his legs before him, splitting them wide, and rested his hands behind his head.

"Have you ever been with a man?"

"No," she croaked, cold sweat breaking out on the small of her back.

He turned his head sideways and gave her a sly look. "Are you sure?"

"Of course," she said. "I think I would remember such a thing." She didn't know if it was risky to make that kind of talk.

But Hassan actually smiled. She was relieved. Her mother—bless her soul—had told her there were things a woman had to do for a man and that it was best to just get used to them. Make the best of it so that it would be over sooner rather than later.

"The women are going to make sure, you know."

"I have nothing to hide, Hassan al-Hassan," she said. It was getting difficult to talk. Her lips were dry. Her mouth was dry. She felt dizzy.

"Stand up," he said.

She did, hands trembling as she smoothed out her robe.

He made a circular motion with his hand. It was obvious what he wanted her to do.

Disrobe.

Shaking, she took off the robe, stood there, in just the roomy panties and ragged camisole the women had given her.

He seemed as surprised as he was interested. "Where are your clothes?"

"They were filthy. I washed them out and hung them to dry while I bathed." Hopefully they were still in the bathroom.

He nodded with apparent satisfaction. "Come here."

She took quivering steps toward him.

He made another motion with his hand.

Doing her best to control her breath, she removed her top.

"Stand up straight, woman."

She straightened her back.

"Arms back," he said. "Don't be shy."

She drew her arms back.

"Hmmm," he said.

She'd heard the stories of the rapes. Best if it were one man, and best if he liked her, at least a little.

"Good," he said. "That's enough."

She didn't quite understand. "I'm sorry?"

"Get dressed," he said, sounding impatient.

He didn't have to ask twice. Besma quickly pulled her camisole and robe back on.

"Sit," he said.

She did.

He got out his mobile phone and made a call. She assumed he was going to sell her, but the stories she'd heard said they took you first, passed you around like a doll before you were sold to some greedy man who could only think about getting his money's worth before he sold you again.

"Darwish," Hassan al-Hassan said to a man he was obviously on friendly terms with, "praise Allah, I wish to speak to Abu Nadir's secretary."

Even Besma knew that name. Abu Nadir was the highest Islamic cleric presiding over Mosul, now in the hands of Jihad Nation, where Sharia Law was strictly enforced, with public beatings, beheadings and floggings the norm. His sermons drew thousands and he was treated almost as a god himself. He was responsible for governing the entire region that had fallen under the jihadists. Her father had told

Besma a story of how Abu Nadir had ordered a shopkeeper to have his hands chopped off for not closing his business in time for prayers.

Hassan al-Hassan was put on the phone with Abu Nadir's secretary. After a lengthy exchange of formalities, Abu Nadir's secretary appeared to question Hassan al-Hassan harshly.

"Yes, Sayid," Hassan said. "I know that the French police have captured Kafka and that he was not able to shoot Dara. But rest assured I have the situation well in hand." He listened for a moment before he replied. "Please dispel your fears, Sayid. You see, we have something important to Kafka. Two important things actually—his mother and father. Yes. Right here in a cell, in this very camp. As we speak."

Abu Nadir's secretary spoke again.

"Sayid," Hassan said. "I am confident that, although he is a traitor, Kafka won't see his parents beheaded. I promised him video of the very same if he were to divulge anything about Abraqa." Another pause. "Yes, I realize that the caliph is not pleased. Which brings me to another point." He cleared his throat and looked at Besma with a smile as he spoke. "I have something for the caliph Abu Nadir. An exceptional bride. Yes. Striking. Blue eyes. Slender. Beautiful. No older than fourteen. *And* she knows the Koran."

Hassan nodded while Abu Nadir's secretary spoke on the other end of the phone.

"Of course she is untouched, Sayid. This young woman would make a fine wife. She's not like his others and he would find much to like in her. And it would be my deepest honor to present her to the caliph as a gift."

Besma shuddered as Hassan's words reverberated in her ears.

35

Maggie hung up the phone with forced composure, sitting in the red chair in the corner of her hotel room. She checked the digital clock on the dresser. Just past seven AM.

She was ready to throw the damn phone against the wall.

Ed said he didn't have the necessary clout to keep her on Abraqa. Now that Bellard had Kafka in custody, the Agency had nothing, despite the threat of protesting Kafka's beating. Ed had a call in to Walder but hadn't heard back.

"In the meantime, Maggs, you better get your butt out of France."

She had to be at Le Bourget in a little over an hour to catch a C-130 back home.

John Rae had gone out to find decent coffee. He had slept on the floor last night. She had let her guard down the other night and, as promising as it had been, she wasn't going to repeat it. John Rae seemed to feel the same way. Seemed.

Nothing was working out.

A few minutes later she heard the two-person elevator ding on the third floor.

John Rae came in with two cups of coffee.

"What's this?" Maggie said, taking the cup he held out for her. "No croissant?"

"I didn't know the French word for 'croissant'."

She gave JR a smirk and took a sip. Lots of sugar and cream. Just how she liked it. John Rae had noticed that. "I was thinking," she said.

"I thought your brow looked painfully furrowed."

"We have to leave France, but who says I have to go back to the US? You're heading back to Berlin, right? I'll tag along. That way we're only a few short hours away from gay Paree when Walder hands Bellard a ration of shit."

"Just one problem," John Rae said, drinking coffee. "Walder doesn't want his name on this, remember?"

"Even though Bellard's people used Kafka for batting practice?"

"Walder got his hand smacked by the White House. He'd rather let Abraqa go down in flames under Bellard's watch—which is what is going to happen without your help."

"Talk about a case of 'I told you so'."

"You got it." John Rae shrugged. "But I made a call or two myself while I was out, not getting you a croissant."

"I hope she charges by the hour—because we have to leave France soon."

John Rae sipped. "Just some friends of mine."

"As in your 'off the books' friends?"

"You got it."

John Rae had an underground network of people he could call in.

"I thought Walder didn't want to know," Maggie said.

"Walder *doesn't* want to know. But that doesn't mean he doesn't want me to go ahead and stick it to Bellard while he doesn't know anything. Off the books. Out of sight, out of mind."

"Benign ignorance."

"You're trying to blind me with big words again but, yeah. Seems that Senator Brahms has breathed new life into Abraqa, thanks to you and dear old Dad."

"What about getting kicked out of France?"

"I'm going to rent a car, drive to Berlin. In theory."

"And you think Bellard is going to be happy with that?"

"I know he is."

"And who told you that? Your psychic?"

"No." John Rae drank more coffee. "Bellard."

Maggie reared back in surprise. "You spoke to him?"

"While I was out not getting you a croissant."

"Huh." Maggie sipped. "Seems Bellard likes you better than me."

"As James Brown sang, 'It's a man's world.'"

"It sure as hell is."

"Well, maybe a little. But you and he were getting into it with fervor. I, however, stayed on the sidelines, so it was easier for me to mediate. And once Bellard calmed down, he realized he just got a high-grade terrorist handed to him, and that we—i.e., you—did most of the work, and he really doesn't want some formal complaint about prisoner abuse coming his way from Washington."

"And you threatened that."

"You did, actually." John Rae drank. "That's what I told him you were going to do, anyway. Call your good buddy Brahms. If he kept acting like a supreme pain in the ass."

"Hey, thanks for letting me know."

"He's not letting you back on Abraqa though. And we do have to leave. But he did cut us some slack."

"How much slack?"

"Leave France by tomorrow."

It wasn't much. But they weren't out yet. Like Ed had said, it was one of those operations. All she needed was another break.

"Since we're here for a little longer," Maggie said. "I'm going to call my old man again, see if I can rattle Brahms's cage—like you had me threaten to do."

∽

"THE MEETING IS NOW ADJOURNED," the young woman in the purple, yellow, red and green headscarf said. She had the characteristic striking blue eyes and dark hair of the Yazidi. She was standing in front of a dozen or so other women and men of Yazidi descent in the Armavir Tea Room that Amina owned in Montmartre. "Stay strong!"

"Stay strong!" the others said in unison.

Maggie sat with Amina. People had turned their chairs to face the speaker but were now resuming their original positions around tables in the small café. Private conversations resumed. A waitress in a green apron pushed her chair back with a screech, got up, and returned to her station behind the counter, turning the music back up and making a fresh batch of coffee. A basket moved from table to table, collecting coins and bills for the Yazidi effort to send a representative to the United Nations to make the case for peacekeepers to be deployed and hopefully stem the ongoing genocide by Jihad Nation. A big man in a red beret guarded the door. Maggie made a donation and passed the basket along.

"You going to be okay?" she said to Amina, sitting across from her.

"I'm going to be fine," Amina said. She was dressed in a smart dark pant suit, with her big hair perfectly coiffed and sprayed and full makeup expertly applied, smelling wonderfully of some authoritative perfume. One would never have suspected that her niece had been brutally murdered less than a week before. "I'm just angry. So angry."

"Easily understood," Maggie said, drinking white wine.

The strident minor tones of singer Xate Shingali's recorded music wafted through the café, simple and haunting, set against the plaintive picking of an oud.

"Perhaps we should be more like her," Amina said, nodding at the loudspeaker in the corner of the room. "Xate laid down her instrument and picked up a rifle to head up the women's Sun Brigade to fight Jihad Nation." Amina set her teacup down with a *clink*. "But how will *that* end? A few woman against a hundred thousand psychopathic killers with endless funding?"

"I'm not giving up yet," Maggie said.

"But the French police already have Kafka."

Maggie set her glass down. "I need you to promise me to be vigilant, Amina. Look over your shoulder. Have someone walk you home after work. Better still, take a taxi. Don't answer the door unless you know who it is."

"Yes, yes. You told me this several times already."

"Then take my advice. Thanks again for the drink."

"When will I see you again?"

"I'll be back for the funeral," Maggie said. "But you may not see me until then."

"Are you really going to see this through, Maggie?"

Or die trying sounded a little heavy handed. "Absolutely. Why do you even ask?"

Amina nodded, as if coming to some decision.

"If you know something, Amina," Maggie said, "you must tell me. *Must.*"

"Very well," Amina said, reaching for her gray leather handbag. "I have something I found in Dara's things." Amina retrieved a black-covered document and handed it over to Maggie.

Maggie took it, read the cover.

White Arabic writing claimed the passport to belong to the State of the Islamic Caliphate. Maggie opened it. It took her a moment to translate the inscription: "If the holder of the passport is harmed we will deploy armies for his service."

A photo of Dara in a hijab. Close enough that Maggie could pass as her. In a pinch.

"They're issuing their own passports," she said, flabbergasted. "I'd heard of these, but no one's seen one—until now. That's how confident Jihad Nation are that they'll own the entire region. The whole Levant."

"That is, after all, their goal."

Maggie read the signature authorizing the document.

"It's signed by Abu Nadir," she said. "The caliph who resides in Mosul. The highest known Jihad Nation figure in Iraq." Maggie leafed through the document. Genuine, stamped. The real deal. "How on earth did Dara ever get one of these?"

"Perhaps you can put it to good use. But whatever you do, please be careful. For your sake, and Dara's memory."

"I will," Maggie said, standing up, pocketing the passport. It felt like an omen, having it in her possession. One more reason to see this through.

36

As Maggie took the stairs up from the Maison Blanche Metro stop, heading back to the Shangri La, her phone buzzed in her pocket with a voicemail notification. Rain was beginning to sprinkle the pavement.

Her father. How odd it felt; no communication for years and now this—regular contact. Just like a normal father and daughter.

Call me when you get a chance, Maggie.

Such a curt message did not seem to bode well.

She ducked into the doorway of a café idle between lunch and dinner and dialed her father on his cell phone in Alexandria. Fortunately he was his way to work and had a moment to talk.

"Anything to get you out of the house," she said.

"Stefania is a wonderful woman, Maggie."

"I'm sure you're required to say that under pain of torture. Is this a fun call?"

"Not in the slightest."

She had suspected as much. "I hope you're using

RedPhone," she said, meaning the encryption app. "Or something similar."

"Comes with the territory," he said.

"Any good news?"

"I spoke to Senator Brahms," he said quietly. "She's doesn't think you have a case with the prisoner abuse complaint. If anyone turned too bright a light on what went on with Abraqa from our end, not notifying the French that we were running it, we'd be in deep you-know-what."

"What a collection of gutless wimps Washington is."

"That's news to you?"

She was disappointed but not surprised. "Well, thanks," she said.

"But Walder and crew know she's still good supporting Abraqa."

Maggie hoped it wasn't all going to be a wasted effort. "I really appreciate it."

"Hold on," her father said. "I haven't finished. Brahms called me back—not long afterwards."

Interesting. Her dad and Senator Brahms. Still pretty close. Well, Brahms was kind of statuesque and well preserved. And she wielded power. Did she call him Robert? "And?"

"Between you and me and the deep blue sea, Maggie, SDAT is just about to relocate your friend."

That made Maggie stop and listen. "Kafka?" she said. "Any idea where?"

"Of course no one will admit any of this, if it were to rear its ugly head on CNN."

"Who watches CNN anymore? And I don't talk to anybody in the press. I just threaten to."

"And, more importantly, Senator Brahms's name doesn't come up—at all. Not ever. Never."

"If you could see me now," Maggie said, "you would see me making a little zipper motion over my mouth. Just like you always did." It was one of the memorable things during her infrequent times with him as a child.

"Some place called *La Ferme*," her father said. "Do you know of it?"

The Farm. "No," she said. "But it sounds intriguing. I shall find out."

"You better hurry. They're trying to get him there today. They're getting it cleared with their ministry of Foreign Affairs as we speak."

"Bellard wants to cover his ass. He's already pushing it with the prisoner abuse thing."

"Well, that's all I have."

"It's a gold mine," she said. It might be the break she needed. She just wasn't quite sure how to leverage it yet. But John Rae would know. "I don't know what to say."

"Try, '*I'm coming home and not getting involved.*'"

"Sorry—that's not the first thing that comes to mind."

"I guess I expected as much," he said. "Take care? If *that* does any good?"

"It does. I will."

"Got to run," he said.

"Take care . . . and thanks, Dad."

"You bet." He rang off.

Encouraged, she dialed John Rae. He was in a bar, a noisy one. There was much shouting, a lot of excited young men hooting and hollering. ZZ Top's "Legs" was pounding away in the background.

"I'm glad to see you're using your last day to see the real Paris," Maggie said.

"I'm a culture sponge."

"Are you in a freaking strip club, JR?"

"They're called 'gentlemen's clubs' these days."

"How classy."

"I'm actually meeting an old friend. He picked the place, not me."

"That sounds like an excuse."

"I know," he said wistfully. She could hear John Rae drink something. "Any news from Pop?"

"As a matter of fact, yes," she said, excitement building in her voice. "Where *are* you, exactly?"

"I'm kind of embarrassed to say. And I'm not sure I want you to come here."

"I already know that men are pigs. Where are you? I'll grab a cab. I think we need to move fast."

"Some place called Miss Ku's."

"In the meantime, see what you can learn about *La Ferme.* It's a place SDAT seems to take special guests."

"It means *The Farm* in English, Maggie."

"I'm glad you're working on your French," she said, flagging down a cab.

37

Miss Ku's was located in the 9th Arrondissement, in the heart of tourist Paris, but stashed away on a narrow backstreet where most people wouldn't see it. Where it belonged. A pink and lavender neon sign over double matte-black doors proclaimed the club to be "international." It featured a nude girl on her back resting on her elbows with her feet pointed seductively. She flickered in the moist air that hinted at more rain.

When Maggie entered the club she was overwhelmed by more glaring pink and lavender neon strips around the top of the bar, making her squint as the bouncer, a big guy with a spiky haircut and a barbed wire tattoo around his muscled bicep showed her to a table at the front of the stage. John Rae and a slight young Turk in western garb were watching a slinky Asian woman in a leopard skin bikini and high heels dance badly to a '70s disco number. The song vocals seemed to be centered around a woman moaning the word *more* orgasmically.

Apart from the woman onstage and similarly clad waitresses strutting around under flashing lights with trays of drinks, Maggie was the only female. She sat down in a low puffy vinyl seat, trying not to think of who or what might have preceded her, and gave John Rae a shake of the head.

"Imagine my disappointment, JR."

John Rae returned what might have been called a shit-eating grin. "Not nearly as disappointed as I am. She's a terrible dancer."

"I can see you blushing, dude, even with all this damn neon."

He shrugged, signaling for a waitress. "If it makes any difference, you're the most striking woman here. *And* you've still got most of your clothes on."

John Rae turned to introduce his friend, who was now watching Maggie with his hands clasped tightly together in front of him. He had dark skin and piercing eyes, and wore a loose blue track suit and brilliant white Adidas sneakers that reflected the black lights placed strategically around the room. A reserved flat line of a mouth gave little away.

"Maggs, this is Abd Allah. I call him 'Bad' since I can't really pronounce his first name. And he is pretty bad to boot."

Bad stood up, leaned over the mirrored table to shake hands with Maggie in a most formal manner. "I am very sorry to hear about the loss of your friend," he said in perfect English.

Bad seemed to know Maggie's recent history, which meant JR trusted him enough to tell him.

"Do I really call you '*Bad*'?" she said.

"Others do. I am fine with it."

"Call me Maggie," she said.

"Bad is ex Millî İstihbarat Teşkilatı," John Rae said as they sat back down.

Turkish intelligence. *Ex*. Interesting.

"Now where is that waitress?" John Rae said.

The leopard skin woman was twirling on a brass poll in a haphazard manner, using centrifugal force to propel her around as she held on for what seemed to be dear life.

A woman with dramatic black bangs down to her eyes appeared. A gleaming shock of red lipstick accentuated what looked to be a permanent pout. She wore a red mesh see-through bikini that left little to the imagination. The only part of her not exposed were her lower legs, which were encased in black PVC platform boots.

They ordered drinks and she slouched off.

The music changed to whimsical and the Asian dancer exited the stage to a smattering of applause. The DJ announced a special international act. A rotund swarthy woman in an orange clown wig hopped up onto the stage, grunting at the effort. She wore a purple and white polka dotted dress and purple sneakers.

"I yam 'Little Annie Fannie'," she said in heavily accented English. "But I yam not so little, eh?" She pointed at an Asian man in a three-piece suit sitting in the front row, trying to slither down in his chair. "Not like you, eh? I bet you are little in quite a few ways, eh?"

One lone guffaw bounced from the back of the room.

"You know," she continued, "My 'usband, 'e ask me: 'why don' you dirty talk to me during sex'." Annie patrolled the stage with the microphone in her fist, glaring at the patrons. "I tell 'im: 'It's because I don' 'ave my phone handy, eh?'"

Laughter, but not much.

"Oh, you fuckers don' like sex? Or you just never 'ad it?"

Maggie turned to JR as she sipped a watery Black Russian. "Is there a *good* reason you came here, JR?"

"Believe it or not, there is," John Rae said, drinking from

a long neck Heineken. Bad sipped a bottle of Perrier. "He's just running late."

"I live in anticipation, then," she said.

"Wait no more," John Rae said, looking over her shoulder to the door.

Maggie turned to see an older man, slim but fit, gray crew cut and gold-framed grannie glasses, giving John Rae a nod as the front door shut behind him. He wore faded blue jeans and a dark floral shirt under a black ribbed motor racing type jacket with zip-up pockets. He approached them in a sprightly manner, defying his sixty-plus years.

"I do apologize for being late," he said in good English tinged with a German accent. "I can blame no one but myself." He had his share of wrinkles and crags but light blue eyes to carry it all off.

He reached out to take Maggie's hand as they all stood up.

"Dieter Fromm," he said. "You must be Maggie. So very nice to meet you. Again, my apologies." He held her hand the entire time he made his introduction but it didn't feel as creepy as it might have. Despite his relaxed manner, there was a military bearing about him.

"'Ey, old fart!" Little Annie Fannie shouted at him with a screech of microphone feedback from the stage. "Don't talk when I'm doing my jokes."

Dieter turned to the stage, bowed. "So sorry, mademoiselle. Please allow me make it up to you in some way."

"Oh, you will," she said, flashing her thick eyebrows. "You will."

"I only ask that I don't have to take you to dinner. I'm not sure I could afford it."

More laughter.

Annie placed a hand on her ample hip. "I don't see what

else you got to offer, Siegfried. Not unless you been doing push-ups with your tongue."

Even more laughter. Random clapping. Another serious guffaw from the back of the room.

"Touché!" Dieter gave Annie a lazy salute and sat down. "Whose idea was this anyway?" he said, looking at Maggie. "Yours?"

"I'm drawn to the ambience," Maggie said. "And the intellectual repartee."

Dieter sat forward, elbows on his knees. "Let's get serious, shall we?" He rubbed his hands together. "*La Ferme.*"

38

"*La Ferme,*" Dieter repeated as he sipped an espresso the pouty waitress had thumped down on the mirrored table before she shuffled off, wiggling a derriere Bad Allah couldn't seem to stop watching. "The Farm—a DGSE black site SDAT uses from time to time."

DGSE—*Direction Générale de la Sécurité Extérieure*—was France's external security.

"Black site?" Maggie asked. Little Annie Fannie had left the stage amidst hoots and hollers. There was a welcome moment of silence before the next exotic dancer was to begin. She waited by the stage, straightening her fishnets.

Dieter was retired from BVT—Bundesamt für Verfassungsschutz und Terrorismusbekämpfung—the Austrian antiterrorism branch. He set his cup down neatly on its saucer. "Meaning: *La Ferme* doesn't exist—not officially. But a few people know about it. People like you." He gave Maggie an inquisitive look, as if wondering how she did know.

Maggie realized how good her father's information was. "I don't know anything beyond the name," she said, sipping her drink. "And the fact that they're taking someone there I would dearly like to talk to."

"This Kafka?" he said, raising his eyebrows.

"Indeed." Dieter was another one John Rae obviously trusted enough to share information with.

"Can I ask how you even know about *La Ferme*?" Dieter said. Bad and JR were following along, although Bad was keeping one eye on the girls.

Maggie shook her head. "Just that it comes from a very reliable source."

"I see," Dieter said. "Well, back in the day, before I retired, I had the opportunity to interview a few—ah —*guests* there."

"Where is this farm?" Maggie said. "It sounds so rustic."

"Near Dieppe."

The northern coast of France. The site of a major battle during World War II. The Allies got their heads handed to them by the Germans during a poorly planned raid. It was the precursor to the Normandy invasion. "Far enough from Paris to be discreet."

Dieter nodded as he sipped coffee. "Close enough to get there in an hour or two. A nearby airport and port, in case the interviewee needs to be moved offshore. Traded. Taken to some island hellhole. Which is what frequently happens. A good spot to stash someone. Do you know when Kafka is being moved there?"

"Tonight I gather. SDAT is getting it cleared with the Ministry of Foreign Affairs."

"So we have a little time."

"Time for what?"

Dieter sat up and gave John Rae a bemused look. "Did you not tell your friend Maggie about our outing, John Rae?"

John Rae took a sip of the Heineken he was nursing. "I didn't want to promise something that might not happen."

Maggie's and John Rae's eyes met. The disc jockey announced that there would be a special on lap dances for the next half an hour. That info seemed to pique Bad's interest.

"Clue me in, JR," Maggie said, although she had a pretty good idea.

He set his unfinished beer down. "We're going to get to the farm before SDAT does."

"You're proposing we kidnap Kafka?" She had to admit she didn't hate the idea of continuing an op that had been snatched away from her. But the consequences were a concern.

"*Kidnap* is such a loaded word, Maggie," John Rae said. "I prefer *rescue*. SDAT has not treated Kafka well. And 'rescuing' him will put him squarely on our side. He'll be happy to play nice with you then. Tell y'all about his Abraqa Darknet. Probably tell you a few other things as well."

Maggie let that sink in.

"Has any of this been approved?" she said, squinting. "You know—*authorized*?"

"What? And take all the fun out of it?" He picked up his beer. "Walder knows what he wants and doesn't know what he doesn't want to know." He drank. "Off the books means no authorizations."

She could live with that, if John Rae could.

"What do you two get out of it?" she asked Dieter and Bad.

"We're doing it for John Rae," Bad said in a solemn tone.

"And because we don't like Jihad Nation very much," Dieter said. "So we will get you your Kafka, and he will tell you what he knows. And everyone will have a very nice time."

John Rae was calling in more favors. He had done something similar in Ecuador, breaking some prisoners out of a clandestine prison on Maggie's behalf. There were times she didn't trust him, to be sure. He played multiple angles. But there were times he delivered, and this looked like one of them. She began to feel Dara's legacy, one that had been slipping away from her only hours ago, coming back within reach.

"I don't know what to say," she said, looking at Dieter, then Bad, then John Rae. "Except *thank you*, gentlemen."

"Dieter's running this little junket," John Rae said. "He knows his way around The Farm."

Dieter consulted his wristwatch. "We best leave now to be assured of getting there ahead of Bellard's men."

"How far exactly is *La Ferme*?" Maggie said.

"One hundred and eighty kilometers," Dieter said. "Two hours if the roads are clear. One and a half if Bad Allah here is driving, regardless of road conditions." He gave Bad a smile. "The man is a bit of a maniac behind the wheel."

"Please give a warm welcome to the lovely Angelique," the DJ said as Fishnets took the stage and blew a kiss to the crowd.

Dieter shook his head. "Shall we?"

Maggie, Dieter, John Rae and Bad all stood up, Bad taking one last look at the stage.

39

"Turn right, up ahead," Dieter said, monitoring the iPad on his lap from the passenger seat.

Bad Allah was at the wheel of a black Peugeot Boxer delivery van, bouncing along the N27 in upper Normandy. Maggie sat in the bench seat behind with John Rae. Dusk was descending on the lush rolling countryside, turning a deep green in the falling light, and the commute traffic in and out of Dieppe was winding down. Bad Allah made a tight right turn onto the narrow country road, the long van fishtailing.

Lead foot, Maggie thought. She had changed into fresh jeans, turtleneck sweater and a roomy windbreaker before checking out of the Shangri La a few hours ago.

"*La Ferme* is approximately one kilometer away," Dieter said. "On the left. We'll park farther up. There's a lay by."

"And you're sure this is going to work?" Maggie asked.

"Absolutely, Fraulein," Dieter said, turning to look at her, scraps of daylight flashing off his John Lennon glasses. "And if it doesn't, well, we try something else."

The plan was for Maggie to find out whether Kafka was

already at *La Ferme*. There was a good chance he hadn't arrived yet. She was to approach the farm house solo and say she had a dead battery, ask for help. Hopefully, someone would let her in and she could get a look around. Meanwhile, Dieter and John Rae would be outside, checking out the property.

"And just to confirm," Maggie said, "no one's going to get shot—right?"

"Not unless it's one of us." Dieter grinned. "But then that would be our own stupid fault. I believe in talking my way out of things if something goes amiss. I'm a chicken from way back."

Maggie doubted that.

"And no one's going to get beat up, either," she said.

Dieter made a *comme ci, comme ça* motion with his hand as the van bumped over a pothole, making them all bounce in their seats. John Rae grabbed the handle on the roof the van. "Dieter would regard that as an operational malfunction, Maggie. He sets his standards higher."

"I prefer '*absolutely not*' for an answer," Maggie said. "SDAT are our allies—technically."

"Not very cooperative allies, though," John Rae said. "You'd still be sitting in a holding cell if I hadn't intervened."

"We can't afford another nastygram to Washington is all I'm saying," Maggie said.

"Duly noted," John Rae said.

"They won't be expecting visitors," Dieter said. "This is a black site facility. Never more than a handful of people on staff. And this is the French countryside. Idyllic. They'll buy you being lost, Maggie, asking for help."

Maggie was trying to determine whether Dieter was one of those people who thought everything was easy, until it actually came down to all hell breaking loose. That's the way John Rae was.

"Up there, Bad." Dieter pointed out a gap in the wavering line of a rustic stonewall flanking the field on the left. Bad Allah nodded. He wasn't much of a talker. He was too busy driving on two wheels. The squeal of tires seemed to be his favorite sound.

An old ornate wrought-iron sign over an entrance to a darkened dirt road reading *Le Plessis* whooshed by. A *plessis* was an old hunting lodge. It was nestled back up behind a hill of verdant shrubbery. The sloped roof just showed, accented by moonlight.

"Over here," Dieter directed Bad, who swerved the van into a small gravel patch alongside the road, nestled in overgrown hedges.

Bad Allah parked in the lay by. Dieter dispensed an assortment of X3 multi-shot Tasers and Mace OC guns to Maggie and John Rae, along with mini flashlights, then threw a small day pack over his shoulder, no doubt loaded down with other goodies. Maggie got the feel of the Mace gun. It looked like a small blue flare gun made of thick steel, and held a can of the toxic spray. You could shoot Mace up to twenty feet away. No one was carrying a real gun. They couldn't afford another international incident if a tussle broke out. This op was strictly low profile.

"John Rae and I will be waiting for you up at *La Ferme*, Fraulein," Dieter said, retrieving a ski mask, pulling it on top of his head like a cap for the time being. "Bad Allah will stay behind, keep an eye out, wait for our call, ready to pick us up if need be. Bad, you get in the back seat and stay down when we leave so the van appears to be empty. Everybody have their Rinos up and running and set to silent mode?"

Maggie checked her Rino phone, as did the others.

"Yep," she said. She gathered her hair back, pulled a dark beret over her head, to one side, affording a measure of disguise.

"Knock 'em dead, Maggs," John Rae said, putting his fist up in the air for her to bump. He'd pulled a knit ski mask over his face and looked a good deal less trustworthy, along with his good luck pigskin jacket zipped up to his neck. Cool night air was settling in.

She gave John Rae's fist a knock, then did the same with Dieter and leaned forward, followed up with Bad, who gave her a solemn nod as he, too, fist-bumped.

"Let's do it to it, gentlemen," John Rae said, then added, "And lady."

Dieter hopped out, yanked open the windowless side door to the van.

"Be good up there, Fraulein," he said, helping her down from the van. "I know you will."

"This isn't sexist at all," she said. "Sending me up there to pull a 'damsel in distress' routine."

"You think they'd open the front door for an old goat like Dieter?" John Rae said, climbing out behind her. "Or me, for that matter?"

Maggie pocketed her Mace gun. "You're assuming those agents are men."

"We play it by ear," Dieter said. "John Rae and I are taking the back way. You stay on the main road, as if you've just left the van here—broken down. The building you want will be directly in front of you when you get to the top of the private road—an old lodge. I'll be in the small chapel to the right of it. John Rae is going to be stationed in the stables to the left."

"Seems an appropriate place for him," Maggie said.

"See what I have to put up with?" John Rae said to Dieter.

"I don't know, John Rae—maybe she's calling you a stud."

Maggie blushed as she and John Rae traded looks, John Rae's through the eyeholes of his ski mask.

"Come on, John Rae," Dieter said. "Time for a jog." He and John Rae pushed through the tall, thick hedges, then dashed across a fallow field in a low run. Maggie took the narrow country road. The nutty smell of earth wet from recent rains filled her nostrils. Off in the trees surrounding the farmhouse, nightingales twittered to each other. Her eyes adjusted quickly to the moonlight.

At the wrought-iron lodge sign she turned right and marched up a dirt road tunneled under trees to where a clearing laid out the buildings Dieter had described—an old stone stable and other more functional buildings to the left, a lovely old stone chapel to the right, and a stone farmhouse with a slate roof in front of her. It looked like a country retreat where one might spend a relaxing weekend. A single light glowed through a window. Maggie crunched gravel up to the front door, getting out her civilian cell phone, which she had powered down.

Stepping up to an ancient oak door with blackened ironwork on it, she noted John Rae's silhouette to her left, just visible in the dimness behind a Dutch half stable door. To her right, standing inside the picturesque little chapel, lurked Dieter. In the shadows she saw him give her a silent nod. Both men were well hidden.

She banged the knocker several times.

Light footsteps padded up to the door.

Someone eyed her through a peep hole.

"*Oui?*" a woman's voice said. So much for the man theory.

"So sorry to bother you, madame," Maggie said breathlessly in French, "but my van died—just up the road. Battery —*dead!*" She stood back, held up her phone to the peephole. "And now my phone battery is gone too. Can you believe it? I'm hoping you can let me use your phone. To call for a tow truck."

"You won't get a garage to send anyone out here this time of night," the woman said in a curt voice through the grill in the door.

So helpful. "Not even from Dieppe?"

The woman gave a staccato laugh. "No."

"A taxi then?" Maggie said. Whoever was in there was not eager to let her in and Maggie wasn't going to ask and raise a red flag. "They must have taxis in Dieppe, no? They could send one out. I'm willing to pay the cost."

The woman behind the door laughed the laugh again. "Where do you think you are? *Paris?*"

"Or a bus?" Maggie said. "Is there a bus I could take?"

"No buses out here. It's the country, in case you haven't noticed."

"If I could just try to call a taxi then, anyway, madame," Maggie said again.

"I'll call one for you but I don't like your chances."

"*Merci*," Maggie said, adding, "Do you think I could use your toilet? I'm a little bit desperate."

"There are bushes everywhere."

The French. "I'm sorry to have bothered you. Thank you for calling the taxi. I'll be at the end of the road. Good night!" Maggie turned around, walked away, not making eye contact with either John Rae or Dieter in case she was being watched.

She headed back down the dirt road.

Well, that went pretty damn well. But there didn't seem to be a hive of activity at *La Ferme*. No vehicles parked either, although they could have been garaged.

She was halfway down the tunnel of trees, peering into shadows, when her Rino phone buzzed. She pulled it, looked at the tiny screen lit up in the darkness.

Group call in progress, originated by Bad Allah.

She dialed up the volume.

"Dieter," Bad said in a crackle of static, "a French National Police *fourgon* just drove by."

A *fourgon* was a long van.

"Head's up," Dieter said. "This could be our boy arriving."

"It's turning into *La Ferme* right now," Bad said. Not much seemed to faze him.

Down the end of the road, Maggie saw headlights, fuzzy in the darkness, bouncing up the narrow lane. She joined in the call. "He's right, guys. They're coming up the road toward me now. I bet that's our guest of honor. They're bringing in Kafka."

"Stop that van, Fraulein," Dieter said, his lips close to the phone. "Keep them talking. We'll be right there, ready to jump in. Let's go, John Rae. *Mach schnell!* We'll cut across the field. Bad Allah, start your engine and motor down to the entrance. Stay out of sight but wait for us."

"Ten-four," Bad said, the engine firing up in the background.

"Geronimo!" John Rae said, and Maggie could hear him already in a dead run, breathing heavily. "Hang in there, Maggs. Turn your phone down so they don't hear us." He signed off.

Maggie silenced her phone, stuffed it in the pocket of

her jacket. The van was halfway up the dirt road. She stood out in the middle of the constricted lane, waving her arms.

The van slowed to a crawl, headlights blinding, and came to a stop ten feet away.

Maggie dashed around to the driver's window, pulling her best helpless face. The window rolled down. A grizzled man in a police uniform leaned his head out. He had a bushy mustache, like a broom.

"Are you lost?" he said in a working class accent.

"My van broke down," Maggie said, blinking in feigned confusion. She gripped the Mace gun in her jacket pocket. "Just up the road. I was trying to get help up at that farmhouse. No luck. And my phone's dead. Can you call a taxi for me? Better still, can I wait with you while you do? It's a little scary out here. I'd be forever grateful."

"Not sure about that . . ." the driver said, turning in his seat. "What do you think?"

"Wait a minute," a very familiar voice said from the back of the van. Captain Bellard. "I know that voice . . ."

Maggie's hackles rose. Bellard was accompanying Kafka. She pulled the Mace gun from her pocket.

The driver turned back around to face Maggie, mouth open, just as she squeezed the trigger, filling his face with noxious wet white spray.

Almost immediately the driver burst into a coughing jag, hands up to his eyes, his face covered in near foam. He screamed as Maggie aimed the jet to the far side of the cab, hitting the passenger on the side of the face before he could put his hands up. The other occupants in the van began shouting before the window started rolling back up. Maggie blasted the driver again, ear to ear. He collapsed down into the leg well, coughing violently, rubbing his eyes.

"I can't see!"

Maggie climbed up onto the running board, her arm inside the half-open window, spraying into the back. There were seven shots per cartridge but she didn't want to overdo it and cause permanent damage. The inside of the cab became a wet cloud. The driver and passenger yelled out in pain, as the rear of the van echoed with cries and shouts as well.

"Go, go, go!" she heard Dieter yell as he and John Rae leapt from the bushes on the other side of the van.

Dieter yanked open the passenger door, stepped aside as John Rae hauled the man from the passenger seat, threw him down on the ground. Dieter tasered him with a *snap*. John Rae leapt up into the cab and gassed everybody in the rear with more Mace.

Bellard and Kafka, in cuffs, tried to cover their faces but both were clearly hit and out of control.

Maggie stepped down, her own eyes burning and watering copiously. It felt as if someone was holding a cigarette lighter to her face and she had only gotten a mild dose. She battled the panicky feeling of not being able to breathe. Her throat tightened up.

The SDAT crew, including Bellard, were soon duct-taped and coughing inside their van. Maggie got Kafka outside and onto his feet, shaky as a newborn colt, unable to see. Arm around him, she led him swaying down the dark road, his face puffy and swollen where he had been beaten. Tears streamed over his bruises from the Mace.

"My eyes are on fire!" he shouted in Arabic. "I can't breathe!"

"It will pass," Maggie said. She didn't tell him it would take thirty minutes to two hours. "It's Maggie de la Cruz. We're getting you out of here."

"*Shukran*," he muttered between coughs. He kept rubbing his eyes with his cuffed hands and gasping for air.

"We'll cut you loose when we get to our van." She helped Kafka down the dark road. Behind her she heard John Rae and Dieter hurling the policemen's pistols and cell phones into the empty dark field.

"You call that a throw?" Dieter said to John Rae. "My granddaughter could make a better job of it."

John Rae laughed. "Don't forget to lock our buddies inside the van."

"Always got your thinking cap on," Dieter said, and she heard him return to the van where he pulled keys from the ignition. He and John Rae shut the doors and locked the van. Then the keys tinkled off into the darkness as well, landing in the field.

The last thing Maggie heard was the hiss of a tire as someone worked on it with a knife.

"*Merci beaucoup*, everyone." John Rae banged on the van. "*Sayonara*, gentlemen!"

John Rae and Dieter laughed as they broke into a run and came hustling down the road after Maggie and Kafka.

"Feeling any better?" Maggie asked Kafka, her arm still around him as they stumbled along.

"I think so." But his mouth quivered. Maggie stood back while he bent over and vomited onto the ground in splashes. He reared back up, wheezing, his mouth glistening. He wasn't able to get his words out but he made bleary eye contact with her for a moment. Good enough.

Behind her, she heard Dieter on his Rino to Bad Allah. 'Pull up to the entrance by the side of the road, get the door open, and prepare for some of your classic high-speed driving. We are bringing a guest."

40

Under normal circumstances the drive from Dieppe to Berlin took roughly ten hours. But that was for an average human being driving under normal conditions. Bad Allah made a mockery of that estimate, driving at night when the roads were less crowded, along with his disdain for brakes and his fondness for the gas pedal, and managed to shave two hours off the eleven hundred kilometer journey.

The team stopped long enough for gasoline, bio breaks and nothing more. Anything eaten or drunk was purchased in a motorway shop and consumed in the van moving at a high rate of speed. By the time they spotted the Fernsehturm, the infamous television tower erected by the former German Democratic Republic, jutting up out of the misty light of the five AM Berlin skyline, they were less than fragrant and the van's interior was clammy and rank. But their spirits were strong.

Some more than others.

Maggie had wanted to begin questioning Kafka as soon as they got on the road but Kafka was still in a state of physical and mental shock from the beating SDAT had doled out, not to mention the Mace which left him reeling and disoriented. He was given a couple of Vicodin out of Dieter's bag of treats and a blanket and spent the trip curled up in the rear seat behind Maggie and John Rae, snoring while the vehicle hurtled along. His bruised face was shiny in the muted street light as they pulled into the former East Berlin.

"Bellard's welcoming party sure did a hell of a number on him," John Rae whispered.

"And now it'll be twice as tough to coax him out of his shell," Maggie said. Especially with Kafka's parents being held by Jihad Nation and the fact that Kafka failed to execute Dara.

"It'll take some work," John Rae said. "That's for sure."

John Rae leaned back in his seat, clasped his hands behind his neck, stretched himself out. Vertebrae cracked. "Well, we have possession of the ball now."

"Thanks to you and your buddies," Maggie said.

"Take a minute and pat yourself on the back." John Rae looked over. "We'll get settled into our safe house in Berlin soon."

Then she could drill Kafka for intel. There wasn't much time left if she was going to disable Abraqa. "Walder is going to have to give his full approval if we end up in some sandy spot south of Syria. This look-the-other-way thing works for small stuff, but not a rescue op in the Middle East."

John Rae eyed her. "And you think that's where this is headed?"

"If we want Kafka to talk, he's going to insist on getting his parents out. I would. A rescue op needs to be an option."

John Rae frowned, seeming to think that over. "Walder

will have to push everyone to sign off. For that you'll need to give him a nugget first. Something juicy out of Kafka."

"I know," she said. "And then I need to convince Ed to let me tag along."

"Hold your horses, Maggie. Don't get ahead of yourself."

Maggie thought about that. Ed wasn't gung-ho about her running with John Rae's crowd. The more she did, the more he risked losing her to Field Operations. And without her, Ed's fledgling Forensic Accounting team would die a slow death. Truth was, she still liked that part of the job.

But getting anything done always came down to politics.

∽

"Well, the view makes up for the décor," Maggie said, looking out of the industrial windows of an empty office of a derelict warehouse built at the beginning of the last century. Pre-morning light cast a pall over the river Spree on her left, along which the Berlin wall once ran, and on her right the abandoned Betriebsbahnhof-Pankow railway station, forbidding in its decay. The history of the Cold War in one look. The walls of the office were in a state of decomposition and the smell was one of severe damp, which explained the mold. Posters of leather goods still remained on the walls.

"The meeting is about to start, Ms. de la Cruz," Helga, the field op admin, said in a German accent.

Maggie took a sip of instant coffee and turned to the center of the large room.

Tapping into the keyboard of a Mac on a folding card table was Helga, the admin, a woman in her forties with a shiny platinum blonde pageboy, a black denim jacket and a pair of high-heeled boots. She had been dispatched by Berlin Station to assist the operation.

John Rae was stretched out in a folding metal chair, giving Helga the once-over when she wasn't looking. Maggie realized she was just a little jealous. Another good reason to nip whatever had happened between them in the bud.

Kafka was crashed out next door in a former secretary's office on a cot, with Dieter and Bad Allah taking turns to watch him. It made sense to let Kafka recover from his ordeal. He'd be more compliant and it put the agency clearly in the good cop role. But Maggie still hadn't forgotten Kafka pulling a gun on her or the fact that he had seriously wounded an SDAT agent. Or that the woman who had lured him here, Dara, a person Maggie had grown quite fond of, was now dead.

She'd be nice. For now.

She walked over to the table, pulled out a folding chair across from the Marlene Dietrich look-alike, feeling grimy in the clothes she had worn for too long, whiffing of Mace. Her hair felt lank, bordering on greasy, her skin shiny. A real fashion plate.

"Let's do it," Maggie said, sitting down.

Helga positioned the laptop's webcam so it centered on Maggie and fired up the chat window using Black Canyon, the latest in encryption conferencing tools, and split the screen into four. After she dialed in, the upper left corner of the monitor showed Ed, looking not-too-rumpled as it happened, being that it was still early evening the previous day in San Francisco. His famous too-wide yellow power tie was halfway down another blue Oxford shirt that Maggie knew to be extra-large, to fit his equally sized frame. A cloud of blue cigarette smoke enveloped him. She'd get him to quit smoking one of these days.

In the upper right corner Director Walder appeared,

dour and humorless. Nothing new there. He wore his permanent frown, haloed by frizzy thinning hair.

"Do we have a quorum?" he said.

They all agreed.

"Status update on Abraqa, Agent de la Cruz?"

"You want to do this, John Rae?" she asked.

John Rae shook his head, leaning back in his chair again, hands behind his neck, closing his eyes to listen. They had all gone too long without sleep.

"We have the asset in our possession," Maggie began, "thanks to some nice work by John Rae and two contractors." She went through the proceedings of the last eight and half hours.

"All above board?" Walder said, rubbing his face.

"Everything in conjunction with Executive Order 12333," she said. Meaning that no one was killed and only necessary force was used.

"And where is the asset now?" Walder said.

"Getting some badly needed rest. That will hopefully make him easier to interview."

"Let's get started on the interrogation," Walder said. "As soon as this call is over."

Maggie wasn't sure that was the best idea although she was more than anxious to get things rolling herself.

"Can we talk about next steps?" she asked.

"Not until we know what we're dealing with," Walder said. "I'm not going cap in hand to NCS brass unless we get some decent intel out of Kafka."

She noticed that Ed, her boss, had not said a word, merely puffing away while he managed to project his worst grimace. He was pissed, feeling sidelined by the whole operation he had initially authorized but had been taken away, first by SDAT, now by Walder. She couldn't blame Ed. But she focused on the reason for all of this. Dara. The Yazidi genocide.

"John Rae?" Walder said.

"Yo," John Rae said from his chair.

"Ah, so you *are* still there. I didn't see you on camera."

"That's because I'm nothing special to look at."

"Do you have anything to add?"

"It doesn't sound like you've gotten any feedback yet from Bellard over reappropriating the asset," John Rae said.

It was official, Maggie thought wryly. Kafka was now "the asset."

"That means Bellard hasn't decided what to do yet," Walder said.

"Or he's still trying to get out of that damn van," John Rae said.

Walder actually divulged a smile. Maggie was impressed by John Rae's level of rapport with a man who scared the crap out of most of the Agency.

"What are your plans, John Rae?" Walder said.

"Going to stick around here and see what Magg—Agent de la Cruz—needs."

Telling his boss what *he* was going to do. Maggie could learn a thing or two.

"What are you thinking, John Rae?" Walder said.

"Wondering if we'll need to take this party down to the Casbah."

"Iraq?" Walder tapped his pencil on his desk pad. "I'm not sure about that. Let's see if the asset tells us something good, then we can decide. Anything else?"

"I'd got the two people Maggie mentioned on an unofficial contract payroll," John Rae said. "I took the liberty. They're guarding the asset as we speak. I also ran up some van rental fees."

"Just get receipts," Walder said.

They signed off.

"And that's how you manage your boss," John Rae said to Maggie. "Strike or be stricken."

"Not bad," she said. "Not bad." She made eye contact with Helga. "Is there anywhere to take a shower, Helga?"

"I wasn't going to bring it up, Maggie," John Rae said.

Helga didn't respond to John Rae's joke. Maggie shook her head.

"We have a hotel room not too far from here," Helga said.

"I'm thinking of our guest," Maggie said. Although she was never one to turn down a hot shower. She had brought her bag up from the van so had a change of underwear.

"We need to keep this on the down-low," John Rae said. "No wandering."

"I'll have a Giga tent brought in and set up," Helga said. "Portable water heater. Towels and soap. It will be functional."

"A Giga tent it is," Maggie said. "And Kafka will need some toiletries and clean clothes."

Helga got out her tablet. "I'll need his sizes."

"Let me find out. When can we get a doctor here? To take a look at him?"

"No," John Rae said. "I don't want Kafka milking it. We can use that for barter later."

"Bullshit," Maggie said. She said to Helga, "I'd like a doctor, please. Soon."

"Since it's short notice," Helga said, "it will have to be a nurse."

"That works," Maggie said. "Can someone go out and get some food? Middle Eastern? Make sure it's halal—kosher."

Helga wrote that down.

"Jesus, Maggie," John Rae said, "I want to be your prisoner."

"In your dreams," she said.

"The hostess with the mostest. But I'll take some chow, too, Helga. I'm sure the boys will join us as well. And yourself, of course. Do you have any good dining stories you can regale us with?"

Helga gave a small smile, made entries. "Who do I bill it to?"

"The usual," John Rae said.

"Of course." Helga left, already making phone calls.

"Maggie," John Rae said. "You ready to wake up sleeping beauty?"

"Let's wait until things are set up and he's been looked at and had a chance to clean up," she said.

41

"Let's start with those suicide bombers," Maggie said. "The ones who showed up at Café de la Nouvelle."

She was recording everything on her computer. Chill morning air hung in the damp abandoned industrial office, early daylight burning through the dirty windows, highlighting motes of dust.

"You know as much as I do," Kafka said, drinking tea from a cardboard cup with both hands, as if warming them. "Because I know nothing about them."

Maggie wanted to believe him. "We'll circle back to that."

The bruises on Kafka's face were starting to yellow at the edges and the puffiness was subsiding. The cuts on one side of his lower lip had scabbed over, turning thick and dark. He was fresh from the Giga shower, hair still wet and combed, and dressed in new khakis, deck shoes, and a white shirt, the cuffs rolled up a turn. He hadn't shaved, no doubt due to the beating his face had received. Maggie saw a hint of definition returning to his chiseled features.

The two of them faced each other at the folding table.

Maggie sat back, crossing one leg over the other. She was feeling refreshed from a Giga shower herself, wearing a pair of stovepipe jeans, a white cotton T-shirt, and a turquoise V-neck sweater against the cold. Helga had loaned her a pair of smart tan loafers. A sack full of empty food containers sat off to one side, leaving a suggestion of onions and barbecued lamb hanging in the air. John Rae stretched out in a chair, tipped back on two legs against a wall mottled with peeling green paint that was more mold then paint. Catnapping and keeping guard.

Maggie tapped Dara's cell phone, scrolling through the old texts between Dara and Kafka. She'd been through them many times.

"Why were you late for that first meeting with Dara?" she asked Kafka. "At the café?"

Kafka set his cup down, looked her directly in the eye.

"The Metro ran late," he said. "One of the doors got stuck. They took the train out of service."

"The Metro ran late," she echoed, sighing. Was that the best he could do? "What stop did you get off at?"

"Cluny—La Sorbonne, of course."

Of course. Getting defensive. "What train?"

Kafka blinked and eyed her sideways. Maybe he thought she was going to treat him with kid gloves.

"Line Ten," he said.

"Line Ten." Maggie noticed John Rae, his eyes open now, looking their way, listening. "What stop did you originally get on at?"

Kafka swallowed. "Odeon."

"One stop away." She gave him a questioning frown. "Why didn't you walk?"

There was a pause before Kafka responded. "I didn't know it was only one stop."

"You didn't *know*?" she said. "You didn't plan it out? An important trip like this? Probably the most important trip you'd ever make?"

"I mean, yes, I planned it out, but I thought I was running late, so I took Line Ten to La Sorbonne at the very last moment. I didn't want to be late."

"Where did you get on the Metro at Odeon? From the street? Which entrance did you use?"

"I took the train," he said, looking her in the eye. "Light rail. The RER."

"Which one?"

"Line Four."

"Line Four. Line Four from where?"

Kafka's nostril's flared. "Gare du Nord. The train terminal."

"Ah. So you took the train into Paris that afternoon?"

"Yes."

"From where?"

"Marseille."

"Wow." She shook her head. "Wow."

"What does this mean? *Wow?*"

"It means you were playing it very fine, especially considering that Dara and you had an important meeting. I mean, here you were, about to meet the woman you'd been flirting with for months, a woman who was going to get you and your parents out of Iraq. Personally, I would've been there an hour early. But not you."

Kafka blushed, most likely embarrassed at the implication that he had been snared romantically. Nothing to be proud of, especially for a Middle Eastern man.

Maggie lowered her eyes at him. "Did you really think I was just going to let the fact that you missed the appointment slide by?"

"I don't know who sent the suicide bombers," he said. "Someone found out. I don't know who. Someone." He ran his fingers through his hair. "Why won't you believe me?"

"I have to make sure," Maggie said. "We took a huge risk getting you out of the clutches of SDAT. For all I know, you set us up. You sent those suicide bombers."

"Why would I do that?" he said, his eyes darting around. "Jeopardize someone—someone I had feelings for?"

Maggie picked up a pencil, tapped the eraser end on a yellow pad. "For all I know you're still a jihadist."

Now it was his turn to shake his head. "I have nothing further to say."

"Well, that's certainly not going to work," Maggie said.

He sat back again and she saw him take a deep breath, compose himself. "I didn't even know you were going to be there."

"It was going to be a surprise."

"Well, it looks like we all got a surprise, didn't we?"

There was a pause. The laptop fan whirred.

"I have conditions," he said.

"No conditions," she said. "Not yet. We rescued you from a dire situation. That means it's your turn to show good faith. Give us something."

"Conditions," he said, pressing his fingertip down into the table. "In writing."

She leaned over to the computer microphone. "Interview one is over." She clicked *Sleep*, stood up. She looked at Kafka, frowning, then she nodded at John Rae, letting him know she wanted to talk with him in private and that she would be right back. She exited the room, found Dieter sleeping in a chair. She tapped him on the shoulder. His eyes opened slowly, and he looked up, not surprised, but awake and ready.

"Can you please go in and relieve John Rae?" she said. "Watch our guest?"

"Of course." Dieter got up, straightened his ribbed motor racing jacket, went into the office. John Rae came out not long afterwards.

"What do you think, JR?" she asked.

"You were too nice to him to begin with. Miss Hostess—nurse, shower, tea. Kosher food. Now he has high expectations. *Conditions*," he added, mimicking Kafka's voice.

"What would you like me to do? Hit him with a phone book?"

John Rae shrugged. "He's a terrorist. Or as good as. You can't be sure he didn't organize that attack."

"I don't think he would have arranged to meet Dara again if that was the case."

"Unless he's got balls of steel."

"I don't feel it."

"He could still be playing us."

"I've been through Dara's texts a hundred times. Her notes. She got Kafka to fall for her."

"Maybe," John Rae said, frowning, "but he was more than ready to shoot her. *You*."

"Because Jihad Nation have his parents."

"How bad do you want him to work with you? *Soon?*"

"What are you suggesting? Waterboard him? Pull his fingernails out?"

"Maggie, how much time do we have? We can't sit around here all week eating kebabs."

She took a deep breath. There were things she wasn't prepared to do. Torturing a suspect was one. "I want to give him a couple hours to stew in his own juice. While I check out his Metro story."

"Fair enough. But SDAT might be creating one unholy

stink with Langley right about now. The Agency might even decide to hand him back if you don't pull a rabbit out of your hat soon."

"Or maybe SDAT is too embarrassed to talk about how they got caught with their pants down."

"Oh, Bellard's embarrassed all right. But he still wants his ball back. It's a nice one."

Maggie went outside, walked along the River Spree, savoring the morning breeze, thinking about what it must have looked like long before people ever came along, screwed it all up. Thinking about something else. Trying to. To clear her head.

She ended up thinking about Sebi. Sebi.

She called Ed. He had been seriously sidelined. She needed to mend fences. Pull him back in. And build up expectations in case this op was taken up a notch.

They chatted about the 49ers and their dismal season before she brought up Abraqa. She could tell Ed was happy to be back in the loop.

"Ed," she said, as their conversation wound down. "I'm wondering if you can expedite a check on some Paris Metro stats that happened around the time of the café shooting? Line Ten..."

∽

"Let's talk about Abraqa Darknet," Maggie said.

Kafka set his cup down. "First, what am I, exactly? A prisoner?"

"You're a lot freer than you were twenty-four hours ago."

"Because you try to soften me up with a shower and tea? Adana kebabs?" He smirked.

That annoyed her.

"Don't forget the nurse," she said. "The pain pills that stopped you whimpering like a little boy? SDAT weren't taking care of you. You could be in a damn coma by now."

He scowled.

"Dara died because of you," Maggie said. "*You.* So did four other French citizens. So don't push your luck. I'm *not* in the mood."

He raised his hands, shrugged at the gloomy surroundings. "This is your idea of luck?"

"Well, it's about the best you're going to get. And you should be thankful. Thankful SDAT don't have you in some cozy room at *La Ferme,* slapping you around. So let's stop playing games."

"What game am I playing, exactly? Kindly educate me."

"The one where you're trying to get the very best deal. I get that. Just make it quick." Maggie sat back, crossed her arms. "We don't have a lot of time. Your parents don't have a lot of time, and that's what this is about. Or should be about."

He nodded. "That's given. My parents—rescued."

"We can do that."

He rubbed his face. "And then what?"

"They are relocated to the West. Here, Germany, the US, wherever. New identities. You too."

"What do I do for a living?"

"You have an education. A good technical background. It won't be a problem getting you set up. But you work for us, too, on the side. That takes priority. Always."

Her phone buzzed in her pocket. A text. She pulled it.

ED: *Kafka's Line Ten story checks out. Broken door, 4:51 PM, Friday. Train taken out of service at Cluny.*

Well, well, she thought. Kafka was telling the truth.

"What do my parents live on?" Kafka said.

She put her phone away. "They'll be given a sum to start with. An apartment. Connections for employment. Just like you will. There will be a monthly income until then, a stipend of some sort. It will be comfortable. Better than being guests of Jihad Nation."

"My parents will be provided a house in Palm Springs of my choosing."

"Palm Springs?" She smiled. "Why not just go for Beverley Hills?"

His face wrinkled in anger. "One hundred thousand dollars per year. That's what my father will receive. Two automobiles, one for each of my parents: A BMW 750 and a Mercedes 500. Complete health care."

Maggie gave a tired smirk. "You had this all figured out, didn't you? Tell me, was this before or after we saved your ass?"

"Be quiet, I'm not finished. I live in New York. Manhattan. I will receive a condo, also which I will select. An automobile. A Tesla S model."

"You sure you really want a car in Manhattan, *amigo*?"

"A sum of two million dollars to start with. And a senior position earning not less than one hundred and fifty thousand dollars per year."

She sat back, blinking in disbelief. She could see John Rae watching her, shaking his head.

"We'll take care of you," she said. "But there's a limit. You owe *us*."

He took a slurp of tea, sat back. "Those are my conditions." He crossed his arms. "I know what I'm worth. I know what Abraqa is worth. Billions," he said. "*Billions*."

Maggie nodded. "Let me tell you your options at this point: A—make ridiculous demands and risk being handed back to SDAT or B—work with us, knowing we'll get your parents out—no small feat—and then, see what else we have to offer. I guarantee it will be better than the French. Significantly."

He shook his head angrily. "I want to talk to someone who has influence. Not some woman who sends lurid texts for a living. We have a name for women like that."

Maggie leaned forward, dropping her voice. "You want influence, motherfucker? Here's *my* influence. Option C— you go back to Iraq. Right now. Present your 'conditions' to your masters. See how far you get with them. After you explain why you tried to defect in the first place. Wonder what that'll mean for your parents." She drained her tea, stood up, crumpled the cup, tossed it in the sack full of garbage by the table. It fell off, landed on the floor.

Kafka's mouth dropped in surprise.

"You have five minutes to decide," Maggie said. She picked up her jacket, threw it over her shoulder, stormed out of the room. She saw John Rae giving her a thumbs-up.

42

An hour later, Maggie sat back down opposite Kafka. A word came to mind when she looked into his bruised face. Humbled. Gray noon light showed his features to be tense and washed out at the same time.

"Well?" she said, looking at her watch. "What's it going to be?"

"You can guarantee to get my mother and father out of Iraq?"

"I can guarantee that we will do our very best," she said. "With a high probability of success." She signaled John Rae, who had been listening. He stood up, came over.

He crossed his arms. "Do you know where your parents are being held, exactly?"

"A camp about twenty kilometers southeast of Mosul. In the desert."

Maggie sat up. The location sounded familiar. "Is it near a river?"

Kafka blinked. "Yes, the Zab River runs close by."

Maggie's heart rate bumped up. "What is the nearest town?"

"Al Kuwayr."

"Are you sure?"

"I spoke to my mother after my parents were taken there. The commander put her on the phone. I'd also been following my father's cell phone. I installed LifeLine on it. I made a note of the GPS coordinates before the phone was disabled. It's the same place."

Maggie pulled the area up on her mapping application, typing in *Al Kuwayr*. There it was.

Two Yazidi women who had been ransomed back to their families had said they were taken to a camp south of Mosul, near a river, by a town. On the way back they noted the name—Al Kuwayr.

Pay dirt.

"Do you know the Jihad Nation commander who runs this camp?" she asked.

"Of course. His name is Hassan al-Hassan."

"Hassan al-Hassan?" Maggie felt a smack of euphoria and alarm mixed together. "You're sure?"

"I've spoken to him many times. One of my duties is to fund his cells."

She turned to John Rae, having difficulty curbing her excitement. "This is the same man Dara talks about in her notes. Hassan al-Hassan is also involved in the kidnapping of Yazidi woman and children and selling girls on the sex slave market."

John Rae raised his eyebrows.

Kafka said: "Hassan al-Hassan is one of the architects of the kidnappings. He was tasked by the caliph's secretary in Mosul. The caliph depends on Hassan al-Hassan to carry out many of his classified assignments now. He is highly valued."

Maggie couldn't believe her luck, if that was the right word for such a discovery.

John Rae said, "Any idea how many fighters this Hassan might have there at any given time?"

Kafka shrugged. "I would estimate any number from a handful of men to two dozen. The number fluctuates. But they would be heavily armed, regardless. Battle hardened. Bad men. Evil men."

"That helps." John Rae stroked his goatee. "Would Hassan consider ransom for your parents?"

"Not in my case." Kafka gave a cynical laugh. "They want me back."

"In that case," John Rae said, "we need a rescue team. Maybe two helicopters. It's been done enough times. But we'd have to check out the logistics first." He gave Maggie a private, knowing look that said he'd have to get Walder to authorize it. "And then we have to move quickly."

Kafka eyed Maggie. "If you can free my parents, I am prepared to help you."

"Good," Maggie said, "because you'll be going along with the rescue team."

Kafka's face turned to stone for a moment. He'd have to take the same risk his parents' rescuers did. Face a similar fate if it wasn't successful. Perhaps worse.

"Is that necessary?" he said, a trace of fear echoing in his voice.

"Call it insurance," Maggie said. They didn't want to walk into a trap. "And we'll no doubt have questions for you along the way."

He frowned. "Then I have no issue."

John Rae said to Maggie: "I'm going to ask Helga to get

some more equipment set up here. Then I'll contact Creech, schedule drone surveillance of the compound." Creech Air Force Base was outside Las Vegas, Nevada, where much of the drone activity was run. "In the meantime, you and Kafka can sync up on Abraqa."

Maggie said to Kafka, "I'm going to need a full understanding of Abraqa Darknet *before* we commit to anything."

Kafka narrowed his eyes.

"That's the price of admission," Maggie said.

"I will show you how Abraqa works," he said. "All the moving parts. But no passwords. Those I keep to myself—until I see my parents step on safe ground." Kafka pressed down on the card table with his finger. "Here."

"That may not be an option," Maggie said.

"It will have to be," Kafka said. He sat back, crossed his arms. "Otherwise you may send me back to SDAT. Or Iraq. I only go so far."

Maggie took a breath. Maybe Kafka would play games when the time came but she'd worry about that when it happened. She understood his need to keep one last piece back until everything was taken care of.

"I'll need to see a transaction or two in flight," she said. "My superiors aren't going to authorize a rescue mission until they see some kind of confirmation that what you have is what we want."

There was a pause.

"That will not be a problem," Kafka said.

"Then we have an agreement."

43

"Let me make sure I have this all down," Maggie said, reviewing the notes she had typed into her laptop. "Then we can move onto the financial institutions themselves."

Night had fallen, and construction lamps were set up on stands around the room. Kafka's bruises faded in the harsh glare.

For Maggie's part, she was doing her best to contain herself. She was one step closer to turning off one of Jihad Nation's black money spigots. As it stopped, the bloodbath of innocent people dying would also slow, if not end.

John Rae and Dieter were busy at a second table that Helga had set up, John Rae typing with two fingers on a laptop, interacting with pilots and officers of the US Air Force at Creech Air Force Base outside Las Vegas, Nevada.

Maggie and Kafka had reviewed Abraqa Darknet for several hours.

It was actually quite simple and that was the beauty of it. As Maggie suspected, there was Bitcoin tumbling, which involved breaking the blockchain between donors and recipients, keeping everything private and removing any direct relationship with each other. A Saudi Arabian banker, for example, who wanted to fund Jihad Nation, didn't know where his donation was going—technically. And it couldn't be proved legally. Hidden Bitcoin wallets were the norm in this digital shell game. In Abraqa's case several levels of indirection were used, rather than just the one that most Darknet online retailers of illicit goods made use of. All was accessed with a Tor browser and hidden .onion sites for stealth networking. It was technology anyone with some basic hacking skills and a devious mind could figure out.

Maggie knew an entire online world existed a few clicks away, where one could buy drugs or kiddie porn, even put out contracts for executions for one's enemies and then select the highest bidder. All protected with tools anyone with a GitHub account could download. There were even the equivalent of review sites for purchases made on the Darknet, keeping vendors honest at the risk of earning criticism from buyers. Buying your dope online was now safer than going down to some forbidding neighborhood where anything could happen.

The only hole in Abraqa, as she saw it, was that only one person—Kafka—ran it with select manual processes. That was because he had designed it that way. Jihad Nation had recruited Kafka for his technical skills. They hired engineers worldwide for many needs—maintaining oil refineries, power grids, everything a modern society needed. And in Abraqa's case, Kafka seized the opportunity to make himself indispensable, creating a unique niche, because Jihad Nation didn't know any better at the time and trusted him. He had been radicalized at university and impressed the caliph's secretary in Mosul, who bestowed tremendous responsibility upon him early. He was well compensated for his efforts—a new SUV, rent paid on a modern apartment in Mosul, a generous allowance for unlimited electronic goodies and a salary of seven hundred euros per month, a healthy wage indeed for that part of the world. A lowly jihadi fighter made a hundred—the average monthly wage of a typical Iraqi, if a job could even be found. Kafka also received unlimited health care for himself and his family. His mother's heart condition had entitled her to be sent to one of the best hospitals in Dubai, all paid for by Jihadi Nation. If they valued you, they took care of you. Until they stopped trusting you.

All Kafka had to do was manage the servers he had set up, handle electronic banking, update and run websites, upload the odd beheading video to YouTube.

Once in a while a little boy would ring Kafka's doorbell in Mosul and hand him a note—very low tech—and Kafka would be required to run an errand. This might involve a visit to some remote spot in the desert where Kafka might pay someone, take care of some administrative task, set up a device or server.

One day he was provided with video equipment and told to tape a mass execution of prisoners. He balked but they had no one else. This was part of his deepening commitment.

He remembered standing back with the video camera, catching the bodies falling into the ditch like dominoes. He did this primarily to distance himself from the action but the visual effect was one the caliph's secretary liked, calling Kafka up specifically to compliment him on his technique. Kafka had an eye others didn't.

When he hung up, Kafka was sick to his stomach.

What had he become?

Then came the beheading videos. The first one made

him vomit uncontrollably into the dirt after the man's head was slowly hacked off, the sound of the blade against bone and gristle turning his stomach more than the visual, earning laughs from the jihadis and a frown from Hassan al-Hassan, who was overseeing the executions. It was all Kafka could do not to stop filming as the camera shook in his hands.

It was then that he realized he was not one of them. Never would be.

He wondered if Hassan al-Hassan was thinking the very same of him as he watched Kafka wipe his forehead with a handkerchief.

But he edited the tape down, added the necessary captions to make the video worthy of a man's life. The caliph's secretary was pleased with his efforts.

"What I don't understand," Maggie said. "Is how so many hostages seem to be almost willing to be executed in those videos. They go to their deaths like sheep, simply let it happen."

"There's a method to the madness," Kafka said. "Most of the time they aren't executed. Often, it's all staged. Yes, they're held prisoner but told the video is just an act for the cameras. And frequently it is. So they play along, read the scripts they're given. But every so often . . ."

A shiver went down Maggie's spine. "It's the real thing."

"Yes." Kafka took a gulp of tea. "It makes prisoners easier to deal with if they think it's all a fake. Until, one day, it isn't."

"Maggie," John Rae said from across the room where he and Dieter had been working with Creech at a table in the glow of a lamp. "I think we've found your town."

Maggie got up and stood behind John Rae and Dieter at a laptop. On a USAF console a black landscape was highlighted with lights and thermal images of a small town by a river.

"There," John Rae said, pointing. "It's nine PM there, same as here, but the FLIR camera is picking it up." FLIR was Forward Looking Infrared Radiometer—night vision.

"That's Al Kuwayr," Maggie said, looking at the blocks of the town scroll by. A shimmering silver band came into view in the upper right corner of the screen. "And there's the river Zab."

"There's Highway 80." Dieter pointed at a silver asphalt strip left of the town.

"US Forces call it the Highway of Death," John Rae said. "IEDs galore."

"Can you turn up the volume?" Maggie said.

Dieter turned up the sound. A steady stream of military chatter crackled from Las Vegas Creech over the computer speaker.

"Coordinates confirm Al Kuwayr," one of the Creech techs said.

"Let's take a closer look, guys," John Rae said to the techs.

Not long afterwards they were looking down at a man carrying a bundle over his shoulder, walking down a dirt road in a sparsely housed section of town. His white silhouette stood out against the shining gray of the ground. Off to one side a vehicle moved down a street, floating like a ghost.

"Nothing out of the ordinary," John Rae said.

Maggie said, "Some of the women who got out said they thought the encampment was east of the town, south of the river."

Kafka got up from his chair, came over. "She's correct."

"Can you scope the terrain south of the river, guys, east of that town?" John Rae asked the Creech team.

The drone's camera nosed along the river, the water running almost white-gray, heading south.

They spent a fair amount of time searching a blackened area.

"What's that?" Maggie said. Shadowy squared shapes were etched out of darkness.

"Some sort of structure," John Rae said. "Struc*tures*." A rectangular wall the size of a sports field bordered everything.

"The compound has a wall around it," John Rae said.

"It does," Kafka said.

Maggie asked the techs, "Do you guys have Snoopy enabled?"

"Sure do, ma'am."

"Can you give that main building the once-over?"

"They might pick us up," the tech said. "If they've got their ears on."

"I think it's worth a quick scan anyway," she said, getting a nod of approval from John Rae.

A minute later one of the techs spoke. "Snoopy just picked up a cell phone in that main building, searching for Wi-Fi. Some dumb bunny left his phone on after lights out."

Then a tiny strip of light appeared in an area of blackness. "And *that*?" she said, glancing at John Rae.

"Some blip?" he said. "Residual heat?"

"There it is again." Maggie pointed at a slip of light, which was now fading. "What the hell *is* that?"

One of the Creech techs said, "Could be a door or window letting light through."

"They're keeping the windows blacked out," Maggie said.

"Can you take her down some more, guys?" John Rae said.

A few minutes later, they were low over the compound.

"A pickup truck," one of the Creech techs said. "Parked against that compound wall, covered up with netting and camouflage. One or two more in that open garage structure there. You can just see the tailgate on one, sticking out."

Maggie strained her eyes.

"Take it down some more," John Rae said.

"Is that roof starting to glimmer?" Maggie said. "On the main building. Or do I need glasses?"

"Some kind of activity," one of the techs said. "Cooking. Electronics. Or body heat."

"Let's take a look at that one truck," John Rae said. "The one by the wall."

They did. Its hood glowed ever-so-faintly.

"It's been driven in the last few hours," one of the techs said. "Still warm."

"There!" another tech said. He zeroed the camera on a small figure, white with heat, walking from the covered garage across the dirt courtyard to the largest building. The telltale point of a rifle barely showed. "He's packing."

A belt of light in front of the main building flashed, then went dark again.

"He just went inside that building. That was the door opening and closing."

"Doing a patrol," John Rae said. "Maybe a perimeter check."

"Maybe he's a farmer, guys," Dieter said. "They can be armed, too."

"With his windows blacked out?" John Rae said. "Multiple vehicles stashed? Camouflage?"

"If it was a farm," one of the Creech techs said, "the place would be lit up. They don't want to get hit by drones so they let it all hang out."

"I think we found your compound, Maggie," John Rae said.

A jolt of exhilaration lifted Maggie's spirits. "Sunrise at 6:51," she said. "We'll be able to see more then." She turned to Kafka. "In the meantime, you can show me who funds Abraqa."

~

"So the money is funneled primarily through Wahhabi mosques," Maggie said. "Most of it from anonymous donations."

They had covered the technical aspects of Abraqa. Now it was time for the parties involved. Maggie knew the mosques in question were used worldwide to fund terrorist activities.

Kafka sipped tea from a paper cup. The construction lights cast a shadow over his face.

"And who are these anonymous donors?" Maggie asked.

"The great majority are Saudis," Kafka said. "Donations are channeled through about twenty charities and foundations. These institutions in turn give money to the Wahhabi mosques who distribute cash to local fighters and resources."

"Using hawala?" she said.

"Often." Hawala was an ancient Arab form of money brokering, handled primarily through word of mouth. No paperwork. If one needed to send a thousand dollars from New York to one's brother-in-law in Pakistan, a local broker would contact an agent there. The brother-in-law would be given a password with which he would go to his local contact, who might be a simple merchant in a market, and be given the cash. Everything happened informally. The brokers earned a small fee for their efforts but the primary reason for hawala was to provide a network free from scrutiny. People dealt solely in cash. Hawala stretched worldwide and was time-honored.

"I'll need the names of those charities and foundations."

Kafka gave Maggie a squint. "When my parents are freed."

Maggie returned a stare. "We've located the camp. But we're not going to be able to get boots on the ground unless I can offer the higher-ups some proof that Abraqa works as advertised."

Kafka eyed her with wariness.

"If anybody's going to free your parents," she said, "it's us. You're going to have to trust me—just like I have to trust you."

Kafka looked at the wall behind her, as if coming to some decision. "Islami Bank of Saudi Arabia, Sina Trust, Sangram Foundation, Coral Trust, International Aid to Children, Center for Peace, University of Bahrain . . ." He looked at her. "There are nineteen in all, to keep the money diversified."

"I'll need them all, account numbers, contact information of the key people, and most importantly, names of the donors."

Kafka returned an impassive look. "All in good time."

"That time is now," Maggie said. "*Now*."

Kafka sighed. "I need to get to Google Docs."

So all of this information was kept in the cloud. Hidden in plain sight. Along with recipes for guacamole and kids' homework. And hundreds of millions of other documents. Maggie turned her laptop around so that Kafka could access it.

Kafka gave Maggie one last hesitant look before he made

an entry, downloaded a spreadsheet. He turned the computer back around. By now John Rae was standing behind Maggie, arms folded over his chest, watching.

Maggie perused the spreadsheet. "Some of these donors are allies to the United States," she said. One or two had close ties to Washington. One she thought she recognized as a contributor to the Worthington Group—the lobbyists her father had mentioned—the same group that supported Senator Brahms. Maggie shook her head in disgust.

"Even I recognize one or two of those names," John Rae said.

Kafka gave a cynical smile. "There are allies and then there are allies."

"When do these donations become anonymous?" Maggie asked.

"These foundations use the Darknet accounts I set up for them," Kafka said. "There are two levels of folders. One public. One private. Donations are made on the public tier. All above board."

"And you transfer funds through the Darknet to the private folder, using the foundation's private key. The connection to the donor disappears."

"The multiple Bitcoin wallets I mentioned enforce that."

"I still need more," she said.

Kafka shook his head. "No passwords until I see my mother and father, safe and sound."

"I'm not asking for passwords yet," she said. "I need you to kick off one transaction, one money transfer, so we can see everything from point A to point B."

"No," he said. "No."

"Look," Maggie said. "You've given us an overview but I need to see this at work."

Kafka sighed. "And then you'll be satisfied?"

"I'll tell you when I see it."

Kafka rubbed his face. Then he reached over, pulled the laptop toward him. He opened a Tor browser, anonymous, blinked in thought for a moment and typed an address into the address bar.

He was presented with a directory structure. The parent directory was named Abraqa Foundation.

Maggie got up, stood next to him.

"I drill down." He made an entry.

He was presented with nineteen subdirectories. Each one corresponded to one of the nineteen financial entities he had described.

"That one," Maggie said, pointing to one at random. "'Helping others—Friends of Islam'."

"Fine." Kafka navigated down to that folder, which contained lists of deposits and transfers.

"The third one," she said.

He selected the file and was presented with a transfer of 1000 Bitcoin, a deposit from a prominent Saudi Arabian oilman.

"About four hundred thousand dollars," Maggie said. "A charitable contribution."

"Exactly." Then he went back to the parent directory of the institution, selected *Transfers*, entered *Create new*, filled one out, hit *enter*.

He was then taken to another portal where two-stage authentication required him to enter a password. "Turn your heads," he said to Maggie and John Rae.

John Rae gave her a quizzical look. She returned with a short nod, as if to say, *It's fine*.

They turned their heads while Kafka made an entry. Maggie counted ten keystrokes.

"It's done."

They turned back.

"Unless I receive specific instructions, I simply go through the various mosques periodically in a round-robin fashion. As a rule I divide the donations twice a month by twenty and transfer a roughly equal amount to each mosque. They take it from there."

"Why not automate the process?"

"Tempting," Kafka said, "but then I lose control." He gave a sly smile. "It would mean embedding passwords in a program or on a server somewhere."

Kafka wouldn't want that. Jihad Nation would be able to replace him more easily. "Makes sense." As much as any of this made sense. "Let's see it at work."

"I usually start with the entity that has been waiting the longest." He sorted the transfers by date, oldest first. He then created a transfer to a mosque in Mosul, for fifty Bitcoin. He hit *enter* and it went through, displaying a status of *Pending*.

Then he logged off.

"And that," he said, "is that."

"How does the mosque retrieve their money?"

"They have banks. There are many. It's technically not against the law in Iraq to process money in this way. The contact at the bank converts the money from Bitcoin."

"What Bitcoin exchange do you use?"

"BitOasis." The Middle East's multi-signature leading exchange.

"How do you receive your instructions if a specific payment is required?"

"A clandestine mail server."

"I need to know about that too."

"And you shall—as soon as I am hugging my mother."

Everything hung on rescuing his parents. The buzz of

the lamps seemed to amplify that reality. "How much money do you process?"

Kafka frowned in thought. "Last year—two million, seven hundred and fifty thousand Bitcoin."

"Just over a billion dollars."

"Give or take a few million."

All that money directed at hatred and killing. Trafficking young women. Children. Investing in misery. Maggie looked at John Rae. "Well? Got enough to convince our people?"

"Are you kidding?" John Rae said. "When top brass hears about this, they're going to be salivating."

"I need a few minutes alone with Kafka," she said.

John Rae narrowed his gaze, as if to say, *Are you sure?*

She confirmed with a slight nod.

John Rae spoke to Dieter. "Come on, old man."

They left the empty old office, leaving Maggie and Kafka on their own, amidst the buzzing of the lamps.

44

Maggie and Kafka sat alone in the abandoned office, the chill of night taking hold.

Maggie brought up the subject that had been silently plaguing her. "Who knew about you meeting Dara that day at Café de la Nouvelle?"

Kafka grimaced into the darkness past her shoulder.

"If you have any idea who set up that suicide attack," she said, "you need to tell me. Otherwise all our lives are at risk. Your parents too. And possibly the lives of many others. "

"I told my parents," he said, looking down. "I told them that I'd met a woman, that she wasn't Muslim. But they would never betray me."

Was that so? "And how did they respond?"

Kafka looked up, eyes glistening. "Both of them accepted it. My father is—was—a university lecturer. Political science. My mother has a degree from the London School of Economics. Just because they're Muslim doesn't mean they're jihadists."

No, Maggie thought, it was their son who had

succumbed to radical Islam, for whatever reason. "Did your superiors know you were planning to meet Dara?"

He gave a wry frown. "Of course not."

"What was the excuse you used to come to Paris?"

"I told the caliph's secretary I had an appointment with a doctor. Jihad Nation is generous with benefits in that regard, as I have said. Higher ranking people come to Europe frequently, and doctor visits are often the reason."

"And did you actually make an appointment with a doctor?"

"Oh, yes. With the ENP, The École des Neurosciences de Paris. I said I was complaining of dizzy spells. Which happened to be true. In my case, it was stress. I had gotten myself into a situation I didn't know how to escape. The beheadings I was forced to videotape brought that to bear. But I laid the groundwork by describing conditions of Ménière's Disease to my doctor in Mosul. He wrote a recommendation. I did my best to justify my trip, in case anyone was watching."

"Do you have to clear such plans with the caliph's secretary?"

"Oh yes. They don't tolerate you wandering off on your own—especially if you're leaving the country."

"Well, it seems you were thorough, but someone got wise." And Kafka was still able to access the Abraqa network, thanks to his cornering the responsibility. It was one of the reasons Maggie had wanted to see the operation in action—to make sure he was still in control.

"I'm the one who set up Abraqa. I'm the one who runs it. As you can see for yourself, it's not complicated. But to the uninitiated, it's smoke and mirrors. For the time being, Jihad Nation has to let me live."

For the time being. "How much time?"

He shrugged. "In my part of the world, we have a different philosophy about these things. Life for us is much more tenuous. In my world, you could be gone"—he snapped his fingers—"like that. Nothing is certain. Unlike the United States."

She smiled. "We only *think* our future is certain."

"Tell me which is better—the land of freedom and prosperity for all, an illusion created by your annoyingly positive outlook that actually applies to very few of your citizens? Or knowing that no government can be trusted? No business? No institution?"

"Is that why you were radicalized?" she said.

"One doesn't have to look far to see the injustices our people have suffered. Much because of your government's policies. One only has to open one's eyes. But one needs faith to survive. Something sorely lacking on your side of the globe. Allah provides that. What do you have? Disneyland?"

"I prefer a faith that includes women. It has nothing to do with Disneyland. But I'm curious. You grew up in a Muslim home."

"Oh, yes. A comfortable, upper-middle-class home. A soft life. An easy life, bending the rules when it suited us, adopting your culture. While most of my people had nothing, couldn't read or write. Thanks to the oppression of the United States."

How they loved to blame the US for their problems. "Seems to me you're subject to the oppression of Jihad Nation right now."

"You Americans gave us no choice."

"Do you honestly believe that? Saddam's ex-generals run Jihad Nation—not the US."

"That's an argument that could fill a hundred books. And still we would not come to the same opinion."

"Perhaps."

"What are your religious beliefs, Maggie?"

She shook her head.

"You must have something. You have to believe in something."

Her mother had believed in Indian folklore that had served her people for a thousand years but she died poor and brokenhearted. Her father . . . she didn't know what her father believed—if anything. Maggie had her code. There was right and there was wrong. You didn't need a book to tell you which one to follow. And talking about it made no difference. You just did it.

"That's my business," she said.

"Disneyland?"

"Fundamental Islam or Disneyland," she said, giving a wry smile. "Both fantasies if you ask me. But one is far more dangerous. One requires blind faith. Last time I checked Mickey Mouse wasn't beheading people."

"The Koran has much to offer."

"Seventy-two virgins? For holy jihad?"

"I'm not saying I agree with *that*. I understand what it means, though—to struggle. That's the pure meaning of the word 'jihad'."

"But Dara made you see an alternative."

He blinked. "Dara opened my eyes."

Even though he was prepared to kill her. "How?"

"You wouldn't understand." He shook his head disdainfully. An Arab man would not discuss matters of the heart, especially with a woman. But the irony of it was that Kafka barely knew Dara. He saw what he wanted to see. And Dara knew that. Pictures and flirtatious chat did the work. Kafka's heart, such as it was, had betrayed him.

"What I need to know," Maggie said, "is whether you're really willing to go through with this. Willing to betray Jihad Nation, the people you once believed in."

"All I want is to see my parents safe. I'll take whatever consequences come with that."

"Even your own death?"

He looked away, then back. "Even that."

Such courage was possible—in the abstract. But when one was put to the screws—having water poured up one's nose, fingernails pulled out—it was a different matter. Everything Maggie had seen so far, however, seemed to imply Kafka was willing to go through with it. Then again, her precious instinct, that elusive characteristic she valued so highly, had failed her before.

"Good enough," she said. She got up from the table, went to the door.

She found John Rae and Dieter talking.

"Let's go for a walk," she said to John Rae.

45

Moonlight cast harsh shadows around the abandoned train station near the safe house as Maggie and John Rae tramped through the skeleton of industry. The quiet rush of the Spree river was audible in the distance. Beyond that the indistinct sounds of a city at night reminded Maggie of where they were.

"The sixty-four thousand dollar question," John Rae said, "is do we trust him?" His hands were jammed in the pockets of his pigskin jacket as Maggie walked alongside. Cool night air hinted at coming winter, helping her focus her thoughts.

"It's too risky for Kafka to give us everything at once." She could see her breath as they walked. "The moment he turns over Abraqa, his parents are compromised. He can't afford to let that happen until they're safe and sound."

"If they're still alive."

She couldn't disagree. "He was telling the truth about the Metro being late. That means Jihad Nation were probably planning to blow him up too. He has no love for them. I don't think he ever did. He was easily lured away by Dara."

"He was still ready to kill her."

"Circumstances changed. They took his parents. And besides, he knows what happens if he doesn't deliver Abraqa to us. *We'll* have his parents as collateral."

John Rae kicked a stone out of the way. "They're a lot safer with us than Jihad Nation, regardless. That might be all he wants."

"It would be Guantanamo Bay for him and a bleak future for his folks. He could be water-boarded until he talks." She took a breath, exhaled vapor. "He knows that."

"I still don't like those suicide bombers," John Rae said.

They stopped, looked at each other in the moonlight, both with hands in their jackets.

"Join the club," she said, "but that's the only wild card I see. We have to trust him at some point. And we have to do it soon."

"You know what this means if it's a fail, Maggie? If Kafka's parents aren't there? If they're dead? If something goes wrong? Do you know what it means for your career at the Agency?"

Did she? She'd be relegated to that basement room on Golden Gate Avenue, sorting data cards no one cared about.

"Well," she said, "I've always wanted to learn how to play the tuba."

"I'm going to call Walder."

"Thanks for the vote of confidence," she said quietly, watching her words turn to fog.

He gave her a quick, intimate smile. Was he thinking about the other night? "You bet."

Maggie felt a blend of relief and tension take hold. She was getting what she wanted. "I'm not going to feel good until his parents are safe."

"But you'll be sitting in San Francisco while that happens, drinking your nonfat latte."

"No," Maggie said, "don't even bother. I'm coming with you. This is *my* op."

"Maggie, your job is done for now. Until we get back with his folks. Then you can take down Abraqa."

"I speak decent Arabic—unlike you. I look the part—unlike you. I even have a Jihad Nation passport—unlike you. So tell me again why I'm not suited."

John Rae stood with his legs apart. "Because I'm not going to let you go down there."

"You're being protective. Sweet. But misguided."

"I don't care."

"Kafka is going. I'm going, too, keep an eye on our *asset*."

"He's the tall Arab guy with the bruises face, right? I can watch him."

She brushed her hair back with her fingers. "In that case, I'm going to have to dig up that 'I don't see how I can honestly work on this op anymore' card."

John Rae shook his head. "Not again."

"A woman's prerogative," she said. "You said so yourself."

John Rae took a deep breath. Twin streams blew out of his nostrils. "I should've known that would come back to bite me in the ass. I guess that's all there is to it, then."

"I like a man who knows when he's beat."

"It's not just me you got to beat. Try Walder, especially if Ed throws a conniption. You're not on Walder's team. Yet. And even though this is the new millennium and all, sending a woman into harm's way when they don't need to just goes against the grain."

"Even though a woman already gave her life for this."

"Touché," he said. He pulled a hand from his jacket, made a fist.

She did the same.
They touched.

~

"It's a go," John Rae said. "Walder gave it the thumbs-up."

He was standing at the foldout table in the warehouse. Helga was packing away the computer they had used for the Creech drone session, and the rest of the gear. Maggie was helping her. Echoes bounced off the high ceilings as the lamps buzzed.

It seemed a bit twisted to be excited. But that's what Maggie was.

"So what's next?" she asked John Rae.

"Pack your bags," he said. "We need to move fast."

46

İncirlik Air Base, Turkey

A burnt orange sun slipped into the Mediterranean, setting fire to swirling particles of fine airborne dust as Maggie and the others waited on the tarmac to board the MH-60G Pave Hawk helicopter. With its long refueling nozzle poking out front, the chopper lingered in the falling shadows like a giant metallic wasp, ready to do battle. Waves of heat shimmered off the runway.

This was it. No going back. Maggie's temples pulsed with anticipation.

Maggie, John Rae, Kafka, Bad Allah—all four decked out in Arab attire, John Rae and Bad in full black Jihad Nation gear, weapons slung over their shoulders, Maggie in a custom blue abaya, which she wore over a T-shirt covering her bra buddy and replacement pistol, and her yoga pants. Kafka wore a simple beige linen tunic over his khaki trousers.

Two pilots, one flight engineer, one gunner.

Three heavily armed PJs—Pararescuemen, including one woman, of the Air Force Special Operations Command 66th Rescue Squadron—dressed in khaki desert fatigues. Tan boots, helmets with cameras mounted on top, their bodies crisscrossed with harness belts loaded with ammo and grenades. A trio of M4A1 carbines, replete with night vision sights, stood in a short swivel stack nearby.

With the internal auxiliary fuel tanks inside the Pave Hawk, they had just enough room on the return flight for Akram and Fadila Tijani, Kafka's parents.

Provided everybody came back, of course. And that Kafka's parents were indeed still guests of Hassan al-Hassan. Everything pointed to it but they hadn't been positively ID'ed by Creech drones as being at the Bunny Ranch. Langley's code name for the Jihad Nation encampment had made Maggie shake her head when she first heard it.

When the sun fell they would take off, fly east along the Syrian border, refueling mid-air, and then into Iraq. Make the three-hour trip to the Bunny Ranch where, under the cover of darkness, they would find a way into the camp, locate Kafka's parents, and then ...

Maggie's phone buzzed. She reached through the opening in her abaya robe, pulled the phone, hoping it might be Ed returning her call. Their last call had been more than tense, Ed unhappy with the fact that Maggie was once again heading off on an operation managed by the clandestine Directorate of Operations.

"Hey, Maggs," he said and she could hear him smoking, his voice thick. It was early morning in San Francisco. "You guys still on the ground?"

"Just about to take off."

"Just wanted to say good luck. Needless to say, I'll be watching everything."

She wondered if he was thinking what she was thinking.

"You still wondering about those two uninvited guests who showed up?" she said, meaning the suicide bombers in Paris.

"Oh, only every five minutes or so."

"We need to get to the bottom of that," she said.

"One thing at a time."

"I like to worry."

"But that won't affect today," he said. "Today is going to be a non-event."

The sun was losing the battle against night. The Pave Hawk started up. The flight crew gathered around the chopper door as the twin turbo shaft engines fired up with a high-pitched whine. The rotor blades were not engaged yet.

Maggie stepped away, turned her back on the noise, one finger in her free ear, and shouted, "Ed, I don't want to leave Forensic. Hopefully this op will help keep it afloat. But I've got to see this thing through."

She heard him take another deadly drag on his smoke. "I know," he muttered.

"I like working with you. I want you to know that."

"Same here," he said. "Take care of yourself, Maggs. I've got money on you."

"Ciao."

After all the pushing she had done, Abraqa had to pay off.

She turned back to the copter.

Heading into the crucible. The Pararescuemen had picked up their carbines and were climbing on board.

47

Three hours later they saw Mosul in the distance, the city lighting up the night. The constant punishing of the air by the rotor blades was second nature to their ears now.

They cut a wide swath around Mosul, staying hidden in darkness, and met up with Highway 80—the Highway of Death—following it but staying well away from the road.

Maggie sat up behind the pilots with the flight engineer, between the gunner's windows. The gunner stood at the ready, manning one of the M134 Miniguns. There were two of the six-barrel, electrically operated Gatling style machine guns, one either side of the craft. In front of the gunner the pilot managed the FLIR stick, while the copilot scanned the infrared readout of the terrain.

Behind Maggie, to her right, the cabin doors were open and two of the Pararescuemen sat with their legs hanging out, the female PJ, whose name was Sergeant Terri Kaminski, in her battle helmet, grinning as if she were on a hayride.

Maggie spotted a grouping of haphazard lights on the

ground fast approaching. A small town. Her heart beat faster.

"That's Al Kuwayr," she shouted to John Rae, sitting on one of the canvas jump seats behind her, next to Kafka.

"That's the place," John Rae shouted over the rush of the chill air, peering between Sergeant Kaminski and a stocky PJ cradling his carbine.

The village passed by quickly. They followed the Zab river, glowing with reflected moonlight.

John Rae got up from his jump seat, leaning forward, hand steadying him. Maggie was still getting used to seeing John Rae dressed in black jihadi fighter gear. She had seen quite a few sides of him on this op. "Once we pass a small tributary feeding into the Zab, we're getting close," he said. "About five kliks from the Bunny Ranch. That's where we set down."

They needed to land a safe distance from the compound where the engines wouldn't be overheard. Maggie, Bad Allah and John Rae would make the rest of the way on foot; the PJs would stay behind with the chopper, awaiting instructions.

"There it is," the copilot shouted, pointing at a thin gully on the black and gray translucent screen, winding its way to the Zab river.

The pilot trimmed the stick back, cutting the airspeed down to zero, dropping the craft vertically toward open terrain. The activity on the Stability Augmentations System lit up the five screens in the front of the copter like a light show as the pitch of the engine fell.

They landed on the ground with a soft bump. The copilot turned to the pilot. "You owe me five bucks, dude."

"Oh, come on," the pilot said, "that landing was sweet."

"For government work maybe," the copilot said. "I distinctly felt it."

"We all know about your sensitive ass."

The engine was shut off, bringing relief to their ears. And soon they were outside, in the cold night air descending after a warm day, listening to crickets in the distance. It wasn't yet midnight.

Maggie pulled her abaya off as John Rae and Bad Allah checked their weapons—GWA drum-fed full auto combat shotguns, short and stocky with angular magazines jutting out, holding thirty-two 12 gauge shells each. Each gun had a boxy silencer at the end of the barrel. She rolled up the abaya, which she had been wearing to combat the cold flight, stuffed it in her daypack, and got out her Rino phone. Now she wore just her yoga pants, her black Nike sneakers, a roomy white long-sleeved T-shirt over her bra buddy containing the Sig Sauer nestled underneath. She was chill but that would change once she got moving.

Kafka was the last to climb out of the helicopter. In the moonlight his face was tense, still dappled with bruises, even in the semi-darkness. He blinked nervously.

The flight engineer came over, stood by Maggie with his hands on his hips.

"I'll make contact once I'm outside the compound, P One," she said to him. The plan was for Maggie to run point, assess the situation. With the abaya, she could pass for Arab if she encountered a patrol. John Rae and Bad Allah would follow. The rest of the team would be called in once it was confirmed that Kafka's parents were indeed being held inside the Bunny Ranch.

She fitted the lightweight headset with its miniature boom microphone over her ear and plugged it into her Rino.

John Rae and Bad Allah set up their phones too. "Remember," John Rae said to P One, "keep the volume low and chatter to zero until you hear from either Maggie or me."

"Got it," P One said.

"Ready for a refreshing jog, guys?" Maggie said to John Rae and Bad Allah, strapping her phone into an armband. The high-sensitivity, WAAS-Enabled GPS receiver had the coordinates of the Bunny Ranch plugged in.

"Hell, no," John Rae said. He was fitting 36-inch bolt cutters into his daypack. The handles stuck out the top. It would be a heavy load. "But lead the way."

Bad Allah gave a single nod. Sergeant Kaminski and her companions gave lazy salutes as they stood at ease, awaiting further instructions.

"Semper Fi, John Rae," Maggie said.

"That's the Marines, Maggie. I was with the Rangers."

"What do the Rangers say?"

"Yabba Dabba Do?"

The others laughed.

She shook her head, smiled, raised her fist chest high. "One of these."

They all gathered in small circle—PJs and even Kafka—and fist-bumped.

"Milk run," John Rae said.

"Don't even bother." Maggie smiled. John Rae had made such promises before, with disastrous results.

"Creech are going to be monitoring the whole shebang so you'll be under watchful eyes."

"I can live with that," she said.

Maggie turned to face the murky desert. This was indeed it. She took off, soon sprinting across rocky dirt, headed southeast. She heard John Rae and Bad behind, breaking into a run as well. But they were ten-minute-milers at best. Maggie would soon put them in her wake.

It felt good to stretch her legs out and ease the tension. Back in San Francisco she savored her five daily miles. This was only three. The bumpy desert ground blurred under her strides in the moonlight. Her muscles soon warmed and the desert chill evaporated.

Every few minutes she would slow down for a moment, consult her Rino, change course as needed.

Twenty minutes later, breathing evenly, she saw the mudbrick walls surrounding the encampment rise up against the midnight horizon.

48

The darkened walls of the compound loomed in the distance.

Maggie set her daypack on the ground, retrieved her rolled-up abaya, unfurled it, slipped the garment over her warm, glistening body. Picking up her pack, she walked toward the structure.

A deep guttural howl on the far side of the compound sent a shiver shooting down her back. A pack of wild dogs. Maggie shook off the jujus, pulled the handheld FLIR camera from her pack as she snaked around the corner of the mud brick wall. The complex was the size of a football field; she had seen that on the Creech video, but it didn't make an impression until she was actually standing before it. She kept close to the wall, in the shadows.

She spotted the entrance from an angle. The dirt road was rutted with tire tracks. Quietly she approached, pressing the point-to-talk button on her headset.

"Coming up to the Bunny Ranch gate," she whispered. She realized her voice was shaking with adrenaline.

"Entrance is on the southeast side as noted. Can you read my coordinates?"

A moment later, a buzz of static was followed by John Rae saying, "We're five or so minutes behind you."

She got closer. The old wooden gates were shut. Open, they'd be big enough for large vehicles to pass. She pressed the PTT button.

"Gates are locked," she whispered, "but not with a chain. Looks like they're barred on the inside. An iron pipe or something."

"So glad I huffed these freakin' bolt cutters all this way."

"It builds character, JR," she said. She eyeballed the wall. Eight feet of old mud brick, patched here and there with whatever came to hand, razor wire running along the top.

"We'll find a way over," she whispered. "Maybe we can use your bolt cutters to get through the razor wire along the top of this wall."

"We'll figure something out."

"P One to Abraqa Lead," a voice interrupted.

"Yo," John Rae said, never one for radio protocol.

"Update from Creech," P One responded. "You're not gonna like this."

"Lay it on me, anyway."

"Drone coverage is unavailable at this time."

"Say what?" John Rae said. "No drone coverage?"

"Roger that."

"But we need that intel."

"Coverage was pulled for unexplained reasons, we're told. Probably another mission. There's an unestimated delay."

John Rae let loose a few choice expletives. Maggie's chest went into knock mode, knowing that the eye in the sky wouldn't be looking down on them and providing them with badly needed guidance.

"Do you want to abort the op, Abraqa Lead?" P One said to John Rae.

There was a pause. Maggie could hear John Rae's and Bad Allah's feet thumping while they ran, JR obviously thinking it over, his PTT button down. "Request we stand by where we are, P One, wait one hour for Creech to possibly reengage drone coverage."

"No can do," P One said. "We have air refueling scheduled for our return. It's a tight window we can't afford to miss. It's *go or blow*."

They might not make it back.

There was another long pause.

"Maggie?" John Rae finally said. "You want to bail?"

They wouldn't get another chance. How could the most powerful military on the planet be so inadequate?

She thought of Dara, dying in the ambulance.

"No, JR," she said. "You?"

"Hell, no."

There were times when JR drove her crazy but right now she was just so glad to have him on her side. "Waiting for you here, then," Maggie whispered. "At the gate."

"Let's get this party started," John Rae said. "Bad Allah, quit talking so damn much."

John Rae clicked off.

The wind shifted, carrying the howl of the dogs on it, and along with that a stench of something so rotten, Maggie's stomach turned. A mouth full of bile rushed up her throat and she had to choke back vomit.

There was only one thing that smelled like that. But she knew she had to confirm, just to make sure there was no one there.

"Going around back to check out some noise," she whispered. "Probably just some dogs."

"Whoa, Maggs. Wait up."

There was a pause before Bad Allah spoke. "Those won't be dogs, Maggie," he said quietly. "They'll be hyenas."

Jesus, she thought. "But I want to be sure there isn't a patrol of some sort. I'll be careful."

"Ten-four," John Rae said. "We're a couple minutes away."

She walked farther south, her hackles raised, out beyond the wall.

She drew closer.

A long open pit lay ahead. The stench was unbelievable. She could hear the dogs feasting down there.

And although she knew what lay ahead, she kept walking toward it anyway. Like a black magnet the pit drew her.

She got to the edge. All lit up by moonlight.

Oh my God, she said to herself. *Oh my God.*

There had to be hundreds of bodies. Some decapitated. Yazidi robes and scarves. There, a woman. Twisted. Human wreckage. And a child. A small boy.

An image she would never unsee.

Breathing through her mouth and not her nose, she spun, staggered back to the gate, blinking to settle her nerves.

When she got to the gate, she thought she heard footsteps from within the compound. Her heartrate shot back up. She pressed the talk button and whispered, "Someone coming up to the gate, JR—from inside the compound. Proceed with caution."

The footsteps got closer. She heard a man muttering, as

if to himself, in Baghdadi Arabic. *I'll give that little bitch a thrashing she won't forget.*

Maggie wondered who he was talking about. Someone in the camp by the sound of it. Quietly she unslung her daypack, pulled a lightweight black burqa hood, slid it over her head. Just her eyes showed. From the side mesh pocket of her pack she withdrew a long narrow syringe, half a milliliter of Etorphine mixed with saline. M99. Animal tranquilizer.

She stepped quietly up to the edge of the gate.

The footsteps approached from the other side. She heard a low screech of metal on metal and saw, through the gap between the doors, a length of plumbing slide free. He was unbolting the gates.

One of the doors creaked on its hinges as it swung open.

Recalling the day when she sat with Dara in the ambulance, Maggie put the hypodermic up to her mouth, pulled the plastic cap off with her teeth, gripped the syringe in her hand. Waited.

John Rae and Bad weren't here yet. She'd deal with it herself.

49

Earlier that evening, inside the Jihad Nation compound

"Did you do well at your lessons today, Havi?" Hassan al-Hassan asked, scooping lamb stew up with a piece of pita bread, stuffing it in his mouth. He wore a black robe with a tan shoulder holster, seated cross-legged on the floor at the low table. Havi sat next to him, wearing a beige Kufi skull cap. He looked down at his plate, picking at his food.

Besma and Abeer sat quietly on the other side of the room, watching, waiting their turn to possibly eat. But what was more important to Besma was getting hold of that phone of Abeer's she had secreted under the bed.

"I asked you a question, Havi," Hassan al-Hassan said. "Speak up when I talk to you. You're going to be a Muslim now, not one of the sheepish people you left behind. Be proud. That means looking a man in the eye when he talks to you."

"Yes," Havi said, looking up, stealing a glance at Besma before returning Hassan's gaze.

"That's better," Hassan said. "Now, how are your lessons?"

"Good, God be praised, Hassan al-Hassan."

"Of course. You are a *cub of the caliphate* now. A star pupil. And what did you learn today?"

"Shooting pistols."

"Shooting!" Hassan nodded multiple times. "Excellent. Did you enjoy it?"

"Actually, it hurt my hand, Hassan al-Hassan."

Hassan laughed and slapped Havi on the shoulder. "Oh, it does at first, my boy. That's because your hands are soft. We're going to change that. You need to practice. And practice. Allah will give you the strength you need."

"Yes, I know. But Hassan al-Hassan, the gun is so big."

Hassan laughed again. "You grow into the gun!" He took a quick sip of tea, spilling some on the carpet. Then, as if something just came to mind, he said, "Here." He reached under his left arm, pulled his pistol, a 911 style semi-automatic, making Besma's heart jump. He racked the gun's slide back and forward with a practiced hand, yielding a noisy ratchet sound. Then he handed the big gun to Havi.

Besma's nerves shot into high gear.

"Take it, boy," Hassan said.

Havi eyed the gun.

"Come on! Take the gun!"

Havi grasped the pistol with both hands. He examined the weapon. "The safety is off."

"I never use them, boy. Allah protects us. He protects all of his warriors. Just as he now protects you."

Besma could only hope that was the case. Allah's protection, as much as she doubted it, would be welcome in Havi's situation.

"It's loaded?" Havi asked Hassan.

"Of course it's loaded, boy. You saw me rack it. Now, stop stalling and show me how you shoot."

"What?" Havi screeched. "In *here*?"

Besma was beginning to feel faint.

"You don't always get to choose where you must shoot, boy. Or when. Do you think a battle will only happen where you wish it? Yes, in here."

Havi blinked in confusion as he held the gun, which looked enormous in his small hands.

"But what do I shoot at, Hassan al-Hassan?"

Hassan stroked his long beard as he gazed around the room. His wild eyes seemed to settle on something above Besma's head.

"There!" He grinned, pointing above Besma and Abeer's heads. Besma turned to see the fat Teddy Bear on top of a cluttered bookcase. "Shoot Teddy!"

Besma gulped back her nerves, noting that Abeer seemed just as uneasy. The thought of a six-year-old firing an automatic pistol in an enclosed space near their heads was not normal, she gathered, even for this place.

"But my sister..." Havi said.

"That's why you must shoot well, eh?" Hassan said, laughing. "So you don't shoot your sister. It will be a good incentive for you. Go on, now. Fire."

Havi clasped the pistol in both hands, raised it, his small arms quivering under the weight. He closed one eye, squinting with the other. Abeer ducked down to the floor. Besma did the same.

Minutes seemed to pass. In another part of the house Besma heard laughter.

"Go on, boy!" Hassan said. "Don't take all night."

"I'm aiming, Hassan al-Hassan."

"Yes, yes, I know you are. But in real life..."

Bang! The gun went off, sounding like dynamite in the enclosed room, accompanied by Abeer shrieking, followed by the clatter of something heavy hitting the floor.

"You got him, boy!" Hassan shouted, laughing with glee. "You got Ted! Excellent shot!"

Besma and Abeer sat back up. Besma glanced at the Teddy Bear, now turned askew on top of the bookcase, stuffing hanging out of his round tummy. A direct hit. She looked across the room at Havi, who seemed to be as surprised as she was. The gun was no longer in his hands.

"Where's the gun, boy?" Hassan said.

"It flew out of my hands, Hassan al-Hassan." Havi held his hands up, shook them loose. "They're buzzing."

"Never mind," Hassan said, looking around. "Ah, there it is! Behind that cushion, Get it, will you, Havi? There's a good boy."

Havi retrieved the gun, handed it back to Hassan, who reholstered it. Besma had been entertaining a wild fantasy of getting hold of the gun herself somehow.

Hassan clapped his hands at Besma and Abeer. "Time for bed, you two. You are dismissed."

Besma was hoping beyond hope that she could stay a while and chat with her brother. But she knew better than to ask such a thing.

Abeer stood up, stormed to the door in silence, obviously not happy with being relegated to the women's room for the night.

Besma stood up as well.

"May I congratulate my little brother's fine shooting with a good night kiss, Hassan al-Hassan?"

Hassan sat back, resting on his elbows. "I don't see why not. Havi, go give your sister a kiss. Be quick about it. It doesn't do to be a mama's boy."

Havi hopped up quickly, stepped around the low brass table, came over to Besma. He wore a fine beige linen robe, which fit him well, and good leather sandals.

"Look at you!" she said. "So handsome! Give me a hug."

She reached down and embraced her brother, holding him for as long as she could, terrified for him. She kissed his neck and whispered in his ear in Kumanji, their Kurdish tongue, "There's a phone, Havi. Under the bed. When Hassan's not looking, get hold of it. Hide it in the toilet. On top of the cistern. Got that?"

He nodded quickly into her neck.

"Good boy, Havi," she said in Arabic now, louder, "I love you."

"That's enough of that," Hassan said, clapping again. "Don't mollycoddle him."

∽

"Where's my phone, bitch?" Abeer shouted, grabbing Besma by her robe, holding her so close that her spittle hit Besma's face.

"How should I know?" Besma said, recoiling, her arms up.

"I know you took it!"

Besma threw Abeer off. "It's not my fault you lost it! Hassan forbid you to use it anyway."

"Stop fighting!" another young woman said. "If Mustafa comes in and reports us, it'll be beatings all round."

"She's right," another said.

They were standing in the middle of a stifling hot room.

There were bunk beds, a pair of twin beds pushed up against the wall, mattresses on the floor, and more than a dozen women to share it all. One small window with bars on it was all they had for ventilation, the curtain draped over it barely moving with the cool night air that didn't come fast enough. A pair of dusty fans sat still, the generators turned off at night to avoid attracting the Yanki drones. There were clothes everywhere. And the smell, the smell of so many bodies, so close together, bodies compressed by space, by heat, by desperation.

"If I find you took my phone, you whore," Abeer said to Besma, storming back to her bunk. "I'll kill you."

An older woman by the name of Gala, a dark-skinned Egyptian who had obviously once been a great beauty, spoke up. "You need to be careful, Ameriki," she said to Abeer, pronouncing the last word as if it were something profane. "Besma here is destined to be a wife of the caliph." She raised her eyebrows and smiled. "She might just put in a bad word for you."

Abeer grabbed her pillow, fluffed it angrily. "And I might just put in a bad word for her," she snapped. "With Hassan al-Hassan. And he's right here. Right now."

"Not quite, Ameriki," Gala said, sitting down on a bed next to another woman who was reading a well-thumbed copy of *Cosmopolitan* in Arabic by a battery-operated lantern. "He's way over there." She pointed to the other side of the house. "And you're *right here*." She smiled, not a nice smile. "With the rest of us. He doesn't want you as much as he used to, does he? There's nothing special about a fat Ameriki."

"Shut up."

"Maybe you should stop stuffing your face, Ameriki," another one said.

"You'll all be sorry," Abeer said, throwing her pillow down on the lower bunk of a bed, climbing in, turning her back to the room. "You'll all be sorry."

~

Middle of the night, Besma awoke, not that she had been sleeping well to begin with; other women were snoring, talking in their sleep. She climbed off her bed—she now rated a single bed since she was destined to be a bride of the caliph—and pulled on her abaya. She stepped carefully over the sleeping bodies on the mattresses on the floor, maneuvering her way to the door of the woman's dormitory. The door had been left open a foot or so, to let some badly needed air into the room.

Craning her neck she peered out. Mustafa the guard was asleep in his chair, head slumped forward over his big belly as if dead. If only.

As quickly as possible, she tiptoed out into the hallway, around him, so as not to wake him, and made her way down the hall. Her nose stung as she approached the toilet. She went inside, shut the door silently, trying to forget the poor girl who had slashed her wrists. Besma would never forget having to wheelbarrow her body out to the pit. She stood, adjusting her eyes to the darkness. She stopped, listened. Distant snoring. An action film played on a laptop computer somewhere. During the day when the generator ran, they charged the computers back up.

She straddled herself, one foot either side of the Turkish toilet, and reached up, touching the very top of the cistern, praying.

Her fingers brushed the edge of something square and plastic.

The phone!

She marveled at how resourceful her little brother was. To get it way up there. So brave.

She couldn't have asked him to call father himself. She'd already put him at far too much a risk. He had done more than his share.

She grabbed the phone, stood down, gave it a quick once-over, made sure the volume was muted. She didn't need some silly music to give her away. Concealing the phone within her robe, she left the bathroom.

She went back out into the hallway.

Mustafa was still asleep in his chair. The others made fun of him behind his back. "The harem guard," they called him. "Mustafa makes his money the easy way," Gala had told Besma, "escorting women to the toilet. Fetching a midwife now and again. No beheadings or gunfights for him." She doubted if his gun even worked anymore, Gala told Besma with a wicked grin, winking. Besma blushed, getting the joke although she had no experience with men. She hoped she never would, not in this hellhole. She knew it didn't matter whether a jihadi guarded women or wore a suicide vest. They were all just as deadly. Mustafa had eyed her in a way that made her nervous, as if she were naked. She knew what he was capable of.

Besma looked at him again, sitting there, and realized the time to call her father was now. The blood in her ears roiled.

She turned around, padded down the dark hallway to the door leading to the outside, where she stood for a moment, the brilliant stars piercing the sky over the compound. The training facilities were to the left, the open garage to the right. A Toyota pickup covered in netting and camouflage was parked along the wall. Two trucks were parked inside the garage. That looked like a safe place to call her father. Perhaps he could try and raise ransom money to buy her and Havi back. The thought of being the caliph's wife terrified her as much as being Hassan's toy.

She darted across the packed dirt of the courtyard, dodging shell casings and stones, getting to the garage quickly, nestling herself between the two trucks inside.

She checked Abeer's phone. So many text messages for the American Terror Bride. In English.

Dear Traci—please call home. It doesn't matter what you've done. Please call. Please let your father and I know you're all right.

What did it mean?

She dialed a number she had memorized.

Crouched between the pickup trucks, Besma listened to the ring drone on. And on. Four rings. Five. Six. Where was her father? It had been days since they had been taken. Was he still at the refugee camps, looking for the lost women?

Was he safe?

The call rolled over to voicemail.

She left the clearest message she could, trying not to break down into tears like a little girl, telling him that she and Havi were alive, along with others, being held by Hassan al-Hassan. She told him where they were, as best as she knew how. Near the Zab river, off highway 80, near a town. An old school of some sort, a Jihad Nation compound now. She had been collecting this information over the last two days, eavesdropping, listening to the women, and she had rehearsed the speech.

When she was done, she told her father that she loved him.

She couldn't bring herself to tell him that Mother had been killed. Perhaps he already knew.

She hung up, powered down the phone, noting that it had very little battery left. She went to a dark corner of the garage and found a cinderblock on the cement floor against the wall. She slipped the phone in one of the two holes, covered it with an empty paint can.

Then she thought she heard something. She shuddered in fright.

The slapping of sandals against feet. She jumped up, darted into the dark garage, stood at the back behind a pickup truck. She peered out into the yard.

Mustafa! Walking around the courtyard with a flashlight lighting his way, the silhouette of his AK-47 over his shoulder outlined by moonlight behind him, his big belly sticking out. Had someone—most likely Abeer—told him she'd slipped away? Abeer would have.

Mustafa would be in serious trouble if the caliph's new bride disappeared. It might be more than his fat head was worth.

He turned, headed her way, straight for the garage. She ducked to avoid the beam of light.

The truck's tailgate was down. Besma climbed into the back as quickly and quietly as possible. The hard metal bed hurt her knees as she inched forward. She lay down between a pile of rope and an old tarpaulin. Ever so quietly, she reached over, pulled the tarp over her. Her nose reeled with the stink of oil and manure.

Mustafa came plodding into the garage, mumbling. *Wait 'til I get my hands on that little bitch.*

Besma lay there frozen. The only part of her moving was her heart, hammering away.

Mustafa went back out to the courtyard. Her breath escaped in a torrent of relief. She heard him wandering around, patrolling the rest of the compound. It seemed to take forever.

And then, when she thought he might be done, she heard him, still beseeching Allah to let him find the girl Besma, as he headed toward the gates.

She heard him pulling the bar that locked the gates.

Opening them.

Mustafa was going outside, to continue his search.

50

Maggie waited by the front gate. In her left hand, behind her back, she held the syringe full of animal tranquilizer. Her thumb was on the plunger, ready, pulsing with her heartbeats.

The guard finished opening the gate. He was a short fat man in a robe, with a big unruly beard.

He jumped when he saw Maggie in her naqib. His flashlight shook in one hand. He clutched the pistol grip of the automatic rifle with the other.

"Besma?" He brought the gun up, level with her midriff, making Maggie jump now.

Think fast.

"My apologies, Sayidi," Maggie said in her best standard Arabic, her Jihad Nation passport ready. She held it up against the flashlight's glare. "I somehow managed to get myself locked out."

"Locked out?" he said, letting go of his weapon, the barrel nose-diving to the ground as the gun hung on its shoulder strap, bringing Maggie immediate relief. Leaning forward, he reached for the black passport. "Who *are* you? One of the new ones?"

"Yes, Sayidi," she said. She let him have the passport. He raised his flashlight to examine the document, squinting in concentration.

Maggie leapt forward, bringing the hypodermic up and back down in one swift motion, making him rear back, his mouth opening in surprise as she jabbed the needle into his shoulder, like a dagger.

"*Al-La'anah!*" he cried, jerking, raising the flashlight like a club.

She blocked his arm with her elbow, leaned in, pressing the plunger all the way down before the needle snapped off in his shoulder. He swore, dropping the flashlight, the beam bouncing. He grasped his shoulder and Maggie landed on top of him, slamming him to the ground with a thump, seizing his throat before he could cry out for help. The flashlight beam came to rest nearby, highlighting the two of them.

He fought against the drug but she straddled his chest, squeezing his throat. He stared up at her with wild, fearful eyes. He flailed and kicked as she rode his big belly with her thighs, like a bronco, hanging on for the duration. It seemed to take forever until she saw his pupils begin to slip into unconsciousness. The synthetic opioid did its work, but not quick enough for her liking.

Finally his eyes shut and his body slackened.

She let go of his neck, sat up, watching him. He mumbled some gibberish in Arabic, drool running from the corner of his mouth.

And then he was out.

She climbed off, straightening herself.

He was still breathing. Sometimes that was debatable

with M99. But the dose had been dialed down from *elephant*. She picked up the flashlight, doused it, collected her Jihad Nation passport, swiped off the dirt, put it away. She dusted herself down.

Two pair of feet thudded toward the gate from beyond, quiet enough that if she hadn't been expecting them, she might not have heard them at first.

John Rae and Bad Allah came jogging up in their black fatigues, shotguns over their shoulders. Although they wore black turbans, neither man had his face covered yet. They slowed to a walk as they reached the gate. Maggie pulled her hood back.

"Looks like you've been busy," John Rae whispered, nodding at the comatose guard.

"You guys move him," Maggie said, unhooking the AK-47 from the man's limp shoulder, slinging it over her own.

John Rae went around to the man's head, lifted his shoulders. Head lolling in a drug-induced coma, he mumbled something unintelligible in Arabic, while Bad took the man's feet, huffing with the effort.

"What the hell is he saying, Bad?" John Rae asked.

"Something about wanting to go to the cinema."

"It won't be as good as the movie playing in his head right now."

"True."

They carried him outside while Maggie quietly shut the gate and joined them. In no time, the guard's ankles and wrists were secured with plastic ties. A strip of duct tape covered his mouth. They left him face down in the shadows.

"Hope the scorpions don't get him," John Rae said.

"It's no less than he deserves," Bad Allah said.

"I don't think anyone saw me deck him," Maggie said. "But somebody could be waiting for him to return. We better move." She opened the gate again a couple of feet to let them inside the compound and then shut it behind her but didn't secure it with the iron pipe. "We'll leave this unlocked. The PJs might need access."

"Can you radio that info in, Bad Allah, along with our status?" John Rae pulled his black wrap across his lower face, covering it, while Bad whispered their current status to P One.

"Now to see if Kafka's parents are here," Maggie said to John Rae.

The three of them crept across the dirt courtyard, staying in the murkiest shadows on the far side of the buildings. They stopped by an open garage, two pickup trucks under a ramshackle roof. A third truck sat out in the open under camouflage netting. They had seen that from the drone.

She had to tell someone about the bodies.

"There's a mass grave out there with hundreds of dead bodies in it," she said. "Yazidis. Some of them children."

John Rae took a deep breath, let it out. "Jesus," he said quietly.

"Animals," Bad Allah whispered, spitting on the ground. "No, I shall rephrase that. I've never seen an animal do anything so wicked."

Now they had to make the mission count.

"The guard asked me if I was one of the new ones," Maggie said. "Evidently, this place is a drop-off point for Yazidi prisoners. It was in Dara's notes. But nothing about a mass grave."

"Focus, Maggie," John Rae said. "Were here to pick up Kafka's parents. Nothing more."

Maggie shook her head angrily. "You can't ask me to forget those corpses."

"One thing at a time. A skeleton crew like ours isn't equipped to stop genocide. We're here to get Kafka's folks."

He was right. But she couldn't let it go. It was, after all, the reason she and Dara had pursued Kafka in the first place. The grave was just grisly proof of what the operation meant.

"I'll go first," she said. "Check things out. See if I can find Kafka's parents."

"You can't very well go inside carrying an AK-47, Maggs," John Rae said, nodding at the weapon over her shoulder. "Not if you want to blend in."

In her preoccupation with the grave, she had forgotten about that. She unshouldered the rifle, leaned it against the mud brick wall of the garage. "I'll start with that main house. That's where the drone's FLIR cameras showed the most activity. As soon as I find something, I'll radio it in."

"Be careful," John Rae said. "Don't let what you saw out there cloud your judgment."

"Got it," Maggie said tightly. "Got it."

With that, Maggie adjusted her earbud, set her Rino's volume low, pulled her Burqa hood back up. She headed across the courtyard silently to the main building.

∽

From where she lay in the back of the pickup truck, Besma heard the three of them whispering in English just outside the garage. They were planning something. They weren't jihadis. She'd heard them silence Mustafa, carry him out, shut the gate. A jolt of hope surged through her. Maybe she and Havi would escape this nightmare after all.

She heard light footsteps padding quickly across the ground toward the house. She pulled the tarp off of her quietly and sat up in the bed of the truck. A woman in a dark abaya and hood entered the main building from the side door, bold as you please. Then she saw two men in black jihadi fatigues run silently across the courtyard as well and stand, one either side of the door. They wore night vision goggles, making them look like creatures from another world.

51

The inside of the main house was pitch black, stuffy and oppressive, the cold night air slow to filter in. The fetid tang of a nearby toilet curled Maggie's nostrils. She pulled her handheld FLIR Scout imager from her bag and raised it to one eye. A short hallway forked left. According to Dara's notes, previous occupants had been held in a room on that side.

Drone coverage would have been ideal.

She'd just have to find Kafka's parents for herself. She hoped they looked like the photos Kafka had given her.

Maggie tiptoed down the hall toward the lavatory. The FLIR camera lit up the bathroom door. It was ajar. She approached slowly.

No one inside.

She stopped, removed another syringe full of Etorphine from the mesh pocket of her bag, leaving it capped. This she placed, carefully, in the inside breast pocket of her abaya, for quick access.

Through the viewer, Maggie spied an empty plastic chair down the hall, outside a door. She crept down, sweating in the burqa hood. As she passed the room, she heard snoring. More than one person. She stole up to the door, removed the viewer, stuck her head inside so that anyone awake might only see a woman in a burqa, not some stranger with a high-tech device up to her face.

She saw a multitude asleep in the muggy room that hummed of too many bodies in close proximity. She raised the viewer. All women by the looks of it. Sprawled in bunkbeds, single beds, mattresses on the floor. A standing fan by the door stood motionless. No power at the moment.

All women indeed, most of them young. A sleepover from hell. The women's quarters of the encampment. But no sign of Kafka's parents.

She stepped back out into the hallway, the FLIR viewer up to her eye, making her way down to the rear of the building. At the corner of the hallway she stopped, peered around.

At the end of the hall there was another hallway to the back of the house. Maggie proceeded quietly. She found a door on the left. Dara's notes had flagged this room as one where prisoners were sometimes kept. But the viewer showed no heat coming from inside.

She stood before the door, reached for the handle, twisted it, pushed the door open. It creaked, setting her nerves on edge, more than they already were.

She found one or two unmade beds, mattresses on the floor, but the room was otherwise empty.

Then from the front of the building, she heard a noise. Someone moving about. The thud of heavy feet. Someone coming down the hall. Someone big, judging by the footfalls.

Her heart jumped in her chest.

Should she call John Rae and Bad Allah? If she did, this

could easily escalate into a firefight before they confirmed Kafka's parents. She'd stay hidden for the time being.

Ducking into the empty room, behind the door, she slowly removed the needle from her breast pocket, pulled the cap off with her teeth through the synthetic material of the veil, held the cap in her teeth, in a pocket of cloth, ready.

Footsteps pounded around the corner of the hallway. Coming her way. Then the unmistakable ratchet sound of a weapon being racked set her nerve endings alight.

She stood behind the door, the needle poised to strike.

The guard, or whoever he was, approached, stopped on the other side of the door.

"*Who's there?*" a man said in Arabic.

No one, she thought. *Go away.*

A flashlight beam broke the darkness, bouncing around the room. She could hear the man breathing.

Maggie held her own breath, the hypodermic up and ready.

In another part of the house, someone coughed. Maggie tensed. It was from the women's room she had passed.

The man turned, the flashlight beam leaving a trail of dust motes as he headed back the way he came. Momentary relief splashed through her.

She heard the man stop at the women's room, where people were stirring now.

"Where is Mustafa?" the man asked the women.

"Who knows?" a woman replied. "Probably off asleep somewhere."

"He's doesn't do his perimeter check until later."

"Well, he's not here, is he?"

"Go back to bed," the guard muttered, storming off down the hall. But one or two women were now talking in low voices.

Maggie clicked her talk button, dropped her voice to the merest of whispers. "JR, a guard is most likely coming your way. He's just found out that the guy we tied up is missing. I bet he heads outdoors."

John Rae clicked his talk button in response, leaving it at that.

Several of the women were chatting. Maggie couldn't go that way without being noticed. She listened to the guard's feet plod back to the front of the house and then the front door squeaked open.

~

Squatting between the pickup trucks in the open garage, Besma watched the two men dressed as jihadis in the shadows crouching either side of the door to the main house with their weapons ready, as if they were expecting someone.

A moment later, the door opened and, slowly, Qasim, Hassan al-Hassan's private guard, wearing a black robe, appeared. No hat to cover his long wild hair. He held an AK-47 by the pistol grip, ready, a flashlight in his other hand. Besma's stomach flooded with acid. Qasim was merciless, and she'd seen the English-speaking woman in the abaya enter the house just before.

Besma wondered if she should alert the two men with the night vision goggles who were hiding. But that would give her away. What would that mean for Havi?

Then, as if sensing someone, Qasim turned in the doorway, swinging his flashlight and AK in the direction of one of the crouching men in black. The man rose quickly, pointing a short rifle with a long box-shaped extension on the end at Qasim.

Qasim opened fire first, his AK jumping amidst the chatter of gunfire. The other man in black sprang in, firing at Qasim at close range. His gun emitted a silenced *poff,* and in the tumbling beam of Qasim's dropped flashlight, Qasim collapsed in a sprawl in front of the doorway. The man who had jumped out of the way grabbed his arm but didn't shout.

∼

From inside the house, Maggie heard a spatter of gunfire out front, then nothing. Her heartbeats quickened. A flurry of anxious voices erupted from the women's dormitory. Movement. People getting up, floorboards creaking, someone heading down the hall. She was still in position behind the door of the empty room. Before she could talk, John Rae broke in. "Man down," he whispered. "One of theirs dead."

"It's just a matter of time before the rest of the fighters respond," Maggie said. She knew from Dara's notes that most of the jihadis slept out back in a separate building.

"Calling P One," John Rae said over the radio. "We have engaged, need your involvement ASAP. Check the buildings out back."

"Ten-four."

Outside, behind the main building, Maggie heard men shouting in Arabic. A generator fired up, making the back wall shake. It chugged away as lights popped on in the hallway outside the room Maggie was hiding in.

Between the women shouting in the next room, the commotion in the hallway, and the generator, it was difficult to tell how many men there might be, but it was more than several.

"Fighters on their way, JR," she said. "Behind the main building. Take cover. I'll stand by here."

"Stay safe, Maggs," John Rae whispered.

Maggie drew a deep breath as she put her needle full of dope away. Men shouted threats of jihad behind the house. Guns popped bullets into the air.

And then off in the distance, she heard the *wup-wup-wup* of the Pave Hawk approaching.

∽

BESMA HEARD the jihadis shouting from the rear of the compound, firing their guns. That's where they kept the middle-aged couple in a separate room, the parents of the man who had run to Paris.

Across the courtyard, the two men in black who had attacked Qasim ran for the garage. Straight for her. Looking for a place to hide. Her heart raced. The one man was still holding his arm.

She emerged from the shadows between the pickup trucks, waving her arms to show she had no weapon. The two men saw her and the one man raised his weapon and pointed it directly at her. Her insides twisted into a violent knot.

"No!" she shouted in Arabic, hoping they might understand. "I was taken captive by the jihadists two days ago. My little brother and I."

"OK," the man with the bad arm said, speaking to the man with the gun in English. The man lowered his gun as they got to the garage. "Get to safety." He spoke Arabic. She ducked back into the garage. They followed her as he explained something else in English to the other man.

"How many other fighters?" the man asked Besma. He

could obviously hear them, as could she, as well as an approaching helicopter. His arm was bleeding but he seemed to be coping with it, gripping it tightly.

Besma found a towel in the back of the pickup, helped apply it to the man's arm as she spoke. "Half a dozen or more," she said. "At one time there were women fighters, too. Al-Khansa."

"How many prisoners?"

"Just two left." She finished wrapping the man's wound. "They sold three girls, moved the others. One boy was executed. One boy died. We're Yazidis."

The two men spoke in English for a moment, then the Arabic-speaking man said: "Is there an older Iraqi couple here?"

"Yes."

That got the man's interest. He recounted it to the other man, a westerner, in English. The westerner nodded, spoke to someone over a radio of some sort. He seemed to be giving directions to the helicopter getting closer.

"Where are they being kept?" the Arabic-speaking man asked her.

"Out back," she said. "In a room next to the barracks—where the jihadis sleep."

"Is it under guard?"

"From what I have seen."

"Do you think you can show us? Once we clear the area?"

"I think so," she stammered. "But my little brother is being kept in Hassan al-Hassan's quarters." She pointed to the main building, where the blocked-out window to Hassan's room was. "And there are women in the building, too. Wives and mistresses."

The two men turned, regarded the boarded-up window

to the left of the doorway. It was now lit around the edges, thanks to the electricity generator thumping away behind the main building. The two men spoke to each other again. The man who spoke Arabic turned back to Besma.

"Is that the window to Hassan's room?"

"Yes," she said. "But my little brother is in there, too. His name is Havi. If you do anything, you must be careful."

"What is your brother doing in there?"

"Hassan is trying to radicalize him."

"I see." He nodded, frowning. The two men spoke again.

Her nerves were getting the better of her as she tried to stay clear-headed. It looked like help was here but Havi was right in the middle of the trouble.

The sound of the helicopter grew deafening as it hovered off to the side of the encampment, waiting. The dust swirled up off the ground in small tornados. The jihadis were yelling behind the main building, guns popping in the night air. But they were not going to risk coming out front with the helicopter. Cowards.

The two men conferred with each other as the helicopter hung in the air, battering the dust into whirls while the jihadis kept up their distant bravado. Besma's heart pounded as she agonized about Havi. What must he be going through?

~

"P ONE, STAND BY." Maggie heard John Rae's voice crackle over the radio as she stood in the empty room in the back of the house. The helicopter drifted over in front of the house, the whip of its rotor blades beating the roof. A piece of metal clanked and blew off.

"Maggie," John Rae said, "here's the situation. We've

taken out one guard. Kafka's parents are being held behind the main house, next to the barracks. Six or more fighters."

"How do we know all this, JR?" she said.

"A prisoner who escaped," John Rae said. "A girl. A teenager. We found her hiding in the garage. Hassan is holed up in his room in the front of the house, along with the escaped prisoner's six-year-old brother. He's a Yazidi being radicalized. FLIR is showing us six or so fighters out back, holding two prisoners as human shields."

"Kakfa's parents," she said. "Stand by, JR. I'm going to try to get a closer look."

"Don't go out there yet, whatever you do," John Rae said.

Maggie ventured out into the hall, turned left, to the end and then right. There was a door with a window, bars over the outside. Inside, the door was boarded up, huge nails securing it. No one was getting in or out. The thrashing of the generator made the dirty window vibrate. Men were shouting.

Maggie pulled her niqab back off her head, wiped the grime off the inside of the window with the heel of her hand. Slightly better. She pressed herself in close, peered out.

Half a dozen fighters holding two people at gunpoint. One was a middle-aged man in a short-sleeved shirt, thinning hair crowning his round head. He was wearing glasses. The other was a plump woman in a filthy burqa, the hood off. She had a round face and ear-length dark hair. One jihadi held an AK-47 on her. She was swooning and probably would not have stayed upright without another man holding her by the arm.

Kafka's mother. Well, at least she was alive. For now.

The view was partially obstructed by the generator thrashing away. On the other side Maggie saw a HESCO defensive barrier, a prefab wall that could be quickly erected. It was probably being used to protect a giant fuel bladder feeding the generator.

All US equipment, left behind after the Iraq war, appropriated by Jihad Nation.

The man holding the woman's arm put a pistol to her head and screamed in Arabic but his words were dwarfed by the copter out front. She shook violently and jerked back, crying out. Kafka's father broke away from his guard, pleading with the man holding the pistol to the woman's head.

The man struck Kafka's father across the face with his gun. He fell to the ground. Another jihadi kicked him, screaming for him to get up.

Kafka's father climbed to his feet. His glasses were gone. Blood ran down over one eye.

Maggie said: "P One, JR—they are indeed holding Kafka's parents as hostages. We've got to proceed carefully."

"Ten-four," P One said.

"Anything else, Maggie?" John Rae said.

"There's a generator, a mobile AMMPS unit, located behind the primary structure. And a HESCO defensive barrier, probably protecting a fuel supply."

"P One," John Rae said. "Can you take that generator out with your mini-guns?"

"We can try," P One replied.

"No!" Maggie said. "They're on the verge of killing Kafka's parents."

There was a pause while rotor blades chopped the air out front.

"It's not a matter of shooting our way in," Maggie said. "JR, can you get somebody on the roof, take up position? Get someone in the house, too, by the women's dormitory—

on the right-hand-side down the hallway? Maybe someone on Hassan's door, as well?"

"And then what?"

"Then have P One back off—outside the compound. The guys out here are at boiling point. We don't want to push them over the edge. Once P One is out of the way, we'll negotiate with them."

"*Negotiate?*" John Rae said. "With Jihad Nation?"

"My guess is they might want to save their sorry asses rather than die."

"I wouldn't count on it."

"It's worth a shot," Maggie said. "Let's get the women out of the main building. Open the front gates. Let them leave. Once that happens, we'll make the same deal for the fighters out back—provided they leave the prisoners behind. If they leave, they have to lay down weapons and go. I bet one or two take us up on it. Others will follow when they see that happen. That'll leave us with less fighters to deal with and just Hassan al-Hassan and the boy in the main house."

The line popped with static before John Rae replied, "It's a stretch."

"If it doesn't work, you can take the generator out. But that might mean losing Kafka's parents."

A pause.

"You got it, Maggie."

"Someone join me and we'll get the women out."

"P One," John Rae said, "drop a PJ on the roof, set the other two down here in front, and then back away from the compound."

"Ten four," P One said.

Maggie heard the Pave One moving overhead, the air whipped into a frenzy by the rotor blades buffeting against the roof. Behind the building, the jihadis were firing at the chopper.

"Taking fire," P One announced.

"There's got to be a power distribution box somewhere," John Rae said to P One. "Whoever gets on the roof, keep an eye out. Drop the other PJs up front by the garage. Then get the hell away. Go!"

"Ten four."

The structure shook as the Pave One descended, hanging directly overhead. One PJ stepped onto the roof above Maggie's head. The helicopter lifted off and moved to the front of the house, the sound of the engines fading.

"I'm coming into the main building with two PJs, Maggie," John Rae said.

"I'll be in the hallway to your right, past the bathroom. Someone meet me at the door of the women's dormitory. Two of you cover Hassan's room."

"On our way."

Maggie reached into her abaya and from under her T-shirt, pulled her Sig Sauer from her bra holster, her body taut with apprehension..

52

Gun drawn, Maggie stepped out into the hallway, which was lit by one bare bulb now the generator had kicked in. She could hear the women in the dormitory room around the corner talking at ninety miles an hour.

When she turned the corner, she saw two of the women standing outside the room, clearly in a state of agitation. They saw her approaching, gun in hand.

One woman shrieked.

"Stay calm," Maggie said in Arabic, lowering her weapon. "None of you are going to be harmed."

Sergeant Kaminski appeared at the other end of the hall, with her M4A1 carbine. She gave Maggie a nod. Maggie returned it.

"Who are you?" an older Arab woman said to Maggie. She was in her early forties, with long gleaming hair and dramatically arched eyebrows.

While Sergeant Kaminski stood, rifle ready, Maggie explained to the women that the Americans were taking over the compound, but that the women were going to have to leave. One or two expressed disbelief but most got dressed quickly, gathering up belongings, packing them into any kind of bag available—carry-ons, plastic bags, anything.

"No time for that," Maggie shouted. "Let's go, ladies."

"Where's Besma?" another asked.

"She must have already left," said another.

"You're sure we're free to go?" one young woman said in English, taking Maggie by surprise. She was American, a heavy teenager with acne.

"If you leave *now*," Maggie said. "We can't guarantee anyone's safety. Especially once we start dealing with those jihadis out there."

The girl grimaced, pulling on big camouflage fatigue pants. Others filed out under Sgt. Kaminski's watchful eye.

"Where are you from?" Maggie asked the girl.

"Milwaukee."

"What on earth are you doing *here*?"

"It's a long story," she said.

Maggie bet it was. The girl was probably a jihadi bride, recruited over the Internet.

Behind the building, the jihadi fighters were shouting anew. Maggie went out into the hallway. The women hurried out. Maggie followed, counting them off. She was one short.

"Where did that American girl go?" she said, turning back to Sergeant Kaminski. "The one in the camo?"

Sergeant Kaminski ducked into the room just as a shot rang out, a tight *snap* followed by Kaminski bolting back into the hallway, slamming against the wall, more surprised than anything else it seemed. She'd been hit. She raised her carbine and, gritting her teeth, fired a burst into the room. The narrow hall echoed with shots. Shell casings clattered on the floor.

"You OK?" Maggie said.

"Yep," Sergeant Kaminski said, patting her rib cage. "Kevlar. Just hurts like a mother. Hopefully didn't break a rib."

Maggie followed her into the room. The American girl was sprawled across a bed, her arm hanging down to the floor. A Tokarev pistol lay by her motionless hand. Maggie kicked it away.

"What the hell?" John Rae said over the radio.

"Unexpected resistance," Maggie said. "It's over." She turned to Sergeant Kaminski. "Go out and cover the women. They have to leave the camp."

"Got it." Kaminski jogged down the hall.

"Are the front gates open?" Maggie asked over the radio.

"Ten four," one of the PJs said.

A few minutes later Sergeant Kaminski contacted Maggie. "Two of the women won't leave. They think *we're* getting them out of here."

"We don't have room—do we?"

"We do *not*," P One interrupted.

Damn. "We deal with it later." Maggie headed down the hall, turning right. She found John Rae and one of the PJs outside Hassan's room.

"No movement," John Rae said. "Door's locked. He's lying low. Coward."

Maggie knocked on the door, hard. She announced herself in Modern Standard Arabic. "This is a United States military mission. We're here for Akram and Fadila Tijani. Tell your men to hand them over to us and we'll leave—no one will be harmed."

"Death to America!" a man yelled.

That's what she was afraid of.

"We don't have a lot of time, Hassan al-Hassan," she said. "Last chance."

"I've got the boy!" he shouted.

Maggie stood back, eyed John Rae. "I'm going out back to talk to those guys. Maybe when they see the women have left, they'll follow suit."

"Are you crazy?"

"No more than you."

"Maggie," John Rae said, "there's a window out front to this very room. We shoot a grenade through it, take out Hassan al-Hassan. With him gone, those jihadis will be a lot more pliable."

"There's a kid in that room, though, right? The little brother of the girl who helped you, told you where Kafka's parents were?"

John Rae grimaced. "It's called 'collateral damage,' Maggie. Yeah, it's a euphemism, but the bottom line is, we get Kafka's parents out, you can break Abraqa Darknet, your Yazidi genocide comes to a halt."

"No, John Rae. I'm not ready to go that route. Not with a kid's life at stake."

"You know what? One school of thought says we could have shipped Kafka off to Guantánamo, got the information we needed out of him there. Without being so damn nice."

"I must've missed school that day."

Sergeant Kaminski broke in. She was up front by the garage, with Besma and the two women who wouldn't leave. "God damn, Maggie! One of Jihad Nation's finest just took off. Some guy with a red beard. Must be a foreign fighter. Ran right through the gate like a bunny. Look at him go!"

That was what Maggie wanted to hear. "Let's hope others follow," she said. She looked at John Rae. "Where's the emergency cash?" Rescue operations carried reserve funds, for repairs, bribes, what have you.

"P One has it on board," John Rae said. "Bad can get it."

"Did you copy that, Bad Allah?" Maggie said. "P One?"

"Ten-four," both parties replied.

"Think you can buy them off, Maggie?" John Rae said, jerking his thumb toward the back of the building. "Jihadists?"

"One is already gone. One or two more are probably thinking about it. If we can buy *them* off, that leaves fewer to deal with. The guy on the roof is a good shot, I take it?"

"He's the best," Sergeant Kaminski interjected on the radio.

"I'm going round there to talk to those jihadis," Maggie said to John Rae. "Bad, get me that cash, please." She looked back at John Rae, who was giving her the red stare. "JR, if this doesn't work, you can storm Hassan's quarters. But give me a shot at it."

John Rae seemed to think that over. "*I'll* go out and talk to them."

"How? You can't speak Arabic. You can barely speak English."

"So come with me. Translate."

"No. This is one case where being a woman has its advantages."

"I can think of a few more. But I'm going with you, at the very least."

"No. They're too jumpy. It's less intimidating if I go on my own."

"It's also a hell of a lot more dangerous for you."

"I'm hoping Sharpshooter on the roof has me covered," she said.

"You got that right, Ma'am," one of the PJs said, presumably the one stationed on the roof.

"Do you know the Arabic phrase '*alhamdulillah*'?" Maggie asked him.

"Doesn't it mean '*Praise be to God*'?" Sharpshooter replied.

"Indeed it does," Maggie said. "When I say that phrase, it will be your cue to open fire on the jihadis. But only then and not until."

"'*Praise be to God*'," Sharpshooter said in Arabic. "Got it."

"In that case," John Rae said, "I'm getting on the roof, too." He turned to the PJ guarding the door with him. "You good here, keeping an eye on Hassan's room?"

The PJ returned a nod. "I'll call Kaminski if I need help."

John Rae turned back to Maggie, gave her a softer look. "I'm going to be in a hell of a lot of trouble if you don't come back, Maggie."

"You can't get rid of me that easily." She gave him a wink, and their eyes met for a moment. Maggie turned, went back outside.

A few minutes later, armed with ten thousand in hundred dollar bills, Maggie headed down the side of the main building toward the back, where the jihadis were holding Kafka's parents. John Rae had clambered onto the roof and joined the PJ up there.

As she approached she caught a glimpse of the five remaining fighters, who had lost some of their bravado. One man sat on the ground, smoking a cigarette. The others stood in a circle around Kafka's parents. The tension in Maggie's body tightened so that her strides became shorter and slightly jerky.

"Stop!" a man shouted at Maggie in Arabic, followed by the unmistakable sound of an automatic rifle being racked into firing position. Her nerves responded appropriately, making her shake.

She raised her hands above her head. One held the thick wad of currency.

"I'm unarmed," she shouted back in Arabic. "I just want to talk."

The tall gunman, wearing a black afghan turban, saw the cash. People could spot that a mile away.

"Come," he said, keeping the weapon trained on her. It had a large round magazine. Gas powered no doubt. She pushed away the thought of a hundred bullets riddling her body in seconds.

She took a deep breath and pressed on, hoping that her scheme would pay off.

She got within ten feet. The man who had been sitting on the ground stood up. She stole a glance at Kafka's parents. His mother's worried eyes followed her every move. His father, an older, heavier version of Kafka, with a wisp of hair on his crown, stood next to her, a smear of blood on the side of his face where he had obviously wiped his wound, as evidenced by the red smudge on one of his shirttails.

"You have two minutes," the man in the turban said.

"What we have here is a stalemate," Maggie began, digging for Arabic that was not in dialect but would convey her meaning well enough. The more she spoke the language the easier it became. "We want those two," she continued, nodding at Kafka's parents. "That's all we want."

"And why should we give them to *you*?" he said with an ugly smile.

Maggie gave her hand, the one that held the money, one half-twist above her head. All eyes were upon it.

"We could take that money from you," he said. "We could kill you. Easily."

"You could," she said. "And then in practically no time at all, the chopper strikes. This camp will be nothing but a smoldering pile of rubble. Well, just between you and me, friend, that's what's going to become of this place anyway when the drone strikes arrive. Very soon. Very soon indeed. But you still have an opportunity to avoid that and fight another day. Provided you lay down your weapons and leave now. Most of the women have already left. Hassan al-Hassan is cornered in his room, hiding. He won't be getting out of here. But the rest of you—well, we don't care about you. I count five of you. I have ten thousand dollars. You do the math. Some of you have families. Two thousand dollars for any one of you that wants to put down your weapon—right here, right now—and leave." She knew what that kind of money meant in a country where a man made a hundred euros a month—if he could find a job. It was life-changing. Already she could see the deliberation in the eyes watching her intently.

"We just lay down our guns?" a short man at the back said.

"On the ground," Maggie said. "And I pay you. And then you leave. That's it."

"How do we know someone won't shoot us?" another said.

"If we wanted to kill you," Maggie said, "we would have struck this camp with drones and been done with it. We just want those two." She nodded again at Kafka's parents. Then she looked at the tall man in the turban. "May I lower my hands, please?"

The cash had made them all curious.

"Go ahead," the tall man muttered, gesturing with the rifle. "Just don't try anything."

"Very well." Maggie lowered her hands and counted off

twenty one hundred dollar bills, making eye contact with the short man.

"Do yourself a favor." She held the cash out. "Lay down your gun. You'll be out of here in minutes, a man with money in his pocket. *Real* money."

Tense silence hovered in the cold night air.

"Step aside," the short man said, pushing forward. He came up, laid a battered Kalashnikov at Maggie's feet, then stood up.

"No, Ahmed," the tall man in the turban said, "I won't allow it."

"You don't speak for me. Hassan al-Hassan is my chief. And where is he now? Hiding in his room with his Ameriki bride. I have a wife and six children in Saudi Arabia." He put his hand out. "Pay me."

Maggie counted off the bills.

"Allah will punish you, Ahmed," the tall man said.

"Allah can punish me when I'm dead," he said, folding the money, putting it in his robe. He turned and, without looking back, walked toward the open gate, his arms swinging. He walked through the gate, the others watching him, and disappeared into the night. No shots were fired.

"Who's next?" Maggie said.

"Me," a light-skinned young man said, unslinging his rifle.

Minutes later two jihadis were left—the tall man in the Afghan turban and a scary-looking man with a big nose and one good eye. But they seemed more concerned with watching Maggie's money and each other than Kafka's parents, who hovered nearby.

Maggie counted her money. She prayed that the PJ and John Rae on the roof had her covered.

"Who's next?" she said again.

"No one," the tall man said.

She had expected as much. But now there were only two of them to deal with. Her heart pounded in her ears all the same. She took a breath, made eye contact with Kafka's mother, repeating a telegraphed look that said run when the opportunity presented itself. She had been doing the same with Kafka's father during the interactions with the men. It seemed they understood what Maggie meant.

"It's your decision," she said to the tall man, folding the rest of the money. She cleared her throat. *"Praise be to God."*

A shot rang out from the rooftop and the tall man bolted sideways, his turban blown away, brain matter flying as he collapsed to the ground in a heap, landing on his weapon. Kafka's mother screamed and ran, her husband following. The one-eyed man spun to fire at the two of them but before he could raise his gun, his head disappeared as the crack of another shot reverberated from the roof.

Maggie ran to Kafka's parents.

53

The sixty-five foot Pave Hawk helicopter set down in the dirt courtyard of the compound between the garage and the main house, spewing sand and dirt as its engines screamed and rotor blades spun.

Kafka and his parents, reunited amidst a flurry of joyful tears, ran towards it, Kafka's arm around his mother. The gunner and copilot hopped out and helped them aboard. Maggie followed, her heart beating rapidly after the showdown with the jihadis. She still wore her abaya, sticky and dirty now. She was filmed with nervous sweat, but overall a feeling of exhilaration prevailed.

They'd pulled it off.

Bad Allah, his right arm hastily bandaged with a rag Besma had applied, ambled toward the helicopter.

Off to one side, in the shadows of the garage, stood Besma and the two women who had opted not to leave the compound. One was a striking older Egyptian woman named Gala. They watched the activity with reserved faces.

Sgt. Kaminski stood by, her carbine pointed to the

ground, watching Hassan's boarded-up window. One PJ was still stationed in front of Hassan's room for the time being, where Hassan remained in hiding with Havi. As Maggie got to the front of the house, she saw the silhouettes of John Rae and the third rescueman appear up on the roof.

Holding his shotgun in one hand, John Rae hopped down from the roof in a jump that confirmed his fitness, landing on the dirt with an easy spring of his bent legs. He stood up, shook himself out, came striding up to Maggie. He patted her shoulder with his free hand. She had just about gotten used to his black jihadi outfit.

"I take back everything, Maggie," he shouted over the roar of the engines. "I should never have doubted you. You got them out. You got Kafka's parents out with a minimum of bloodshed."

"We," she said. "*We* got them out."

John Rae gave a smirk as he peeled off his jihadi head-covering, tossed it to the ground. "Remind me to take you along when I buy my next car. Talk about negotiation skills."

JR's approval was just an added bonus.

"We have to get going!" P One said over the radio. Maggie turned to see him at the chopper door, fastening the chinstrap of his helmet. "Refueling in less than an hour. We still have to make the border."

"Roger that," John Rae replied.

Maggie flinched, turned back around to face John Rae.

"What about Hassan al-Hassan?"

John Rae shrugged. "I wish. But there's no time. We got what we came for."

Maggie's guts churned. "But he's got Besma's little brother in there with him."

John Rae gave a somber stare. "I don't like it any more

than you do, Maggie. But we don't have a lot of choice. Mission accomplished."

"*Mission accomplished?* We can't just leave a child here with that maniac. What about his sister? Besma? She helped us. What about those two women over there?"

"They could've left."

Maggie shook her head. "We're getting her little brother out of here."

Kafka and his parents had boarded the chopper. So had Bad Allah.

"Thank you for flying USAF Airways, folks," P One said over the radio. "Ship sails in five."

"Maggie," John Rae said, his face serious in the broken darkness. "Believe me, I wish we could mop up. But we don't have room for any more passengers, anyway. We're at our limit. It would've been nice to have two choppers, but we know how *that* went."

"Give me that," she said, reaching out for John Rae's shotgun. "Someone can take my spot. I'm sure it won't be Besma. She's not going to leave her brother here."

"Maggie," John Rae said. "You've gotten everything you wanted. Abraqa. I've come through for you. But this isn't a humanitarian issue. We came for Kafka's parents. Nothing else."

The chopping of the rotor blades filled her ears, adding to the pressure.

"You have a safe trip back," she said. "Tell them to send another chopper. We should have had two in the first place. I'll be here, waiting. Now give me that gun."

John Rae rubbed his face, leaving a grimace. "OK," he said, "you win." He spoke to the P One. "Shut 'er down, Boss. We got one more thing we got to do."

Maggie breathed an inner sigh of relief.

THE PJ on the roof said over the radio, "I think I found the power distributor up here, in the back, hidden under a crate. Looks like it's connected to the generator down below."

John Rae said: "Take it out, Bud."

A rattle of automatic gunfire over their heads did nothing. Then, after two more long bursts, the building was plunged back into darkness. Maggie stood next to John Rae and the other PJ in front of Hassan's door. The PJ's infrared helmet light lit up the doorway.

With the lights out, Hassan al-Hassan started shouting. She could hear Havi yelling in fright.

Maggie banged on the door. "You're the last one, Hassan al-Hassan," she shouted in Modern Standard Arabic. "Your fighters have either fled or been killed. It's up to you how you want to get out of here—on your feet or in a body bag."

"I've got the boy!" he screamed. "I've got the boy!"

"Let Havi go and you live. That's the deal."

Hassan al-Hassan laughed maniacally. "You think *I'm* afraid of dying?"

"Your body will be covered with pork offal and dumped in the pit outside. You won't reach paradise."

"Allah won't forsake me! I'll take the boy with me. We'll both be glorious martyrs. Won't we, Havi? Won't we, boy?"

Inside the room, Havi cried out.

Maggie's heart pounded frantically. She looked at John Rae. "He'll do it."

"I know he will." John Rae rubbed his face. "We can pop a smoke grenade in through that front window, create a diversion. Maybe the kid can get away while we break down the door."

Maybe. "Can someone bring Besma in here?" Maggie said over the radio.

Shortly after, Sgt. Kaminski appeared, her helmet light lighting her way. Besma was with her, wearing an abaya with the hood down, her pretty face a mask of worry.

"When I give the word, Besma," Maggie said, "I need you to talk to your brother in Kurmanji. Tell him we're firing a smoke grenade through the window. When that happens he needs to get away from Hassan. We're going to break down the door and storm the room."

Besma gasped air as she nodded in agreement.

John Rae turned to Sgt. Kaminski. "Bring me the Blackhawk. Have your partner on the roof come down and load up an M18 and get ready to pop it through the window. He'll have to blast the plywood out first. Bad and the P One gunner can help. The rest of us here will be waiting to knock down this door. Hurry."

"Roger." Sgt. Kaminski went thumping off down the hall, back outside.

One of the PJs was positioned in front of the window with a grenade launcher. The P One gunner stood by with a carbine. Kaminski returned to Hassan's room with a Blackhawk battering ram, a two-foot long black cylinder with grip handles. John Rae took it from her.

Maggie said to Besma, "Talk to Havi now. And pray Hassan doesn't speak any Kurmanji."

Besma gulped back what had to be fear, turning to the door. "Havi?" she shouted, her voice cracking with anxiety. "It's me—Besma."

"Besma!" Havi shouted back, his muffled voice clearly terrified.

"The soldiers are going to shoot a smoke bomb through the window. When that happens, you must get away from

Hassan and away from the door. Soldiers are going to come in and there's going to be shooting. Do you understand?"

"Yes! Yes!"

"I love you!"

Besma turned to Maggie, shaking. "He's ready."

John Rae held the battering ram, spoke into the radio: "Let 'er rip, guys."

A moment later they heard a salvo of automatic rifle fire taking out the plywood covering the window out front, then a crash as the M18 bounced into the room.

Hassan shouted from within: "Havi! It's a bomb!"

"Go!" Maggie shouted to John Rae.

By the PJs' helmet lights, John Rae heaved the battering ram repeatedly into the reinforced door. After several crunching blows, the door gave.

John Rae dropped the battering ram, readied the shotgun that had been hanging over his shoulder while one PJ kicked the rest of the door in. Bright green smoke poured out into the hallway. Sgt. Kaminski raised her carbine.

Pistol shots rang out from within.

"Go! Go! Go!" John Rae shouted.

They charged into the room, guns up.

"Havi!" Besma shouted. Maggie lit the way with her FLIR. Meanwhile John Rae and Kaminski moved over to the far side of the room, weapons raised, circling a bed, Kaminski's headlamp focused on a figure lying on the bed. Hassan al-Hassan.

"*Bas!*" John Rae bellowed, one of the few words of Arabic he knew, as he aimed his shotgun at Hassan.

Hassan's hands went into the air.

Maggie scanned the room with her FLIR viewer. A small white shadow crouched behind the sofa. "There he is! Havi!"

They soon had Havi out, coughing and spluttering, Besma carrying him outside in her arms. Tears pouring down her face, she held her brother, hugging him and kissing the top of his head.

John Rae and Sgt. Kaminski emerged, escorting Hassan al-Hassan, his hands over his head, POW style, wearing only a pair of boxer shorts. He was muscular and furry.

The third PJ stood by with his rifle. A grenade launcher was attached to the end of the barrel.

Maggie wiped her face with her hand, trembling with relief.

John Rae and Sgt. Kaminski tied Hassan's hands behind his back with plastic cuffs. They took a moment to put their weapons down, grab a bottle of water.

Hassan, for his part, glowered at everyone.

Maggie succumbed to a wave of gratification. Both of Kafka's parents had made it. Besma and her brother had made it. Hassan was theirs.

"Where's my sister?" she heard Havi say.

Maggie turned, saw Havi looking at her. He wore a dirty beige linen robe and sandals. His eyes were wet with tears from the smoke grenade and who knew what else. "I don't know, Havi."

Then she heard Besma speak.

"You *bastard!*" Besma said through her teeth.

Maggie spun to see Besma striding calmly from the garage, holding up the AK-47 that Maggie had taken from the gate guard and left leaning against the wall.

Besma came to within a few feet of Hassan al-Hassan, the barrel of her weapon pointed directly at his head.

Hassan's face dropped in a rush of panic. "No!" His arms struggled behind his back. "No! Please!"

"You killed my mother, you filth," Besma growled.

"Besma!" Maggie shouted, breaking into a run. "Don't!"

Before anyone could get to Besma, the AK went off, rattling and jumping in the girl's hands as she narrowed her eyes.

Hassan's head erupted in a cloud of red mist.

54

A grainy red horizon crept up the blackened sky as the Pave Hawk finished air-to-air refueling. The HC-130P flew less than a hundred feet in front, its four engines groaning. Then the giant transporter retracted the fuel line from the helicopter's nozzle and the drogue basket fluttered back toward its parent like a giant floppy shuttlecock.

Maggie blinked away the last of night and gazed around the jam-packed chopper. Everywhere she looked there was a human being, sitting, sleeping, one or two simply watching the sky drift by as the wind rushed, some savoring their newfound freedom with hopeful looks and anxious smiles. The Pave Hawk was well over its limit of eleven people. But everyone understood it would be a death sentence to leave Besma, Havi or the two women behind.

Maggie glanced at Besma, sitting cross-legged on the floor by the door, stroking her little brother's head in her lap as he slept. Although Maggie could not hear her over the whine of the twin engines, Besma's lips moved with soothing words. The reddening daylight and the intimate image made Maggie experience a physical release, a welcome weariness softening her muscles after so much tension. Even though there were many more to follow Besma and Havi, it *was* a beginning. And there was no way Washington could ignore the Yazidi genocide now.

Besma's assassination of Hassan al-Hassan was a fact that would never leave the confines of this group. No one held it against her. John Rae simply took the warm AK-47 from Besma's hands, ejected the magazine, and set the gun to one side as he gave Maggie a knowing look. Maggie returned the same.

In the seats next to Maggie sat Kafka, in between his parents, an arm around each one of them. His mother slept deeply, the hood of her burqa pulled off, her head resting against her son's chest. His father, the blood from the wound over his eye wiped clean with a medical wipe, stared out the open window, seemingly at peace. Kafka wore an exhausted look of serenity. He seemed to sense Maggie's eye and turned to give her the first real smile she had ever seen from him.

There was still work to do, deactivating Abraqa, but much of that she could do on her own. And no one would be killed in the process.

For Kafka and his parents a new life would exist, once they were settled in the United States.

55

"I take it Kafka and his parents have arrived safe and sound in Langley?" Maggie said to Ed. Her cell phone was set in conference mode, sitting on the pink rococo soap dish of her miniscule bathroom in the Shangri-La Hotel on rue Philibert Lucot while she plucked her eyebrows and sipped from a tall paper cup. After Iraq it was bliss to be back in this funky little hotel with its simple pleasures she took for granted far too often—coffee, hot water, clean sheets, electricity twenty-four hours a day.

"If 'by arrived' you mean running up bills for room service and sending out for gourmet ice cream," Ed replied, his gruff voice echoing off the tiles, "then, yes. I just had to approve a request for a tailor for a private fitting in their hotel suite."

"Nice to see they are adapting so quickly to the Western world," Maggie said, starting on her left eyebrow. She had bags under her eyes. She needed sleep. "What about Kafka?"

"Getting debriefed before your arrival to finalize the taking down of Abraqa."

"I know how to have fun," she said, sipping coffee.

"You *are* going to be on that C-130 tonight, right, Maggs? I mean, no taking off at the last minute the way you ditched John Rae—leaving him in a taxicab without a word of French to help him." Ed gave a chuckle. Maggie knew he had told that story many times already.

"I'll be there," Maggie said, her tone serious now. "Debriefing Kafka. Taking down Abraqa. I just need to settle up a few things with Amina. Did that request I submitted go through?"

"Yep," Ed said, and she could hear him lighting up a cigarette.

In addition to covering Dara's funeral expenses, the Agency was paying off the lease on Amina's tea shop in exchange for her services as a potential future intelligence contact. A sleeper agent. Amina would most likely never be called into service. It was accounting sleight of hand that Maggie didn't have a problem with. Amina would accomplish more for the Yazidi community with that tea shop than half a dozen agents ever could. Besides, the agency owed Dara.

"Any word from Bellard?" Ed asked.

"Not so far," Maggie said. "But I came in from Germany under an alias."

"Wonder how he's holding up—after getting skunked out at *La Ferme*."

"I kind of feel sorry for him," Maggie said. "He *did* get skunked. Even if he had it coming."

"Now that is what I call being magnanimous. Bellard threw you in a cell. He stole the op from you."

"It is his country. And we did promise him credit for the op. I think he should still get it. If nothing else, it might put us back on friendly terms. And it means we don't have to sneak in and out of France until he retires."

"Not a bad idea." She could hear Ed take a deep drag on his cigarette. "I'll float it by Walder."

Maggie's left eyebrow was nice and smooth now, perfectly arched, like the right. No more gorilla bristles.

"Got to run, boss. See you tomorrow."

"Make sure you're on that C-130 at Le Bourget."

∽

THE SUN BROKE through the clouds over Passy Cemetery as the six men lowered the plain wooden casket draped with a red and white Yazidi flag, a gold multi-pointed star in its center, into the ground. The men ranged in age from sixteen to elderly and all wore the best they had for the occasion, from a well-tailored Italian suit to a simple pair of gray polyester slacks and pressed well-worn shirt. A few red-and-white keffiyehs adorned heads.

Around the gravesite a gathering of Yazidi and Armenian mourners chanted prayers amidst the plaintive sound of a lone flute and the banging of a single drum. The women wore scarves, many weeping openly, symbolically beating their bosoms to summon grief, others beginning to toss mementos and hand-written notes and money into the grave.

Amina, dressed in a deep blue pant suit and long white head scarf, came forward, holding a crown made of peacock feathers. She stepped up to the foot of the grave and stood, closing her eyes, which were glistening at the rims, before she lowered her head. She tossed the headdress onto the top of the coffin. She then made the repetitive beating of her chest as well.

Maggie, dressed in a somber black business skirt suit, black flats and black chiffon hijab scarf, blinked away the tears welling up as she silently said goodbye to Dara.

~

"And what of the people?" Amina said, composed now as she sipped tea. "The ones you saved?" They were gathered for a simple wake at the Armavir Tea Room. The music was livelier and the mood upbeat as mourners sought to look forward. Dara was, after all, a hero.

"Still in Turkey," Maggie said. "Two are seeking asylum in the west. But that's a lengthy process, as you know. Besma and her little brother will be repatriated with their father in Northern Iraq."

Amina shook her head. She had removed her scarf and her big hair was back to its former bouffant, reeking pleasantly with hairspray. "Is that so wise?"

Maggie shrugged and sipped a glass of white wine. "It is Besma's people. And her home."

"But her little brother is only six years old, you said."

"I feel as you do," Maggie said. "But their conviction is greater than mine."

Amina drank tea. "You did a wonderful thing, Maggie. And dismantling that evil money machine."

"Thanks to Dara. None of this would've been possible without her."

Amina drew a breath as she appeared to stem what might have been the beginnings of fresh tears. "You don't know how proud she would be of you."

"I'm honored to think so," Maggie said softly.

"And what of this famous Kafka? The man who would shoot my niece? And now is being treated as some sort of hero, too? It seems all he did was benefit from this whole miserable event."

Maggie nodded in agreement. "Some people seem to come out on top no matter what. Kafka will be handed a nice life in the US—new identity, job, money. His parents are safe. They'll get the same. All with our blessing. While Besma goes back to a bombed-out village, caring for her little brother. But once we break Abraqa, it will be worth it. I head back to the US to begin that process tomorrow. Over one billion dollars of Jihad Nation money will be frozen. Think how much good *that* will do."

"You mean how much evil it will prevent." Amina sipped tea.

"Yes."

"I can't help but feel that Kafka took advantage of my niece," Amina said. "Whether she really had feelings for him or not. The thought of that opportunist alive makes me sad. May Dara rest in peace."

∽

"Captain Bellard just left for lunch," the receptionist said.

"A late lunch," Maggie said, checking her watch. "He must be working too hard."

"He ran down to Café Lepic. Can I take a message?"

"No. I just called to say hello."

"And whom should I say called?"

"Dara," Maggie said. "Tell him it's Dara. I just wanted to say thanks."

Maggie hung up.

The clouds had cleared completely and it was turning into a beautiful day. Café Lepic was a twenty-minute cab ride from Montmartre. She wanted to thank Bellard in person, apologize as necessary, patch things up.

Not long afterwards she paid off the taxi half a block down from Lepic. The working class café was half-full as she arrived, most of the regular lunchtime crowd gone.

Through the full-length window outside, she spotted Bellard down at the standup bar against the wall, across from the cash register and serving counter, where she'd found him the first time she'd been here. He was wearing his light blue suit.

She headed in and stopped when, to her surprise, she saw someone with him.

John Rae.

She stepped back outside, pulled her hijab back over her head. She fished her sunglasses out of her handbag, slipped them on.

She strolled by the café, head down, glancing through the window as she passed to confirm what she just saw.

Bellard. And John Rae. The two men appeared to be in a deep discussion, Bellard nodding at something John Rae was saying.

John Rae was supposed to be heading back to Washington for Kafka's debriefing.

Maggie was the one with a detour, to attend Dara's funeral. Why had John Rae not told her he was going to be in Paris?

And why was he being buddy-buddy with Bellard?

She walked down to the end of the street, mulling things over.

A taxi approached. She flagged it down.

∼

MAGGIE WAITED in the tiny hotel lobby for a cab to take her to Le Bourget. Her cell phone rang. It was a Paris number she didn't recognize.

"Maggie?" a familiar Frenchman's voice said.

"Bellard," she said. "How are you?"

"Call me Alain," he said in French. "I'm flattered you recognized my voice."

"How could I forget? It's the same one that had me put in a cell."

He laughed. "I knew it had to be you when my secretary said Dara called. Congratulations. I heard your operation was a success."

"Who told you?"

"Walder."

"Really? When?"

"Earlier. He called me—with some news."

"Oh, I thought someone else might have mentioned it." *Like John Rae. Since he met with you.*

"No. I got it straight from the horse's mouth. He wanted to tell me that SDAT would be getting the credit for Operation Abraqa. I think a word of thanks is due."

Why was Bellard being less than transparent?

"Well," she said, "it was the least we could do after that little stunt we pulled out at *La Ferme*."

"The less said about that the better, eh? At the end of the day, Maggie, as you say, we are all on the same side. And the operation *was* a success. That's what counts."

Her only wish was that he meant it. But she simply didn't know. "You, monsieur, are a true sport."

"How's it going with Kafka?"

Did he want to know if she'd broken Abraqa yet?

"No problems so far," was all she said.

"Come on!" Bellard said. "You tied us up in a van—after tear-gassing us! Give me a little something."

"I suspect we'll be wrapping things up soon. Very soon."

"When are you heading back to the US?"

"Tonight," she said.

"Ah," he said, giving a sigh. "Next time, then. And when you return, dinner will be on me."

Did Bellard have an evil twin? "I hope it will have a tablecloth underneath it and not be served on a plastic tray in my cell."

Bellard laughed.

∽

Night rain pattered on the roof of her taxi as they pulled up at Le Bourget. She was never so happy to get on a C-130 and go back home.

All that remained was to dismantle Abraqa. She already knew the nuts and bolts. It was just a matter of going through the motions, now that Kafka's parents were safe.

Nearly there.

56

An early morning knock at his hotel room door woke Kafka from a deep sleep. He was still adjusting after jet lag, months of apprehension over the situation with Jihad Nation, even more intense worry over his mother and father. God be praised, they were safe now, in a suite in the very same hotel. For the last day he had slept in a near blackout, recovering.

They'd made it. The United States. Freedom. The land of plenty.

He almost didn't get out of bed. He began to drift back off.

But another knock pulled him out.

Kafka threw off the covers to the king-size bed and climbed out, stumbling over to the door in his new silk pajama bottoms, rubbing his eyes.

"Who is it?" he said in English to the door, head cocked.

"Maintenance," a voice responded.

He opened the door on the chain, peering out.

A hotel maintenance worker in a brown uniform and cap. Tall. Fit. Trimmed neat gray mustache. Wearing glasses.

Holding a toolbox. "Water leak downstairs," the man said, pointing down with a finger. "I need to make sure it's not coming from your bathroom."

"I was sleeping."

"I do apologize, sir," the man said. "Won't take but a minute. If there's any complication, we'll be happy to move you to another room."

"Very well." Kafka sighed as he unlatched the door, stood back. "But I expect to be upgraded."

The man came in with his toolbox. Kafka shut the door.

The maintenance man went into the bathroom; he set his toolbox down on the floor. Kafka heard him banging around in there. He turned on the faucet, turned it off. He opened a cabinet door. He turned on the shower.

"Can you come in here, sir?" he said. "I think I've found it."

"Where is this leak?" Kafka said, going over to the bathroom.

The maintenance man was kneeling by the toilet. He had removed a red tray of small tools from his toolbox and put it on the seat lid.

"Shut the door, will you?"

Kafka did, starting to get annoyed. "Where is the leak?"

The maintenance man stood up, stared through his glasses. "I'm looking at it."

Kafka froze when he saw the hypodermic needle in his hand.

"What?" Kafka said stupidly. He turned to escape but he had shut the bathroom door.

The prick of the needle jabbed his midriff.

Almost immediately he stumbled, only recently having woken up, after days of exhaustion. His head began to swim.

Shout, he thought. *Scream.*

He couldn't.

"Did you really think you could get away with it?" he heard the man say, echoing in his ears. "Did you really think you could betray us?"

Kafka opened his mouth. Words, slow and laborious, started to come out, but they were words without sound, landing with dull thumps, like stones underwater. And he fell with them, falling softly onto a submerged layer of wet sand, to remain there, forever.

~

"Dead?" Maggie said. "*Dead?*"

She could not believe it.

She'd barely slept on the flight back. Now she stood on the runway at Langley Air Force Base, having disembarked the transport, planes roaring as they took off and landed, talking to Ed on her cell phone.

She was shattered.

"How?" she asked.

"Found on the bathroom floor by the maid. Shower still running. Looks like a heart attack. But we won't get the coroner's report for some time."

"*Heart attack?*" Maggie said. "Kafka was thirty years old."

"Thirty, working for Jihad Nation while he worked us as a double agent, under an unbelievable amount of stress, trying to get his parents to safety. Thirty going on eighty as far as his nervous system was probably concerned."

"And the timing doesn't cross your mind?"

"What do you think?" Ed said, and Maggie could hear him sucking on a cigarette. "Right before we were scheduled to dismantle Abraqa?"

"Exactly."

"And now we can't."

"Says who?"

There was a pause.

"I thought Kafka wasn't going to give up the passwords until his parents were safe and sound and settled in the US," Ed said. "When your debriefing was complete."

"Ed," she said. "You really are a Luddite."

"Wait—did Kafka ever log onto Abraqa from your laptop?"

"Bingo. In Berlin. Before the rescue operation."

"Of course you would have some kind of Trojan keystroke recorder program on your computer."

"Apple and Android are doing the same thing to the entire cell phone public. Why not me?"

"I've said it before, Maggs. I'll be working for you in a year or two."

"Only I don't want your job."

She heard Ed take a drag on his cigarette. "For the time being we keep this strictly between you and me, Maggs. Until Abraqa is shut down."

"I was going to say the very same thing."

"Shouldn't you get a jump on it?"

"Disable Abraqa Darknet? Whoever killed Kafka thought I was going to have to wait until after the debriefing Kafka is now never going to have to begin the process. So I have a little time. But yes, I will be doing it very soon." All she really had to do was change the passwords. "But I need your okay, Ed. If I do it on my own, you know it's going to piss more than a few people off. Perish the thought we violate protocol."

Ed took another puff on his smoke. "You have my okay. But do it when this phone call ends. Not that I'm paranoid."

"I'm way ahead of you."

There was a pause while a plane groaned into the sky.

"Kafka's demise feels like more than simple retribution, Ed."

"I know, Maggie," Ed said. "And then again, I don't. That's the way this game goes. You don't always know. It could be just what it looks like. Jihad Nation took Kafka out when they had no other option."

But *she* knew. Or thought she did.

She just had no idea who.

57

"Disabling Abraqa was almost an anticlimax," Maggie said. "It was simply a matter of changing Kafka's passwords on the private folders so that nobody would be able to log in and transfer funds."

She watched Director Walder gaze out of his spacious fourth floor corner office which overlooked an expanse of trees. In his crisp blue shirt, with his hands in the pockets of charcoal gray slacks, he appeared to be studying something in the distance. She couldn't get a read on him.

Ed sat next to Maggie in a desk chair, chunky legs crossed at the ankles, his mountain man beard in need of a trim and his glasses amplifying droopy lids from last night's redeye from San Francisco. John Rae, never one to be intimidated, leaned back on two legs of a chair against the far wall, hands clasped behind his head. He wore a blue poplin suit, white shirt and black bolo tie, and a pair of his signature cowboy boots, these in beige. Now that the op was complete, he had shaved off his scruff, leaving a neat goatee and sideburns again. His hair was freshly cut. He did not look like someone who had spent the last few days running across Europe and the Middle East dealing with terrorists.

"Well, that's a relief," Walder finally said. "Abraqa was shut down without Kafka's help."

A relief? Someone certainly didn't think so—whoever had attempted to short-circuit the process by killing Kafka before his debriefing with Maggie.

"Officer de la Cruz was adroit enough to harvest Kafka's passwords when he logged onto her computer in Berlin," Ed said.

"So we didn't really need that rescue mission after all?" Walder said, turning to narrow a look at Maggie. His frizzy hair caught a scrap of morning light. "Once you got his passwords, you were good to go. Is that correct?"

"Yes," Maggie said slowly. "But we were hoping to gather additional intel. And ..." She cleared her throat. "... we had an arrangement—Kafka's parents were to be brought to safety."

Walder gave her a flat-line stare, making her realize it wouldn't have bothered him not to deliver on that promise.

"Are his parents safe?" he asked.

"Distraught to say the least," John Rae said. "But alive. We've got a guard on their hotel door and have expedited their relocation process."

"I see," Walder said, turning back to the sea of green outside. "So where do we stand on Abraqa now, Maggie?"

Maggie looked around the room. Ed, Walder and John Rae—normally, three people she trusted implicitly, even Walder, with the less-than-perfect relationship she shared with him. Above reproach. Normally.

But since Kafka had been killed, she didn't know. Caution weighed. "Five hundred thousand, thirty seven million dollars' worth of Bitcoin assets frozen. Moved into a private wallet I set up. I've catalogued the nineteen banking entities involved and they are now on record."

Walder turned back around, looked at Maggie, blinking.

"Weren't we expecting more money?"

"About twice as much," Maggie said. "Somewhere in the region of two hundred million Bitcoin, according to what Kafka told me in Berlin. Abraqa handles one billion dollars per year."

Walder raised his eyebrows. "How do you explain the difference?" There was a tone of admonition in his voice.

Maggie looked around the spacious office again.

"I request that this be a Class Four discussion," she said.

Walder nodded. "Very well. Everyone is on notice that what is said here does not leave this room."

Everyone agreed.

"Continue," Walder told Maggie.

"From what I've seen, more than half the institutions made withdrawals from their public wallets in the last twenty-four hours."

"Meaning they got wind of Kafka being dead somehow?"

"I expected the raid at the Bunny Ranch to scare a few people off but I wasn't expecting this."

Walder frowned. The implications were serious.

"I think we've had a leak since Quito," Maggie said. "Maybe longer."

Silence hovered while everyone eyed each other.

"I've been here for a good while," Walder said. "'Mole' is a word one doesn't use lightly."

"Agreed."

"I know this agency better than anyone. It's my life. I would know if something wasn't right."

"Certainly you would know better than anyone, sir,"

Maggie said. "But no one is infallible. The Agency is a huge organization."

Walder pursed his lips. "What do you suggest?"

"We start putting the nineteen institutions involved in Abraqa under the microscope. Find out who ditched early. Pull those threads. Follow the money."

Walder thought that over too. "We'd have to make it look like we're doing something else." He didn't want panic from the rank and file.

"We'll call it *due diligence*," Maggie said. "We can set up a financial front that's looking to invest in Middle Eastern banks."

Walder nodded.

"Maggie needs approval and budget, Eric," Ed said to Walder. "And this needs to be Class Four from top to bottom. No approvals from the Senate Committee, nothing that gives the game away."

"This is the time to find out," Maggie said. For her part, Maggie had almost been killed in Ecuador when someone had gotten wind of her escape from a situation there.

Walder tapped his chin. "Nothing impacts this organization more than something like this."

"Maybe it will be for the better. Maybe it will be a good thing."

"It's a good thing if we're on the right track," he said, eyeing her. "A patient should never be operated on unless they're actually sick. I need to review the details, think it over."

Maggie took a breath, nodded. "In the meantime, I'd like to continue my analysis."

"Report any findings directly to me," Walder said. "Only to me. No one else."

Maggie caught the look of displeasure on Ed's face. He was being cut out of the loop again.

"Let's focus on where we are now before we conclude here," Walder said. "This was a major setback for Jihad Nation—half a billion dollars of their funding cut. Significant indeed. But not the end of the line. Like the head of a hydra—you cut off one, two grow back."

Ed said, "I just want to say that despite the results, this is still a major win. Kafka—one of their top people—out of action. Their banks scared off, if temporarily. A facility near Mosul disabled. Three terrorists removed. Jihad Nation are hurting. And with the minimal resources that were deployed. We also have half a billion of *their* money."

Not if any new potential defector learns of what happened to Kafka, Maggie thought. She couldn't help but reflect on an earlier op again, a mysterious driver who was sent to pick her up in Quito when she was on the run. He turned out to be an unknown agent, killed in an automobile accident. Someone had infiltrated communication between her and Ed. And that had never been resolved.

As much as she hated to admit it, the Kafka hit was classic Agency. Remove an agent in play. Make it look like a heart attack.

Or someone who wanted it to look like an Agency hit. Jihad Nation weren't stupid.

So much of what she did came down to trust. Trust and instinct. For all of her electronic tools, things still boiled down to the basics.

"A victory," Walder said.

"I just want to say one thing," John Rae said. "I think what Maggie did deserves real recognition. Jihad Nation money frozen? With a skeleton crew? One helicopter when we requested two? Almost no casualties on our side. Nailing

Hassan al-Hassan? *And* getting those women and Yazidi kids out of there? Putting the genocide up front and center. Talk about two birds with one stone." He gave Maggie an appreciative nod. "More like a flock."

Yes, she felt pretty good with that. Dara would have felt the same way.

Maggie's phone buzzed in her pocket. Her private phone. A text. She pulled it out, even though she was in a meeting. Maybe it was Amina. She hoped Dara's aunt was coping with the aftermath, now that the funeral was becoming history.

SEBI: *Limo picking you up tomorrow at your place 8 PM. Courtesy of 999 Records. You better not stand me up!*

Sebi's record release party.

She thought for a moment.

She texted him back: *I wouldn't miss it.*

Maggie pocketed her phone. "If we're all done here," she said. "I'd like to get back home." A real flight. Business class. Not the jump seat of some noisy C-130.

Eric Walder turned around. "I see no reason why we can't let you go." He acknowledged Ed. "Do you, Ed?"

"No," Ed said. "Maggie shouldn't have to sit through the post-mortems. That's what we're for." A smile tried to break its way through his beard.

Maggie gave him a wink.

She got up, headed for the door.

"Maggie," she heard Walder say.

She turned, looked at him.

"Yes, sir?"

"Good work," Walder said. "Damn good work."

A red letter day.

"Thank you, sir," she said.

She closed the door behind her, left.

A moment later, she heard the door open and shut.

"Hey, Maggie," John Rae said.

Maggie turned.

"Hey, JR."

"What's your hurry?"

"Just ready to get back home."

"You knocked it out of the park," he said. "I hope you know that."

"*We* did."

"Right," John Rae said. "But Abraqa was your baby, from the get-go."

"I inherited it from Dara. But thanks. And I couldn't have done it without you and all the other little people." She laughed at her own joke.

John Rae smiled and then his look turned softer and she knew he must be thinking of that night, not long ago, the two of them alone in her hotel room.

"Better savor it, Bud," she said. "Because that's all there was."

He shook his head. "When I'm an old man sitting in my rocking chair, and I rock a little faster, you'll know what night I'll be thinking of."

"Me too," she said.

"I thought we might go out and celebrate tonight. *Just* celebrate. I've got a few friends, believe it or not, and they'd like to meet a bona fide hero. I'm buying."

"I'd love to JR," she said, "but I promised someone I'd be home tomorrow."

"I see," he said. "Everything OK? With you and me? Besides that one-time thing and all?"

"Why wouldn't it be?"

Their eyes met.

Kafka had met the kind of end that was tailor-made for

John Rae and his crowd. Although it made no sense, no sense at all. If anyone had championed her case, it was JR.

Maybe she just didn't trust anyone anymore.

But she had seen him with Bellard. At Café Lepic.

Intuition and instinct. What nebulous companions.

What was she thinking? John Rae? No.

She just needed some sleep. Some down time.

"We'll get together soon, hey?" she said.

"Ten four."

John Rae raised his fist.

"Good luck with the *guitarrista*," he said. "He's a lucky man."

"He was."

They fist-bumped.

EPILOGUE

Erbil, Northern Iraq: several weeks later

"Now we defend ourselves from the evil," Captain Rozaline Kalesh said, standing before the one hundred plus Yazidi women dressed in camouflage. "Whereas before we were its victims."

Young and pretty, her blue eyes were accentuated by a red beret and a red and white checked scarf tucked into her camouflage tunic. With her infectious smile, no one would have suspected that the commander of the Sun Ladies had only recently escaped being a Jihad Nation sex slave, given to fighters as a reward for holy jihad, and that she would see her baby beheaded for crying.

And that she would now be commanding a unit of Yazidi paramilitary women with like backgrounds, fighting for vengeance against their former captors.

Women.

Some as young as fourteen, like private Besma Erol,

standing ready, also in camouflage, with her red beret at a slant, her Kalashnikov by her side.

Havi was back home safe with Dadi, *back home* being the seat of a pickup truck, travelling endlessly to the far-flung refugee camps in Turkey where her father sought to reunite their people. But never alone. Their village destroyed and deserted, Havi would never be left alone again.

Not until he, too, was old enough to fight.

THANK YOU!

Thank you, dear reader, for purchasing (or borrowing, or stealing) The Darknet File. If you enjoyed this book, please consider leaving a review on Amazon, where it really counts. No need to write a thesis; just a few words will do. Not only do reviews help authors get their work noticed but they also provide me with valuable feedback. There's a reason I sit in a darkened room, banging out stories about people who never really existed, doing things that never really happened, and it's all about people like you, who read my work. So have at it! And check out my other books. If you haven't read THE CAIN FILE, it's the first book in the Agency Series. Another Agency File book is in the works.

Please visit my Amazon author page for the latest:
https://www.amazon.com/Max-Tomlinson/e/B006DI55LM/

ABOUT THE DARKNET FILE

Although THE DARKNET FILE is a work of fiction, much of the story is taken from current world events, as of 2016, when the first draft was written.

The genocide of the Yazidis of Northern Iraq by ISIS is a tragedy that has received far too little attention, and it is this theme that inspired THE DARKNET FILE, as well as the ongoing problems with terrorism in Europe. The Yazidis have suffered at the hands of many since day one. One can hope that as ISIS is pushed back, they will be able to recover as a people and reclaim their ancient legacy. The Sun Ladies, by the way, are real, and battle ISIS as we speak. These are indeed turbulent times we live in.

CPSIA information can be obtained
at www.ICGtesting.com
Printed in the USA
LVHW041936210523
747621LV00003B/705

9 781097 304776